Rebecca F. John was born in 1986, and grew up in Pwll, a small village on the South Wales coast. Her short stories have been broadcast on BBC Radio 4. In 2014, she was highly commended in the Manchester Fiction Prize. In 2015, her short story 'The Glove Maker's Numbers' was shortlisted for the *Sunday Times* EFG Short Story Award. She is the winner of the PEN International New Voices Award 2015, and the British participant in the 2016 Scritture Giovani project.

Her first short story collection, *Clown's Shoes*, is available through Parthian. She lives in Swansea with her three dogs.

The
HAUNTING
of HENRY TWIST

REBECCA F. JOHN

First published in Great Britain in 2017 by Serpent's Tail,
an imprint of Profile Books Ltd
3 Holford Yard
Bevin Way
London WC1X 9HD

www.serpentstail.com

Copyright © 2017 Rebecca F. John

1 3 5 7 9 10 8 6 4 2

Designed and typeset by sue@lambledesign.demon.co.uk
Printed and bound by Clays Ltd, St Ives Plc

The moral right of the author has been asserted.

The characters and events in this book are fictitious.
Any similarity to real persons, dead or alive, is coincidental
and not intended by the author

A CIP record for this book can
be obtained from the British Library

ISBN 978 1 78125 714 2
eISBN 978 1 78283 289 8

For Matthew
and
for my parents

RUBY

It is not only because of the smog that Ruby Twist fails to notice the grumbling approach of the bus on this cold, spooky morning. Though the mist is thick and fast-swirling and London squats behind it like a fading dream, Ruby hardly notices. She is not thinking of the weather, or of stepping carefully, or of the danger of the road ahead. She is thinking only of Henry. It is an embarrassing habit – one she is glad to have kept secret – but sometimes, when they are apart, Ruby finds herself rebuilding his face in her mind. She fits one fine feature over the next, word by careful word, until he stares back at her from behind her own eyes. She does it just so that she can look at him, and every time, she discovers something different about the face she knows so well.

'Your hair is the colour of wet sand,' she'll say to him afterwards, as though the observation is a casual one. 'Your hands belong to an artist.' Today, she considers that his eyes are the deep, soft shade of green olives and that perhaps, if they have a girl, she will have her daddy's eyes. They chose their names months ago. After a night full of 'nos' and 'maybes', they laid them out in the silence of a splintering dawn, pleated into each other beneath the quilt Ida had patchworked for them as a wedding gift. It was before the real cold came, when the baby was still a tight, invisible knot only Ruby could feel or know.

'Harold?'

'No! Bleddyn?'

'What?'

'Gruffydd?' She was teasing. She didn't want a Welsh name.

Henry huffed. 'I can't spell it, or even say it. Billy?'

'Yes!' she squealed. And that's how they had continued, slinging names around until something stuck.

When Ruby suggested Elizabeth, after her own middle name, and Henry said, 'Yes, Libby,' Ruby had bounced up, swung herself astride him, and kissed his nose. 'You, husband, are a perfect genius,' she said. 'You ought to father a thousand children and find them all perfect names. Billy for a boy. Libby for a girl. Those are the ones, definitely.'

And the choices did feel definite, in a way their earlier ideas had not. Ruby had imagined then, though she had not admitted it to Henry, that they would have at least one of each; that neither name would go to waste. Now, with only two weeks more to wait, she feels comfortable despite the taut pull of her belly. She feels light. She feels confident she can do this again and again, for Henry.

She takes a detour onto narrower Stanhope Terrace. She has time to waste and she wants to break the monotony of the straight track onto Oxford Street. Here the mist, trapped between closer buildings, spins in darker circles, and Ruby waves a gloved hand at it, as though she can persuade it to clear for her. She feels this powerful. Her heels clip–clip against the pavement. Her bright red coat flashes with each forward step. The lipstick she swept on to match it clings heavy to her lips, but it is a weight she enjoys: it reminds her of how pretty she felt this morning, when Henry stood behind her in the mirror, his hands around her stomach, and winked at her as she twisted the thick ends of her hair one way then the other.

He's the kind of man who can deliver a wink, she thinks;

he's handsome enough for that, her Henry. She shakes her head, laughing at herself. Even here, alone, she is being smug.

As she walks down Brook Street and re-joins Bayswater Road, the world grows lighter again, and Ruby tips back her head and peers past the buildings laddering the sky to look for signs of snow. It is cold enough, crisp enough. It is the only thing that could improve today. But she knows she cannot ask for more, not so much as the ghostly flurry of snow in this early winter morning, because she has everything she has ever wanted. Almost everything. All along the street, the dark curves of men's hats gleam in the damp air. A corner of grey suit-jacket pushes out of the whiteness then disappears again. Briefcases swing in and out of sight, gripped by disembodied hands. And Ruby reaches for the rhythms of the city. She has come to love these sounds: the clacking of feet on the pavements; the talk, passing or sustained, which gathers like rain clouds before dropping its stolen words onto strangers; the low rattling pulse of the traffic, nosing through London's labyrinthine grid. Each is reduced to a whisper by the next. Nowhere in Wales could you locate that same jumbled din.

To her left, a long row of white Georgian houses wear the fog as a dancer might a feather boa, draped over a shoulder or looped around an arm, half-revealing themselves. Ruby had thought this place impossibly grand the first time Henry had shown her to the flat. Now, she is comfortable here. She knows every small street which darts away from the park. She has walked this way – from home to Monty's private garden – a hundred times.

A short, round-hipped woman passes and returns Ruby's smile, nodding at the dome of her pregnancy as if to say, 'Yes, I know, I remember that', and Ruby stands a little taller to push out her stomach, delight rippling through her. One day, she thinks, she will step past a younger woman and do the very same thing; she will send the most profound sort of satisfaction rushing through another expectant mother. Because Ruby knows what it is to endure a wait. She waited so long to come to London, to find a job, for Henry to propose, for the eventual dawn of their wedding day. And soon, very soon now, she will be able to stop. Then, she has decided, she will sit in the wide bay which fronts their flat, look out at the private comings and goings of the street through the opened window, and write a letter to her parents and Ida which might just persuade them to pen a real reply.

She has already planned how she will begin. She will simply say, My son has arrived, or, My daughter has arrived. And then, she realises, she will begin waiting all over again.

All Ruby has gained in these last three years, and somehow, along the way, she has managed to lose three whole people. They have not exchanged angry words, nothing like that, but a gap has opened up between the Myrtle Hill house she used to race around, trying to tempt Ida into adventure, and her Bayswater Road flat, which words do not seem able to straddle.

Sometimes, when Henry is at work and Ruby is alone, she closes her eyes and feels her way around that big detached house, trailing her own distant spirit from room to familiar room.

She enters the living room and sees her father, drying after his bath and dozing in the fire heat, his half-lit face smooth and tired, his still-straight shoulders wrapped in a towel worn flat by so many identical evenings. She sees her mother, hunched, small-eyed and content, over the next in a great line of books she has stacked into an alcove, already in the order she has decided they must be read. She wanders into the kitchen and sees Ida crouched below the sink, clutching the leg her mother has slapped and blowing the skin pale again. Elizabeth's hands always could deliver the most unavoidable slaps, administered with a deep breath on both parts when Ruby snuck down to the sea and clambered over the rocks or tore her skirts fighting with a boy at school.

And she hears them, too.

Her mother calling from the kitchen: 'What's on the wireless, John?'

'Nothing but dust, Elizabeth.'

This is how Ruby communicates with her family now – in the past. But she is sure not to mention this sadness in the letters they reply to with such brevity. She feels she would be letting John and Elizabeth and even Ida down, to set out on her big adventure and then admit to missing any one thing she had been forced to leave behind.

Twenty minutes later, Ruby is still strolling towards Monty's, her pace slowed. She is unused to the breathlessness which comes upon her now during longer walks, but she will not curse it. She has decided not to. The houses to her left have grown into sprawling department stores. Bunches of people press their faces to spotless windows, shivering in the rectangular shadows of rolled-away awnings which drop over their heads; shop signs loom outwards, their giant letters distorted by the perspective of those on the pavement below; doorbells shake frenziedly as doors are flung open and never properly closed. The hard scents of Capstan Full Strengths and Woodbines thicken around her.

On a side-street corner, two hulking black horses stand patiently, snorting hot plumes of steam into the bitter air and shifting from leg to leg while piles of newspapers are unloaded from the cart they are harnessed to. Ruby pauses to put a hand to one of their noses. She removes a glove and touches the soft heat around its nostril. She inhales their strong, earthy smell.

Somewhere down the street, a shout bursts through the crowds and the horses prance backwards, worried. The cold reclaims Ruby's hand and she shuffles it back into her glove, squinting towards the growing commotion. People are bobbing around, their jolting and pushing drawing attention even through the sheets of mist. More shouts go up, clanging against each other. And then there is a quicker movement amongst the shoppers, and a sharp clatter as something is dropped or thrown to the ground, and a smaller figure, a boy, pushes his way out of the ring of people and tears up the street towards her, a bag of something flying behind him like a balloon, bouncing to the rapid thump-thump-thump of his feet. Despite the month, he wears only a vest, a scarf and a pair of shorts, his socks pulled high to his blueing knees. His breath wheezes out from beneath the peak of a too-small cap. His shoes slip on slivers of invisible ice, but he does not slow. He cannot slow. He is a thief.

Ruby steps down into the road as he rushes by. Two passing men flatten themselves against a shop window to avoid a collision, and as the boy pounds away, fast as a dream, Ruby finds herself nodding a greeting to them.

'Someone should get after him,' the larger of the men says. His slighter companion grunts in agreement.

'No,' Ruby says. 'He was hungry.' The larger man raises his eyebrows at her. 'Apples,' she explains, because she had seen them, fleetingly, hard and green and beaded with watery cold, bumping against each other in the bag. 'They were just apples.'

The man shrugs. He considers the length of her through uneasy eyes, the way people do when your stomach is stretched round with a new human being. 'Are you hurt?' he asks.

'I'm fine. Thank you,' she answers. And why shouldn't she be, she wants to add. But she doesn't. She never does. Ruby Twist is not interested in causing offence. She watches them straighten their coats and move off, already beginning to embellish the details of what has just happened. 'He could have killed someone, barrelling about like that,' the slighter one says, and while the other hums his concurrence, Ruby turns back to the horses.

'Don't people tell themselves the oddest things sometimes,' she whispers. 'Don't they? Hmm?'

The horses watch her through sad brown eyes and chew

on their bits, mouths moving as if they have something to say. Ruby wonders if the metal sends sparks of pain through their teeth in these temperatures; she wonders what it would be like, to know pain and not be able to say so. Then one of the animals pushes his warm, pink tongue out to taste the sleeve of her coat, and she laughs. Later, she will tell Henry about this, and he will ask her questions as though a simple disturbance in the street were the most important thing in the world. Henry has always done that for her – made her feel important.

At first, she had thought he was poking fun at her, this serious-looking man who had his jacket buttoned though they were at a dance; who kept his tie perfectly knotted while the rest of the room came undone; who smiled with just the two crescent-shaped wrinkles around his mouth. But Henry has never poked fun at anyone. Humour is something he only receives, with a twitch of a smile and a cough which flutters in his throat like a trapped bird.

The thrill of discovering these details has faded now, in comparison to the early days. It has been dulled by the everyday proximity of her husband. But still Ruby can't keep her mind from wandering presently towards the pull of his neck: the specific way his beard sneaks under his jaw and down into two tapering points when he's been too lazy to shave; of how, when she puts her lips to the thinner skin there, it is always warm. There is a width to Henry's arms and chest which makes her, in some incidental way, proud. It shows him, she thinks, to be superior to the strings of skinny boys who parade around London, draped in all manner of vibrant, girly clothing, lamenting the fact that they missed those four unknowable years Henry refuses to speak about.

Women, she knows – every variety of woman, young and old and married and widowed – are jealous of her. But Ruby can't hold that against them. She would be jealous, too.

She does not linger at the shop windows. Now and then, she sneaks a sideways glimpse at her hefty reflection and finds herself pleased with the new solidity of her frame, but she does not pause. She did not come out to buy anything. She came out because Matilda had asked her to and, though she and Henry had stumbled out of Coco's Café with Matilda and Grayson only ten hours previously, Ruby is keen now to get to Monty's garden and listen to what her friend has to say. It is Matilda's way to be dramatic, yes, but there had been something, a cut to her voice perhaps, which had persuaded Ruby that Matilda really was hurt this time.

'Come to Monty's by ten,' she'd whispered, while the men were distracted. 'There's something I need to ask you. Something important.' And Ruby had promised she would.

Near the entrance to the Tube, she stops to check the road. She watches soft shadows sliding through the gloom and tries to distinguish their shapes. She listens for the mounting drone of oncoming traffic. A train of suited people rattle past her and disappear below ground, knocking her bag from her shoulder as they go, and Ruby grabs the strap of it with her opposite hand and drags it back up her arm. She has only to cross the road, turn through a complicated but rapid series of lefts and rights, and she will arrive at Monty's. Within five minutes, she will sit down with Matilda and proffer her best advice.

She suspects that what Matilda wants to discuss is Grayson. She has noticed the snippy exchanges between them lately, the way they move gradually apart when they sit to a meal. She has thought about it carefully, just this morning in truth, in the hour before dawn when Henry flinches through his worst dreams, and she has already decided on the right words. Give him another chance, she will say – because she likes Gray, and really, deep down, she thinks he has just got a little bit lost in his love for his wife. Ruby can appreciate that. There are times when Matilda's mood veers towards a less predictable place than the rest of them know; than they have perhaps ever known.

But, as Henry keeps reminding her, it is not her job to right all of Matilda's wrong moods. And as she glances about herself one last time and decides it is safe to cross the road, Ruby vows that, once she leaves Matilda this morning, she will not think on other people's troubles again today. Today, just for a while, she wants to think only on herself, and Henry, and the surfacing inkling she has that, yes, she is definitely carrying a girl. Today, somehow, the baby feels like a girl. A little Libby. Ruby allows herself to acknowledge that she has wanted a girl all along, and then she steps off the pavement.

Off the pavement and into the deafening blast of a horn.

Off the pavement and into the screech of a stranger's scream.

Off the pavement and straight in front of one of those bright red, big-wheeled, double-decker buses which had so thrilled her the day she arrived in London; which had made her believe, finally, that she'd done it, got here; which she'd pictured, right down to the way they would shine when the rain fell on them, from her bed in the back room of her parents' house in Pwll.

She does not recognise the impact. She does not have a chance to. The bus hits her, and the driver shuts his eyes, and the brakes squeal and groan as she is flung limply forward, and the vehicle stops just short of ploughing over her, and Ruby Twist – twenty-four, nine months pregnant, and happy, happy – is left lying in the middle of Oxford Street, her arms and legs splayed out in fractured points, the surface of her domed stomach rolling as her daughter moves about inside her. And all she can think of is the pram she can now see, upturned before her, its wheels at right angles to the pavement; the baby's mother lying on the ground, mouth open to a silent scream, still gripping the handle between white fingers; the pram's black hood, hooked forward, hooked forward, yes, but surely not substantial enough to protect the baby from the fall it must have had when it was tipped to the ground.

Ruby tries to step forward, to help right the capsized child, but she finds she cannot move her legs. She reaches out, but there is only a trembling from her arms. She does not understand why no one is rushing towards them, this mother and baby, and so she calls.

'The baby. The baby,' she says.

And then there is a voice at her ear, a man's voice, and it is saying, 'Don't worry, love. We'll take care of the baby. Don't you worry now. We'll take care of you both.'

And she wants to say, No, no, not me. The baby. *That* baby. But she has lost all her words, and she closes her eyes with the effort of trying to find them, and there is no trace of Henry behind her lids now; there is nothing there but the black square of an upturned pram against the white glare of the morning, and the heart-stopping possibility that the baby is hurt. That heart-stopping possibility.

A JANUARY FUNERAL

He lies with his arms behind his head, hands folded under his neck in an inversion of prayer, and watches the fluid seesaw of long branches against the paling sky. Around him, music plays on, words and laughter and sighs slotting into its happy rhythm, but he has ceased to hear any of it. He looks to the sky. Far above him, a distant bird, elevated by invisible twitches of feather, weaves through shrinking patches of clean blue space; the clouds stroll steadily along on their endless carousel rotation. And above the clouds ... Heaven, perhaps. Perhaps.

Henry is not so sure any more.

He follows the bends and springs the wind forces out of the branches. The tree is alive with them, the twigs reaching out like fingertips, except that the cracked brown is too dark against the sun-shone white to resemble skin. He has dedicated the last half an hour to fathoming what the colour reminds him of and he knows now: last year, he'd found a nest of robins outside the flat, huddled uselessly close in their bowl of twigs, dead. And he wonders now whether the mother bird abandoned them voluntarily or was taken by a predator. It is important today, in a way it could not have been then, whether she made a choice; whether she fought hard enough to stay with them.

He hadn't shown Ruby the robins. Not because she would have been disgusted, as other women he's known might, but because she would have mourned their loss. She would have held one in her delicate palm and inspected its tiny, curled-in potential, and hated that she hadn't noticed them tucked down beside the steps and brought them inside. She would have hoped the mother to safety. And so Henry imagines it fluttering around above him now, brown wings trembling and tilting, separated from her offspring but very much alive. Still very much alive.

He chooses this as his truth, because that's what the truth is to him now – something he must choose to believe in – and what he believes is that her last minutes were the most serene. He has to give her that much.

At intervals, shadows pass over him, but he does not move to see who they belong to. He would rather guess at Yeoman's clipping pace, or Green's polite coughing, or Daisy's stifled sobs. He does not know who informed these people. It was not him.

As each person passes, and Henry decides on their identity, he invents a scenario in which he shows up on their door-step with the news. He watches himself steered into a kitchen where bread is baking and he finds sleep, face down on the table, to the heavy tick of a grandfather clock. He sees himself perched on a leather settee in a drab green lounge, staring at an untouched whisky glass. And when he runs short of guests to invent stories around, he can't help but suppose himself back on a distant field, the sun squeezing the last trickle of moisture down his neck as mercilessly as a hand wringing a sponge dry, his feet aflame with infestation of a sort he refused to investi-gate. He would wish himself there today, if it were possible. Even that place was preferable to this.

What he had been thinking on then he can't imagine now. He knows that he and Bingley had long ceased exchanging vulgar words about the time elapsed since they'd last seen a woman. He suspects they had abandoned talk altogether at that point, but he cannot be sure and he doesn't want to dwell on the issue, so instead he runs his mind over every last shape that view was comprised of: the long ripple of the land; the flat wedge of black sky; a far-off, delusory block of darkness which might just be a farmhouse, with a family inside, laughing and eating and dreaming and washing in cold, clean water.

Henry is using thoughts like these – remote, unremarkable ones really – to keep himself together. Because he is sure now that he could let go, just as the leaves of this tree did as the summer blew away, and allow the wind to take him. He could leave his body behind. He is capable of that – of releasing himself from it, like a man from his suit jacket at the end of an impossibly long day, and flinging it aside. What is the use, in any case, of a body that can fail him so spectacularly; that can begin to crumble, from the heart outwards, until there is nothing left? Because that is how he feels. As though, soon, there will be nothing left.

Through last summer and the one before, he and Ruby had lain beneath this tree and watched the leaves shiver and flip and rest; watched darkness slot into their puzzle-piece gaps; watched each other's faces claimed gradually by strips of shadow.

Now, they are bare, he and it – so bare that they do not feel the day's frost settling its intricate web over them. Henry is in his shirt sleeves, the white cuffs folded up to his elbows, but he does not notice the goose bumps which dot his skin. He does not notice the specific movements of the people around him, or the shift from song to song, or the dancing. He notices only the sky, and he stares hard at it, trying to forget that, with the dimming of the day, it is beginning to turn the same chalky colour as dead skin – a colour so dense and definite and ugly that it can etch itself permanently onto your brain.

'Henry. Henry, darling,' she says. 'Please get up now. You're going to freeze.'

She speaks to him as though he is a child, despite having none of her own. Women are born with it, he thinks, this way of looking and feeling and wanting to care; of promoting other people's needs above their own. He is not sure he can find the same will within himself. If it was the other way around, would he ignore the guests in favour of leaning over her, his face tight with worry as he patted and cooed and pretended he could empathise? He suspects he would not. And so, if he were capable of summoning any feeling at all now, Henry supposes that he could manage, just, maybe, some admiration for her selflessness.

She is good to him, Matilda. She is kind.

Kindness, though, is not what the other guests at the funeral see. They hint at what they see with glances and frowns and lifts of their eyebrows. They will talk about it when they get home, allowing the words they've been storing like held breath to spill out as they fold their mourning clothes away. They have seen the way she watches him, fusses over him, screws the heel of her shoe into the ground whenever she is near him. They have seen the way her hands reach, quite independently, towards him. And they have thought already today, and many times over, that perhaps Matilda and Ruby were not such good friends after all.

Grayson stands near the gate, sipping his drink and ignoring the suspicion that foams up around his wife. He ignores it because he must; because he knows from experience that not ignoring it would only make matters worse. Matilda has always presented him with these sorts of choices – between bad and worse, between worse and worse still.

That she loves Henry is clear. The knowledge of it thunders through Grayson's veins, the way his own blood did in those newest of days, when he and Matilda would wait for the spread of darkness and slip hand in hand through London's streets, just walking, their need for each other tightening with every step. It makes for a swimming sensation in his ears, to see her bent over Henry, wishing his eyes towards her when it's clear all the poor sod wants to do is gaze up at the sky and pretend his own wife is not dead.

Grayson leans back into the dubious wall of greenery behind him. The branches give slightly, sucking him in amongst the foliage, but they soon find a way to support his weight and he takes a cigarette from his inside pocket and props it between his lips.

If it was Matilda, he wonders, would he lie on the ground as though he was not surrounded by people? Would he block out the chattering of guests and the pattering of cold shoes on hard ground with the belief that, if he watched the heavens for long enough, his soul would simply detach itself and go chasing off after his woman? Would he appear, to all intents and purposes, to be dead himself? He thinks probably not. And that is why Matilda loves Henry over him. Because Henry Twist is a man improved by love, sustained by love, made more than a man by it. And Grayson Steck is a man who sees it as something of an illusion, really, now that his lust for Matilda has long since been satisfied.

When he looks at her these days, what he sees is a tall, drawn woman he doesn't know all that well. A woman he wouldn't conceive of making love to in daylight, as he suspects Henry did Ruby. A woman who once during their courtship dragged him, laughing, up the steps of someone else's house, pressed him against the front door and murmured, 'Let's pretend this is our home. Open the door and call to me, Gray. Call to me. I'll always come.' Who, when he could not find his black tie this morning had barely looked at him before spitting, 'Is there anything you can't ruin, Grayson?'

Is there anything you don't want me to ruin, Matilda? was what the voice in his head had said. What had escaped his lips was only, 'Tilda …?' And she had not answered the question the way she used to, with her hands.

Her hands had mapped their courtship from the start: told him when to kiss her, when to embrace her, when to first dare to unbutton her blouse. And that is why he stands, pressed into the scratchy hedgerow and smokes and smokes when he should be helping his friend – because he can't bear to watch her put her hands on Henry's shoulders and beg him to sit up and mourn with the rest of them. He manages to smile when he is smiled at first: the guests are all at it, throwing tight-lipped grimaces back and forth, their grief not quite allowing happiness into their eyes. But Grayson understands that they are enjoying, in some quiet way, the funeral Monty has helped organise.

They had returned from the church expecting nothing more than food and drink on the ice-packed earth. They were huddled in layer upon layer of clothing, their hands pushed into gloves, their chins tucked inside scarves, their backs already hunched against the temperatures since they couldn't possibly all squash into the summer house. What they had found between the high stone walls of the garden was a small jazz band, positioned neatly in the middle of the weather-waned space, the four men clad in dark suits, their polished brass instruments poised in stiff hands. Eight flapper girls surrounded them, their slim legs almost hidden by their long, straight dresses, their jewelled hairpieces glinting in the afternoon glare. As soon as the wrought iron gate was opened, the music had begun and the girls had started to dance. And later, warmed by two or three songs, they had thrown off their coats and pulled people away from their companions to join in.

Since, the funeral has become something resembling a party: the drummer turns his sticks between nimble fingers; the trumpeter arches backwards and dips forward, following the undulations of his notes; couples twizzle and flick their feet to the stop-time beat, dancing the black bottom. And between dances, guests tip flutes of champagne into open mouths and kiss each other's cheeks before swapping stories about a young woman who has been dead for exactly seven days.

A young woman whose husband has lain unmoving on the ground since Grayson steered him into the garden.

Grayson has not partaken. Neither, naturally, have Matilda and Monty. The activity was intended for those who knew Ruby less well, and, looking around again, Grayson begins to suspect that perhaps some of these people didn't know Ruby at all. There are too many of them. They are familiar only by type. Monty, he realises, has populated the garden with his cronies. But it suits Ruby, this easy chaos her funeral has danced into. It has an optimism about it, and he is glad Monty thought of it. He is glad that, for most people at least, today has not been entirely miserable.

He takes his cigarette from between his lips and raises his glass to the sky: his own private salute. To Ruby.

Two hours pass. A little more. The musicians pack their instruments back into battered cases. The guests start leaving, two or three at a time. Despite the dancing, they are shivering; their fingernails show purple-blue curves. But they smile as they touch hands with Matilda – who has taken control since Henry lay down beneath that tree – and say things like, 'I'm glad we did something different, for Ruby,' or, 'She would've laughed at this, Ruby.' Her name is like sour fruit in their mouths, uncomfortable and welcome at once. And they smile through this, too, because they remember, today, that someone else has it worse than them.

Though his inertness unnerves them, some edge closer to Henry and say difficult things before they go. 'We're sorry, Henry.' 'We'll miss her, Henry.' They stare at the perfect symmetry of his face, the subtle uplift of his nose tip, the thickness of new hair around his lips, and they imagine, while they wait for him to respond to their words, that he will be remarried within the year with looks like his.

Henry does not hear their words. He only continues to stare, unblinking, at the liquid routine of the bare branches above. He moves with them. He writes Ruby across the clouds with his eyes. Ruby Twist, as she has been for just two years. He should be glad she will be buried with some small part of him, that her gravestone will flaunt his love for her, but he cannot conjure the feeling.

She had been Ruby Fairclough when they met, at a party he didn't want to go to and didn't want to stay at until he saw her, young and small-seeming under the white, high-arched ceiling. She wore a dress of the unnameable colour inside a shell and pink lipstick. She appeared so sure of herself that he was afraid to offer her his company − afraid in a way he'd never known before around a girl, because of a girl. So instead of introducing himself, he just watched her, turning and shaking her feet, sending the pearly fringes of her dress flapping, swinging her arms in time with her girlfriend, her dark, tucked hair loosening, and her smile never faltering through all the minutes of that frantic Charleston. He watched and he waited and eventually her dark eyes found him, playful, in the spin of that bubbling room. And before that − before she came to the bar and stood in front of him, hands to her hips, and said, 'So, are you going to wear that awful worried look all night?' − he had been as alone as he is now. Except he hadn't felt it.

There had been other women. He'd never pretended otherwise. He'd never needed to, because, whatever had happened before her, Ruby had understood right away that he had never loved. He unleashed something almost savage on her in the beginning: he held her too close; he worried too much; he grew tense and angry through the shortest absences. And she struggled to tolerate the force of it, until she found him tearful with the fear of needing her one night and began, slowly, to teach him how to love simply.

'Henry, love,' Matilda says. 'Why don't you eat something?' She is sitting at his side. She has been there for some time, a mostly unmoving weight which Henry is aware of only occasionally: when she does move; when she speaks. Monty is there, too. And Grayson, further away, moving amongst or away from the people who stand about now the music has stopped, glasses in their hands, plates in their hands, hands in their hands. They laugh, some of them. He hears them, though only faintly, because they are far away, these people he knew. He cannot remember their names or their faces. He does not try to. They will move off, pair by pair, into bigger crowds of people he does not know or care to know. They will walk the city streets, passing strangers without so much as a smile or a hello, passing strangers with suspicious nods and closing fists. On every city street, at this very moment, people pass and pass and pass each other, their feet clicking and slapping faster and faster, their steps echoing through the stacked crates outside grocers' shops, or rattling the windows of clothing boutiques, or bouncing off the thick, proud walls of heaped up one-room homes and towering, sharp-roofed churches. And amongst all of that, cars hoot and puff and grumble, horses snort and toss their manes, birds snap their wings and panic from chimney to chimney. And below and through the press of London, trains smash their straight-tracked ways, stopping and starting, sucking people in and spilling people out. This is the way of the city. This is its endless life. It does not stop when starving boys thieve bags of green apples from careless shoppers, or when wives lock their husbands out or in to end their faithless ways, or when girls tire of teasing men and take other girls as their lovers, or when men make the pavements their pillows, or when young women in their final easy weeks of pregnancy fall under the wheels of too-late-in-braking buses.

It will not stop because a man has lost his wife and feels

like his body is crumbling from the heart outwards.

But a person can stop within it. A person can choose to fight its drag and flow. And outside the flat Henry and Ruby shared, standing on the frost-wet pavement, his hands pushed far into his pockets, his cap pulled low, surveying the white stone exterior of the building through dark, deep-set eyes, is a man who has chosen to stop. A man who will not move again until he encounters Henry Twist for the very first time.

THE STRANGER

When the garden is finally empty and the sky has collected all of its light up into one tight, brilliant ball, Grayson and Matilda walk Henry home. They stand one on either side of him, Matilda talking continuously and Grayson filling the spaces she must use to breathe with hums and agreements. They walk backwards along the route Ruby took that day, but Henry does not remark upon this. He still has not spoken. The night is icy and sharp-smelling and where Ruby saw crowds of shoppers, they see only shards of moonlight on glass; where she stopped to put her hand to the muzzle of a horse, there is no sound beyond Matilda's voice but the crackle of the secret parts of the city lighting up and shutting their doors against the dark, miserable, workaday parts of it.

By night, while the workers sleep, London is transformed into an enormous playground. Henry, Matilda, and Grayson are au fait with this only because of their association with Monty, who is rich enough to secure invitations to the treasure hunts or swimming parties the newspapers attribute to that wealthy bunch they have dubbed the Bright Young People. They do not get invited. Though Henry wishes now, idly, that they could stumble upon one of those Chelsea or Mayfair gangs, fancy-dressed and tipsy and piling into a fleet of cars to zoom out to the country and drink away whatever worries they think they have. He wishes he could get tangled up in one of their fantasies, and allow a mob of hysterical girls to dress him up as Mozart or King George or an Indian chief, and stride around some country mansion trailing flirts and admirers behind him. He wishes himself into an easier existence.

The wish, though, is an empty one. He doesn't really want to drink Ruby away. And with his next footstep he finds himself certain that if he saw such a gang the very next time he turned a corner, he wouldn't even pause. He is going home, to what is left of his wife.

———

Matilda, too, is thinking of parties – or rather, of being outside them.

There was a time, before years of trying and failing, before years of blame and awful silences, when Matilda and Grayson had enjoyed these unquiet city hours. They would stand in the shadows of buildings, listening for the music within, wanting to enjoy it but unwilling to share each other with a room full of people to move nearer to its beat. They would shuffle together through the streets then, her head on his chest, improvising an awkward, forward-moving dance and laughing because, however awkward, it was theirs and only theirs. Matilda sighs. As so frequently happens when she drops accidentally into her memories, she wants now to reach around Henry and grasp Grayson's fingers between her own. She looks for the slim span of his hand but, finding it hooked on the wedge of Henry's shoulder blade, she is instantly repulsed by it again; by the way it hangs, limp, weak, off the proud strength of Henry's bones.

Not once since Ruby died has she seen Henry slump under the weight of it. Not once has she seen tears roll into his eyes. And she knows this is because he is strong, but there is a small, spiteful pulse, deep in the core of her brain, which forces her to wonder if maybe he isn't as devastated as everyone supposes he is; which wonders – though she scrunches her eyes shut when it surfaces and tries to persuade herself that the idea does not float there – if there might be a chance.

It does not occur to Matilda that she has always wanted what she cannot have. In childhood, she would leave her evening meals to waste whilst she scurried round the table, pinching tastes off everyone else's plates. In her teenage years, she would chase herself into loneliness by trading other girls' secrets or eyeing other girls' boys. In early adulthood, she filled her head with impossible ideals and refused to settle for anything less: she would go on to teach only if it was at the academy she'd happened past that time, with the little windows that flashed just so as the sun dropped and turned the trees to magenta, and the ivy that scampered all the way to the roofs, and that doorway you could only imagine emerging from in a wedding dress; she would marry only if the man who asked her was five feet eleven inches tall, and had a pleasant nose, and ears which did not protrude too much, and eyes which slanted downwards just enough to call to mind a kindly dog but not so much as to appear miserable. Grayson had matched that description. She'd been lucky to find a man who did. But then, for all her planning, none of it had happened as she had expected it to. None of it. Gray, it transpired, was not the candidate she had advertised for.

Matilda lets him know that every day. It is Henry she wants. And she refuses to delve far enough inside herself to question how or why, or to realise that she didn't know she wanted him at all, until Monty showed her. She remembers the revelation now as he presented it to her – as though it were fact. With his gentle hints, his explanatory looks, Monty was not suggesting the possibility of her feelings for Henry, he was making her understand them. And Matilda did not notice that the deeper she sunk, the more buoyant Monty's mood became. She was too busy struggling to stay afloat.

They'd met Monty at a party, she and Gray, three years earlier. They got talking over the hectic blare of a particularly bad band and he'd soothed their fractious moods with talk of a private garden he owned, not so far away, which he allowed his friends the use of. It was, he claimed, cupping an arm around Grayson's shoulders, a corner of paradise crammed into London's commotion. And he was right. They visited that very night and were introduced to a young couple they found lounging over a basket of half-emptied wine bottles. Matilda has no recollection now of what they looked like, that couple, but they were entertaining, she remembers, and not so impressive as to intimidate Matilda, and it seemed, for a while, that whiling away easy, romantic evenings in the garden with them might bring she and Gray closer together again. That was why when, months later, that couple argued themselves through the gates one final time and Monty ushered Henry and Ruby through it in their place, Matilda was so disappointed.

They were too comfortable together, this new couple; too tactile. And far too beautiful. She feared that Ruby would draw Grayson's eye away from her. Until, that was, Monty commented quietly one day on how closely she was watching Henry. She stopped worrying then about the direction in which Gray's eye was travelling.

After that – in the long days and nights they spent, the five of them, sitting between the high garden walls, picnicking under the tree, sleeping in the squares of sunlight which managed to push through the mesh of buildings, getting drunk as the mottled moon cruised overhead – Monty whispered all manner of surprising things to her. Later still, he started appearing in her dreams: the white tufts of his hair; his skeletally thin face; his pale, starry eyes. His laughter had echoed through the depths of her nights, and bit by bit, he had made her understand. Montague Thornton-Wells, he had assured her, is a man who knows about love. And what he knows about Matilda is that Grayson was never the right choice for her. Henry Twist is the man she should have been with all along.

As they approach Henry's flat, Matilda steps slower. She gazes after a motorcar as it bumbles away. She lingers at the park railings, pretending she has seen some animal nosing through the dark. And the men slow with her, not thinking about it, not considering that she is only eking out the minutes she can spend with the length of her arm curled into the crook of Henry's, pretending that Grayson is not there at all. Imagining, in a careless way, what it might be like if he had died too.

Henry allows himself to be steered up his front steps like an invalid. He pauses for Matilda to open the door and follows her into the hall. He leans against the doorframe while she turns on the lamps in the front room and draws the curtains. He watches the floorboards while she fusses around, unable to look up and see another woman occupying that space. Exchanging words with her is impossible, so he waits. Then, when she has touched his face too many times, and Grayson has fidgeted in the doorway and suggested they leave, and they have let themselves out and squabbled their way down the steps − 'You have to let him be, Tilda.' 'Mind your own business, Grayson.' − he turns off the lamps and opens the curtains. He breathes out.

Streetlamps defend the street below against the relentless shove of darkness and enough of their gentle yellow spread reaches Henry's window for him to see the room by. He stands in the curve of the bay and studies the light which falls across the crumpled foot of the bed, settles on the sharpest edges of the wardrobe to his right, the dressing table to his left, and slips away between the cracks of the floorboards. Near the fireplace − again to his left, but nearer the window − there is a deep green two-seater settee, the cushions still plump with disuse. On top of the fireplace are two framed photographs: one of

Henry and Ruby on their wedding day; the other of Ruby as a child, sitting with her sister at her parents' feet, a Welsh wind chopping up the sea behind them. There is no photograph of Henry's family. Scattered across the dressing table are Ruby's hairbrush, her powder, her metal lip-tracer, and, pushed far into the corner, the lid removed and lost, the round tin of Henry's hair cream. He has not used it in a week.

The streetlamps pick out the shiny items, the larger surfaces. They do not find the small, empty chair pushed under the dressing table, though. They do not illuminate the wooden back of that shaky object, and so Henry concentrates on pulling the details of it out of the gloom; remembering the way Ruby used to sit on it, her legs crossed at the ankles; remembering the way it used to creak whenever she shuffled closer to the mirror. He traces the shape of her into the darkness. And this is not healthy, he knows, but he does it anyway: he begins working like an artist, thinking out the colours of her, the textures, the sweet vanilla scent of her perfume, the way she would sit in that mirror and fiddle and fiddle with the hair she could not quite bear to bob but wore forever curled and pinned away from her heart-shaped face. He works slowly, savouring his creation. He paints her into the long cherry dress which was her favourite, her arms and shoulders bared, her feet bunched up because she has not yet put on her shoes and they are cold. She is not quite three-dimensional. He continues his work, adding finishing touches to her hair, threading the different shades – some chestnut, some almost gold – through the darker brown.

And slow minutes, or hours, later, he is still there, challenging himself to recall the exact difference in length between each of her fingers.

Upstairs, Vivian and Herbert start bumping around and, passing over the point where a bronze helmet-shaped light fitting attaches to the ceiling, one or other of them sends its three glass bell shades swinging. Henry glimpses it as it sways into stillness. When he looks back to the dressing table chair, he finds the item empty again. It is as though the house is reminding him that they are waiting, Vivian and Herbert, Mr and Mrs Moss – Viv and Herb, as they call each other and like to be called.

He shouldn't keep them any longer. Them or Libby.

He steps back through the hallway, outside, and around the side of the house to climb the staircase to the upstairs flat. They might have opened the interior dividing door, he and the Mosses, especially this morning, when Henry had knocked to ask a favour of the neighbours he and Ruby had so rarely spoken to; but it hadn't felt right, considering how long it had been closed, and that neither party had suggested it.

As the rain begins to fall, he puts his knuckles to the exterior door again and waits for someone to answer.

When Vivian swings it open, she immediately lifts one erect finger to her lips to shush him. 'She's not long settled,' she whispers. 'Why don't you come in?'

'Thank you,' Henry answers, 'but I ...' He can converse with Vivian, just about, but he cannot sustain it for long.

Vivian nods. 'You're tired. Of course. I'll bring her through. At least come in out of that weather.'

Henry takes one deliberate step inside and Vivian disappears to fetch his daughter. His daughter – the words do not come easily to him yet. He is not sure they ever will. It is so much more of a shock, to have a daughter with no mother than it would have been to have a son. He glances around the kitchen: at the pale blue paint on the cabinets, the rug trapped under the table, the blue and white patterned plates Vivian has lined up in every available space. The stove hurls out heat, which rolls away into the night because Viv did not trouble him to close the door and he is still standing between it and the frame. On top of the stove, a kettle and an iron warm. It is a homely room, Henry decides; a room a mother might have decorated.

Perhaps Vivian will be the woman to ask for help when they crash, he and Libby, into the first of so many walls nature has stacked up between them.

Vivian reappears, Libby slung low in her arms, and she and Henry creep through the series of awkward manoeuvres it takes to pass the sleeping baby over. Henry remains for a moment in the doorway, Libby held slightly away from his body, the rain falling heavier behind him.

'You'll know,' Vivian says, pushing her hands into the front of her apron. 'If there's a problem, you'll know.'

'I'm not sure.'

'You'll see,' she insists with a quiet smile. 'Trust me.'

And Henry wants to wrap his arms around her then, this prickly looking, certain little woman: not because of what she is saying, but because of what she is not saying. Sorry for your loss. Blessed is the corpse the rain falls on. All those things, uttered at so many other funerals, are not for his Ruby. Ruby. He wants to say her name over and over again, to anyone who will listen, because, what else is there to say which encompasses her so completely? On her headstone, he has opted only for

Ruby Elizabeth Twist
1901 – 1926
Wife and Mother

They had tried to persuade him into including a verse or something from the Bible – Matilda, Monty, the black-suited men he hadn't seemed able to shake for so many hours. But, no. No, he had said. And Grayson had backed him up. What more could there be than this?

Except, of course, *sister* and *daughter*. But he had not thought, at the time, and he doesn't need to have met John or Elizabeth or Ida to know that they will not forgive him that lapse. He can only hope now that they will not travel to London to view his mistake. Ida has already vowed, in fast slanting writing, never to excuse him for burying her sister hundreds of miles from home. It might be, however, that the distance will keep them all from one more hurt, and he wants that for them, truly he does – the evasion of one more hurt.

Moving back around the side of the house, Henry bends over Libby, catching thick trickles of water on his neck and shoulders and letting them soak into his shirt. Libby sleeps, bundled into four white layers of clothing and pressed to his chest. She is so small and light that, were he not able to see her – the frowning, not-yet-grown eyebrows; the scrunch of tiny nose; the tear caught in the corner of one closed eye – he would doubt he was holding anything at all. His eyes stay trained on her, constantly surprised by her existence, until he reaches the corner of the house. There, he lifts them to the street, searching the night for anyone who might be a witness.

The doctor had told him he couldn't take her from the hospital: that she was too weak; that she needed a mother; that the child was lucky to have an aunt who might take over the role. And Henry had watched this man – who had been quick and confident enough to cut his daughter from his wife's belly; who, with every word he spoke, gave a wave of those unnaturally long, hairless hands he used to preserve lives – and fought the urge to contradict every well-considered, educated remark he made.

Ruby's child could do nothing but survive. Henry was certain of that. And she would do so with her father. That was why he had taken her.

Far down the road, a couple stride further into the darkness, hands locked, their legs moving together, their uneven shadows springing into existence as they pass under streetlamps then lurching out in the blacker stretches between the posts. They disappear around a corner and Henry sighs and moves on again. They have no interest in his daughter. They have not come to take her away. The street is empty.

The park, though, is huge and unknowable and could be

concealing more or less anything. Reaching the bottom step, he stops and squints into the black columns between the trees. He senses a movement there beyond the usual shuffling of the wind over grass and water; a purposeful movement. Someone has seen him, he can feel it. Panic jolts down his throat to pierce his stomach. He thinks he is going to vomit. It is his greatest fear now that someone, some doctor or official, will come to reclaim Libby. Despite all his smaller worries, he is loosely aware that, whatever the circumstances, this is what learning to be a father means – the acceptance of constant fear – but since he has no one to share it with, he means to fight it. And fight it hard.

'Who's there?' he calls, the words bounding through the night.

And immediately, without self-consciousness, without shame, a man takes a forward step out of the shadows.

He is tall, about Henry's equal, but slighter. His coat is a tad too big and stands emptily out at the shoulders. His newsboy is pulled so low that his eyes are lost beneath its stiffened peak, but the deep spill of a bruise remains visible, leaking out from his nose and down towards his earlobe and the hinge of his jaw. His hands are bunched into the pockets of worn brown trousers which grow darker spot by spot as the rain hammers heavier. He bares his hands and, holding his arms out to his sides, palms up, shrugs before he speaks.

'Henry?' he asks.

Henry reverses slowly up the five steps which lead to his front door, just to stand higher than this stranger who knows his name, and once he feels the shelter of the house behind him, its three high storeys keeping the cloudburst off his back, he straightens his shoulders and curls Libby up into the dip of his neck. One hand presses her close. The other makes a fist at his side, his fingers aching with the effort of staying calm.

'You didn't answer my question,' he says.

The man pushes his cap back and Henry sees that he is

frowning as he feels his way up and down his body with slaps of his hands. Finding nothing, he removes his cap completely and studies the inside of it before flipping it on again.

'Jack Turner,' he says eventually.

'Are you sure?'

'As sure as I can be.'

There is a stillness to this man which appears to run right to his middle. Even when he moves, he does so leisurely, as if he has just woken and the lethargy of sleep has not yet worn off. His failure to recall his own identity does not seem to trouble him.

'How do you know my name?' Henry asks.

'I don't know.'

They stand, the width of the road apart, and as Jack pushes his hands into his pockets and takes a couple of languid paces back and forth, looking up at the house and frowning again, Henry feels a flicker of recognition. Was Jack already here when Matilda and Grayson brought him home? He can't be sure. But there's something familiar in the way he stands, perhaps; not the physical shape of him, but the attitude, open and easy in the quickening shower.

Jack Turner, as he claims to be called, looks like a man who is pleased with the world; like a man who takes pleasure in every new experience. And it makes Henry uncomfortable. She used to be that way.

'Why are you waiting here?'

Jack squints at Henry as though he had forgotten he was there. He smiles. 'I liked your home,' he answers.

'I'd like you to leave,' Henry says. He is sure suddenly that Jack Turner means to harm him. There is no other explanation, though he fumbles for one.

Jack lowers his head, as though he is bowing to Henry, and without another word, walks away, removing his cap as he goes so that his wetted brown hair grows instantly wavier. He swings the cap at his side. His stride is light and unhurried.

When he is nearly out of sight, he begins whistling a tune, scattering cheerful notes in amongst the silvery jets of rain-water, and Henry lets himself into the flat.

'It's fine,' he murmurs to Libby. 'It's nothing to worry about. He's gone now. He's gone.'

Later that night, though – when Libby has woken for the umpteenth time, grumbled, wailed, been fed and dropped into sleep again – Henry finds himself sneaking to the window and peering out through the beaded glass in search of the man he sent away. He sleeps only sporadically, and each time the baby wakes him, he returns to the window. Sometimes, he thinks he sees Jack – the phantom outline of him dashing into the shadows, the wet sag of his trousers over his scuffed boots, the shine of his curls in the still-falling rain. Other times, he scans the diminishing lines of pavement to left and right until he is dizzy with it before wrapping himself back into his blankets and attempting to recapture his taunting dreams.

Whether he sees some sign of Jack Turner or not, though, in those first moments of waking, as his eyes adjust to the intimate, lonely dark of the room, he is sure he hears two steady sounds beyond Libby's cries: the tapping of the rain on the windowpane; and, lacing through that insistent beat, a man's voice, whistling.

THREADNEEDLE STREET

L ess than a week later, he returns to work. Ruby is haunting the flat. She is held within every crease of it: the loose sheets of writing paper flapping along the windowsill, left there, probably, so she could write home later that day; an errant thumbprint on the mirror-glass; the chip she made in the skirting board by throwing a shoe at him, heel-first, during an argument about, of all things, the fact that they had not argued in a while. She worried about things like that, Ruby. Their arguments, she said, were as important as their lovemaking. She believed it when she warned him that if you reached the point where you could no longer entice yourself to argue, well, then there wasn't very much left of your soul.

Henry had laughed at that claim. A soul was a far more complicated apparatus than she allowed for. Not that he'd said that to her. Sometimes, he felt the twelve years between them, but he would never once admit to it.

He rides the Tube most of the way to the bank. His Tube journeys are his substitute for the nights Libby wakes through: they jolt him in and out of sleep. Before that, though, he parcels himself into his suit and sneaks Libby upstairs in the inky well of early morning. Then, having delivered her with whispered thanks to his neighbour and a kiss of his daughter's hand, he cuts across the park to the underground entrance. Vivian has agreed to care for Libby through the menacing January days, and he is appreciative.

On those days when the sun doesn't puncture the clouds, he sees Ruby more frequently, more clearly. He could count her eyelashes on a dull afternoon.

In the park, he passes a memorial bench. It is mostly unused: nearly a decade passed and memories and ghosts still keep people away. Now and then, though, he sees a man resting there, a trouser leg tacked up or the arm of a coat dangling hollowly over a sown-flat shirt sleeve, trying not to remember how it felt, six, seven, eight years ago, to sit watching the trees under the illusion of healing. He nods to them on those infrequent instances, and sometimes they nod back or hold out a cigarette to him, inviting him to share in forgetting. Sometimes, they are incapable even of that.

Henry could avoid the bench on the way home – he could avoid it altogether – but he doesn't. Occasionally, you need to remember why you have to forget.

It is not the same with Ruby. Grief, he thinks, is as unique in each of its incarnations as any one person is in comparison to the next. His grief for Ruby is loud inside him. And yet, he has not crumbled as he thought he would. Now, it is as though his heart has paused partway through shattering and is held forever in a new fragmentary state, its brittle splinters scattered through his chest, like stitches, keeping the rest of him together.

This, he is sure, is the only reason he can manage getting to work and stooping over his ledgers and moving his hand as though he is recording words and figures that mean anything.

For the larger part of a year, since Churchill ushered them back into the gold standard, conversation at the bank has been of approaching disaster. Henry, though, has never managed to muster much enthusiasm for the doom talk that shoots off the brims of top hats and filters down into the gossip of his fellow clerks. Within the institution, they are seen as a lowly sort, clerks, and he doesn't mind. He doesn't need to be 'in the know' as some do – like O'Keefe and Green and even Yeoman, thrusting their noses up and pretending at importance because they've risen above the average working man. Henry's aptitude for numbers had dropped him into banking before the war, and really, he should never have come back. He has no patience for the politics, the men who come blustering in and out worrying endlessly that this estate has been carved up, or that that house has been sold in so-many bits, or that this family has lost its god-damned-priceless history on account of the farms. Agriculture is a dirty word at the bank, but, if anything, Henry has always relished it. Its four hard syllables have the lumpy swell of unspoiled land embedded within them, and he has spent whole days before now lining other people's wealth up into orderly columns and dreaming of shovels being thrust into wet soil and marches over muddy hillsides.

After particularly tedious days he would try to coax Ruby into returning to Wales, where they could build a home of their own in the verdant roots of a valley invented entirely in Henry's mind. But Ruby wouldn't be enticed. You don't know anything about living off the land, she would say. Besides, she had spent most of her life getting out; she certainly wasn't going back voluntarily. Not when she had all this.

And that is why he defied the Faircloughs and buried her under London – because she loved the city.

He does not think, any more, about staying at the bank or leaving the bank or what will come next. He does not think of the place at all once he steps out through its doors onto Threadneedle Street. Keeping his eyes down to avoid the attentions of the waistcoated, shiny-shoed droves – men who know him well and yet distantly enough to still ask after Ruby – he heads towards heavier traffic, then strides along with its fumy flow as the Morris Oxfords push their bullnose fronts into the paths of beeping Baby Austins and black Model Ts. He drops down into the cocoon of the Tube and stands braced against the train's electrical shudder, inhaling other people's smoke without complaint though he has never smoked himself. Despite it not yet being six o'clock, he emerges, long after his eyes have adjusted to the stuttering artificial light below ground, into the murk of near-night and crosses the park again.

And it feels much the same, this moving through the city, as moving through the working day. Everything which surrounds him shares the blurry quality he imagines a page of text presented his father with when viewed without his spectacles. All the detail is there, but bringing it into focus is impossible.

There is one thing he does look out for during these journeys back and forth to Threadneedle Street, though. He does not intend it, but each time he turns a corner or crosses a road, he slows a little and peers around. Sometimes, he stops and puts his hands in his pockets as though seeking a wallet or a key, though he needs nothing. In the park especially, he watches every tree trunk, every hedgerow, hoping that a figure will emerge from behind them.

He is looking for a man named Jack Turner, because he is sure, isn't he, that he caught a flash of him on the Tube that first morning he returned to work. As a bump in the track shoved him into waking, Henry is positive he saw that strange chap stepping away down the carriage, his brown trousers slack about his legs, his newsboy tipped lazily back on his head, and he needs to know what the man wants with him. He means to get an answer out of him, the very next time he sees him. He very much means to get an answer.

―――

This evening, he does not go straight upstairs to collect Libby from Vivian. He lets himself, as quietly as possible, into the flat and locks the door behind him. In the hallway, he notices the soft smell of dust roaming on the air. It needs cleaning. The whole flat does. But he has no intention of doing it. He is not incapable; he looked after it himself before he met Ruby. Neither is he trying to preserve some fading scent of his wife, or the smudge her hand last made on the wardrobe door, or the shape of her sleeping body in the bed sheets – as he supposes other people might imagine if they visited. These are things his mind possesses; he does not need the proof. He simply cannot see the purpose now of anything so ordinary as cleaning.

He wanders into the kitchen at the rear of the flat and momentarily considers making tea. Before lifting a cup or the kettle though, he wanders back into the hallway and through to the only other room he rents – the large, over-furnished square he and Ruby conducted their lives within.

All their most important decisions were made here: where they should marry; whether they had always wanted children; what they should christen their first baby. Libby's cot is wedged between the fireplace and the settee, where Ruby had insisted it must be positioned, sitting cross-legged on the bed, belly round but not yet enormous, and directing him to shove the cumbersome weight of it two inches this way then that way so she could watch his shoulder muscles tauten with the effort. It was only when he turned and caught her grinning to herself that he realised her game. By that point, he was sweating, and he rushed over to press her face into his clammy chest as punishment.

He puts a hand to the place where her laughter blew against his skin and, when he looks back to the bed, sees an echo of her there, feet arranged sole to sole so that she could rest her arms in her lap and cradle the growing protrusion of their daughter. He begins again his new practice of applying specifics to the memory. Her hair was free, he knows, falling in unshaped curls which tightened into spirals at their ends. Her face was bare, showing the weak red scar on her left temple. She pursed her lips at him and said, 'What? I'm not allowed to ogle my own husband?'

'I wouldn't have you ogling anyone else.'

'Exactly,' she replied. 'Now, ogle me back.'

It is not painful, this remembering. It happens by some unknown, perhaps inherent, process, and Henry wonders if it might be a mechanism of grief. What he will come to understand, though, is that really it has nothing to do with grief at all – it is only another symptom of needing someone.

Removing his jacket and looping his tie over his head, he drifts back into the hallway and climbs to the top of the stairs. There he sits, back to the wall, knees bent into a pyramid, and puts his ear against the heavy dividing door. Heat from the Mosses' flat bleeds through the thick wood. Seeping cold rises towards him from his right and trickles along his arm and around his neck. He is a man of halves: half warm, half cold; half anguished, half euphoric; half here, half staggering lost through the mists of a January morning in search of his dying wife.

He listens to the wordless sounds of Vivian and Herb's conversation lifting and falling and sometimes breaking off. Even at their age, they have the luxury of time to fill.

Libby is silent. She sleeps long and deep with Viv, but Henry doesn't fret about this. It is comforting up there in the always-warm rooms, Viv and Herb's gentle voices revolving around her like the easy eddying of water. Their movements are slow and calming, smoothed by maturity. He guesses they are both into their seventies, though Herb is frailer than Viv. Where Herb has started to shrink in on himself, Viv has retained, or developed, a harder edge. They speak his wife's name in the same generous tone, though. Did he mind, Herb had asked, reaching up to clap a palm to Henry's shoulder, if they said Ruby's name to the child now and then, so she could get used to hearing it? Henry had not known how to respond and Herb had explained himself slowly: things could get difficult, he said, when names stopped being spoken; he'd seen it happen.

Henry wondered then, for the first time, if they had lost a child to the war. He'd thought them saved from that – any child of theirs would surely have been approaching middle age ten years ago – but there was something in the old man's greying eyes that told him otherwise. Something, too, in the way Viv held Libby. And anyway, look at him, Henry – by the time Libby turned twenty, he would be fifty-six.

He did not enquire about the possibility of a son: a Gunner or a Corporal or a Sergeant Moss who never made it home. He knows better than that.

He dislodges a layer of dust with his foot and a little shower of it puffs outwards before sprinkling back down onto the steps. He watches it resettle, then straightens an index finger and with the tip exposes the wood beneath by carving out four letters:

R u b y

And once the letters are there, formed, he can't help but repeat them. And before long, he is crouched halfway down the staircase, writing Ruby Ruby Ruby in perfect rows around the two distorted imprints his legs make where he kneels.

It is then that Matilda knocks the door. He knows it is Matilda because she calls as she knocks. He stops and stands, rubbing his hand in the seat of his trousers. He curses himself for turning on the lamp in the hallway and emitting evidence of his presence. He wants to stay silent and wait for her to leave, but he is casting a giant's shadow across the flat and he knows she will see it if she so much as glances through the window.

'Henry,' she calls, over and over, hardly stopping for breath.

When he opens the door, her fist is raised, poised to bang the black paint again. She crinkles her forehead in an expression of sympathy.

'Henry,' she says. 'Darling, Henry. Where have you been?'

Without invitation, she enters, shuffling past him in the doorway and stepping through to the front room. Her heels thump the floorboards. Her dress swishes noisily and her coat swings wide about her legs. She is thunderous in his quiet space. She is, as always, too much.

'Working,' he answers, but Matilda does not react to this as he expects her to, with talk of it being too soon and appeals for him to come and stay with her and Grayson. She is frozen in the doorway, one hand to the frame, the other to her mouth. Side on, her face is flat, the cheekbones lengthy and wide enough to eclipse her bony features. Henry compares the pointed bridge of her nose to the fleshier design of Ruby's and finds Matilda's face wanting in anything resembling friendliness. It is a deficiency he has never before noticed.

'Oh, Henry,' she mutters finally. 'It's still here. Why didn't you tell me? I could have had it removed.'

Not knowing what she is referring to and lacking the desire to find out, Henry does not respond.

'You don't have to be embarrassed. I understand why you'd want to keep it. Really. It's just, don't you think it would be better, to pass it on to someone who can make use of it?'

He frowns, waits.

'The cot,' Matilda says.

Henry straightens up, pinches his lips between a thumb and forefinger, then pushes his hands into his trouser pockets. He hadn't wanted to say this to anyone – not even Tilda and Gray. It had felt safer for her to be a secret, shared only with Viv and Herb, because everyone else had made an assumption he hadn't felt able to correct, and the doctor had said he mustn't think selfishly about keeping her for himself, and he was sure the man had reported him by now for abducting his own child.

'It's for Libby,' he says.

'Libby,' Matilda repeats. 'You would have had a girl.'

Henry sees her tears growing, glinting, and speaks quickly.

'We did have a girl. But listen, please, don't tell anyone. They told me not to bring her home, and that I had to give her to Ida, and —' He swallows the panic in his voice and closes his eyes. 'I'm afraid someone will take her away.'

Matilda moves towards him and wraps a hand around his forearm. 'Where is she now, Henry?'

'Upstairs.'

'Upstairs? Then go and get her.'

It is obvious she doesn't believe him. Her fingers are at her mouth and she chews at her thumbnail, looking up at him out of a newly pale face.

When, five short minutes later, he returns with the sleeping baby hugged to his chest, she is paler still, but she smiles wide at the sight of Libby, bundled in wool, and her tears spill abundantly then. Precisely as Henry had hoped they wouldn't.

'You called her Libby,' she says, scooping the little girl to her breast.

'It's the name her mother chose,' Henry replies.

'Libby Twist.'

'Elizabeth Ruby Twist. Libby for short.'

'Of course, of course,' Matilda answers, but she doesn't seem to be listening. She is staring down at Libby, her tears still falling, and there is a look about her eyes that Henry can't quite fathom. He's never seen it on Matilda before. Though he is reminded, loosely, of something or someone: perhaps his mother. 'She's perfect. It's perfect,' Matilda says, and when she says 'it', Henry is not entirely sure what she is referring to.

They go through and sit in the window, as tiny and close — it would seem to any onlooker — as a new family under the moonless sky. But Henry and Matilda are miles apart really. Matilda prickles with hope while Henry is made serene by his daughter's proximity. Matilda plans for a future while Henry mourns the one he's lost.

'Have you got a nurse,' she asks, 'to feed her?'

Henry does not explain that he has been guessing, thus far,

at how to tend a baby. He does not mention that he spent more than an hour deciding whether he should give her Liebig's formula or SMA, and that in the end his choice was without reason; that at first he rubbed the stuff onto her tongue with a little finger, ignorant of whether she could suck or swallow; that when he is completely clueless he probes the old woman upstairs for advice, though he has never asked her whether she raised a child of her own.

Libby half-wakes with a short clucking sound and Matilda hands her, slowly, back to Henry.

'Gray and I wanted children, you know,' she confides.

'It's not too late.'

'I'm forty-one years old, Henry. Besides, we hoped for years. It just didn't happen. Eventually, we gave up hoping.'

'Sorry.'

'Yes, anyway ...' She gives a little shake of her head, as though she is trying to rouse herself from a deep sleep. 'I did come here for a reason.'

'To check up on me,' Henry says and, made comfortable now by Libby's heart beating against him, he almost smiles. Almost. He steps back and forth in front of Matilda, bobbing the baby up and down as she squawks and punches the air. She does not cry often and Henry has wondered if this is normal, but he will not risk visiting a doctor to ask. She seems healthy enough to him, despite her size. And hasn't Vivian promised him he will know if there's a problem? He has no option but to believe her.

'To tell you that there's a party on Friday,' Matilda says. 'And that you must come.'

'I can't go to a party.'

'Of course you can. You'll have to some time. There's no occasion or anything, it's just, you know what that bright young lot are like, and well, Monty's in with them apparently, so there we go. I think it might just be because it's the first of the month. You don't have to stay long, but you do have to speak to people at some point.'

'I'm speaking to you.'

'Yes, and don't think I haven't noticed it's the first time.' Matilda stands and rests a hand on Libby's back to still Henry. He obliges. 'You're doing well, but you mustn't let yourself get lonely.'

'I'm not.'

'Of course you are ... So, Friday,' Matilda says. 'Midnight. I'll pop an invitation in so you have the address. Oh, and there's a theme. Everyone wears white.' Then, though the effort it costs her verges on painful, she kisses Henry's cheek and lets herself out of the flat.

From the pavement, she watches him pull the curtains. A pillar of muted lamplight shows at their centre, where the fabric does not quite meet, and Matilda stands in the bitter night and waits to catch glimpses of his shadow as he moves around the room. A baby! There's a baby! She cannot calm the thrashing of her heart. She cannot grasp how she has persuaded herself to stand and walk out of his home when he so badly needs her. And he does need her now. Now more than ever. He can't raise a baby alone. And here she is, and here is what she has longed for, and surely there is nothing to stop her from taking it now – though of course it must all be done well, sensitively. For tonight, she must content herself only with one more glimpse of him through a window.

But she does not get it. The light does not fall right. And long after her hands and feet have started to sting with the cold, she submits and turns to walk away.

With every forward pace, though, she wonders if Grayson will let her go, when the time comes. Will he give her up to a better man, or will he fight for her?

MIDNIGHT WALKS

He begins wrapping Libby into her pram and pushing her through the depths of London's early hours, where they might just be safe. He has begun to worry for her health, being always indoors, and he cannot risk taking her outside in daylight. Anyone might see them, then. Anyone might grow suspicious of a man alone with a child so young, report him to the authorities, congratulate themselves for doing their civic duty as his baby is stolen from him. And so he waits for the night to age, for the day's innocence to be chased off by drinkers and party-goers and women with a price, before he walks Libby through the city.

Ruby would laugh at his caution; at the inverted logic of it. Hadn't Ruby laughed all his worries away? Hadn't she tried to hide all her own from him? One flat Saturday, when she was experiencing the very first flutterings of her pregnancy, they had taken a stroll around Regent's Zoo. The place was quiet, emptied by the scowling threat of rain, but Ruby had thrown back her head and squinted at the clouds and decided that it would 'hold off, for an hour or two at least', so they had stayed. And it was them alone who stood and watched the Arabian oryx dropping their masked faces and using their horns as fencing swords, who laughed as the orangutan scratched at the orange globe of his belly, who marvelled at the size of the polar bears as they rose onto their hind legs to sniff out their dinner.

Ruby was transfixed by the polar bears.

'She must be eight foot tall,' she said, 'standing up like that.'

'How do you know she's a she?' Henry asked.

Ruby smiled and, sliding one arm around his waist, tilted her head onto his chest. 'Oh, she has to be a she,' she answered quietly. 'Look how powerful she is. I'd love to be a polar bear.'

'You would?'

She turned to look up at him. 'Don't you laugh at me, Twist!' she warned, screwing a knuckle into the gap between two of his ribs.

He wriggled away from her, one hand still at the small of her back. 'All right, all right. I'm not.' They settled into each other again. 'Why do you want to be a polar bear?'

There was a long silence as they watched the two bears, startlingly white against their sandy enclosure, trundle towards their feeding cage on too-big paws then rise up again, their triangular heads searching the bars, their wide black noses pushing at the air.

'Because,' she said eventually, 'when you're that strong, you mustn't be afraid of anything.'

It was probably the closest Ruby ever came to admitting being scared. Her bravery was something she prided herself on. But Henry came to know it, her fear: it was what prompted her anger, what woke her at night, what caused her to stand straighter when she had an audience. It was what made other people think she was the most confident woman in all of London.

He lets Libby's pram roll to a stop when he realises that, without thinking about it, he has walked all the way to Regent's Zoo. He can see nothing from here. He stands at an exterior wall and pauses, his ears searching the night for the sound of some animal within. What he needs now is life. Just that. Life: the affirmation of it. Overhead, the moon dips and weaves between the clouds in a complicated game of hide-and-seek, lighting then darkening the world below. Henry waits in the shadows, breath held, for another thread of moonlight to find him. And God, doesn't he long to be found. That's what Ruby had done for him – she had found him sinking in memories of mud, and held onto him, and now, without her, he is lost again.

Henry closes his eyes and reaches once more for a sound, a shuffle of evidence to prove that he has company. He had done the same thing in France, hunkering low in the dark and searching for a stifled cough or sob in the quiet chorus of the night. Then, he had needed to confirm that there were still men alive out there. Now, he needs only to confirm that he is. He waits. And maybe a minute later he thinks he hears it: a deep-throated, meaty kind of bellow that he decides must be coming from the camel enclosure. He can compare the sound only to something demonic, but it is issuing from another living animal, and it relaxes him enough to slow his breathing, to persuade him to open his eyes. And what he sees when he does, far along the street, is the figure of a man: a tall man, a slight man, his hands shoved into his pockets as he walks away, trailing a whistled tune behind him.

'Jack,' he breathes.

But Henry cannot move more than two steps to chase after him. He is not sure, any more, why he should want to. This is not the anger he was expecting to feel. There is no surge of fury to entice him to run Jack Turner down, as he'd imagined he would, and beat answers out of him. There is no pounding temptation, rushing through his blood, to take action. Henry is motivated only to stand and watch him saunter through the city, and he is shocked by this passivity. It is born, undeniably, of relief. But why, why should this stranger in an oversized coat bring him relief? He cannot account for it.

From her pram, Libby lets out a whimper. Perhaps she is beginning to feel the cold. Or perhaps, being able to view only the shifting sky from where she lies, she feels she has been abandoned. Henry returns to the front of the pram to allow his daughter to see him, then, dropping himself into a crouch, puts his hand to the soft protrusion of her belly. She is so delicate that he could injure her with just two fingers. She is so perfect that he aches just to look at her. And that is why he is terrified of being her father – because she is perfect and delicate and he doesn't know if he can protect her from the world.

'We'll go home, shall we?' he asks her, the way Ruby would have done, the question turned about on itself. He experiments with this, sometimes; with constructing sentences as Ruby did. He wants Libby to know the cadences of her mother, of herself.

Libby considers him seriously, those little eyes filled with some unknowable logic.

'Yes, we'll go home.' He curls his hands around the pram's handles. 'Home,' he says as he steps forwards. 'Just me and you.'

Though he's not entirely sure why, some part of him thinks he should invite Jack to come with them: to warm himself at the fire or drink a cup of tea. But when he lifts his head to check how far down the street he has gone, there is no trace of Jack Turner.

The man has disappeared.

He reappears though, for fleeting visits. He does not leave Henry alone. When Henry rides the Tube to and from work, he dances on and off it, never venturing close enough for Henry to call out to him. On Threadneedle Street, Henry catches glimpses of him peacocking through the crowds. When Henry sets out on his midnight walks, he is sure Jack follows him, echoing his footsteps, managing to conceal himself for the most part but neglecting, now and then, to hide the tell-tale stretch of his shadow. He becomes Henry's very own phantom.

And Henry begins to welcome the arrangement.

He hadn't realised it until tonight, when he was disappointed to see nothing of Jack on his walk, but truly he is growing comfortable with this haunting of his. It is all the companionship he is capable of just now.

Wandering over to the window, he puts his nose to the glass and peers out past the fogging of his own breath. The rain has polished the road to a gleam, and Henry can see the house reflected back in it: a squat, faded version of reality. A woman stutters past, tipped forward on her heels, her head down as she swerves around the deeper puddles. He recalls a similar night, before they were married, when he'd stood waiting on Ruby like this. He had promised to take her somewhere fancy for drinks, though he was hoping, as he always did, that she would be too tired to venture out when she reached him. It was for that reason that he kept the flat a little too warm when he was expecting her. He wanted to lull her into staying here, where he could keep her for himself, where he wouldn't have to tolerate the touch of other men's want on her skin. The rain, working in his favour, was falling ruthlessly. He was anticipative of hours spent together; only together.

He watched until Ruby dashed into view, her flowered umbrella bobbing and spinning above her head, her feet made invisible by the speed at which they covered the pavement, her handbag flapping in the gale that was picking up. The rest of the street was nothing more than a smudge the weather had made. But it was as though Ruby had been stencilled over it, she was so unspoiled, so sharp a picture. Henry could distinguish her every line: the red arcs of her lipstick; the black flicks at the corners of her eyes; the pendulum swing of a single pearl necklace across her chest. She was flustered – he could tell by the set of her shoulders. Pinched fingers holding her umbrella's canopy in place, she swept her head left then right before scurrying across the road. There, she paused for a moment to flatten her skirt. Then, with a huff, she glanced up towards the window Henry was standing at. Foolish, he dropped to the floor, a soldier again caught in enemy sights. He blushed even as he did it. But he couldn't possibly be observed waiting on her; couldn't possibly show, though Ruby was shrewd enough to see it anyway, any sort of dependence on this bold little woman who had crashed into his life.

He was still crouched on the floor when she rapped on the door. He was just striding into the hallway when she pushed open the letterbox and, putting her mouth to the new space, called, 'Hurry up, Twist. I'm soaked through and desperate to take all my clothes off.'

They had kissed there in the hallway, time punctuated only by the tap of rainwater on the tiles as it dropped from the hem of Ruby's skirt, until Ruby had started to laugh.

'What?' Henry frowned down at her. 'What's funny?'

'Nothing. It's just … I spent two hours getting ready and look at me.' With a shrug, she flicked at the dripping strands of her hair. 'How is any woman supposed to impress her man when the sky is falling in?'

Henry smirked. '*Her* man?'

'Her man. A man.' She rolled her eyes, slapping at his shoulders.

Later, though, in bed, she ran a fingertip through the wing-shaped spread of hair across his chest and whispered, 'You are mine, you know, Henry Twist. I chose you because I knew you were supposed to be.'

Henry wakes to find himself curled in the window-seat, one hand opened to the woman who should be sitting alongside him, his palm cold and empty. Groaning against the old aches the war deposited through his limbs, along his spine, he sits up and stretches. These are the worst moments, the waking moments. He is not alone when he sleeps. Turning, he looks out into the night again, seeking another human being. There is always this now. Always this imprecise need … And then there, as if by some dark magic, as if Henry himself has summoned him, is Jack. He leans against the nearest street-lamp, his hands bunched in his pockets, one foot cocked up over the other, and he smiles and smiles and smiles.

Henry knocks his knuckles against the glass. 'Jack!' he calls. 'Jack!' He is breathless suddenly. He is, he realises, excited. Here is his opportunity to invite Jack inside, to speak with him properly, to learn where he's come from and where he's going and what it is that he wants. But then Henry blinks, and in that trivial slice of a second when his eyes are closed, Jack vanishes. He vanishes so quickly that it is impossible he was ever there to begin with.

And, 'Ah,' Henry says, because he needs to tell his sleeping daughter that he understands now. He does. He thinks he does. He'll go to that party Matilda invited him to.

THE WHITE PARTY

He is somewhere in Belgravia, sloping about in search of the rear gates the invitation has specified he must enter by. He has been walking for half an hour, maybe a little more, and he is appreciative, as ever, of the gradual loosening of his muscles. Each time he steps his city's streets, he remembers how much he loves this movement, just for the rhythmic pleasure of it. He ought to take more exercise, he thinks. And soon he will: one day, he'll remove himself from the bank and never again sit to a desk. He'll like that.

Rounding a corner, invitation in hand, he checks the road name again and, when he looks up, realises he needn't have. Ahead are a pair of wide black gates, their iron curls laced through with white ribbon. This is the place.

He approaches quietly, not wanting to draw attention to himself, and eases the gate open. At the crest of a rolling grassy wave, the house floats: squat and old and riddled, lopsidedly, with climbing ivy. Henry does not need to have visited before to know that these people have money. It is apparent, too, that the gardens have been transformed for the party. He stands at the entrance to a dream.

At the garden's centre, moated by circularly arranged flower-beds, stand three ancient trees. They are leafless of course on this first day of February, but they are not bare. From every branch, loops of white material have been suspended, tied at each end so that they form low-hanging, soft-seated swings. Presently, three slender ladies lift their feet off the ground and sway themselves into action. Henry pauses a moment to watch their pendulous game, but his eye is soon drawn away, because everywhere there is something to look at. A white dance floor has been laid over the grass: it is slack, and possibly fashioned from bed sheets, but under the midnight sky it looks like foot-printed snow. Tables and chairs have been spotted around, each draped in its own colourless cloth, and at the centre of each table, a single candle burns inside a glass jar. Four or five waiters swerve between multiple burning braziers, carrying shiny trays of white wine.

'You made it,' Grayson says, appearing at Henry's side with a smile and offering his hand. They shake, touching shoulders briefly. 'Thank God. This isn't for me at all. They were silly-drunk when we arrived, the whole crowd. Can't find a sensible word between them.'

They stand and survey the gardens, Grayson dragging on a cigarette. There are perhaps fifty guests present, each dressed as the invitation dictated, though some more elaborately than others. A handful of ladies wear plain evening dresses with long gloves and appear, despite the hour and the temperature, not to be frozen to the bone. A few men have procured the correct colour trousers and teamed them with simple shirts and jackets. Most people, however, have made costumes of furs and scarves and even masks, beaded or pearled, which they hold before their faces only for brief spells before removing them to take their next drink. They battle the cold with pale velvet capes and greatcoats and ushanka hats.

A young woman passes and, without stopping, inserts a white rose between two of Henry's shirt buttons.

Grayson shrugs and indicates his own jacket pocket. 'One for every guest. Don't bother trying to rid yourself of it.'

Henry feels he has stepped into a theatre, or a circus, or a fantasy. Instantly, he is glad he decided to come. Do the normal things, Vivian had said. Don't forget the normal things. And he supposes that is advice he has to live by, if he wants to keep Libby a secret; if he wants to push Jack from his mind. He had known without searching that he didn't have any suitable clothes, and he hadn't tried to find any, so he wears a white shirt, a vest beneath it, a pair of lightest brown slacks, and a coat, which he removes now that he is in the midst of all this pale decoration, to make himself less conspicuous. Tonight is his first attempt at enjoying company and he doesn't want to attract attention. Rather, he wants simply to be functional amongst people again. And he is glad he does not have to attempt that at Monty's. Not yet.

It had occurred to him that he might not return to Monty's at all; that it was a place too full of Ruby. But he cannot avoid every street she walked, every room she entered, every place he stood or sat or passed through and thought of her. He cannot avoid London.

'Gray,' Henry ventures. 'I meant to thank you, for that week. I –'

'Don't you dare,' Grayson says, his words carried on a cloud of smoke. 'I won't have you thanking me for a damned thing. I'm surprised you survived that week, Twist, I really am. But I'll tell you something, I would've done a lot more than I did do if I'd thought it would've helped.'

Henry nods at the ground.

'I've tried to tell Tilda to lay off, you know,' Grayson continues. 'She's just ... headstrong. I'm sure she'll calm down soon enough, once the grief eases a bit.'

———

Grayson knows this is not true, but he thinks his delivery fairly convincing. Henry will not reflect on something so insignificant as his words anyway. Not yet.

Grief, for Grayson, has only visited once – when his mother, the only parent worth investing anything in, submitted quietly but moodily to the Spanish Flu. He had always thought she would be the stoic sort, slipping away with squeezes of hands and promises that she'd be watching, but that flu left her confused and nasty and, though he still doesn't want to admit it, bloody frightened.

'So,' he says, to keep his thoughts in the present. 'You're back at work.'

'Unfortunately,' Henry replies.

'Needs must, I suppose.'

Henry nods and Grayson tries to think of something hopeful to say, something inspiring, but he is distracted by the idea that he is experiencing a sort of grief too: a different, lesser sort, yes, but he is grieving all the same. For his marriage. And though it is not intentional, Henry is the cause of that. And for a moment, a shot of time as ephemeral as a raindrop, Grayson hates him for it.

'I'll get us some drinks,' he says, and strides away, persuading himself as he goes that when he returns with two glasses of wine and a fresh cigarette, he will have forgiven Henry. It is Matilda, after all, who does not deserve his understanding.

—

Four or five emptied wine glasses later, Henry stands near a piano, listening hazily to Monty as he teases the keys. In this white world, the deep polished mahogany draws the guests towards it as though it has a gravity of its own, and they sing along as Monty skips from song to song, sometimes finding the right notes, sometimes stumbling onto the wrong ones. Voices drown out his mistakes.

Eventually, Monty stands and stretches out his arms and everyone groans.

'That's all I've got,' he declares, holding up his old hands. 'Who's next?'

A woman in furs is thrust forward to take his place, and as she settles herself on the stool and runs her fingers along a scale to get a feel for the instrument, Monty curls an arm around Henry's shoulders and steers him towards the deserted trees. There, they slump into a pair of fabric swings. Monty clears his throat to speak, but Henry beats him to it.

'I can't talk about her yet,' he says.

'Actually, I was going to ask you about you,' Monty replies.

'It's the same question, isn't it?'

'For the moment, perhaps.'

Monty straightens his legs to push himself backwards and his trousers lift to reveal a pair of skinny ankles. Henry studies the fine taper of ageing bone beneath the socks, thinking that Montague seems decades older now than when they first met, just a few weeks after he met Ruby.

Henry was waiting for her outside the theatre, where they had arranged to see a late showing. It was half past ten and should have been dark, but it was midsummer and the sky retained a thin, royal blue hue: against it, the street-lamps looked too yellow, like the flesh of a pineapple. Midges swirled on the air. Each time he heard approaching footsteps, he scanned the street, anticipating her new dainty presence. Ruby was living at that time over on Strawberry Hill, sharing a muddled, slanting-roofed attic flat with a large-chested girl named Daisy, and it took forever to get there. As a result, they usually met halfway between Strawberry Hill and Bayswater Road. Tonight, though, Henry had insisted Ruby come closer to him, so that he could persuade her back to the flat and keep her until the next day.

He was unsure how well received this plan would be, but he was chancing a bad reaction, because he couldn't quite believe his initial attraction hadn't faded. In fact, it was getting stronger, and he'd never known that before.

By eleven o'clock, he was still standing on the same spot, just in front of the poster for the film they had missed.

As Henry recalls, it was some drama of Daisy's that kept Ruby away that night. She appeared on his doorstep at seven the following morning with a bag of jelly babies, a smile, and no apology. Before he gave up on her and left the theatre, though, Monty had stepped out of the café across the street and, when Henry snapped his head around at the sound of shoes on the pavement, laughed and said, 'If you're not waiting for a woman, I'll give you all the money on my person.'

'Guilty,' Henry smiled.

'Shame,' Monty replied, pulling a wallet from his pocket to show Henry the stack of pound notes within. He winked. 'A single ticket might have made you rich tonight. But then, perhaps you're rich enough already. What's her name?'

Henry flicked his eyes at the ground then back at Monty. He didn't know how to talk frankly, as this stranger in an expensive silk cravat seemed to. He'd never learned. 'Ruby,' he said.

'Ah,' Monty nodded. 'A jewel. Then you're a wealthy man indeed. But since she's late, how about a nightcap?' He indicated the café he had just stepped out of, dimly lit but clearly still serving. Low, slinking conversation slipped out under the door. Shadows hunched over table tops, dealing and laying cards. 'We're one short for the next hand.'

When Ruby knocked at his door the next morning, Henry did not tell her that he'd been asleep for only two or three hours. He did not tell her either that he was so many pounds richer than before. Instead, he bought her a ring.

'Why did you introduce yourself to me, that night outside the theatre?' Henry asks now. Suddenly, there are so many obvious questions that no one has bothered to ask Monty; questions that hadn't occurred to Henry when he was happy. Perhaps they haven't occurred to the others either.

Monty begins swinging, without lifting his feet off the floor. 'Because you looked lonely.'

'And what about you?'

'I looked pretty swift, I'd say, for a man of my age.' Monty lets out one of his crackling laughs, and Henry turns to face him.

'Were you ever married, Monty?'

Monty stops swinging and looks at Henry properly. 'No.'

'Is that why you fill your garden with people, because you're lonely?'

'I suppose so.'

'Then why didn't you marry? Even after the war, you could have. For companionship, even.'

'Would you have married any of the women you had before your Ruby?' Monty asks, and Henry colours a little at the old man's phrasing. His father would never have spoken such a sentence. These were the kind of things Ruby said though, in private, and gradually Henry had learned to stop blushing. In private.

'No.'

'And I wouldn't have married anyone apart from my Alice. Still wouldn't, for that matter.'

'You've never spoken about an Alice before.'

'It's not a very happy subject.'

'Did she die?' Henry blurts, and instantly he regrets his candour.

'She did not. She still lives in Bloomsbury, with her husband. They had four children, so I imagine she has a few grandchildren by now too. What else would you like to know?'

Ordinarily, Henry wouldn't say anything more. But Monty is wearing a little smile and nodding encouragement, and Henry thinks maybe Monty needs to talk as much as he needs to listen.

'Was she already married when you met her?'

'No. I proposed myself, the next day, but –'

'The next day!' Henry interjects. 'No wonder she turned you down.'

They share a quiet laugh and Monty shoves Henry so that he rocks away from him. 'That's more like it,' he says. 'Always so hard to shock lately. I knew you weren't gone forever. Now, do you want to hear about it or not?'

'Yes,' Henry says.

'Good. She was nearly as tall as you are, my Alice – though a deal more pleasant in the body; of course – and she had the brightest red hair, and the gentlest way of laughing. It was her eyes that really did it, though. They were the purest green you could imagine. Clear as a good cut of diamond. Clearer, even.' He tries not to sigh, but Henry can hear it, gathering up inside him, the breathy sadness.

'Why do you stay so close?'

'Because she loved me, and I loved her, and being further away wouldn't change it.'

The woman in the fur stops playing and a cheer goes up around the piano. Henry sees Matilda peering around her, neck stretched long, as another player is pushed forward; then Gray, at her side, putting a hand to her waist and speaking into her ear. Perhaps he is inviting her to dance. She doesn't meet her husband's eye. Instead of enjoying the party, she continues to search it. For Henry.

'Why did she refuse you?' Henry asks.

'Because she loved him more,' Monty answers.

'I'm sorry, Monty. I shouldn't have asked. I probably wouldn't have if I weren't so drunk.'

Monty laughs and he and Henry watch as the guests divide into pairs to jitter around the dance floor. Within three or four bars they're up to speed, some intuited knowledge spinning them away from collisions. From where Henry and Monty sit, they blend, one couple into the next: ashen limbs tangle up in each other; the dance floor crinkles and shifts under scores of feet; dark hair whips around dizzyingly. Above, the clouds peel away to reveal a perfect spherical moon and everything below is turned to silver.

'I probably wouldn't have answered if you weren't so drunk,' Monty admits finally. 'But listen, if second-best does come along, well, I'd say second-best isn't so bad, that's all. In time.'

———

Dawn crawls up the sky, the delicate pink of flushed skin. London is not yet awake. They lie, the guests, all across the garden; arms spread wide or folded under their heads; heads back to view the beginning of the day or resting on lovers' chests. They are warmed by last night's drink and the morning's new light and the still-burning braziers and the somnolent pleasure of a successful party. Deep within the host's rambling house, a cook clatters pans and the sound rings distantly through an open window slat, but it does not disturb them. Occasionally, a lone figure passes on the other side of the boundary wall and they count its progress together, the creak of every frosty forward pace loud in the silence of this, the most clandestine part of the day.

'Who are the most miserable people in the world?' someone asks. They take turns to speak, holding one sprawling conversation rather than breaking into smaller groups. They are subdued and peaceful. It is the perfect time to talk nonsense.

'Our parents,' someone answers.

'Prime ministers' wives,' a female voice offers.

'Lovers,' a man suggests gruffly.

Monty interrupts. 'This is a depressing subject,' he says. 'I propose a change.'

'Proposal approved,' says the boy Henry believes to be the owner of the property. He is young and foppish and embodies the Bright Young People perfectly, Henry thinks. 'New subject,' he calls. 'Anyone?'

'All right. Who are the happiest people in the world?'

'The ignorant ones.'

'It's got to be us, surely?'

'Not compared to children. I say children.'

'I say lovers,' the gruff man suggests again.

'You can't use the same answer for both questions.'

'I can if it's true.'

'Adjudication Mr Chairman,' someone calls, and they titter as one, like a flock of birds turning on the same invisible current, feathers twitching in perfect unison.

'You've got to appoint a chairman before appealing to him.'

'Well, that sounds like an awful lot of effort. I submit new subject.'

'I concur.'

This time, Matilda suggests the topic. 'The most important people,' she says. She is lying with her head propped between Henry's feet. Grayson is to her left, hands slotted into each other over his stomach. He could easily put an arm around Tilda or pull her to him, and Henry wills him to move, but he doesn't: he breathes the slow, unbroken breaths of a sleeper.

'You can't say "lovers" this time.'

'Soldiers, then.'

'Not much call for soldiers these days.'

'Charlie Chaplin.'

'Anyone but Baldwin, ay?'

They cheer this, but not too loudly. They know the right volume, the right pace for their words. The immutability of the hours between these perimeter walls has led to a regression. A hundred years might have passed since they stepped through those ribboned gates, and they have become, in the interval, an embodiment of the more primitive version of their species. They are a pack of humans.

At least, this is how it feels, to be so drunk and so tired and so free. Work calls none of these people, especially on a

Saturday morning, and Henry wonders how many of them have children to return to – though most, he supposes, employ nannies. He soon empties these thoughts from his mind, however, because he has an uneasy feeling that even his thoughts are not confidential here; that they might be accessed by some telepathic trick. Still, he does not banish Ruby. He will willingly share Ruby before he will push her aside, and today he sees her sulking at the foot of the stairs, the early weeks of her pregnancy making her nauseated and slow-eyed. He shapes her from the head down – as though he is encountering her from the front doorway, as he did months before – urgently recalling the slope of her tired shoulders, the tilt of her head against the stair spindles, the curl of her arms around her legs, the layers of clothes she had piled on because, she said, she couldn't remember what warm felt like.

'Enough of people,' someone says. 'Let's do words.'

'What, the saddest and the happiest?'

'I have one that's both. Happy and sad.'

'Well? Don't keep us in suspense.'

'Home,' the woman concludes. 'Happy when you're there, sad when you're not.'

'Or the other way around, dear,' an older woman quips.

And so it continues, until the pavements beyond the property are noisy with walkers and motorcars stutter into life and horses snort against the weight at their backs. The beginning of real life, it seems, marks the end of the collective night-time existence of all these bodies, and they rise from the ground like ghosts and glide away.

Henry suspects he will never meet any one of them again, and that is apt, really. Last night, he stepped out of his life. Now, he is disgusted by his behaviour. However well he might have dressed it up, he had come here because he wanted to escape.

On the corner where Matilda and Grayson part ways with Henry, the three stop. They slump at the window of a bookshop, turned away from the displayed spines and pages, puffing heat into their hands. Shoppers swerve fluidly around them, bags bumping legs.

'Why not have breakfast with us?' Matilda asks. Though all three's eyes hang heavy in their faces, though she aches for her bed, though she knows Henry will want to get back to Libby, she cannot relinquish the hope of extending their time together.

She has not told Gray about the baby. She knows she should have. Yes, she knew that as she walked home from Henry's, alone but not frightened by the city; and when, that night, Grayson brought her a drink and settled by the fire to ask how Henry was doing; and later, as she lay beside her sleeping husband, trying to recall the last time they had touched. Keeping her secret, though, was more of a thrill. It was something she and Henry could share. For now, its promise will have to be enough.

'You're more than welcome, Twist,' Grayson says. 'You know that.'

'I can't,' Henry answers. He fixes Matilda with one of those looks. She knows it is not for her – he snares everyone the same way, with a narrowing of his eyes and a hardening of his jaw as he takes in every detail – but she feels it: it breaks over her, like a raincloud collapsing just inches above her head. 'Will you explain everything, to Gray, when you get home?'

'Of course.' She nods. 'But you know –'

She stops because Henry's head has snapped up. He is not listening. He is staring instead down the street, in the direction they have just come. She and Grayson follow his gaze, but they see nothing unusual about the swirl and flow of Londoners, bundled into thick coats and wool scarves, their hats making each one indistinguishable from the next.

'Henry, darling,' she begins, but Henry holds a palm up

for her to stop. His lips purse to shush her. Then, without so much as a glance at his friends, he launches himself forward and sprints away down the street.

Matilda watches him go, mouth still half-open. She measures the rapidity with which each foot flicks up behind him. She notices that his loose coat lashes people as he speeds around them. She gasps when the crowds grow too heavy and he jumps down into the road and keeps running, running, as cars beep at him and a bicycle is forced onto the kerb and its rider is thrown sideways, and someone shouts after Henry to 'Watch it!'

'What was that about?' she says.

'Haven't a clue,' Grayson answers, and as he does, he reaches to take her fingers in his. Feeling the cool proximity of her husband's flesh next to hers, Matilda crosses her arms over her chest.

'Home, then,' Grayson mutters, and they turn and continue on their way, moving quickly through the arctic breeze, an unbridgeable gap no bigger than a newborn child between their marching arms.

When they reach their building, they are silent and still confused. Gray fumbles around for the key and Matilda snipes at him for taking too long, stamping her heels on the door-step. They did not see the man Henry saw sauntering through the morning crowds, his worn brown trousers held by limp braces, his newsboy tipped to the back of his head, his wavy brown hair gathering at the nape of his neck into smaller, tighter curls. They did not see him. And even if they had, they would not have recognised him as the man who has invaded Henry's mind. How could they have? Henry is still struggling to recognise it himself.

ENCOUNTERS

He fills Libby's days with promises. Her nights, too.
Though they are alone, he cannot bring himself to sing
her lullabies. He runs through them in his mind, he invents
the words he fails to remember, but when he opens his mouth
there is nothing waiting behind his lips. Strings of crisp black
letters melt away. He has become a sort of mute. He thinks
it is because he can envisage Ruby so clearly, stuffing the flat
full of songs, and it makes him feel inadequate: Libby has been
denied more than half the parenting she would have known.
So instead, he whispers promises into the smooth peach perfection of her ear. Promises of gentle hills and greenest fields and
long bleak winter beaches they will visit, the bleached sand
snatched at by frothing salt waves. They will look out at all
these things, knowing that her mother looked at the very same
views at one time or another, knowing that it is the land which
birthed and moulded Ruby Elizabeth Twist.

Now, he carries his daughter to the window and inspects
the street below. Henry had told him to come quietly, and not
until after midnight, and that he must not knock the door, but
he doesn't trust him to abide by these rules.

Jack Turner, it seems, is something of a loose cannon.

When Henry caught up to him after the party, he had been

trying to persuade a red-faced costermonger – cart stuffed with crusty flashes of dark-silver fish – to let him 'help out with the heavy work' with grins and flourishes of his slim but big-knuckled hands. 'I'm a grafter,' Henry heard him say. 'The most honest-to-goodness grafter this side of –'

He did not finish the sentence. He felt Henry rushing towards him and turned away from the coster, who immediately resumed his bellowing. Seeing Henry, Jack smiled and let out a friendly little grunt, then dropped his hands into his pockets.

'Henry,' he said simply.

Henry stopped in front of him, chest heaving. He could not remember the last time he had run anywhere. 'Jack,' he replied, holding out his hand.

'Where are you flying off to?' Jack asked as they shook.

'Here,' Henry answered. 'Just here. I wanted to ... say sorry, I ... I've had a lot of apologising to do lately, and I ... Sorry, that's all.'

'Sorry?' Jack laughed. 'What the hell for?'

'Being so rude that night, outside the flat.'

'You had every right to be rude.' His hand flew out and grabbed an apple from a second costermonger's cart while the owner's head was turned. He tossed it into his other hand then slipped it inside his jacket. 'I was loitering. With intent, probably.'

Henry frowned at him. He was starting to regain his breath now. He was standing taller. He was still measuring the physical threat Jack posed. Though something made him want to talk to this man, be near him; if he could have, Henry Twist would have taken a measuring tape to Jack Turner and compared their every dimension.

'You were going to rob me?'

'Maybe,' Jack answered, shrugging, his dark eyes widening into a look of faultless candour. 'That, or knock and enquire after a room.'

When Henry did not speak, Jack continued. 'Are you going to punch me for that bit of honesty? Because really, I don't think my old brain is up to another wallop.'

'No,' Henry answered. 'No, not at all. The bruise on your cheek?'

'That was the first wallop, yes. Now, what can I do for you, Henry?' He raised a palm. 'Wait, before you answer that.' He spun around and, without waiting for the coster to pause in his shouts for custom, flexed his lean arm like a strongman. 'I've just the build for the work, don't you think?' He winked at the man, who raised a fleshy fist and pumped it at him, though without any real aggression. Retrieving the stolen apple from inside his jacket, he turned to the second coster. He spun the apple like a cricket ball then, catching it, took a large, loud bite. 'And I particularly like your apples, sir. Best in the city.' He began to back away and Henry followed him. The second coster shone red with the effort of staying put: he could not leave his cart unattended to chase after a thief. 'You know where to find me if you find you need a second pair of hands,' he called finally, then to Henry he said quietly: 'Right, where were we?'

By that point, Henry had not known what to say. He doubted in fact that he'd had anything to say in the first place, but stepping along next to Jack, the shouts of a few street sellers bulging in the smoky air, the smell of earth-wet vegetables forcing its way into his nose and mouth, his only thought was this: how can I keep this man nearby? So he stopped, planted his feet, looked Jack straight in the eye and said, 'Do you still need somewhere to stay?'

It was probably one of the more foolish things he'd ever done, and thankfully, Jack had already found lodgings, but it got them talking at least and Henry – undeniably relieved to be conversing with someone who had never clapped eyes on his wife – found that he didn't want to stop. He listened as Jack told him how he'd woken on the floor of a pub some weeks ago, blood on his tongue and a pain in his head as intense and sure as hell; how the landlord had relayed an account of his being set upon the night before, for an unknown or concealed reason, and beaten halfway to death before a couple of drinkers intervened; how he could not remember a single thing preceding that hazy moment when he was roused by the glare of first light breaking through the dusty window of the Prince of Wales and found himself flat on his back, his every bone aching against hours on wooden floorboards, laid out at the mercy of God Himself and every man beneath Him.

Henry did not comment on any of this. He waited for Jack to stop talking and told him, in the most honest way he could, that strange as it might seem he was in need of a new friend. They arranged to meet three days later: after midnight, Henry had insisted, though he hadn't explained why. And oddly, Jack hadn't asked. This only begins to bother him now that it is five minutes to one, and he has been watching the clock tick since a minute past twelve, and he is anxious – though he refuses to dwell on the potency of this feeling – that Jack will not come.

He is still worrying his entire body into a state of rigidity at ten past two, when he hears footfalls fast on the front steps.

Opening the door, he finds Jack with his head bent down, concentrated on the ankle he is flicking about so that his snapped bootlace dances like a charmed snake. He wears the same tatty ensemble, his newsboy at the wrong angle, his braces still flaccid across his chest. His shirt, though, remains white. Henry suspects he scrubs it every night.

'So, why all this mystery?' Jack asks, without lifting his head. 'Don't know if I'm one to do as instructed, really, but it seemed I ought to in this case.'

'Come in,' Henry answers, moving sideways in the door to clear a path. For some reason, he is standing as though steadying himself for a fight. He shakes his free arm out at his side, releasing the tension.

'How do I know it's safe?'

'What?'

'Well, you could have something to do with my ...' Jack points to his head.

'There's nothing in there but a sleeping baby,' Henry says. He has already deposited Libby safely upstairs, with Viv, just in case – but the mention of a new child is so far from threatening that surely Jack will stay now. 'But if you don't want to take your chances ...'

Jack peers around Henry into the dusky space beyond. The lamplight seeps like low cloud between the spindles of the staircase and Henry remembers the carved out letters that fill the top steps. He hopes they are not visible.

'I'm not sure I do,' he says, smiling wide. 'Let's go and have some fun. You're a man in need of fun, aren't you, Henry? How about the dog track?'

'I can't go far.'

'Just over to the park then,' Jack suggests. 'You can watch the house from there, and I can watch my back.'

'Are you always so suspicious?'

'I suspect only since I started getting attacked in pubs, but then, perhaps I'm just a suspicious fellow. Either way, we certainly won't find out tonight. Shall we begin with proper introductions?' He offers Henry his hand again and they shake roughly, each squeezing just a touch harder than is necessary. 'Jack Turner,' Jack says. 'I'm pretty convinced about that much now.'

'Henry Twist,' Henry returns. 'And that was never in doubt.'

They sit languid with companionship in the park, their feet dampening in the grass, their mouths shaping smile after smile. They are discovering that they like each other. And this is as much a surprise to Henry as anything, because he knows he should not be here. Tonight, it seems reckless, how often he leaves Libby with Vivian. The woman is old and tired. Each time she drops into sleep, she is chancing one more dangerous descent towards death. And he'd know nothing of it, sitting here, chatting with a man he barely knows. And what of Jack in any case? Jack might be a diversion. This might all be a set-up.

But, no. He's being foolish now. Yes, Henry knows he should not be here, but somehow, Jack has persuaded him that it will be all right. He is persuading him, word by empty word, that he is exactly where he ought to be.

Mostly, Jack talks and Henry listens, and this suits them both. Henry still finds it difficult to sustain conversation, though it is coming back to him – like a memory long discarded then felt for again with the most tentative explorations of fingertips. Perhaps Jack's memory will come back to him this way, Henry thinks, but he opts not to voice the thought: he does not know him well enough to offer him hope. He has made that mistake before. The first time it was his young sapper friend, Bingley, who he preached so ignorantly to of belief and fortitude when the boy was missing most of his internal organs. The second time it was his father. Twice is too often to have made that mistake. He will not make it again.

'All right, what about work?'

Jack closes his eyes and hums while he thinks. 'No,' he decides. 'Not a single thing.' He raises his hands in front of him and cups the damp air. 'Although, I feel like I might have worked with my hands.' His eyes spring open and he spreads his fingers to consider their lengthy shape. 'These, my friend, are an effective pair of hands.'

They sit side by side on the bench, the lamp-lit flat diagonally in front of them on the opposite pavement, and Henry glances to his right: Jack lounges back, his elbows propped on top of the seat's wooden slats, his legs stretched long. He is grinning.

'Maybe you were a carpenter,' Henry suggests.

'Maybe,' Jack answers. 'But I'm thankful now, whatever I was. I'd never have found anywhere to stay if it weren't for these hands.' He lifts them from the wrists and presents them again with a wink.

Henry shakes his head, not understanding.

'I've got no money,' Jack explains. 'How do you think I'm persuading the old lady to let me stay?'

'You're … sharing her bed?'

'No. God, no! I'm in the attic. I let her share mine, though, from time to time. I mean, it's only been a couple of weeks, but it's working out well enough so far.'

Despite himself, Henry begins to laugh. In the empty night-time park, the sound expands as though funnelled through a megaphone. Jack sits up straighter.

'What?' he asks.

'It's just … Is she *really* old?'

'No.' Jack punches Henry's upper arm. 'I don't know. Forty-five, maybe.' Then, sheepishly, laughing too, he adds, 'Definitely not fifty.'

Henry scrunches up his nose. 'Of course not. Forty-nine would be fine but fifty, that would just be, indecorous.'

'Indecorous! Christ, Henry, what are you, a man or a minister? Say it as it is.'

'I try not to.'

'And why the hell is that?'

Henry's father blares through his mind. Not a picture of him exactly, but a sense, like a blast of crisping meat through an opened oven door. It is not as pleasant though, this sense. It is sharper, more complex – like an architect's pencil design, perhaps, held close to the face, the level of detail overwhelming. Henry's father had always been an overwhelming sort.

'No reason,' Henry says.

'Good, then try it.'

Henry smiles, but it is not as free as his laughter was. He

feels his cheek muscles pushing against it.

'Ah, come on,' Jack coaxes. 'How am I behaving, Henry, playing with the old girl's feelings like that?'

'Charitably?' Henry offers.

'Is that the best you can do?' Jack jumps up and stands in front of Henry, arms folded across his chest, head tilted in a parody of inquisitiveness. 'Be disagreeable. It's liberating.'

'Unpleasantly.'

'Unpleasantly,' Jack yells. 'Come on, Henry. Imagine the scene: a lonely woman, an absent husband, a handsome young bugger like me turning up on the door. Give me a word.'

'Disgusting,' Henry says.

'I'd say fucking revolting,' Jack laughs, but immediately Henry sees the sadness behind the joke. The tears prickling Jack's eyes are not born of amusement, and Henry wants – no, needs – to ease the fear Jack has been hiding so well, for his own sake as well as Jack's.

He stands. 'Revolting, then,' he says, louder.

'Revolting,' Jack cries, throwing his head back and flinging out his arms. Though he still laughs, his stance reminds Henry of a writhe of pain. He looks like a man tormented.

'Revolting,' Henry shouts, to distract him from it. 'Revolting.'

'Revolting,' Jack shouts, even louder.

And that is when the rain begins hammering down on them. They stand for a trice, their heads tipped back, their eyes to the heavens, and let drops of the sky fall onto their faces. Heavy beads drum against leaves, bending the flat membranes into gleaming curves. Grass blades cower under the downpour. On Bayswater Road, the streetlamps direct the water to the pavement like kindly theatre ushers. The entire world, it seems, is looking downwards, downwards, but Henry and Jack are looking up, and it does not escape Henry's attention that, were it not for Jack, he would never have lifted his head.

'Run,' he says.

'Run?' Jack asks.

'We'll be soaked otherwise,' Henry answers, pointing towards the flat, and they take off together, he and Jack, bolting across the road and up the front steps. Within seconds, they stand huddled on the threshold as Henry fiddles with the key. Rain batters the road, turning now to noisy hail, and a passing motorcar slows under the onslaught, its headlights marking two dribbling columns on the tarmacadam.

On nights like this, Ruby would stay awake for hours, sitting at the opened window and inhaling the smell of the rain. It was different here, she used to say: thinner in the nose. But she still loved the crackling music it made on the window-panes. She would turn towards him in bed and say, 'Come here a minute,' and he would grin at the funny construction of her sentences and her easy beauty, hair untamed, legs gathered up under the fluid folds of her silk chiffon nightdress, face eerily grey but alive, alive with the shifting reflections of water on glass. She'd never thought she would miss the rain that blew in off the sea at Pwll, relentless as the waves, driving, driving until you thought you could drown in it. She'd told him that a hundred times. London rain was powerless in comparison and it made her long for the drama of the coast. She did not want to go back, not one bit; there was simply a duality within her which meant that, though she was happiest here at the heart of the country, with him, she could not rid her bones, her tissue, her every atom, of Wales.

He pushes open the hallway door and steps through into the front room. And as he does, he almost feels Ruby sitting in the bay window, turned away from him, that nightdress draped like a fan over the seat. He breathes in, expecting her vanilla scent. Then Jack moves behind him, his weight forcing a creak out of a floorboard, and she fades gradually away, like a portrait left in the light and accelerated through a century in a matter of moments. It is as unalterable and devastating as that. Henry loses Ruby a thousand times a day.

The fire has been smouldering for hours, and they move towards its mellow heat together, Jack eyeing the empty cot charily.

'Where's the baby?' he asks. 'Upstairs,' Henry answers. 'She stays with the old woman upstairs. I should fetch her, really. I ...' He doesn't have a good reason to present to Jack. Why should he fetch her, really, in the middle of the night? He simply wants her close by, where he can watch over her. But he doesn't know how to explain that to a man who has either never had children, or forgotten them.

'Then fetch her.' Jack nods, shrugs.

And Henry does. He knocks Viv awake and explains that he is back early from the party he'd invented, that he'd been missing Libby too much to stay. He carries Libby back downstairs, cradling her, shushing her. He settles her in her cot by the fire as Jack, perched now on the arm of the settee, watches him, because suddenly he trusts this man. He does. He cannot fathom it, but he does.

'She died, didn't she, the baby's mother?' Jack mumbles the question, and Henry is confused for a moment. Surely he knows this. Surely everyone knows this. 'Was it the birth?'

Henry takes a deep breath and explains all he can, his voice trembling, his eyes focused on the raindrops which dot the floorboards, like flung stars, between his and Jack's feet. They have almost dried when he runs short of words.

'I'll find you a change of clothes,' he mumbles abruptly then, and steps out into the hallway, away from his wardrobe.

Hand to the banister, he pauses and listens for a movement upstairs, paranoid now that Vivian or Herb will hear Jack's voice. But why, he wonders, should that pose a problem? He would introduce him as a friend, fallen on hard times, who needs a settee for the night. And that would almost be true. Except that Henry does not look at Jack and see a friend. He realises it all at once. He sees in Jack some echo of her.

When he returns with a towel he has retrieved from under

the stairs, Jack is bending over the cot, a smile tweaking the corners of his mouth as he flips his cap over his face and away again, over and away. Henry pauses in the doorframe and watches. Libby, so recently awoken, burbles happily at the game.

'I think she likes me,' Jack says.

'I think she does,' Henry answers, opening the wardrobe and pulling out the trousers and shirt he needs for work the next day. 'Here.' He tosses the clothes onto the bed. He is not going to work anyway.

Jack lowers his cap into the cot towards Libby's waving hands and she makes clumsy grabs for it. Then he unbuttons his shirt and drags it off, wincing as his shoulder pivots out of his braces. The firelight shimmies over his bare torso, revealing the still-dark welts from his beating. All down his left side, along the ridges of his ribs, the bruising is a confusion of ripe red and purple; below, his hipbone is smashed and healing badly; across his chest and stomach heavy blows have split the skin, which still struggles to knit itself back together.

'Christ, Jack,' Henry whispers. 'It's been weeks. I didn't realise it was so bad.'

'It's getting better,' Jack answers. 'It's taking longer than I thought but the pain is lessening, almost every day.'

Henry pinches at his nose and sniffs deep, trying to draw back the tears which clog his throat. Though he does not want to think it, the thought is as obvious as the injuries strewing Jack's body, and it fills him with relief and sadness and, more than that, doubt. Definitely doubt. In fact, he hardly dares to believe it, but he cannot deny that Jack does not look like a man who has simply been beaten. The wounds are too great, too long in mending. He looks rather like a man who has been struck, once, hard, irreparably on his left side. Struck by something huge and unyielding. Something vehicular.

'Throw it over, then,' Jack says, indicating the towel Henry is still clutching.

But Henry does not. He steps across the room, temporarily dumbed. He raises the towel and wraps it around Jack's shoulders. Then, as softly as he can, he gathers the material into his palms and begins running his hands over Jack's body.

Streets away, around corners where streetlamps stutter and past doorways so deep with shadow they can hide love or hate or anything between, through flocks of feathered and sequinned girls filing into dances and the men who hold umbrellas over their heads, and up three narrow flights of stairs, Matilda and Grayson lie in bed, coiled into one another.

They have spent the evening at Monty's, pressed together under a blanket, sitting with their backs to the trunk of the big tree. Matilda knows it is a sycamore, but she has never mentioned the fact. She had not wanted to admit, in front of Henry and Ruby and their simple consuming love, to having the occasion to read about the identification of trees. They would never have considered engaging in such a wasteful activity while the other was close by. Now, with Ruby gone and Henry shrinking in on himself and absent, for the most part, from the garden, she could have told Grayson. She hadn't wanted, though, to make things any less familiar.

Since the White Party, Monty's association with the Bright Young People has grown deeper. They have begun popping in and out of his garden now, and Matilda doesn't like or want the company. It had been their own secret place, just the four of them, and she feels it has been invaded.

Tonight, when a few of the newspaper lot had showed up, she and Grayson had risen and left without a word of discussion. They had arrived home to find the flat depressingly dank and climbed into bed, more to avoid the cold than to be intimate, rolling themselves into their sheets with shrieks and shivers. It was Matilda, in the end, who had reached out to Grayson.

Now, surrounded by nothing it seems but violent hail, her cheek against his chest, she begins to laugh. She had forgotten this feeling; of knowing a body, of expecting hands here or lips there. It is so far removed from the panic and need of loving Henry that she feels relieved. Here, right here, with her husband's slow-softening biceps curled under her neck, she even considers that Monty has talked her into believing in something which is not real. After all, he is handsome, Henry: handsome enough to make you deem his silent brooding interesting, exhilarating, even. Maybe she has been fooled.

'What are you laughing at, woman?' Grayson asks, smoothing her hair back as if she is some breed of lap-pet. She has always been disappointed by her curlless ash-brown hair. She moves her head slightly against his hand to extend the contact.

'I don't know. I just feel like I haven't laughed in such a long time.'

'You lost your friend, Tilda. No one's expected you to.'

The mention of Ruby sobers her and she props herself up on her elbows to look at her husband. Easy, uncomplicated Grayson Steck: his jaw a thicker version of what it was on their wedding day; his light-blue eyes made smaller by amassing wrinkles; his hair greying in three distinct streaks which travel backwards from his forehead to make him look badger-like. She runs a finger back and forth along the shallow V of his collarbone.

'Gray? Do you think there's a reason it was Ruby? I mean … do you think she was too happy?' It is the first time Matilda has spoken Ruby's name since the funeral, and it catches in her throat. Henry, Henry, Henry – that's all it's been. And yes, he lost Ruby, but Ruby lost him too, in a way. Him and everything else, her baby included. It's Ruby she should have been thinking about. The tears are tripping down Matilda's face before she feels the heat they create behind her nose. They are formed from pure shame.

'No, love,' Grayson answers. 'I think she was unlucky. Very unlucky. And I'll tell you something, I miss her more than I thought I would – when it first happened, you know?'

Matilda hums in response. She doesn't want to have to commit to a yes or a no.

'I don't know how Henry does it,' Grayson continues. 'With the baby as well. I wouldn't have the foggiest. Wouldn't even know where to start.'

Matilda says nothing. Suddenly, her husband uttering Henry's name makes her baulk. She doesn't want to hear it. She doesn't even want to think it, or share a bed with a man who is thinking it. Henry has been between their sheets too long.

Pushing herself up onto her knees, Matilda shakes her head. 'Let's not talk about it.'

'No, wait.' Grayson grasps her wrist and pulls her back down into the sheets. 'I've been wanting to talk about it, actually. I didn't want to mention it at first, in case it was a daft idea, but the more I think about it, the more sensible it seems.'

'What seems?'

'We should have the baby,' Grayson replies, sitting up himself now and settling against the wall.

'We can't *have the baby*,' Matilda mutters, closing her eyes. 'He's not going to give her away.'

'But he can't care for her himself, and go to work, and all the rest of it. And he'd be able to see her all the time, if she lived with us. Whenever he wanted. We could even tell her he's her father, when she's old enough. Think about it, Tilda. Properly.'

'It's a terrible idea.'

'It's the best thing for her.'

'Maybe. But what if she was yours, Gray?'

He stops, mouth open, chest puffed, then lets out a long sigh and presses a thumb and a forefinger to his eyebrows. He grows smaller. 'Of course I'd keep her.'

'Of course you would.' She shuffles closer to him and spreads her palm over his heart. 'You're a good man, Gray. My good husband. My good love.' She kisses his nose between words. 'But she wouldn't be ours.'

'No, I suppose not.'

'No.'

Grayson had never once considered, before his marriage, that he would be incapable of fathering children. Or that his wife would be incapable of mothering them. Or both. They do not know whose fault it is, though they are both careful with words like 'fault' and 'problem'. Once, early on, in a conversation held imprudently at a small, wobbling café table, Grayson had called them a failure – not her, *them* – and the fallout had been a long, hideous thing to see. Since, they have shaped their blame in other ways. With sulking, mostly. And embarrassment.

Matilda's flirting, her attention-seeking, the shame she brings him, is another aspect of his marriage he could not have predicted, but then, so many of his ideas have changed in the last twelve years that he cannot say with any certainty what his thirty-year-old self thought or did not think. He believes in his memories of being happy with Matilda. He especially treasures a day they spent on the Tube, permitting the other a brief head start and taking turns to chase or be chased around the city before meeting eventually in Regent's Park; and later, outside a favourite café; and as red evening crashed onto the sky, on the Mall, where they had pretended to be King George and his Queen consort. But he cannot be sure that it truly existed, this happiness. It is possible it was only a trick played on him by infatuation.

As Matilda bestrides him, he searches her face for a flicker of her younger self. He sees traces of her tonight, hidden, and all too often now, beneath hardening layers of disappointment. Soon, he thinks, they will be gone.

'I love you,' he says, testing the sound of that terrible sentiment. Perhaps he will never know if he really means it. Perhaps the only way to test it is to see her dragged under a bus.

'I love you,' she answers, but the response only makes him doubt the concept more. Something plunges inside him. He could say the rest now – the speech he'd planned on using all along, once she'd dismissed the baby idea. It wasn't Libby she did not want: it was him, Grayson. So, if you love him, go to him, he would say. And he had no doubt she would take up the offer.

She kisses his nose again and again before straightening up. 'Listen to that,' she says, smiling. 'The rain has stopped.'

'Has it?' Grayson asks. 'Really?'

'It really has,' Matilda promises. And she is right. Outside the window, the sky is quite abruptly calm. The torrent has hounded the clouds into the distance, to burst over the English countryside. Thousands of Londoners have already ducked through their front doors, though, slamming them against the night. The city's voice has been swept away and in the new silence, Gray puts a hand to his wife's slender neck and whispers a different offer to her.

'What if we tried again?' he says.

AN UNWELCOME LETTER

When the single white envelope drops through the letterbox, Henry is sitting on the stairs in his hallway, counting and recounting the ten days which have passed since he last saw Jack.

True, they did not plan to meet again. Jack has not broken an arrangement. But Henry had thought an agreement implicit in the fact that Jack had not retreated from his touch. In truth, he had seemed to want it, once his initial shock had lessened and the stringy pull of his muscles had loosened. He had stood, still and relaxed, and allowed himself to be dried, then removed from his wet trousers and fitted into Henry's, which swung an inch or so wide at the waist. He had lounged on the settee before the sputtering fire, his chest still bare, and permitted Henry to feel his way along his ribs in search of fractures.

'We used to do this in the army,' Henry said.

'Maybe I did, too,' Jack answered.

It was different, of course, with just the two of them present, but Henry was not uncomfortable, and Jack didn't seem to be either. It was not what it might have looked like, to cynical eyes. It was the first time since that January day that Henry had felt normal.

He considers the letter on the floor below him and decides

not to fetch it yet. He has the only word he wants here, beneath his fingertips. He continues from where he left off: Ruby, Ruby ... It is feasible that Jack grew disgusted by their behaviour later on, when he went back to his attic and his old lady, or when he persuaded some younger woman he had flirted with at a nightclub to disappear into a dark corner with him and recalled the feel of a woman's skin against his own. Henry does not know how he spends his days – but perhaps, under those circumstances, he might have looked back and labelled the whole episode as just a little bit odd. No, Jack would not employ such a bland word. It would be one extreme or the other for him. Because, whatever Henry had said about the army, it was not a time of war. They had not felt their bodies pulled together by the blood-deep fear of taking or sustaining lives. They had stood, face to face, and Henry had touched Jack with the same hesitant need with which he had touched Ruby, before they were married.

Jack had let him.

In the next room, Libby squawks awake and Henry descends the stairs. On the way, he picks up the letter and deposits it on the table beneath the hall mirror. There, he hesitates, and catches in the glass the reflection of the last seconds he and Ruby spent together. At six o'clock in the heavy dark of this March morning, his wife, weeks dead, appears before him piece by piece, like a jigsaw being slotted together. She smiles at him across one imperial foot and the afterlife.

'Ruby,' he murmurs.

She was wearing red, her coat pulled over her swollen stomach – over Libby, who was still a balled-up wealth of possibilities then. Boy or girl. Dark or fair. Henry has come to know her as an uneven mixture of her parents: Ruby's dark eyes; Ruby's ruddy skin; his own sandy hair. Ruby's temperament, he suspects. But then – then he had thought more about the tight sensation of Ruby's distended abdomen as he looped his arms around them both. He had winked at Ruby – the best way he knew to tell her she looked beautiful. And now, he performs these movements again, gently applying his hands to the emptiness that used to be her, and whispering into her neck, 'I've got you. I've got you.'

He returns to the bank sporadically. They excuse his absences – at Yeoman's persuasion, he expects. They excuse his silences, too, as he sits before his adding machine, pressing the numbers, pulling the crank, watching the wheels turn and never once considering whether or not the figures displayed are the ones he ought to be seeing. They excuse his mistakes. He is surrounded incessantly by the pecking of typewriter keys, the clacking of heels on the floor, the undertones of philandering male clerks and the giggles of their female targets. Uninterested in the work, he has turned down promotions in the past but he wishes now he had taken them, solely for the benefit of a more private office.

Today, he is first in. The flat ejected him with the first breath of dawn and the promise of something unpleasant inside that envelope. He knows from the hand who has signed it, with a formal 'sincerely', and he is afraid to liberate the slanting sentences within. He sits at his desk, barricaded from the sad, high-ceilinged magnificence of the office by a deltoid of lamp-light, and, palms flat on yesterday's ledgers, rests his forehead on his arms.

He is not aware of Yeoman, standing behind him, until he speaks.

'Go home, Twist,' he says quietly.

Henry lifts his head. 'I can't.' What he means is, he shouldn't. He is embarrassed when he remembers all those people who carried on after the war; carried on without their husbands or their sons. He has lost only half of what his colleagues think he has lost and still he cannot function properly, cannot complete a working day, cannot speak as he used to speak. He wonders if a man can be stripped of his bravery. Or whether the thing itself is more a commodity than a trait: like money, which can be known in plenty at one moment and entirely depleted the next.

'You can. Look, you're not doing anyone any favours here. You haven't had enough time.'

Henry studies Yeoman's sagging face; the downward slope of skin around his eyes and mouth. In the past, they have wasted evenings together, he and Yeoman, laughing themselves drunk at bars or eating dinner with Mrs Yeoman. They are friends. They used to be.

'What if there isn't enough time?' he says.

But he takes his friend's advice, anyway. He stands, claps Yeoman on the shoulder, and steps out of the bank long before nine o'clock ticks around.

By ten, he is sitting at Vivian's kitchen table, nursing his daughter and conversing in murmurs as Herb naps in his armchair beyond the lounge wall. Heat from the stove smothers the room. Libby purrs in her sleep, her lips clamped around the tip of Henry's little finger. He would like to believe she holds some link with her mother that can't be severed by death — they say, don't they, that children are more open to communication with the spirits. But he doesn't believe it. Not really. He knows that if Libby has any sense of Ruby at all, it is only of the sightless black protection of her womb, the steady drumbeat of her heart.

'What could it say that's so awful?' Viv enquires, pouring tea into two blue-flowered cups. The letter sits on the table between them, made all the more threatening by the tiny neatness of its envelope.

'Perhaps she knows,' Henry says.

'Perhaps you should tell her,' Viv suggests, giving him a playful sideways glance.

'I know, I know. It's just … I'd hoped I could delay until Libby's older. That way, they could see that I'm capable. They wouldn't have any reason to fight me for her.'

'And you think they'll forgive you that, do you?'

'Probably not.'

'Right. Well, then. Open the thing and put yourself out of your misery.'

Henry pushes it towards Vivian. 'You do it. Please, Viv.'

'No chance.' She laughs quietly. 'It might not be from her. Maybe it's a love letter, from that friend of yours.'

Henry's blood quickens at her words. Abruptly, he can feel his own heartbeat, storming in his ears. She saw, then. She saw Jack. Perhaps she happened to look from her window as he skipped down the front steps and away, dragging on his jacket, and presumed. Perhaps she has sympathy for the sort of men she will think them. But then, perhaps not, in the long run. Perhaps her words are her warning, that however well she might like him, she will have no choice but to involve the police eventually.

'What's her name?'

'Her,' Henry repeats stupidly.

'The friend. The tall one. You know.' Viv puts her hands to her cheeks and draws the skin down, sucking in her lips. 'The one looks like she's missed a meal or two.'

'Oh, Matilda,' Henry answers, breathing again. 'Matilda.'

'Hmm. A little older perhaps, but attractive enough, in her way. Is there –'

'She's married.'

'Shame,' Viv muses. 'She loves you something terrible. I've seen her, standing out there, deciding whether to knock or not.'

'When?' Henry asks.

'Some nights.'

'Which nights?'

Vivian frowns at him. 'You're growing snappy in your old age,' she says. 'Drink your tea. And then tell me more about this Matilda. How long has she been married?'

Henry obliges and takes a sip. The tea is weak and over-sugared: it hacks steadily through his teeth towards the nerves. 'Ten years or so,' he answers. Then, to change the subject, he adds, 'How long have you and Herb been married?'

'This anniversary will be our fifty-bleeding-seventh.'

He smiles. 'You must have hundreds of love letters.'

'From him?' Viv scoffs. 'The seas would dry up before Herbert Moss penned a love letter.' She glances towards the door to the next room. Only his feet are visible, the left crossed over the right, one brown slipper on, the other kicked away. 'I wouldn't change that for a minute, though,' she continues. 'He's a bit like you, my Herb. So tough on the outside he's brittle, so soft on the inside he's at risk of melting.'

She winks at him over the top of her teacup and Henry fights back a little cough of discomfort.

'I knew a woman once who wrote a love letter to London,' she says. 'She lost two boys to the war. The first in '16; the other right at the end. She was never the same after that. It wasn't always obvious, you know, it was just that sometimes she'd lose parts of herself, and walking around the city, seeing certain buildings, still the same as they'd been before, and the parks, all reliably where they always had been – that was the only thing that made her feel ... solid.' Viv takes another drink. 'So she wrote this letter to the city, because she couldn't bear to address it to her boys. She wrote it over and over again, one every morning for a long while, and she spent each day sitting at the base of the Cenotaph, ripping them up and scattering them for the pigeons.'

'For the pigeons?'

Viv nods. 'So they'd eat them and fly them all around London. Don't you think that's a beautiful story?'

'I don't know,' Henry answers. 'It's a bit sad.'

'Oh, it's a lot sad,' Vivian agrees. 'You're right there. Doesn't mean it can't be beautiful, though.'

———————

Later, when he gets into bed, Henry considers these words again. He watches the world – so often dark – churn on outside the window and begins to long for the next flash of passing headlights: on occasion, he has learnt, a person's sanity can be bound up in the simple hint of another human being.

ARRIVALS

At half past twelve, he begins wandering up and down platform one, the great wrought iron skeleton of Paddington Station curving above him. He is surrounded on all sides by the dashing and scurrying of passengers, whose hats and coats turn from black to amber as sunlight filters down over them through the gaps between the ceiling-ribs. The place smells of tobacco and oil. He takes a bench beneath the Dining & Tea Room sign. On platform two, huge mounds of mail sacks wait to be thrown on board, and as he watches, one shifts and tumbles down the others like snow down a mountainside, dragged along by its own weight. He stands again and checks the clock mounted high on the wall. The curling black hands have barely crept past the six. He must be patient for twenty-nine more minutes.

He replied to Ida the same day he opened the envelope. *You'll find me at the memorial on platform one*, he wrote. Then, feeling as idiotic and bashful as a man arranging a date, he added, *I will be holding your letter.*

He has only a vague idea of what Ida might look like. The photo on his mantelpiece shows her as a girl – just two years younger than Ruby but so much less confident for it, clinging to her mother's knees while Ruby pushes out her chest and grins. What he imagines he will see when the train arrives is a smaller, thinner version of his wife: her eyes cast low, her back not so straight, her mouth less inclined to smiling.

It was Ruby, after all, who had escaped what she had described as an empty village full of empty people. This was an exaggeration, Henry knew, shaped by drink and Monty's constant pleading for her to tell him everything about the 'ancient mystery' he considered Wales to be. But Henry also knew that Pwll was tiny and home to more grandparents than grandchildren, and that Ida had never been brave enough to run away in search of work or excitement or love. She'd never been brave enough to run towards anything. Until now.

He shuffles through the crowds back towards the memorial. He is twenty-five minutes early, but still he worries he will miss her; that she might have caught an earlier train; that she has not received his reply and will travel to the flat without waiting for him and that, once there, Vivian will see her from the window and come down to send her away, accidentally introducing her to Libby before he gets a chance to, and that then, wild and angry, Ida will snatch his daughter away and disappear, completely, forever. The implications of his dread are far too elaborate to ever translate themselves into reality. This does not make Henry capable of dismissing them, though. He has not known rational fear since 1918.

The bronze soldier stands, legs braced, on a plinth adorned with a plaque inscribed, *3,312 Men and Women of the Great Western Railway Gave Their Lives in Service of King and Country*. Henry reads and rereads the dedication, lining ghosts up into neat battalions in his mind and trying to envisage what that number of people looks like, stood one next to the other, filing into eternity.

Ruby had asked him about the war only once. Henry sits down again on the nearest bench and closes his eyes to savour the remembering. It was the Christmas after they got married. Or the New Year, rather, since Ruby had travelled home to visit her family over Christmas. She had refused to take him with her – next year, she'd said; once they'd had a chance to get used to the idea of him – and when he had collected her from the train upon her return, they had walked past this very memorial.

Ruby stopped and felt for his hand. Her smile failed as she took in the statue's Brodie helmet, slightly askew, and the greatcoat flung about his shoulders.

'Did you have a tin hat like that?' she asked, without facing him. It was a fragile thing, Henry's past, which must be handled only with gloved hands. She had learned as much with minimal help from him.

Henry wondered if she knew that 'tin hats' was what they had called them, or whether she was simply describing what she saw. 'Most of the time,' he answered. 'When we were lucky enough.'

'I wouldn't say you were ever lucky, Henry.'

He stared down at the top of her head, nearly a foot below his own, and ran his eyes along the soft outward whorls of her hair-roots. And this is what he concentrates on now – the sweet simplicity of the top of her head, the bow of which he slid his chin over so frequently. That New Year, though, he only put his hand to it and pulled her into his chest. He had not decided to bring silence down on his war before that moment when she asked him to be vocal. He just couldn't find the words he wanted. And Ruby felt it and spoke to save his struggle. 'Well, until you met me, that is,' she said, wriggling round in his arms to look up at him. 'I mean, that was the luckiest night of your life, wasn't it, husband?'

A passenger zips by, catching Henry's foot with a swinging briefcase, and Henry opens his eyes to the unbroken bustle. The crowds divide and funnel towards one of Paddington's twelve platforms, and he stands and moves against their pull to take his place before the memorial.

He leans back into the cold stone wall and pulls Ida's letter from his pocket.

And when, twenty minutes later, Ida disembarks and glances around in search of Henry, what she sees are two soldiers standing side by side, their shoulders broad and proud, their heads lowered over the words of a woman.

'Mr Twist?' she asks, dipping a little to catch his eye.

Her voice is so familiar that, briefly, Henry is unwilling to lift his chin. He considers the round, shining-black toes of her shoes, the hem of her wool dress; then, slowly, the book she clasps one-handed in front of her; and then, finally, her face. 'Miss Fairclough,' he manages. And she smiles, easily, widely – precisely as he had thought she would not.

'Miss this, Mr that,' she says. 'Shall we just stick to Ida and Henry?'

He nods. He is glad now that he looked up. The voice is close to identical. Her build too is much the same: slim but too well-proportioned for the current style. Her face, though, is different. The eyes are smaller, lighter; the cheeks thinner; the lips wider. The Fairclough sisters must surely have shattered a hundred Welsh hearts: Ida, like her sister, is beautiful. But she is not Ruby. Thank God. She is not Ruby.

'I'd like that,' he answers. 'What book are you reading, Ida?'

She tips the cover up awkwardly to show him the title. In her other hand, she carries a small, brown, leather suitcase. '*Wuthering Heights*.'

Henry is not very familiar with the story: there are, he thinks, too many lovers and grudges all tangled up in one another to commit to memory. He does remember, though, that there is an awful lot of sadness held within that story. And not a little beauty, he supposes, if you look at it the right way. Perhaps Vivian's words will prove just right to persuade Ida that he has not behaved too badly.

'Are you a romantic?' he asks, with half a smile. He has already decided that her answer will be 'yes'. Why else read that book, with all its nostalgic wildness?

'Not at all,' she replies. 'I just happen to like reading about the way things were, before all of this.' Ida waves her hand at the shuffling crowds, the men who tap-tap their umbrellas to the ground as canes, the grinding of train brakes, the children who scream against the noise, the blasts and hisses of steam which spread through the station as indoor clouds, the clanging of bells, the hastening chug the engines make as the trains pull away on a new journey.

'All this is progress,' Henry says, more to keep talking than because he believes in the opinion. He does not want quiet between them yet. Quiet will force him towards his admission.

'Yes,' Ida answers. 'And isn't it so much better, to look back in the other direction, than to look forward in this one? We will all be turned into machines one day, Henry, I swear it. And how will we think then, when our minds are turned by cogs? Would I still miss my sister?'

'I think you are a good deal more serious than your sister,' Henry says. 'If you don't mind my saying.'

They are stepping out onto the street now, where they are met by a conflict of warm sun and chilly winds. Henry watches Ida adjust her hat. She seems confident, despite never having visited London before.

'I don't mind,' she says. 'I always was. I took after our mother, you see, and loved to read. Ruby rather took after our father, who loved not to. In fact, I never really thought about it before, but she was always happy to plough forward, wasn't she, my sister? Into anything. Perhaps that's why you liked her.'

'Perhaps so. I was something of a project for her, I suppose. I'm too inclined to dwell on the past myself.'

In response to this, Ida hums. She is distracted, gazing up at the imposing frontage of the Great Western Royal Hotel. Her eyes dart over every clean, white-sandstone column; every window frame; every intricacy of ornamentation which goes unnoticed, largely, by the passing Londoners. Henry can tell she is impressed.

'Have you never wanted to visit London?' he asks.

'Oh, I've wanted to,' Ida answers. 'It's just ... Well, we felt we didn't want to bother her, once she'd set herself up with this exciting life, you know? We felt like a burden.'

'Your parents, too?'

Ida nods, then thrusts her head up higher, battling sudden tears.

'But she thought you were angry at her,' Henry whispers. 'She thought you felt she'd abandoned you. She was going to make it up to you, she said, once the baby came. She was planning to come home for a while.'

'Was it a boy or a girl?' Ida asks.

And, yes, it is Henry's fault that the subject has been broached so quickly, but really he feels he ought to set matters straight. It saddens him that Ruby and her family had wasted all that time, denied each other their company, for the sake of a misunderstanding; for the sake of respect, really. Ida could have come to stay. He and Ruby could have gone to Pwll. He could have afforded the train fares. He nods his head. There will be no more denials.

'Actually,' he says, 'I need to talk to you about that.'

———

And it is easy, talking to Ida. Easier than talking has been for weeks and weeks, because this woman knew Ruby longer than he. She knew her moods and her passions and her anger – and he wants all those things back. He worries sometimes that he will remember more of the good than the bad and that, in doing so, he will retain only part of his wife.

They sit now in the park across from the flat, on the same bench he and Jack chose that night. In the afternoon sun, they are surrounded by laughing lovers and parents with shrieking little ones and slow old couples, all turning their backs to the city and walking it away. Their talk is absorbed into open air. Their working weeks are forgotten. Henry and Ida tilt their faces into a beam of buttery warmth, talking quietly and sporadically when they manage to wade out of their own thoughts.

Ida has succeeded in fending off her tears, even when he broke the news about Libby, and Henry admires her for it. He alone knows how hard she has fought.

'We can go and see her whenever you're ready,' he says.

'Soon,' Ida answers.

'Are you angry?'

'Did you expect anything else?'

'No.'

'Well, there we are then.'

'You know,' Henry begins, but gently, gently. He deserves more than anger. 'I only –'

'I'm not saying you did wrong,' Ida interrupts. 'You did what you had to. We'd never met. Do you think I'd have packaged my own daughter off to you if it had been the other way around?'

He says nothing. He waits. The more Ida speaks, the less of Ruby he sees in her, and he is immeasurably glad. He has found his Ruby again – or she has found him – and, he realises now, he had been afraid that observing her semblance in Ida would make him doubt Jack. But he has thought about this, hard, in the beating depths of every night since, and he is sure now that he should never have questioned Ruby's ability to find her way back to him. He should never have questioned his instincts. Wasn't it on the very day of her funeral that Jack came and stood before him and called his name?

What he can't work out, though, is why Jack has disappeared. Unless, of course, Jack is as confused presently as he, Henry, was in the beginning. It could be that Henry's name was the only definite Ruby managed to convey to the body she stole.

'Later,' he says, 'I'll take you to Monty's. We spent a lot of time there. And to the place we first met, and … You are staying, aren't you?' He nods towards the suitcase, positioned between their feet.

'With Daisy,' she answers.

'With Daisy? Strawberry Hill Daisy?'

Ida nods. 'I wrote to her, asking if I could visit, just to see the place, and she wrote back saying that the girl she shared with after Ruby had left only a few weeks ago, and that I could stay there if I liked, as long as I wanted. She even suggested I make a go of it up here myself.'

'And what did you think to that?'

'I thought it wouldn't suit me very well. And it doesn't so far. But I'll give it a few days. A week, maybe. After all, I have a niece to acquaint myself with now, don't I?'

'You do,' he says, standing and offering her his arm. 'Shall we?'

'Why not,' Ida answers, unable to hold onto her anger when there is a baby to meet. Grabbing her case, she straightens up and smoothes out her dress with a palm before hooking her arm through his.

'You know,' he murmurs as they step towards the flat, 'I'm glad you're going to stay a while.'

Ida laughs at this and Henry frowns at her. 'What?'

'She told me about that look of yours, my sister,' Ida explains. 'She said you could make women fall in love with you with a single glance – this look, all tormented and moody, even when you were happy. And I'm sure that was it.' Henry opens his mouth to protest but Ida carries on. 'But don't you worry, Henry Twist, I am not a woman who falls in love with sad looks. Or with her sister's husband, for that matter.' She is still laughing, her head shaking back and forth in disbelief. 'What a girl, to even know how it is you would look at another person. I never saw her like that … She must have loved you very much.'

'I'm sure she did,' Henry answers softly.

'Me, too,' Ida agrees, the laughter still caught in her cheeks. 'Me, too.'

That first night, Henry escorts Ida to Strawberry Hill and rides the Tube back to Bayswater Road, painting pictures of Ruby onto the blackened windows: the naughty slant of her smile when he returned from work one birthday to discover she had completely emptied half of their front room so that they could slow-dance before the window until the sun came up; the frightened flash in her eyes when she did not fall pregnant in the first months of their marriage; the tightening of her when he sank away into the past and refused to let her follow him; and, always, her arms swinging in time to that Charleston the night they first met.

As he shoots from tunnel to tunnel, Henry pretends he is leaving these images behind him, like a film reel of his married life seen through the rectangular wood frames of the Tube train windows, and imagines how it would be if every passenger who followed him under London saw, along the way, Ruby Twist, brought to cinematic life.

That, he thinks, is the sort of gift he would like to give her – a memorial, like the soldier in the train station. But a moving one. Because Ida was right. Ruby would not want to stay still.

And Ida doesn't seem to want to either. In the days that follow, she learns to find her way from flat to flat. She appears on his doorstep unannounced, with a scruffy teddy she has bought Libby, then a cake she has made, then a bonnet Daisy has knitted. He does not complain about her telling Daisy. Now that Ida knows, and has written to her parents to let them know too, what does it matter? If the doctors try to make him hand her over, he feels sure Ida will take his side. And why should they make him, anyway, with Libby doing so well? They have made it through the worst. He even starts taking her out in her pram during the day – it feels safer, with Ida walking alongside him – and parading her around at Monty's for everyone to admire. In the course of a week, his life changes.

He refuses to consider that he has only three months' rent to his name and ought to beg back his job.

He refuses, too, to seek out Jack, though he thinks about him constantly. But where would he start? He doesn't know the address of the old lady with the spare bed in her attic. He doesn't know where he might find the Prince of Wales pub, and even if he sought it out, Jack would not be foolish enough to return to the scene of his beating. Some days Henry manages to persuade himself, on occasion for hours at a time, that there is no Jack Turner; that his grieving mind simply invented a man with a back straight enough to carry his heaped worries. But really he knows that his mind did not gift him a creation, because there was that time, after the White Party, when he had stood in the street and spoken to a real, living man. People saw him do it. The costermonger raised his fleshy fist.

It seems that a moment's doubt, however, is all it takes to draw Jack back to him, because the night after Ida leaves to return to Pwll, Henry is woken by a whistling.

At first, he thinks it a dream, and turns himself back into sleep. But the sound persists, and when finally he goes to the window and pulls the curtain, there is Jack, standing in the narrow umbrella of light beneath a streetlamp, his eyes raised to the flat, his mouth pursed around his tune. Seeing Henry's head appear between the curtains, he stops and lets his lips open into a smile.

His first words, when Henry opens the front door to him, are these: 'So, who's the woman?'

THE GATHERING *of* HOPE

Matilda arrives at Monty's alone and, slotting her key into the lock, rests a hand on the black iron scrolls of the gate briefly before letting herself through. It is early, before nine, and the sky is low with undropped rain. Laces of liquorice cloud weave their way between the highest buildings. She left home as soon as Grayson departed for work.

They are not meeting until four, but over the last week she has observed Henry's movements and she knows that, most days now, he walks Libby through the city as the first thin chinks of morning appear. Ida has been a good influence on him. And a bad influence on Matilda, who, from the first second she saw Ruby's sister, felt the belief she had so carefully been building race impossibly away from her, like a yacht caught on stormy waves. How could she replace Ruby, when her sister was so much better fitted for the job? How could she mother that child, when a younger woman was there to snap up the role?

The jealousy, upon seeing another beautiful woman standing at Henry's side, and seeing strangers assume she was his wife, and seeing that Ida was somehow immune to the feelings this assumption would bring about in most, no, all other women, was to Matilda akin to the surging hatred she is gripped by when she passes careless mothers pushing prams in the street.

She has been forced, once again, to admit to herself love which will not be returned.

As an adolescent, she had been too arrogant to believe she would ever know this sort of hurt. In her earliest years, Matilda and her parents existed – and exist still – within a triangle of freely given affection. When she first met Grayson, that triangle bulged out into a square. And she had imagined, innocently, that the shape would continue to grow as she delivered one, two, three children.

On her wedding day, she already had their names picked out, ready to present to Grayson on their wedding night. First, there would be Victoria. Then Michael. And finally, little Leo. She spaced them an even three years apart, so that Victoria, six by the time Leo made his appearance, would have the pleasure of helping her mother nurse a baby. There was no detail of these predicted children too small for Matilda to have pictured. The freckles which would scatter Victoria's nose; the lick in the front of Michael's hair which would flick it forever outwards; the shrill rise of Leo's overtired cry; the gleaming black locks they would all share; the squeals they would emit as they chased each other up and down the staircase of the house the Stecks would live in when they were a family of five. Matilda knew these things. Nature, she thought, must have implanted traces of knowledge somewhere deep inside her, to encourage her in the act of procreation.

If she were a better person, Matilda would have asked Ruby if she felt the same way before she fell pregnant; she would have shared the anticipatory joy of it. By then, though, Matilda had been childless for more than a decade. And bitter for at least three quarters of that time. She could not allow her friend the happiness she herself had been denied by ... she does not know what by.

Reaching the sycamore, she drops onto a blanket which sags

sadly on the grass, abandoned by some clutch of Bright Young People last night, no doubt. Matilda wrinkles her nose. An article in the papers yesterday had lambasted them for tearing up an unoccupied house on Kensington Park Road whilst the owners were away on the Continent, and Matilda looks now at the mess surrounding her and imagines the destruction those poor people had returned to. But this is always the way, afterwards: a smashed glass, a wine-stained dress, cake crumbs trampled into the floor – the next day, they make a party a sad thing to remember. Or so Matilda has always thought. But there, in the moment ... She recalls lifting her feet and straightening her legs in front of her on the swings at the White Party; she recalls swaying wildly forwards then back, forwards then back, grinning as she studied the swell and ripple of her skirts. She had anticipated each backward swing, preferring it to the forward tilt which made her feel she was falling, and she wonders now whether it is the same for other people. It could be that it is only she who sees sadness in the mess happiness leaves behind, only she who feels an affinity for the particular direction in which a swing swings.

And, yes, the more she thinks about it, the more she begins to see that she has never allowed herself to venture towards middle ground. It is too vague, and, therefore, too scary a place. So, she loves Gray, or she hates him. She blames her childlessness on herself or, by turns, on anyone and everyone else. And perhaps that is why, when she cannot bring herself to love Grayson, she loves Henry – because he is silent while Gray likes to talk, and he is serious while Gray likes to joke. Henry Twist and Grayson Steck are opposed in every possible way.

Matilda cannot begin to predict how Henry would react if she shamed him as she has shamed Grayson. She does not believe Henry would endure it. Not without retaliating. And though she does not think him capable of it really, she is bombarded by the thought that another man might strike her, should she neglect him the way she has Grayson, and the man in her mind is Henry, and the prospect of him looming over her, fist clenched, sparks within her a flash of excitement.

Sometimes, she deserves to be punished.

———

At midday, when Monty wanders into the garden in search of company, Matilda is still there. Some clutch of younglings has fashioned a swing in the sycamore, like those which were suspended from the trees at the White Party, and Matilda is swinging further and faster than she ought to given the make-shift design, her head tipped far back, her hat upturned on the grass beyond her where the wind has cast it, hours-old tears shining shaky lines down her face. The branch above her creaks and groans like a hundred-year-old man. The liquorice clouds of hours before have not burst: they have ruptured and drifted apart in their own soft way to reveal, piece by irregular piece, a day as mild as single cream.

'Tilda,' Monty calls.

She rights her head. 'Monty,' she says, smiling. 'I was waiting for someone.'

'And did he come?'

'Who?' she asks, pretending ignorance.

'Someone, of course.' He winks.

Matilda thrusts her heels into the earth to still herself, scuffing the navy leather. 'No,' she answers. 'Actually, he didn't. But you're here now, Monty dear, and I couldn't be happier to see you.'

Cheeks are kissed and Monty stands tall – though not quite as tall as he used to, even so short a time as a year ago. He pretends to adjust his tie with a grin. 'Nor I you,' he says. 'Though had I known I had a hot date waiting for me, I wouldn't have lingered so long over breakfast.'

'You should never linger, Montague dearest,' Matilda says.

'It'll make an old man of you. Of all of us.'

'I don't suppose there are many things that could make an old man of you.'

She slaps his arm gently as he settles a shoulder, a hip, against the tree trunk. 'You know what I mean, cheeky.'

'I'm not sure I do,' Monty answers. 'Are we being serious for once?'

'I think we might be.'

'Wait a moment then while I put on my best serious expression.'

Even on those rare occasions when they do discuss the important things, they do so in this same playful way. It is, Matilda thinks, an affliction of their generation. No, of their time. Many years more will have to pass before anyone can complain or worry about anything much without feeling outrageously hypocritical.

'Do you think he is the way he is because of the war?'

'Henry?' Monty asks.

'Yes.' She might well have been talking about her husband. He saw it, too: whatever 'it' consisted of. Grayson had told her once that she would never be able to visualise it, and that she must never try.

Monty sighs kindly. 'What do you really want to know, Matilda?'

'I don't know.' She stares across the garden at the summer house, so that she doesn't have to look Monty in the eye. The wind, which has blown itself into some other part of the city now, has left the door ajar but she has not been inside. They hardly ever use it. You cannot watch the sky from in there. 'I suppose ...' She feels a fool, but she also feels that if she doesn't speak these words, they might just burst out of her some other time. 'I suppose I want to know if there's a chance.'

'What do your instincts tell you?'

'Instinct is a liar,' Matilda answers. 'And a sycophant. It only tells you what you want to hear.'

'Some people might call that hope,' Monty offers.

She swings apart from him so that it seems she is moving forward while he moves back, and they become in her mind the two mechanisms of a clock, one the tick, one the tock, which must never come together. And perhaps this is Monty's curse, she thinks, glimpsing him at perfect arcing intervals, because despite his best efforts to keep them close, people are forever moving away from Montague Thornton-Wells. She's noticed the tendency amongst the Bright Young People lately, too: how they always have to 'rush off' once the wine bottles are emptied; the cruel way they laugh, sometimes, when he asks them to stay a little longer. Monty gives his entire self to his friends, and they are quite willing to take it. Poor man.

She ought to stop this childish swinging and give him her full attention. But she can't, not yet. Beyond the garden walls London clatters on timelessly, never pausing, never resting, and Matilda finds herself exhausted by it today. She concentrates on the clock sounds she is imagining until they start to grow louder in her mind: loud enough to drown out everything but the awful onward march of her hope. Monty is right. It's hope. She has wasted most of her life on hope. And now, at forty-one, she has no choice but to conclude that it is not the positive disposition everyone supposes it to be. Really, she must learn to stop.

———

Some crowded miles away, Grayson stands before the second-storey window of an old Gothic building and addresses five rows of young, uninterested faces. At intervals, he taps his blackboard with his cane, but more to snap the boys awake than to emphasise a fact. 'I would like one of you –' *tap* '– to please tell me –' *tap* '– in which year –' *tap* … Weak sunlight separates into long fingers, like a spread hand, as it falls through the glass, but it does not irradiate the room. There is no penetrating the gloomy depths of Classroom F: the ceiling is too high, the window too narrow, its occupants too eager to be released. Naturally, there are always one or two children who are keen to learn. In this particular class, there is just one – Baker – who sits straight in his chair and writes in his lap in an attempt to hide his application. He knows the answers to every one of Mr Steck's questions, but he will answer none, and Grayson is too sympathetic to single him out.

'Thompson?' he says, sensing the forced response will be wildly inaccurate.

'Not sure, sir,' Thompson replies.

'Then make an educated guess,' Grayson coaxes. The boy next to Thompson yawns, wide and apologetic, behind his hand.

Grayson has never had much time for the Education Officers or the Institute of Education or the Board of Education, or whatever other titles the rule-makers have attributed to themselves over the years, but he thinks there is something in the idea being tossed about recently that open-air schools, or at least upgraded ventilation, could improve learning. Wouldn't it be more pleasant to lift up the desks and shuffle outside with them on a fine day like this than to file behind these heavy wooden things boys were carving their initials into fifty years before Grayson was born?

It would be more pleasant for him, at least. Especially now that the days are protracting, growing milder. He would like to witness the odd flower blooming.

He turns to write something on the blackboard, performing an elaborate rotation so that he can glance out through the window at the sky. By four o'clock, he will be at Monty's, swilling the day away with a glass of something strong.

'Was it 1603, sir?'

'Yes!' Grayson spins back round to face his class. 'Yes it was, Thompson.' He points his cane at the boy. 'I am thoroughly impressed with you.'

Thompson looks down at his hands and fights the smile

which pulls at his lips. And it is in moments like these, when Gray manages to impart some sliver of knowledge, that he remembers he would have made a good father. Possibly even an inspiring one. He mourns his could-have-been children in fleeting public silences. Then he clears his throat, pushes his reading glasses up his nose, and returns to the matter at hand – teaching.

A decade of disappointment is quite enough.

The great dark slab of his classroom door edges open and he calls for his visitor to enter. One hand around the wood, she leans in.

'Miss Emory. What can I do for you?'

'I wondered if we might have a word after class, Mr Steck?'

'Of course,' he answers. 'I'll wait at the end of the day.'

Sally throws him a small, red-lipped smile and ducks back out of the doorway, almost as though she is curtsying. From the corner of his eye, Grayson catches Thompson miming a whistle. He slaps the blackboard, hard.

'Master Thompson, did you have to spoil your moment of glory? I was almost feeling proud of you just then.'

'Sorry, sir,' Thompson mumbles. But Gray understands why he did it. Miss Emory – all of what? Twenty-two? – is the school's newest recruit. Big-eyed and pink-cheeked, she tiptoes through the corridors, sending her skirts fluttering around her slender calves. Her hair, blonde, almost-red, is cut into a pretty bob and forever shining. Her lips part into ready smiles as she fixes you with the unfathomable emerald stare of a cat. And there is something undeniably deliberate about it all, Grayson has decided. Miss Emory is a performer.

As he turns again to the blackboard, Grayson hopes, abstractly, that his students think his face is flushed with anger at Thompson. One night last week, after he and Matilda had one of their quarrels, he had dreamt about Sally Emory. He had dreamt the messy, brain-swamping sort of dream he imagines artists know; the sort that induces them to work at smashing layer upon layer of paint over a canvas, or teasing lines of poetry from pen nibs only to ball up the sheet of paper and begin again. In short, a fantasy seeped into his head – as real and tactile in those sleeping hours as his wife was next to him when he woke – and he's not sure he's ever known that to happen before.

If he were a wiser man, he thinks, he would not meet Sally Emory after school hours for any purpose. And yet, he knows he will.

Grayson does not reach Monty's until gone six o'clock. During his short walk from the train station, darkness plummets over the city, streetlamps flicker on and build to a steady blaze, the cold turns his nostrils to smoking chimneys. As he strolls along the pavement, dragging the back of one hand against the garden's perimeter wall, he spots Henry coming in the opposite direction. They wave, nod a greeting, and, a few steps and a handshake later, push through the gate together to find Matilda already blind-drunk.

Monty sits at her side, passing her glasses of water which she holds but does not imbibe. Over the top of her own coat, she wears one of his, but she shivers and it slips off and Monty is forced to keep wrapping it back around her. All about them, cream-coloured blankets and cushions are scattered, waiting to be settled onto, and at the centre of this familiar arrangement is a large basket full of dark, glinting bottles. Monty has provided again.

'How long have you been here?' Grayson asks, confused by her state.

'All day,' she answers, flinging her glass in his direction so that much of the water slops out. Her eyes stay closed. 'I was waiting.'

Grayson does not ask what for. He knows. He is standing next to him. 'Perhaps we should head home?' he offers.

At this, Matilda throws her arms out to embrace the air and smiles a long, slow, liquefied smile. 'You're here now,' she declares. 'You're all here, all my beautiful men, all together, and I, and I, I –'

'She's really not as bad as she seems,' Monty says. 'The cold air must have got to her, that's all. She hasn't had a drink in hours.'

'Shall I pour you one, Monty?' Grayson sighs, lowering himself onto his knees and reaching for the basket Monty has always supplied, jammed with litres of this wine or that rum or some exotic concoction they've never cared to learn the ingredients of. He really ought to take Matilda home. But he's tired and thirsty and home will be a lonely place tonight. Besides, he needs to drink, to flood his thoughts of Sally. 'Henry?'

He measures three glasses, ignoring Matilda's pleas for another, and they sit to a habitual toast.

Monty raises his hand. 'To ... To what? Anyone have an idea?'

'To the abandonment of hope,' Matilda slurs and the men smile indulgently at one another.

'That's depressing, Tilda,' Monty warns. 'How about, to the gathering of hope?'

'Hope for what?' Grayson asks.

'The future,' Monty suggests.

'The future,' Henry agrees quietly, and they clink their glasses and murmur 'Cheers, cheers,' as they settle onto the mounded material for the evening.

'And to taking Ruby there with us,' Monty adds.

It is the first time since Ruby died that they have done this properly, the way they used to, with nothing but drinks and daft talk and soft furnishings. In the short silence that follows Monty's words, they sip and swig and reposition their tired limbs, and Henry drifts towards the echoes of his wife the place holds. He sees ghostly strokes of her midway down the length of the garden: the flip of her hair as she tosses her head in frustration at her failure to hit a ball through one of Monty's old croquet hoops.

When they had arrived that day, Monty had the game already set up and was waiting for them amongst the hoops, spinning a ball skilfully between his fingers.

'When I was a scrawny young lad,' he'd said, by way of explanation, 'I was something of a competitor. I thought we might give it a go.'

And they had all done quite well, excepting Ruby.

'Do you remember how bad she was at croquet?' Henry says now.

'Oh, no one could forget that,' Monty laughs. 'The way she growled and stomped and growled some more!'

'And kept swinging the stick over her head.' Grayson demonstrates, arcing his empty hand upwards. ' "You've done something to my stick!" '

'Really,' Monty says, 'it's not a stick, it's a mallet.'

Grayson smiles. 'That's exactly what you said to her.'

Henry draws the remembered lines of her onto the emptiness before him, colouring her dress in a deep, charcoal grey – though of course he can't be sure any more what she wore that particular day. What he can be sure of is the scowl which burrowed further into her face with each miss, the way her shoulders rose higher and higher.

'She wasn't sold on your teaching, Monty,' he says.

'She certainly was not.'

'She was as quick-witted as ever, though,' Matilda offers, a little smile creasing her lips. 'Remember, Monty was boasting on about being a croquet champion in '65 or something –'

Monty coughs. 'Excuse me. It was '66 *and* '67, actually.'

'And what did Ruby say?' Matilda smirks.

' "What about '68?" ' Henry replies.

'Everyone started playing tennis in '68,' Monty had

returned, and all – bar Ruby – had laughed. An hour later, when Henry, Monty, Matilda and Grayson were enjoying their second drink, she was still chasing the little ball through the grass, scooping clumps of earth up with her haphazard mallet action and knocking down the hoops with her increasingly forceful hitting.

'Ruby,' Monty called. 'You're beaten, sweet girl. Give up. It's just a game.'

'Maybe,' Ruby replied. 'But then again, most things are. Doesn't mean you should give up on them.'

Matilda sighs. 'I always wished I could quip the way she did.'

'Ah,' Monty replies, 'no one could equal Ruby on that front.'

They had attempted for long minutes to persuade her to sit to drinks with them, but Ruby had not capitulated, and Henry had dropped back onto his elbows and smiled as he watched his woman turn laps of the garden without even marginally improving her technique. When, eventually, a fluke ball rolled beautifully through a battered hoop and she yelped with excitement, he rushed over and lifted her and twirled her about like a child, because he knew it would keep her smiling. There was nothing that brought him more pleasure than to cause Ruby Twist to keep smiling.

'Are you still with us, chap?' Monty asks now.

Henry nods.

'Good,' Monty continues. 'I thought we'd lost you to the beard for a minute there.'

'The beard really is becoming … something, you know,' Grayson says. 'Quite something …'

'Something!' Monty laughs. 'Would you listen to him? He's being polite, Twist. It's a catastrophe, that beard. You look like a wild man. You look like you've been attacked by some mysterious hairy creature. In fact, I shouldn't be surprised if moons started orbiting that beard. Have a shave, man, for God's sake.'

Henry touches his beard and smiles with just his lips. 'I hadn't noticed it was that bad.'

'Oh, trust us,' Monty says. 'It's worse.'

'I can't disagree,' Grayson whispers. They are all whispering now. Matilda, propped against Gray's shoulder, is sliding into sleep.

'The little lady will think her father's been eaten by a bear,' Monty adds. 'Where is she, anyway? With the old woman upstairs?'

'That old woman,' Henry answers, 'is probably younger than you. Or a similar age, at least.'

Monty flaps a hand at Henry. 'Everyone my age is old.'

'Is that why you don't bother with any of them?' Grayson asks.

'That's exactly why,' Monty says, though they all know there's more to it than that. Monty needs something from the young people he surrounds himself with. He's a man moved by nothing so much as desperation. 'And if Henry's going to become one of them,' he continues, 'sitting about in his flat every day, alone, I'm afraid I'll have to ditch him, too.'

'I haven't been alone.'

They turn to him for an explanation, two heads moving as one. Henry can see they're afraid to ask if there is a woman. Yes, no — either way it would be uncomfortable for them: hiding their disgust if he has moved on this quickly; hiding their shame if they have mistakenly supposed he would. And they are right to feel torn. Despite his secret convictions about Jack, Henry is very much still mourning Ruby. After all, Jack does not remember Henry; he does not love him; he does not know how it feels to be loved by him in return. Meeting Jack, however much of herself Ruby has managed to leave with him, is like meeting someone new. And Henry has no idea how to explain it.

'I mean, I won't be alone. An old friend is going to be staying with me,' he says, because he wants to believe it. 'Jack Turner.'

Last night, when Jack had finally appeared, Henry had been beyond anger. He had not attempted to stop him stepping through the front door, though. However angry he was, he still wanted Jack nearby. Making sure the curtains were properly drawn, he demanded an explanation with all the fury typical of any jilted lover. 'So, are you going to tell me where you've been?' he spat. Or something similar. He forgets now. Because when he reeled around, ready for his argument, Jack was sitting cross-legged on the bed, matching the sole of one foot to the other, just as she used to, and it was disarming.

'I'm sorry,' he said, 'I should have told you –'

'Actually,' Henry interrupted, slumping down onto the settee and rubbing at his forehead, 'you shouldn't have had to, should you?'

'Why not?' Jack shrugged. 'I felt I should have, and so I should have. Let's not quibble about it. And I haven't been anywhere. I've just, well, I got myself a spot of work. Not a lot, considering this.' He tapped his temple with a fingertip. 'Just donkey-work really, down at the docks. You know, it's surprisingly hard to find a trade when you've forgotten yours.' Grinning, he pulled off his newsboy and jacket and flung them aside. He moved easier now than he had before. His arm did not stall as it bent.

'You're feeling better, then?' Henry asked.

'Much.' Jack lifted both arms and flexed like a bodybuilder. 'I'm like a new man.'

There was no evidence of bloating muscle beneath his shirt sleeves – he is too lean for that – but Henry has not mistaken his trimness for weakness. He still hasn't shaken the habit of measuring Jack as a threat.

'And what sort of man is that?' Henry asked.

'A cautious one, I suppose,' Jack answered. 'Because, I'll be straight with you here, Henry, I've been keeping an eye on you, on the flat.' He lifted his hands in surrender, but Henry did not want an explanation as to why Jack had been watching.

He wanted only to believe that Jack was feeling something of what he was, that Jack too had recognised that strange pull. 'Now,' Jack continued, 'God knows that sounds creepy, but what choice have I got but to be careful?'

Henry swivelled around and leant over the back of the settee so that he was pupil to pupil with Jack. The masked moonlight made a marble sculpture of his face – all carved angles and flattened surfaces. His usually tanned skin was milk-like. His dark eyes shone. His hair was a confusion of perfect kinks. If Henry were a woman, he might have known then that Jack was beautiful.

'Perhaps,' Henry smiled, 'you're an honest man, too.'

'I'd like to think so. But do you know what I intend to be most of all?' Henry shook his head. 'A happy man,' Jack concluded.

'That's admirable,' Henry answered. He turned back towards the unlit fire, rubbing again at his forehead and the bridge of his nose. Behind him, he felt Jack shifting closer, then a touch on the point where his vest displayed his bare shoulder.

'Tell me, then,' Jack said.

'What?'

'What you're so worried about.'

Henry hunched forward and, elbows pointed into his thighs, pushed his hands over his face. Exhaling loudly, he attempted to summon the courage to speak words he could not yet locate. The thought was there, fully formed in his mind, but he could not translate it into a sentence he could deliver to Jack. He was afraid. Not that Jack would attack him – he could bear that. He was simply afraid that if Jack left again, he would not come back.

'What sort of man do you think *I* am?' Henry mumbled. 'I mean, do you think I'm a … you know, a … Because I'm not. I've never … It's just, perhaps I know who you are better than you do, and perhaps that makes me feel …'

For once, Jack was quiet. He waited patiently for Henry to stumble through his questions, hand unmoving on the smooth orb of his shoulder. But Henry could not say the word he needed to say.

'Do you think I'm a … I'm not a …' He cut out like a car engine.

'Henry?' Jack said, slowly. Without lifting his head, Henry nodded into his hands. 'Do you know what I think? I think, given what you've told me, that maybe I remind you of Ruby. And I think maybe that's all right.'

When Henry felt Jack's lips on his neck — a cool, firm contact — he remained still, bent into his own hands. He was not fearful, not any longer. How could he be now? With one easy movement, Jack had vanquished all his worries. But he did not want to show Jack the tears his lips were drawing from him, as steady and flowing as silk handkerchiefs being pulled from a magician's sleeve. That joy, that shame, was his alone.

'Jack Turner.' Monty repeats his name. 'Jack Turner. Do we know him? Whose circles does he run in?'

Henry shakes his head. 'No, you don't know him.'

'Then tell us more,' Monty coaxes.

'I can't,' Henry says, setting his drink down. It's time he got home to Libby. 'I'm not sure I know him myself yet.'

THE CINEMA

On the first dreary day of April, Henry Twist stands before the mirror in his hallway and listens to yet more rain drumming against his front door. The entire world is the same soft shade of grey. In his right hand, the heavy ball-end handle of his Gillette razor, which he rolls in his palm. On top of the wooden chest he leans against, a bowl of water, releasing wavering panes of steam which rise before him and make him look, in reflection, like an illusion. He dips the razor then slants it against his cheek and pulls it through the thickness of cream there, waiting for the rasp of removed hair. He matches the stroke on the other cheek.

He got rid of the beard as soon as he returned from Monty's a couple of weeks ago, and he feels better for it: a little more like himself. Perhaps, he thinks, these simplest acts – shaving, laughing, cooking – are what healing is made of. And he doesn't feel so guilty now about that, healing, because he is sure that he will always wear the scars Ruby etched on him.

Above, he hears Vivian wake and shuffle around her bedroom. Recently, Herb has been staying in bed more and more, and Henry, when he goes upstairs, sees the pain it causes Viv. It is under her skin: a moving shadow which lightens when Herb struggles to his chair and darkens again when he cannot conjure the fight to move his body across the width of two rooms. She does not talk about it. There are so many things Viv does not talk about, it seems, that Henry marvels at her not swelling up like a great balloon and bursting. He has still heard no mention of children, though he did catch sight of a medal one day when he collected Libby from the cot Viv has set up for her, so he believes now in at least one brave son.

Henry includes him in his prayers – Young Moss – and holds Libby tighter when he thinks of him.

Recently, Libby is a different girl every day. She grabs at his fingers and, when he carries her against his shoulder, his earlobes. She directs her head shakily this way and that. Her eyes dash about in her heart-shaped face. Elizabeth Twist grows more like her mother minute by minute, and Henry is grateful for it.

As he swills his razor clean, he peeps around the doorframe and through the slats of her cot, where she is sleeping deeply, her arms and legs stretched out into a star. She is turned away, showing him the silky-delicate back of her head, and Henry can't help but imagine something sharp piercing the plump place where her neck rolls into her shoulders. He closes his eyes and shakes the image loose. He has been trying to learn from Jack what it is to be an optimist.

There is still a warm dent in the bed sheets where Jack lay last night, sleeping as still as the dead. Before he had bounced onto the mattress and claimed his side though, he had waited, hidden behind the kitchen door, for nearly an hour for Yeoman to leave; hardly breathing at first, but then, as time plodded on, relaxing and causing the door to creak as it swung away from his fidgeting. In the next room, watching Yeoman sip a drink, Henry twitched at every sound. He told Yeoman he wasn't coming back to the bank; he watched Yeoman play with Libby – so delighted by her every accidental sound that he called them 'words' and congratulated her on them; he stole sneaky glances at his watch, calculating how much longer Jack could stand on the same cold spot. And he grew tenser and tenser.

When Yeoman finally stood to leave, the wide plates of muscle to either side of Henry's spine were rippling, and he was struggling with simple pleasantries. He did not know how to explain who or what was concealed in his kitchen.

'You'll stay in touch, won't you?' Yeoman said from the doorstep. 'Bring the baby over for the wife to meet her. She'd love that.'

'I will,' Henry answered. The two men smiled at each other, knowing it wouldn't happen.

'Shall I tell them, at work?'

'Please,' Henry said, and he wondered then if that was the last word he would say to all the people who used to fill his life: please. Please don't tell anyone ... Please don't mention ... Please don't think ... Please don't assume ... He stopped begging the last time his father hit his mother, and now, here it is again – a thing so ugly, and yet so often necessary. There is much, though, that Henry will endure for Jack, if tested. He knows this. And begging – for a man who, as a boy, watched his mother lie and cheat his father, then scream for pity as he beat his response into her – is not such a small sacrifice.

As he scrapes the last lick of shaving cream from under his jaw, he hears a scuffling at the back window which tells him that Jack is home. Every day now, Henry wakes to find him gone then waits through the dawn for him to return, dirtied and exhausted, having completed the first part of his working day before most of London blinks awake. They have settled into this routine easily, quietly, without once discussing what it means. Neither man has questioned that Jack must come and go via the kitchen window, clambering up and dropping out into the little yard in the early dark before checking in all directions for spectators of a crime not committed. The bicycle he uses to get to work they conceal behind the coalhouse and, sure he does not want to hear the answer, Henry has not queried the acquisition of it. He does sometimes suspect, though, that Jack cannot remember his previous work because he never had any. He is altogether too resourceful for a law-abiding man.

Henry would happily go on forever this way, knowing and not knowing, but he is aware that today Jack will want to discuss their situation: as he left this morning, he had whispered to Henry, 'Later. It's important.'

There is a thud as Jack drops onto the kitchen floor, and a breath afterwards he saunters into the hallway, a frozen lump of something meaty hung over his shoulder. With a flick of one arm, he throws it forward and catches it in both hands, presenting it to Henry with a wide smile. 'Dinner,' he says.

As Henry cleans his razor and carries the bowl back into the kitchen, Jack follows him, talking fast and loud, as he always does when he's been at the docks. At first, Henry had thought this would disturb Libby, but it does not seem to break her sleep. Perhaps Jack's voice slides into her dreams and keeps her safe from nightmares.

'Do you know what I was thinking earlier? I was thinking I want to go to the cinema. I've never been, you know. At least, not that I remember. And there's this film I've heard of, all about puppets, and –' He sees the look on Henry's face and stops. 'Of course we can't go together, but … I don't know, we could each buy a ticket. Sit a couple of rows apart.'

'It's an idea,' Henry answers.

'But not possible.'

'I don't think so. Maybe if we go to one of those theatre shows, where the girls –'

'Do you want to?' Jack asks.

'Not really.'

As Henry turns to lower the bowl into the sink, Jack loops his arms under Henry's and presses his own palms to the other man's chest. Henry inhales the salty smell of hard labour on skin before releasing that same long exhalation he makes whenever Jack touches him – part fear, part relief – and listens with closed eyes, frowning gently, as Jack speaks into his hair.

'Last night,' he says, slowly. 'I dreamt about a woman.' Henry waits. 'A hell of a woman. And the house she lived in: the biggest, oldest house you could imagine, with a garden in the front and children playing there. Two boys. Two small boys. And she stood at the door watching them, this woman. And laughing.' Henry feels Jack smiling. 'And she was so happy just to watch those boys. So damn happy ...'

'What did she look like?' Henry murmurs.

'Kind,' Jack answers. 'The sort of woman who would make a good mother.'

'What else? Describe her.' Henry holds his breath, waiting for the details which will tell him whether the dream was Ruby's – some hope she clung to as she died and passed on to Jack, translated into pictures – or whether the dream was just that, an ordinary dream, a messy collection of empty thoughts gathered up together into a story.

Jack rests his chin on Henry's shoulder. 'She was fair,' he says. 'Fair-haired, blue-eyed.' And Henry deflates a little, relieved. He is not ready, yet, to admit his beliefs to Jack. Perhaps he never will be. Perhaps it is only he who ever need know.

'Do you think she was real?' Henry asks. 'Someone you knew, before?' He has not considered until now that there might be a wife, children, who wake up every day and plead for God to bring Jack Turner back to them. Jack, he guesses, is what? Twenty-seven? Twenty-eight? It is possible, likely even, that there is a fair-haired, blue-eyed Mrs Turner mourning her husband somewhere in London right now, and he sees her himself then, projected in miniature onto the window-pane before him, like a tiny film. He sees her standing on the door, watching her boys play, but she is not smiling: her face is undone by the endless crying, and there is a rip in her stockings she has not noticed, and she has curled one side of her hair and forgotten the other, and Henry knows what her grief is like. The idea turns him cold.

Feeling his shiver, Jack pulls him closer and kisses the newly smooth line of his jaw. Henry does not have the strength to tell him to stop. Or why he should stop. Initially, though, he does resist Jack's touch: he always does. He stands taller, clenches his fists, readies himself for a fight. Then he softens as Jack's hands move over him, as strong and weightless as wind off the surface of a cruel sea; as natural as that; as essential. He lets Jack draw him around, around, until they are standing face to face, and Jack catches Henry's head in his hands. 'No,' he whispers. 'She's not anyone.' His lips graze Henry's. 'Do you believe me?' And Henry nods, he nods, because there is Jack's mouth, on his, and all of Henry's own words are suddenly contained within it. He has given them all over to this man, the man his wife chose, the body she fell into, the soul she replaced with her own, and Henry loves him, just as Ruby would expect him to. Just as hard and uncompromisingly and mercilessly as Ruby would expect him to.

He grabs Jack's collar and forces him against the nearest wall. 'I believe you,' he says. And he kisses him again, his arms tight around Jack, his shirt pulling across his shoulders as he battles the urge to lash out, because this, with Jack, is an equal mix of need and honest, core-deep fright, and his body hasn't learned yet how to reconcile the two.

'Close your eyes,' Henry orders. 'You'll spoil it otherwise.'

'Spoil what?'

'Wait and see.'

Henry sits at the head of the bed, propped up by the wall behind him. Between his legs, back to his chest, Jack is sprawled: a warm, casual weight, the sheets wrapped tight around the narrow angle of his hips. They have waited until dark for this, of course, but still Henry drew the curtains when midnight struck and they undressed, peeling off yesterday. To their right, the fire expires with a long chorus of snaps and fills the room with curls of dense, bitter-smelling smoke. Jack sniffs it in.

'I like that,' he says. 'That's a good, real scent.'

'Aren't all scents real?' Henry replies.

'I don't think so. Not the ones you only remember.'

'What about love you only remember?'

Jack thinks about this, and as he does Henry slides a hand tentatively towards his heart: he is cautious still about these simple intimacies. He counts the beats through the layers of muscle and tissue, skin and hair – steady.

'I suppose love you remember is still love,' Jack decides. 'It might even be more real in retrospect; more felt.'

'That's a wise thing for a man with no memory to say.'

Jack tips back his head so he can look at Henry. 'Perhaps,' he says, smiling that wide smile, 'I was a wise man. Perhaps I was a scholar. Can you imagine that? This handsome and clever. If I was rich too, I'm sure there are women in every corner of England crying for me.'

Or men, Henry thinks. It is Jack, after all, who has taken the lead in this … Henry can't bear to call it a love affair, even in the privacy of his own mind. Since that moment when he felt along Jack's ribs for breaks, Henry has left it all to him: every choice; every chance. And it was Jack who first kissed him, not the reverse; Jack who first pulled him free of his clothes; Jack who got into his bed as though it were a normal thing.

'Aren't you afraid?' Henry asks.

'Afraid of you? There's nothing to be afraid of in you. The only person you scare is yourself.'

'How do you know that?'

Jack shrugs. 'Call it intuition. Call it a gut feeling. Call it whatever the hell you like.'

'And what about *this*?'

'Call this whatever the hell you like. Naming it something isn't going to change it.'

'What if someone called you something else?'

'Like what? A nancy? I couldn't give a damn.'

Henry shakes his head. 'I don't believe you.'

'I am that I am, Henry. I am that I am.'

'Who was it that said that?'

Jack lifts Henry's hand off his heart and kisses each knuckle. 'I think it was God.'

Henry's father had employed God in his every argument with his wife. If God had meant you to be a slut, why did he invent marriage? If God had wanted you to have more children, he'd have provided you with them. If God didn't want me to teach you a lesson, why did he make me stronger than you? Henry tries to remember a time when he'd heard his father talk about men, men like them, but he can't. Perhaps he could not speak of them. Perhaps the very thought made him physically sick. But then, they must have encountered at least one, on all their walks together through the city, Henry a small boy ducking from every innocent wave of his father's hands. Henry steps his mind through his childhood, checking every corner, every shop, every green inch of parkland he can recall, but there is nothing. For a while, it seems his father never interacted with another man, let alone a nancy.

And then Henry half remembers an incident on the street below his bedroom window: he had watched with eyes wide, trying to breach the darkness, the soft knuckles of his right hand pressed to his teeth. He could smell the musk of the curtains and the cold off the glass, and he could hear, beyond the silence of an empty house, the gentle thud of repeated punches absorbed into a helpless body, and the wind.

It had been one of his mother's men. One Henry's father had discovered and dragged home to beat in front of his wife. Afterwards, he had been lifted off the pavement and carried slackly away, and Henry's parents had clattered back inside, shouting and clawing.

'I only do it to remind you.'

'Of what?'

'To want me.'

'If God had wanted me to want you, he'd have made you more beautiful.'

Henry had not needed to hide halfway down the stairs to hear this exchange. It was shoved up at him through the floorboards. It echoed off the hard crack of a slap. It rained down on him like an assault of hailstones, and even then he did not understand it. He knew his mother was beautiful, on the outside at least.

Libby snuffles and Jack sits up to check on her. The tendons in his neck shift as he stretches to see over the cot's bars, and Henry puts a hand to their movement before pulling Jack to his chest again.

'She's fine,' he says. 'Besides, you can't just move about like that in the cinema. People will miss the film.'

Jack settles back and closes his eyes, understanding Henry's intentions now. 'So, now that we're in our seats, old man ...'

'I'm going to let that one slide,' Henry says.

'Please do,' Jack replies, flicking his eyes open momentarily to send Henry a wink before wriggling into a more comfortable position, the back of his head cradled by Henry's sternum.

Henry clears his throat and begins. Already, he feels an idiot, but he knows that this is the sort of playfulness Ruby would have enjoyed, and he's sure Jack will, too. 'The seats are too small,' he says, barely above a whisper. 'Our knees are pushed up against the seats in front, and we're trying not to move so that we don't shake the row. At first there'll be chattering. Then, the words 'Pathéscope presents' will come up, and as everyone quietens down, the hissing and crackling of the film will fly over our heads and hit the screen, and what was just a wedge of grey light will be the opening scene: people or a train or fields.'

'Or puppets,' Jack adds.

'Or puppets,' Henry agrees, but he does not like the idea.

He sees himself and Jack, wooden-faced and hooked up to strings, blundering this way and that at the invisible direction of what they think to be instinct, because – they are controlled, really. They are moving at someone else's bidding. It has not escaped Henry's attention that, were they truly welcome amongst the Bright Young People, had they been born into such easy wealth, no one would question the relationship they seem to be building. He has heard about the nightclubs and the private ballrooms. But he has heard, too, of the arrests, and he knows the poor don't come out unscathed.

He finds himself combing his fingers through the tighter curls just above Jack's neck. 'And –' No, he won't tell Jack anything of the possibilities out there for them. How can he, when he doesn't believe they really exist?

'Carry on,' Jack prompts.

'And as the film goes on,' Henry continues, 'you'll find yourself starting to forget you're even there. It'll be like you're standing inside it all, like you're a completely different person, like you could be …'

His voice drops to almost nothing.

'… anyone at all,' he says. 'Like you could be anyone at all.'

On the pavement outside Henry's Bayswater Road flat, soaked through to her underthings by the small rain that has been falling all day, her hat drooping, her make-up running, her shoes being steadily ruined, Matilda Steck stands tall and rigid and sick. Her umbrella hangs loose in her right hand, the black canopy still extended but turned to the ground now, crumpled on one side and sheltering nothing and no one. She ought to be cold, but she does not huddle into her coat or rush for cover. She does not think. She is nothing presently but anger, which shakes her body like an approaching Tube train.

She had been coming to tell Henry about her plans; she had been coming to tempt him away from Ida before he fell into her trap; she had been coming to ask him, finally, if it was time for her to leave Grayson, whatever the consequences. As she skipped up the front steps to Henry's door, her hopes were pinned to a proud man, a good man, an honest, respectable, untouchable man. Seconds later, she stumbled back down those same steps having glimpsed, through a gap in the curtains, a sight which collapsed her every hope.

There, lying ensconced in each other, were two bare-chested men. And there they remain. One fair, the other dark. One well-built, the other slighter. One wide awake and talking, the other drowsy and descending into sleep. Both an insult to God Himself. And one of them, at least, happy for the first time since that January morning when the world ripped his wife away from him.

CORRESPONDENCE

Pen gripped between stiff fingers, she bites words into the paper – long spikes and crude curves replacing her usually mellow hand. She stands hunched over the table, loath to pull out one of the four chairs and settle; loath, in fact, to do anything which might bring her comfort. She is ready to roll her anger out over days, weeks. In this moment, she is certain she will never know happiness again.

How could she? Despite her best efforts, the world has denied it her.

She scratches three short sentences through the paper and into her table top, scrawls her signature, and stuffs the letter into an envelope without rereading it. Sealing the envelope, she splits the skin of an index finger, but rather than sucking it dry, she drops the letter onto the table and squeezes more blood from the cut. She allows a red bead to fall and burst over the paper then, whilst it is still wet, she sweeps it quickly lengthways with a thumb – for the drama of it. She does not let her tears dilute the drying stroke.

Eventually, a boisterous sob escapes her, fracturing the silence and Matilda stops, breathless, and sinks to the floor, letting the noises come. Around her, the flat is in darkness. She did not stop to turn on a lamp. She ran all the way from

THE HAUNTING of HENRY TWIST

Henry's, ankles twisting, coat snagging. She watches the windows tremble with rain and waits for Grayson to come to her. And barely a breath passes before he is stumbling from their bedroom, eyes small, hair stabbing outwards, pyjama trousers twisted sideways around him so that he appears, as he steps towards his hysterical wife, to be a contorted doll, his body facing in one direction, his legs in another.

'Gray,' she manages to howl between sobs, the one syllable stretching ridiculously.

'Yes. Yes,' he says, 'I'm here.' And he crouches in front of her and holds her knees while she struggles to keep her chest from heaving like furiously pumped fireplace bellows. He holds her, though he knows where she must have been at one o'clock in the morning. And, when she is calm enough, Matilda presses her hands over her husband's, because it is not only for Henry that she is crying. Not *only* for Henry. Grayson was two hours late home from work again this evening.

'What is it, love?' he whispers finally, once her tears are falling silently. The 'love' makes her stomach crunch in on itself like a balled fist.

'Everything,' she answers. 'Everything, everything, everything.' Grayson is afraid to question her beyond those 'every-things'. Instead, he humours her. He coos and shushes and strokes. 'That bad?' he says. 'Why don't you get some sleep, then? It'll all seem better in the morning.'

He lifts her and, wrapping his arms around her middle, steers her to bed. He does not disturb the bloodstained letter on the table. He does not see it. He is busy, unpeeling her sopping clothes, pulling her into her nightdress, kissing the parting of her perfectly straight, silver-toned hair. Even before the guilt of the last few weeks blanketed him, he had always admired the smooth silvery sheen of Matilda's long, brown bob. It was – is – he thinks, the best parts of her shining through.

Matilda falls abruptly into sleep, dropping heavy, exhausted by her antics. Occasionally, she shudders – perhaps she is already getting ill from roaming around in the wet night – and moves apart from Grayson, closing around her own linked arms. When she grumbles, Gray touches her bent back, and again she shifts from his reach. He assumes then that what she wants to escape is him. He tucks himself into his pillow, facing away from her. And when he shuts his eyes, he is relieved – though it has led to so many of these nights, sleeping back to back – that he and Matilda cannot see into each other's thoughts. Henry and Ruby had been the sort of couple who could share ideas and hopes without the need for words. Grayson saw it a hundred times. They would sit in Monty's garden together and throw glances back and forth and the air between them would physically tauten with meaning. Grayson had envied that. But now, now, what would Tilda see or hear if she could tap into her husband's senses? A woman half her age whose smile would hit her like a punch: a series of punches. Once glimpsed, Sally Emory's smile alone would become Matilda Steck's life-long adversary. Gray knows it. Just as he knows, or has come to know with age, that love is sometimes nothing more than a long succession of different degrees of pain: a wound of the most splendid sort.

He does not love Sally. She is beautiful, yes, and there is a gravity about her, especially for so young a woman. But at almost twenty years his junior, she is still so close to being a child. Last week, tangled in bed, he had considered her make-up-free face – the last hints of roundness in her cheeks, the even skin surrounding her eyes and brows – and felt rising within him an equal mix of revulsion and lust. The revulsion was directed inward.

'Sally,' he said.

She groaned in response, smiling without opening her eyes and stretching out her back. As she shifted, her leg, slotted between Gray's, pulled at the skin of his thighs, sending a flash of need through him. He breathed it away.

'I have to tell you something.'

'Go on, then,' she replied.

'I'm sorry … about this.' He shrugged to indicate that he meant them, the situation they had blundered into. 'But, I'm never going to love you. I thought I should tell you that. I'm not sure what you –'

'How do you know?' Sally asked slowly. Her eyes were still closed.

'What?'

'That you're never going to love me. How do you know?'

Grayson thought about this for a long while, running his hand over her china-white shoulder as he took in, for the first time, the layout of her single rented room. All of her belongings were contained here, but the space was not cluttered. It was, conversely, quite bare. A small desk, positioned at the window and heaped with books, was the only untidy spot. He imagined Sally sitting in the glare of midday light, face contorting over words she could not cover quickly enough. Though she had pushed the desk under the window so that she could watch the street below – busy with beeping cars and working men and pigeons, all battling for their strip of city space – she did not look up from the pages before her, dimmed by her own shadow, yes, but so much more, potentially, than what was outside her panes of wood-panelled glass.

Of course, he did not know that she lost herself to books this way. He only wanted it. He wanted Sally – he preferred to think of her as Miss Emory still – to be someone extraordinary, so that he could excuse his actions.

'I know because I made a promise,' he answered finally.

'So now you're promising not to love me?' Sally sat up, baring her breasts to him then piercing him with those emerald eyes. She knew how to use her body.

'I promised that a long time ago,' Gray said.

She leant forward and blew her next question onto his lips. 'When?'

Grayson held up his left hand. 'When I married my wife,' he said.

True to the fashion of a man his age, who is just beginning to fear the rest of his life, Gray had not dawdled with Sally. She had offered herself to him that day she asked to meet after school hours – in the most diplomatic way possible, naturally, with a single brush of her hand across his arm – and Grayson had accepted, graciously and gratefully, understanding all at once that he had wanted this for months. Maybe even years. Not necessarily with Sally, but right now, he thinks, she is the perfect candidate. There is no echo of Matilda in her. She is dissimilar in every way.

He turns over and traces Matilda's curved outline in the dark. Her hair has opened out into the long teeth of a garden rake, resting black on her night-greyed pillow. He plucks up a strand of it between his fingers. On their wedding day, they had pledged these bodies to one another: bodies, he thinks, which keep on changing. What of all those other pledges, though? Forgiveness. Loyalty.

The sting of at least one promise broken has not lessened as he thought it would. He should call it off with Sally. Though perhaps after just one more meeting, since that has already been arranged for Monday evening, and it would be more difficult now to abandon the agreement than to fulfil it.

He turns back over and tucks the blankets under his chin, searching sleep amongst memories of Miss Emory, her milky skin exquisite under his hands, her pink-rose lips reaching for his.

He hopes he will not hurt the girl.

―――

Morning drizzles through the window. The white ceiling, cream walls, polished floorboards are all freckled with watery specks. Caught in occasional shafts of weak, ashen light, the specks dance towards and away from each other, forming little rivers of luminosity which flow over the dining table. At the table, which stands proud in the centre of the room, Matilda is slumped, fingering the envelope. On the front, she has scribbled *Ms I Fairclough*, but she does not know the address. She hadn't recognised that problem until she shifted the pen down to mark the first line.

Matilda sighs. It has been raining forever. Forever.

At dawn, she had pulled on a cotton day dress and coat, ready to face the day, but she had failed, like a defective motorcar engine, somewhere between clothing herself and propelling herself out of the flat. She had neglected to brush her hair. Now, she stands and creeps towards the door in her stockinged feet. There, she drags on a plain felt cloche hat, avoiding her reflection. It does not matter what she looks like. No one cares. No one sees her.

She pauses and listens in case Grayson is stirring. When she is convinced he is still deeply asleep, she opens the door and slips out, pulling it closed behind her inch by silent inch. At the bottom of the stairs, she hauls open a second door and regards the sagging city. Funny, she thinks, how on occasion London can lift and refine and make everything that bit more exciting. Funny how, on others, it can be the limpest, weightiest place in the entire world. This city, Matilda decides, it lives with you. And as she steps out of her front door onto the shining pavement, it does, it lives with her. It is grey. The tramlined buildings, the chimney-smoking flats, the arrow-straight street darting ahead of her — it is all grey.

Matilda does not lift an umbrella to it. Today, she wants to feel it.

Next week, at Monty's, the Bright Young People are holding a Kings and Queens Party — one of the naughtiest of all, Matilda is told, since kings and queens are governed by no one — and London will again be a place of laughter and shimmying and stolen kisses. Monty has already forwarded

Matilda and Gray's invitations, and Matilda will go, she determines now, with or without her husband. She wants nothing more than to be one of those careless girls who swap lipsticks and husbands with smiles; who dance like nobody is watching them; who run the streets, lengths of beaded silk or chiffon or satin shining under streetlamps, teasing men and each other. She will have taken up smoking by then. She purchased a cigarette holder after the White Party – an expensive one, already anticipating the need to emulate those wealthier, freer women – but she has not used it yet. Cocktail-length and carved from warm tortoiseshell, it will fit perfectly at the Kings and Queens Party, held casually apart from her, the cigarette releasing its coiling breath into the sky.

Matilda is not concerned with whose company she might manage to acquire at the event. She only wants to feel at the core of something again – the way she had at her school, before she'd married Gray and had to leave teaching; the way she had at Monty's, when Ruby was alive and she hadn't yet started loving Henry or stopped loving Grayson, and they were simply five friends, drinking themselves towards the brilliant possibilities of tomorrow.

She could calculate, if she wanted to, how long ago all of that had ended. But the time would total only months, and those months could not begin to demonstrate how distant it feels, so she does not. More than that, though, Matilda feels herself to be distant, removed, as though all of that friendship had been a falsity. One only she had been tricked by.

Sometimes, when she can't stand her own company any longer, she packs the gaps in her days with false memories of Ruby. Or, if not entirely false, then much altered. She sets them up, like stage actors, at Monty's or a café or a party – places they really did visit together – but she removes the words they truly spoke and substitutes them with those she would rather hear. Sitting at a Park Street café on an early summer evening, leaning on a palm, her head tilted to one side, Ruby smiles sympathy at Matilda and tells her not to worry. 'I've known all along,' Ruby says. Always the same simple words. I've known all along. That is the solicitude Matilda calls, again and again, from between Ruby's perfect petal lips: against the brassy boom of a jazz band on a sharp winter's night; in the still, foggy breath of a London morning as they step, arm in arm, along echoing pavements; with the last swilling of drinks on a gentle weekday evening; or with the first fat drops of spring rain; or in the darkened hush of a row of theatre seats. Matilda imagines and reimagines the conversation they never had. She tortures and consoles herself with it. But most times, it goes her way. She tells Ruby that she is sorry for falling in love with her husband, and Ruby responds with a smile and a forgiving touch on Matilda's arm and a promise that she has known all along; and, coming from the memory of Ruby's dainty, wide-eyed face, Matilda can't help but believe the words.

And Ruby had known. Of course she had. She had known, and still she had agreed to meet her terrible friend. Because if the memories are false, their friendship was real. Though Matilda had grown increasingly jealous of Ruby's looks and love and life, they had laughed together at the start. They'd shared shoes and worries and lipsticks and secrets. They'd delved hand in hand into each other's pasts. They'd conspired against the men when they needed to win an argument. And so Ruby had said yes when Matilda asked her to leave her flat that January morning.

That is why Matilda hasn't admitted to anyone that it was she who begged a pregnant woman to walk to Monty's to receive her apology for acting so disgracefully: for flirting with Henry, and being less of a friend than she ought to have been to Ruby, and embarrassing them all with her treatment of Gray. Matilda had asked and, as usual, Ruby had answered. And that kindness had taken her under a bus. That kindness had robbed her of her daughter.

Matilda cannot disentangle in her mind now whether

she is sending this letter to Ida because, having seen a man usurping Ruby's place, she feels duty-bound to ensure there is a Fairclough woman in Libby's life, or because she knows it will impact Henry's new life in some irreparable way.

As she walks towards the Thames, though, intent on crossing its murky waters onto the south side, she hopes it is the former. She decides that it should be the former. What kind of woman has she become otherwise?

―――

Eventually, late that night, an address is obtained from Daisy in Strawberry Hill, who arrives home to find Matilda curled up on her doorstep, chin to her knees, and invites her in for tea.

An hour later, Matilda pushes the letter into the dark mouth of a red postbox on a street she doesn't know. Blood and all, the envelope drops invisibly away. And then, to Matilda's mind, it is already on its way to its recipient, flying over London's stone-built web and outwards over spring-dewed fields, moon-silvered rivers, sprawling, half-lit villages, and the odd tight-centred city, all the way to Wales.

She will try to forget the particular words she has indulged in.

A ROYAL PARTY

Jack Turner pedals his bicycle towards the first scarlet fissures of morning, the breeze he creates threatening to displace his cap. He enjoys the rush of air about his neck and through his hair. He does not slow. His booted feet impel the pedals, but with very little effort. He is carried along, body upright, by the momentum of his journey's beginning, black wheel spokes spinning into a blur beneath him. Now and then, he releases the handlebars and stretches his arms into wings. He flies towards hours of hard physical labour, smiling at the few people he passes. He is, as usual, happy.

When he approaches a corner, he grips the handlebars and leans far left or right, testing the forces which hold him up. In the last weeks, he has learned to anticipate the buildings he will see as he speeds from one street to the next: the sprawling, ornately arched, red-bricked structures; the rows of skinny, pale-stoned homes; the white-columned entrances to grand private dwellings; the crammed, two-storey houses from whose slate roofs tiny triangular windows protrude like pairs of peeping eyes. Occasionally, he still views these familiar sights. Occasionally, his attention is drawn by some changeable detail – a tabby cat curled on a sill, mewing its presence against the glass; a bicycle like his own propped against painted railings; a young girl breathing steam onto a window then drawing faces in it with an index finger and a grin. But more often now, he watches the sky, because that he cannot predict. And today, it shows him a collection of radiant red cracks.

Red sky in the morning, sailor's warning.

Jack recites the adage in his mind, but he does not believe in it. He has seen fine days unwind out of similar burning dawns, the good sneaking gradually out from behind the bad.

He pedals on, the metal wheel guard rattling, the spokes ticking, the wind hissing past him. Riding under lines of plane trees, he inhales the faint sweet scent of pollen on this first summery day of the year. He thinks past the next damp hours, when the harsh smell of fish will stick in his nose and to his skin, and fancies himself already back at Bayswater Road, washed and enveloped in clean bed sheets. He thinks of going home.

Or so Henry imagines. Because that is what Ruby would have done, in the same situation. Ruby would have appreciated every last detail.

Henry stands and steps towards the window. He holds Libby against his chest, his arm hooked underneath her so that she can kick her legs freely, as she loves to: they drum into his stomach. He stops in the curve of the bay, where Ruby used to sit to smell the rain, and bounces Libby up and down, humming an invented tune. The downpours and showers of the past two weeks have been whipped away and the street below Henry's flat is busy with cars and walkers: people who have apparently hidden away through the long, colourless days. The city sounds of footsteps and chatter, car horns and bicycle bells, slamming doors and clattering cart wheels and the squeal and clank of trams. Small sounds, through the glass. The buses, though, announce themselves loudly, and Henry closes his eyes until they have grumbled out of sight.

'Who's there?' he asks Libby. 'Who's there, hmm? Is Jack coming?'

And when she squawks happily in response, Henry's stomach plummets, as though Libby's heel has made a footballer's connection and sent it whizzing to the floor. His daughter knows more of Jack than the woman who carried her, grew her. Or perhaps not. He will never know, really, but he fears it.

He turns her to face him, her little body pliable between his palms.

'What do you know, ay?' he says. 'Tell your father.'

Libby smiles at him and he lifts her higher, above his head.

'Yes, tell your father,' he demands, wiggling her so that she laughs. And she does. She laughs and laughs, as though Henry has told a joke of timeless brilliance. Her nose scrunches up. She begins to hiccup. Her joy draws tears from Henry, and he tries and fails to blink them away, then laughs at himself as they wet his face.

'You're making a fool of me, Miss Twist,' he tells her. He throws her just free of his hands and catches her again, watching her face change as she finds herself loose in the air. Each time, she registers the same shock, opening her eyes and her mouth wide, then giggles as she finds the safety of her father's hands. It amazes Henry, that there is a human being on the planet who requires only the touch of his hands to feel safe.

He wonders how old his daughter will be when she realises that he is simply a man.

The scent of Johnson's baby powder fills the shadowy flat as Henry and Libby play their catching game. Following Viv's instructions, Henry had bought three gold cans of the powder. The orange and cream labels are arranged neatly now on the shelf above her cot – he hasn't yet emptied the first can, and that reassures him a little. He has had to begin calculating how much these things will cost. Soon, his savings will run out.

'I could beg for my job back,' he mutters. 'Yeoman would help.' He presses Libby to his chest and turns to Ruby. 'I don't think it's good for her, though, being away from us all the time.'

He speaks the thought as if in conversation, but he does not converse with Ruby's ghost. He does not guess at the words she might have said. He only remembers those she did, in whichever order they happen to come to him, and today, though it does not help him with his impending decisions, what he remembers is Ruby reclining on the settee the night after their wedding. She wore a two-piece tweed suit and, over it, tiredness. She twisted her bare feet around and around themselves.

'Do you think we know each other very well, Henry?'

'I've seen you naked,' Henry answered, grinning.

She smirked then stuck out her tongue. 'It's not about *seeing* me naked,' she said. 'It's about *knowing* me naked.'

'And I do. I know the bones of you.'

'Do you promise?'

Henry finished undressing and climbed into bed. 'I promise,' he said. 'I know how happy you are when you dance, and that you miss your sister more when it rains. And I know that you're braver with your body than you are with your feelings. And that you talk too much when you're scared.' He flicked the bed sheets aside for her to get in. 'What I haven't worked out yet is what you're scared of right now.'

'You, of course,' she replied, standing so that she didn't have to meet his eye as she spoke. 'Isn't that obvious?'

'Me? What would I ever do to hurt you?'

'Henry.' Removing only her jacket, she curled into their bed and put her cheek to the breadth of his chest. She sighed her answer. 'You could leave me.'

He sits down on the empty settee. The fire is black and long dead and he pokes a toe at an escaped nugget of coal. Rising morning sunlight slants slowly across his back and he shifts so that Libby can feel its heat on her face. She flutters her eyelids against it. Henry rests his chin on top of her soft, fusing skull. Here she is – Elizabeth Ruby Twist: a complete, living, thriving, laughing person. A person Ruby will never meet.

'It was you,' Henry whispers to the photograph above the fireplace. 'You left me. *You* left *me.*'

But still the idea is not one he can credit. Ruby wouldn't have allowed it. Ruby would have fought, harder than she'd ever fought for anything. And that is why he believes – though he would have sniggered and dismissed the concept in anyone else – that she has deposited some fraction of herself in Jack.

Henry's certainty makes him suddenly desperate for Jack, and he goes back to the window to watch the street whilst he waits. To be desperate for a man – it is at once incomprehensible and entirely ordinary, because he knows, he knows, he knows that there is something of her in there, and he will not let it go.

But perhaps, he thinks, he could consult a medium, someone who deals in these matters, to help him explain it all to Jack. The only theory he can muddle together is that Ruby and Jack died at the exact same moment and that, in striving to return to her body, she found herself in the wrong place. He cannot broach the subject with theories and possibilities, though. He needs definites. He needs someone to tell him, with a smile and a certain nod of their head, that people can come back; and that when they do, they might be slightly different; and that, though their knowledge of the past might be confused, it could reorder itself, given time.

It is what he needs to believe. And he needs Jack to believe it, too.

He could not endure being left behind again.

———

At eight o'clock, short minutes after deep navy darkness has slithered over London, Henry takes Libby upstairs to Vivian for the night, and he and Jack leave for Monty's. City lights spark on and shut off, imitating the stars, and as they walk Henry grows quieter. As if in response, Jack grows chattier.

'So, what are the rules here? I mean, this is all a bit daring, isn't it? A week ago we couldn't even go to the pictures, and … How many people are going to be there, anyway? Henry?'

'I told them I had a friend staying,' Henry answers. 'They're expecting you.'

'But what if someone works it out? Works us out?'

Henry stops and leans in closer to whisper to Jack. 'I thought you didn't care if you were called a nancy.' He smiles shyly. 'You are that you are, Jack. You are –'

'I don't care,' Jack protests. 'It's just …'

'What?'

'Elizabeth,' he says. 'What about Elizabeth?'

Henry takes his hands from his pockets and, removing his hat temporarily, pushes them, left then right, over his slicked hair. 'Ida is happy that she's happy,' he answers. 'Nobody could justify taking a child from her father when the family is content with the arrangement. I've thought about it. And Ida gave me her word she would speak for me, if she needed to. I'm not half so worried about Libby as I was.'

'That would all change, Henry, you know that. If Ida, or her parents … If they knew –'

'They're not going to find out because we arrived at a single party together.'

'You can't be –'

'I am. I'm sure. In any case, we're just two chaps attending a party. Nothing more, nothing less. Not to anyone else's eyes.'

'I think we might be a bit ignorant to believe that,' Jack mutters.

And they might. Henry agrees. But he feels bolder when Jack is standing next to him. He feels braver. Jack fiddles with the lapel of his jacket. He has borrowed one of Henry's suits,

black, and wears the waistcoat buttoned and the jacket loose
– as Henry does, though he wears grey. Each man has on a
fedora to match his suit, the front of the brim snapped down.
Each has his tie smartly knotted. Neither looks very much like
a king, but then neither has the money or the inclination to
play dress-up. They want only to enjoy a night out together.
They have not considered that, handsome as they are in their
sharp ensembles, they will be kept apart most of the night by
various women dressed as various queens.

Henry swings open Monty's gate and steps inside first.
Though they do not touch, he can feel Jack close at his back,
fidgeting with his clothes. Henry, too, is beginning to panic,
but he is soon calmed by the sight of the garden, which has
again been transformed and does not bear the least resemblance
to the place he visited after the funeral.

Fairy lamps, strung from the trees and along the walls,
cast a rich glow around the oblong of land. At the far end of
the garden, as distant as possible from the trees, a long, honey-
coloured, double-peaked tent has been erected. Clearly visible
within it is a heaped banquet table and, where there is space,
circular gatherings of cushioned chairs. In the middle of the
garden, on top of a mahogany table with delicately sculpted
legs, is a large, blaring gramophone, its gold nonagonal horn
glinting. And around that central point, couples spin hip to
hip, necks stretched long as swans, the Charleston and the
black bottom abandoned tonight in favour of a waltz they have
deemed more regal. Men in doublets and breeches and women
in corsets and petticoat-puffed skirts slot themselves seamlessly
into the triple-time music, a few nips of this or that no doubt
aiding their grace.

'Do you remember how to dance?' Henry asks.

'No,' Jack answers, 'but I'm going to enjoy learning.' He
winks and claps Henry on the shoulder, and Henry tenses a
tad, though he thinks he hides it well enough: he disguises it
as an adjustment of his jacket.

'Go and find a partner,' Henry suggests.

'Really?'

'Really,' Henry says, because he can see Matilda approaching now, and fear has seized him. He does not want to introduce Jack to her. Or anyone else, for that matter. Jack feels like his very own secret, like a thought or a dream that might spontaneously fragment should his friends lay eyes on it.

And so, in his peripheral vision, Henry remains aware of Jack — a long, wiry figure, walking away to find a drink and a willing dance teacher — but the person he watches is Matilda, who is strutting quickly towards him, her pace made more maniacal by the orchestral beat issuing from the gramophone. As the insistent piano part is joined by trilling violins, a viola, a more solemn cello, flutes, a smooth oboe and finally a majestic French horn, Matilda weaves through the spinning couples, shoving at those people who swing too close, her face pinched and pale. Henry is sure she will say something nasty about Gray when she reaches him, and he doesn't want to hear it. Grayson is a good friend; a good husband, too, as far as Henry knows. He is hardly ever responsible for the bouts of belligerence which sometimes grip his wife.

'Which Queen are you?' Henry asks, smiling, once she is within earshot.

Matilda stops at his side, resisting, as always, the urge to touch him. The need makes her jittery. 'A generic one,' she answers, swallowing the 'darling' she usually addresses him with. Her anger has not dissipated yet. Already, though, standing beside Henry, she can feel it shrinking, cowering, pulling in on itself like a hiding animal. It is as if she is eighteen again, and so ready to be in love that she can feel it even before she has found the man.

'Where did the crown come from?' Henry asks, nodding at it.

'It's a tiara.'

Although she is corseted, Matilda wears a narrower dress

than many of the party guests. It is of some light, nameless colour, overlaid with lace, and is only just grand enough for the tiara styled into her hair.

'The tiara, then.'

'Monty.'

'Is it real?'

Matilda sighs loudly. She stares at the dancers rather than share a look with Henry. 'I don't know, Henry. I think it might just be ... I see you brought your friend.'

Jack is walking slowly around the garden's boundary, smiling as he goes. Where he finds climbing vines or the trunk of a tree, he drags his fingers over them, enjoying the different sensations. When women catch sight of him – and many of them do, Henry notices – he nods and grins, then moves off before they have a chance to approach. As Henry and Matilda watch, he stops and leans back against the wall: one hand in his pocket, he taps the other against his leg with the music.

'How did you know it was him?' Henry asks.

'I saw you arrive,' Matilda says. She did: the explanation is in part truthful. The memory of he and Henry together, though, churns inside her.

'Jack Turner,' Henry says.

'Where did you meet?' Matilda asks, taking a drag of her cigarette. Determined to wear the look well, she had practised before a mirror prior to smoking in public. She had measured each movement precisely, adjusting her hand or wrist or elbow by the smallest fractions until she had it right. Now, she releases her coil of smoke and positions her arm like a ballet dancer, unrolling from the wrist until her cigarette holder points diagonally away from her and traps the reflection of the fairy lamps in its fiery design.

Henry does not comment on this. He does not seem to notice the change.

'Nowhere. We just ... We've always known each other, in a way.'

'Old friends,' Matilda says.

'Yes.'

'Jack Turner?'

'Yes,' Henry answers.

'Jack Turner,' she breathes, releasing another smoky spiral. 'And Henry Twist.'

———

They dance and drink and flirt and fondle past midnight. Then past one o'clock, two o'clock. Finally, at somewhere around three, someone flops to the floor, and after that rather than dance the guests simply mill from group to group, seeking people to slink away into darkened corners of London with. Henry and Jack have removed some chairs from the tent and they sit in front of it now, Monty to their right, and Matilda and a late-in-arriving Grayson to their left. None of Henry's fears have yet transpired. In fact, Jack is getting along well with the men. Matilda, however, has been in a filthy mood all evening, her silences interrupted almost solely by exaggerated huffs and sighs.

Henry has not enquired as to why. He has no sympathy, and even less patience, with her behaviour. Ruby was the sort of woman who voiced her complaints, stridently. And he appreciates that more than ever now: it gives him one more thing to remember.

Tonight, what he recalls is their very first argument, on the pavement opposite Daisy's Strawberry Hill flat. Him grinding his teeth and hissing at her to be quiet. Ruby shouting, her accent thickened by frustration, because he had messed up and their wedding-day plans would have to be changed. Daisy opening a window, leaning out and warning them, in her most sarcastic voice, that hers was 'a respectable position, where the streets were quiet and the bedrooms were reserved for argumentations'.

'And what are you smirking about, Twist?' Monty asks.

Henry shakes his head. 'Nothing.'

'In that case,' Monty winks, 'I'm sure we didn't want to know anyway.'

'Don't be such a dirty old man, Monty,' Grayson laughs.

'Oh, come on, who would fill the role if I didn't?'

'Nobody. That's the preferable option.'

'Nonsense.' Monty swigs the last of his drink away and throws the glass over his shoulder. It lands five or six feet behind him and rolls to a stop, depositing a glistening trail of clear liquid. 'It's what everyone's here for.'

And, as if conjured by his words, a couple of girls appear from inside the tent, throwing obvious looks at Henry and Jack.

'Come,' Monty calls, beckoning them. 'Come and sit, Your Highnesses. You are most welcome at our humble court.' He stands and bows to kiss their hands, which they offer, slow and deliberate. Soon, the two are sprawled on the grass, laughing at Monty's bad jokes and glancing from Henry and Jack to each other and back again in a flirtatious routine so complicated that Henry thinks they must have choreographed it while they layered up their costumes. They introduce themselves as Muriel and Lillian − names which pass through Henry's consciousness without being retained. At one time, before Ruby, he would have allowed them to seduce him. Now, however, he is incapable of anything but worrying that one of them might interest Jack.

'And what is it you do, Muriel?' Monty is prompting, but Henry is not listening. His head is boiling and his throat is tightening and his stomach is hollowing itself out because Muriel is lovely, and his brain is refusing to show him anything much beyond Jack clambering on top of her in Henry's own bed.

'You've gone quiet, Twist,' Grayson observes a few minutes later.

'He's a shy fellow, our Henry,' Monty puts in. 'But he's handsome enough to make up for it, don't you think, ladies?'

They giggle in reply.

'That handsome!' Jack teases, twirling his glass between his palms and bending forward to rest his arms on his knees. 'You must think him very handsome indeed, Monty.'

Henry feels the blush climbing his body and, whilst he wills it to fade, he cannot take control of it, because he is thinking now of the way Jack's lean shoulders look under his jacket, reaching forward like that, and the gently indented column of his spine, and the slight dimples at the base of his back. They are still accompanied by a trace of disbelief, these thoughts. But he cannot dwell on that trace, cannot justify it by labelling himself a nancy. He refuses to. He craves Jack – that much is undeniable. So he leaves it at that.

'I'm probably not the best judge, I'll grant you,' Monty laughs. 'But these lovely ladies seem to agree with me.'

'You're actually making him colour,' Grayson says.

'Am I?'

'No,' Henry protests. 'You're not, no.'

And the claim would have marked the end of the teasing, he suspects, had Matilda not chosen this exact moment to stand and make some announcement.

She moves abruptly, knocking her chair backwards onto the grass in the process. It lands with a dull thud. 'Jesus Christ,' she almost-shouts, 'are you all truly this stupid?' A few nearby guests squint at her before returning to their conversations, their questions apparent in their shrugged shoulders, their furrowed brows.

Grayson stands with her, raising his hands as though to calm a spooked horse. 'Tilda?'

'No,' she snaps. 'No. You can sit back down. Go on, sit back down.'

Grayson obeys and Matilda stalks back and forth, rubbing her black eye make-up down her cheeks. She wobbles momentarily, her heel sticking in the earth and serving only to make her angrier. Her shoulders are high, prickling.

She's going to say it. How she found out, Henry doesn't know, but she is going to say it, he can feel it, and it's like the dark before a big push again, and dread is spreading through him like fire: that same unstoppable lick and burn. Waiting into those nights, Bingley always at his side, Henry would retreat further and further into himself. He'd close himself off to the sounds of the other men, passing cigarette stubs from mouth to mouth, passing crumpled photographs from hand to hand, passing insults about in an attempt to block out what was coming with the morning. He'd wash, if he could, and ready his boots with the same caring touch with which a mother would tend a newborn. Then he'd lie down, and close his eyes, and fight the loosening in his bowels.

'How is it you're so calm?' Bingley had asked him one time. The night was oven-hot; bugs of some description stuck on the air and to the men's skin, and no matter how fast they were swatted away, each one managed to leave that itchy bump behind them – the swelling red evidence of the fact that soon Henry and Bingley and every other soldier on the continent might be nothing more than rotting flesh, ripe for insect consumption.

'I'm not calm,' Henry replied, opening his eyes and sitting up again, his routine fatally disturbed.

'You do a bloody good impression of it.'

'What else is there?'

Bingley considered this, chewing at the sharp edge of a cracked fingernail. 'There's talking the thoughts away.' The approach Bingley clearly wanted.

'Talk, then,' Henry conceded. He had not known then, of course, what would happen to Bingley the next day, but he was glad in the end to at least have given the boy what he wanted.

'What about?' Bingley asked.

'Tell me about your family,' Henry answered. Earlier on

in the campaign, there would have been jeering at this sort of talk. Men would have cuffed boys about the ears and called them sissies. Boys would have blushed then got their dicks out, to hide their shame. But all that was over with. The few men nearest to Henry and Bingley moved closer to listen, each of them painfully jealous of their own simple pasts.

'At home,' he began, leaning back and locking his hands behind his head, 'I'm apprenticed to a carpenter. And we live in this tiny terraced house – on Hawthorn Road, that's what my road's called – my parents and my three little sisters and me. Fifteen, eleven and nine they are, my sisters, and every morning we have breakfast together, all six of us, and we scream at each other most of the time. Really scream, you know? Because someone has eaten the last slice of bread, or there's no milk left.' Bingley laughed as he said this, the laughter catching wet in his throat. 'Or because it's early and we just want to scream because another day is starting in a way we might not want it to. Selfish things like that. But we like each other best when we scream, I think. Or we will when I get home. 'Cause I'd fight for those girls, you know. I'd bloody fight for them. For all I'm worth.'

Henry had wished then that he'd had someone to fight for. He'd wished hard for that. And now he has Jack, right here with him, to fight for. But he doesn't know how. He's too angry. He's too scared.

'Can't you see it?' Matilda fumes. 'Can't any of you *see* it? You two especially –' With a jabbing finger, she indicates Muriel and Lillian, who gape blankly back at her. 'You're embarrassing yourselves. Really, you are. Would you like me to explain why that is?' She whirls around and points first at Jack then at Henry. She times her revelation perfectly. 'He's *his man*,' she declares finally. 'His *man*. Do I need to carry on? Do I? Do I? Do I?'

She repeats the challenge until somebody stops her.

'You do not,' Monty says quietly, his face stern. 'You do

not and you should not.' Then he too stands and, placing a careful hand to her back, says, 'You'll regret this tomorrow, Tilda.'

In the few short moments that follow, Henry observes them from what feels like a great distance: Monty steering Matilda back to her chair and setting it right for her; Matilda lowering herself onto it mechanically, as though the part of her brain which moves her has ceased functioning; Grayson sneaking away to retrieve fresh drinks rather than admonishing or questioning Matilda. Henry imagines again that he is the man behind the projector at the cinema, and that the people before him are just tricks of light which he alone has the power to turn on or switch off. He brightens their colours in his mind, only to fade them to nothing. He tries to recollect every last detail he described to Jack – the first words on the screen, the crackling sound of the reel – so that he can replay them for himself, in slow methodical order, because it might be the only way to keep hold of his control.

Jack does not move. Henry does not move.

Henry wants to hurt Matilda.

One of the girls on the ground speaks: perhaps to ease her own discomfort, perhaps to ease everyone else's. Either way, she chooses the right words. 'My cousin Wally has a similar set-up himself. He keeps it quiet for the most part. His buddies have never seemed to mind, though, you know. You two shouldn't be so coy.'

There is a wallop of silence before Monty starts to laugh.

'But ... It's not true!' Grayson says, handing out glasses and settling back into his chair.

Were he not rattled, though, he would offer the place to one of the ladies – Henry is positive of that much. Grayson is a gent. Henry peeks at Jack from under his hat brim. Jack shrugs in response, lips twitching into a flash-fast smile, there and gone again. Henry removes his hat, to give himself something to handle. Then, finally, he speaks.

'Actually ...' he says.

And that's all he needs to say. Matilda rolls her eyes and slumps backwards, vindicated but somehow all the more empty for it. Grayson opens his mouth and closes it, like a child blowing bubbles. Monty reaches out and clamps a hand around Jack's knee – Jack being nearest to him – and as he does, the two queens excuse themselves and amble away in search of more suitable men.

'Well, I can't say I was expecting that,' Monty says, the words coming slowly. 'But, there we are. It would be a tiresome existence indeed if we were all of us predictable.'

'Is that all you're going to say?' Matilda asks, her voice like flint. She does not turn to Monty for his answer.

'Perhaps,' he suggests, 'you should head home, Tilda. Why not come back in the morning? I'll be here, supervising the clean-up after this mob. I could do with your help.' He speaks as though to a child, all the while eyeing Gray, who eventually takes the hint and hooks his arm under Matilda's to persuade her up.

And, much to Henry's surprise, she leaves without uttering another sound.

Henry, Jack, and Monty sit in silence then, gazing after the Stecks as they meander away through the constellations of crownless monarchs who lie about the garden, wide skirts and velvet cloaks spread over the grass, legs flung out, cigars and cigarettes releasing matching smoky wisps into the sky as they curl, the Bright Young People the newspapers so passionately love and so readily hate, body into body. Their wedding vows are forgotten. Their homes and their children and their everydays are a far-off joke. They are shaping a ruleless reality, but Henry knows that he and Jack do not belong within it.

This is it for them. Tonight must be freedom enough.

He glances in Matilda and Gray's direction only twice, to make sure they really are leaving. Before they have even crossed the garden, Henry notices, Gray releases his wife's arm. By the time they reach the gate, they are walking two or three feet apart, and when they step through it onto the pavement beyond, they move like two strangers, happening into each other's lives for only the briefest of moments.

And that, Henry thinks, is sad. That, regardless of the situation, is very sad indeed.

Later, someone tires of the lethargy which has pervaded the party and drops the gramophone needle to restart the music. As couples redistribute themselves around the garden – dancing more desperately now, less discreetly – Monty takes Henry aside and sits him in a quiet corner. Backside to the earth, Henry pushes his shoulders hard against the uneven stonework: hard enough to leave little dents in his flesh.

'Have you thought about this, properly?' Monty asks.

'I've done enough thinking, Monty.'

'And you're sure?'

'Yes.'

'Then why is it,' Monty probes, 'that you're facing away from me?'

Henry turns to Monty, to tell him that he is not ashamed; that he had not been avoiding Monty's regard; that he had been watching Jack, who, visible transiently through the shifting gaps between revolving couples, is trying presently to balance three champagne flutes on his fingertips. But he stops himself. Monty has caught him unawares: the man has never looked so old. Henry studies the patches of discolouration which map the whites of his eyes, the pleats of skin folding down over his lashes. He wonders if he, too, has aged tonight.

'Will he make you happy?'

'Why do you care about us so much?' Henry returns. 'We're selfish, every last one of us. Selfish and callous. And we don't do a thing for you. Not a single damn thing –'

'Yes, you do. You ...' Henry hears the wobble in Monty's voice and locks eyes with him, challenging him for once to speak the truth. He can't tolerate another secret. 'You make enough noise to drown out the fear.'

'Of what?'

'The end, of course,' Monty answers. 'What else?'

Henry stops. He can't respond to that. Not when he has ventured so close to the end himself. He understands Monty's fear, he does, but ...

'Now tell me if he'll make you happy. Henry.'

And Henry is about to say 'yes, yes, yes', but before he can utter a sound, a shriek goes up. Short but penetrative, its echo seems to knit itself into the air, where it lingers, another high-ceilinged tent, as panic begins below. One of the fairy lamps, knocked by an enthusiastic dancer, has swung too close to the greenery and as flames begin to spread, and women scatter away gripping their skirts, and men dash forward to make half-hearted attempts at dousing the growing fire, so Monty – young again – leaps up and lopes away across the garden.

Yes – that is the answer Henry had wanted to give. Yes. And for a moment, it had felt definite. As Monty rushes away, though, Henry loses his grasp on the word and, when Jack finally returns to his side, smiling, champagne flutes now artfully arranged in his slim hands, Henry's bravery seeps away too. There will be no celebration for them. How can there be?

He jumps up. He tries, and fails, to speak. And then all at once he is running. Hat tumbling to the ground, tie flapping over his shoulder, he attempts to escape the party – the whole evening, in fact – at a sudden, unstoppable sprint.

Shoved aside, Jack lets the glasses smash to the ground. Then, retrieving Henry's hat, he takes one long deep breath and sets off after him.

DOUBT

He stops running only when he feels his lungs might burst. And even then, he does not stop walking. He strides on towards home, his head pounding, his breath heaving, his arms swinging as an imaginary soldier's might. Henry knows that real soldiers do not move this way. In Belgium, those who still had arms to swing had long lost the drive to force them through such a pointless arc.

Behind him, Jack – the fitter of the two men now, though it might have been different once – matches his footsteps.

'Nobody was angry,' Jack says. 'Come on, Henry. Did you think it could go any better than that, after what Matilda did?'

'No.'

'Then did Monty say something?'

'No.'

'Will you slow down? Christ, Henry!'

Henry stops and spins around. The two men almost collide. 'Christ, Jack,' he spits.

'Christ, *Jack*? What do you mean 'Christ, Jack'?'

Henry scrubs at his face with both hands, trying to ignore the reek of stale alcohol which fumes off them. He paces back and forth across the pavement, shaping more of a circle really in the narrow space. They are on Bayswater Road now, just a little way from the flat. A line of oak trees leads the way home, their branches tangled in their neighbours' and casting a web of shadows onto the street below. Henry grips the black spears of the park railings in tight fists and, like a man imprisoned, rattles them until they make a deep, hollow-sounding twang. Then, unsatisfied, he turns and kicks at the nearest lamppost. There is a clang of shoe on metal and the light sways above them, but neither Henry nor Jack looks up at it. They've made eye contact now, and they cannot break it.

'We shouldn't have gone,' Henry says, quieter this time.

'I know.'

'We can't do it again.'

'We don't have to.'

'But there are things, other things, like … work, and … I have to move out of the flat, and … Libby will have to go to school, you know? Libby will have to …'

'Grow up.'

'Yes. Grow up. And how can she do that, with –' Henry stops and flicks his hand between himself and Jack: it trembles like an indecisive weather vane.

'Two men,' Jack whispers.

'Two fathers,' Henry whispers back. 'And, what should we do, Jack … Jack. You're not even sure that's your name!' He attempts a laugh, but it withers. 'What should we do?'

He hasn't the strength to stop the tears coming. He's had too much to drink, and too little sleep, and he's been collecting them for too long a time. They gather and fall. Jack shifts forward, slides a hand around Henry's back, and pulls them together chest to chest.

'Don't,' Henry says.

'There's no one around,' Jack murmurs.

'Someone might pass.'

'No one will pass.'

Jack wraps both arms around Henry and clings to him as he sinks to the ground. On the pavement, he speaks over Henry's shoulder, not caring if the world hears his words.

'We'll work it all out,' he says. 'I know what you think. I do know, Henry. I don't know if you're right, I don't even know if I believe it's possible, but I do know what you think, all right? All right?'

Henry does not answer immediately. He attempts instead to think his way back to last year, when Ruby was here and Libby was not and he recognised the shape of his life; when it was travelling in the direction he had pointed it in. Already, the reality of that past is being distilled. Each day or week or month he spent with Ruby is being condensed into a singular picture or sentence.

'How?' he asks eventually.

'Because I know *you*,' Jack says. 'I know what's inside you, all right, right down to your bones.'

———

And though this is the very first thing Henry wants to hear, it is perhaps the very last thing Jack should have said, because, sitting on the steps outside the flat, hatted and coated, a small brown leather suitcase at her feet and an angry woman's letter folded into her pocket, is Ida Fairclough.

Morning has not yet begun to open up the darkness and, in the near-black canopy of shade the building creates, she is invisible. In the cavernous quiet of half past four, though, she can hear almost every word Henry and Jack speak to each other as their sentiments echo along the street. She can hear, too, that Henry is crying. She cries with him, silently, hunched around Matilda's letter, because she understands its jumbled message about deviants and perversions now, and because she understands that, wherever he is seeking his comfort, this man, this proud man, is crumpled on the cold ground aching for her sister. Hurting for her. He is made weak by his need for Ruby. Whatever the circumstances, Ida wishes someone would ache for her that way.

She peeps over the wall. Henry and Jack are still huddled into each other on the pavement. She lifts her suitcase and tiptoes down the steps, considering slipping away and returning another time – she is sure Daisy would put her up for a night or two – but just as she turns in the opposite direction, she is spotted by the man she knows only as Jack.

'Hello?' he calls, rising.

What choice does she have then but to turn back and walk towards these two so rudely discovered lovers?

'Henry,' she says when she reaches them. 'I am sorry to sneak up on you in the middle of the night. It's just that, I received a rather dramatic letter ... But first, how are you?' She passes her suitcase into her left hand and offers him her right.

'Ida,' he responds dumbly. They stand, Henry and Jack, side by side, shuffling from foot to foot like bashful children. And though Ida feels she has caught them in the midst of a naughty scheme, she is determined not to show it. She is too proud to allow any sort of hysterics in the street.

'Shall we?' she says, indicating the way but arranging her hand awkwardly, as though she is a shop girl demonstrating the quality of some item of clothing.

And: 'Yes,' Jack answers when Henry does not. 'Yes, we should.'

In the front room, Ida stands in the curve of the window whilst Jack builds a fire. Henry, balanced on the edge of Ruby's shaky dressing-table chair, thinks that it is not cold enough for a fire. He understands, though, that Jack needs a task to occupy himself with. They are uncomfortable, all three of them. Their words, when found and blurted into the silence, are tinny and disconnected – as though they are arriving along a telephone wire.

'It was Matilda, wasn't it?'

'Do you need to ask?' Ida says, allowing herself a tiny smile. 'She obviously fell for that look of yours.'

'I don't think it's about –'

'Of course it is,' Jack puts in. 'It's about you.' The flames are catching now, jumping towards and away from each other, towards and away. He stands, stretches, and settles on the settee, positioned between Henry and Ida. He is ready to play referee.

'I'll have to beg your forgiveness for a second time,' Henry says, his voice low but his head high. 'And in as many meetings.'

Ida lowers herself onto the windowsill and removes her gloves, then lays them out flat beside her, smoothing the creases away. She crosses her legs. 'Perhaps,' she says, 'an explanation, rather than an appeal.'

'You're not furious?'

'I might be. I don't think I should decide before I'm made aware of the details, though, do you?'

Henry hides his face in his hands, trapping the sigh he releases. 'How did you get to be so reasonable, Ida?'

'Why shouldn't I be?'

'Your sister wasn't.'

Ida smiles. 'No,' she says. 'She wasn't, was she? I loved that. Not that I ever would have admitted it … Anyway. I'm ready. I'm listening. Begin at the beginning.'

The two men share a glance and, feeling the privacy of it, Ida makes a show of peering around the room. There is still so much of Ruby here: the photographs on the mantel; a pair of black shoes placed next to the wardrobe; the bits and pieces scattered over the dressing table; a diamanté and white-feathered headband hanging from the mirror there. Amongst these items Ida feels – at the back of her neck and through the hairs on her arms – a certain presence which, she imagines, many people would mistake for a ghost. She knows though that it is not Ruby who haunts her, but her own guilt. Ida Fair-clough begrudged her sister the life she chose. She was envious.

And her envy made her stay away from the woman she so longs to reach now: a woman who is forever unreachable.

'It was the day of the funeral ...'

Ida takes a deep breath and straightens up. Then turns to Jack and nods. 'Please,' she says. 'Carry on.'

And so he does. He guides her, move by careful move, from that night in January when he walked whistling away from Henry for the first time, through his every important recollection – their meeting at the costermonger's cart, his muddled memories of what happened at the Prince of Wales, the lies he told to acquire work at the docks – right up to the moment when he and Henry decided to venture out to a party together. Some of it Henry has not heard before, and he sits, chin resting on the pillar of his forearm, and takes it all in.

Naïvely, perhaps, he trusts Jack to offer Ida only the appropriate details. It is clear that Jack wants to unburden him of telling the story, and Henry is grateful. He hasn't the stomach for it. Not so soon after Matilda's antics. Besides, he does not possess enough words to tell Ida all he wants and needs to tell her. He doubts there are enough words.

Listening to Jack speak, though, he realises that he has asked too little of him really. He should have demanded wheres and whens and hows. He could not ensure Libby's safety around a man he did not know. And yet, he has seen Jack lift his daughter from her cot and cup her so carefully against his chest that you would suppose her made of the finest glass. He has seen him sit her on his lap to play the silly clapping games which so thrill her. He knows – with a certainty so absolute that it cannot be challenged, even in retrospect – that Elizabeth Twist adores Jack Turner, and that the reason for that adoration is familiarity.

Libby recognised Jack the instant she first saw him.

As they talk, another morning blooms gold over the city, spreading in wide warming slants over rooftops and alleyways, streets and parkland, and eventually forming a sort of halo around Ida, who listens intently to Jack, blinking away her tiredness. Henry has seen a thousand London dawns. Now, he wonders again what it would be like to watch the sun emerge each day over the tops of the Welsh mountains. He should have taken Ruby home. He should have insisted. She would have fought him at first, yes; she would have shouted and raged at his going against her wishes. A fight, though – one simple argument or a hundred more complicated contests, it matters little now – might just have kept her alive.

And then there is Jack. Who or what could have kept him alive, as he was before he was attacked?

Henry has not forgotten the woman and the two boys who visit Jack's dreams. When he is brave enough, he sees them for what they are. And he considers then that the smallest of their choices – to meet him from work or to wait for him at home, to take a walk with him or to join him later – might have ensured that a woman still had her husband and two children still had their father. These meaningless moments, these are the points lives pivot on.

'Can I be blunt, Mr Turner?' Ida asks.

Jack, perched now on the back of the settee, opens his hands, as though he is releasing from them a snared bird. 'Of course.'

'Well, it seems to me that there is nothing for you here but Henry. You can't be after his money, or his home. And, in any case, it would be far easier to acquire a rich wife if security was what you sought. You don't have to persuade me of your good intention. But what I can't understand – and you must forgive my impudence here, Jack – is what Henry wants with you.'

They turn their eyes on Henry, who feels his colour rising.

'I mean,' Ida stutters on, 'he's not a man who is inclined towards … men. Not in the way … Not as …' She huffs, exasperated by her own spinelessness. 'You married my sister, Henry. You adored her.'

Standing, Henry removes his waistcoat and unbuttons the

neck of his shirt. He needs breathing space. It has always been the same for Henry – that what he needs most in times of crisis is physical space. War had given him that, at least. But the bank hadn't, and London doesn't, and his parents' house had not. As a young man, he had rushed off in any which direction in search of it. When he was sixteen and his mother disappeared for a fortnight with a man she met at the pub, he had walked a hundred miles – he'd measured them – just to tramp the thoughts out of his head. A year or so later, when his father fell down the stairs and snapped his ankle and his mother lolled about on the settee in tears for days, finally blaming herself for her husband's pain, Henry had cycled London small; he had learned every last ugly angle of it; he had folded the map of it into his mind so that he could open it up again, whenever he needed, and view the sprawling scale of the place.

He hasn't been able to do anything like that since Ruby.

'Ida,' he says finally. 'Do you believe in the afterlife?'

'I do not.'

'No. Neither did I.'

'But,' Ida prompts.

'But –'

From above, as though in response to the subject matter, there comes a loud crack: the sound of thick ice fracturing, or wood splitting under an axe. It makes them all jump. They look around the room, searching the inexplicable interruption. Though it is not apparent they continue, in silence, to seek it – as people will. And then there comes a second sound, a voice, and Henry realises that the crack was that of a door, long since unopened, being wrenched from its frame.

He strides into the hallway.

At the top of the stairs, the heavy oak divide between his flat and the Mosses' creaks ajar. A dust-storm plumes and swirls at ankle height. And, as Vivian steps from her own home into Henry's and descends towards the odd gang below, so she obliterates the letters he had so carefully marked out. Ruby's name, running continually across her path, goes unnoticed as Vivian edges down, Libby pinned to her side. So too does the spot where the letters R u b y are replaced by four different letters: J a c k.

Vivian's bedroom-slippered feet return the dust to simple dust.

'Everything all right?' she mouths as she passes the baby over.

Henry nods.

'You had me getting worried there, you know.' She keeps to a whisper. 'Talk, talk, talk, and you not coming up to fetch the child. I hope you don't mind –' She indicates the door.

'Not at all,' Henry answers.

Jack and Ida appear in the hallway and Vivian, embarrassed at being seen in her dressing gown and fidgeting with its collar, sends them a little smile.

'We had some things we needed to discuss,' Henry explains. 'This is Ida. Ruby's sister.'

Ida offers Vivian her hand and they shake.

'A beauty,' Viv says. 'A real beauty. And you are?' She extends her hand to Jack.

'Jack,' Henry says. 'This is Jack.'

'Jack?'

There is a stroke of silence, as thinly unpleasant as a note dragged out across violin strings.

And then: 'My fiancé,' Ida announces, slipping her hand around his waist. 'He's my fiancé. We came to visit this little lady.' She releases Jack again and moves forward to take Libby from Henry. 'And haven't you grown big?' she says to Libby, who studies her from beneath a serious brow.

'She certainly has,' Viv agrees, standing slightly taller. Perhaps, Henry thinks, she is proud of her part in his daughter's life. And really she ought to be. She has fed her and sung to her and rocked her to sleep.

Henry is proud, too: not of what he has done for Libby,

but of what she has done for herself. Shortly after her birth, when that clever, skinny doctor had told him that her traumatic arrival would make her weak, he had appealed to one of the nurses, who – likely out of pity for a man who had become a widower and a new father on the same day – had insisted that it could go either way. His daughter might long be affected by the circumstances of her delivery, she explained. She might be weaker than the average child, her brain might be slower to develop. Or, she might thrive just the same as any other full-term baby. Libby, like Ruby before her – and like Ida, Henry supposes, considering how she is taking the news of he and Jack – is strong. And he takes no responsibility for that. She has grown strong all on her own.

As if hearing Henry's thoughts, Jack says, 'She's a tough little thing.'

And they all hum in agreement, united and quieted by their admiration for Libby, bending towards her like flowers reaching for sunlight.

When the clock in the next room rouses its hands to shudder and click past eight, Jack, Ida and Vivian are still lingering in the hallway, discussing Libby's many virtues. Standing idly between them, Henry listens, saying nothing. The opportunity to explain Jack to Vivian has, thankfully, been denied him. With it, however, went his chance to inform Ida of the appointment Monty helped him make in a clutch of stolen moments last night. 'Ten tomorrow morning,' Monty had said with a wink. 'Don't be late.'

And Henry doesn't intend to be. He would not dream of keeping Miss Sybil Brown waiting – not when he has such important questions to ask her.

SYBIL BROWN

By ten minutes to nine, Henry already has them seated in a café around the corner from Sybil Brown's flat. He had been too eager in ushering them out, too ridiculous in dashing them down the moving stairs for the Tube. Neither Jack nor Ida had challenged him, though. They are gathered now at a window table – round and too small for the three to eat comfortably from – sipping steaming coffee and watching chains of suited men file to work. Libby, asleep in her pram, is positioned alongside Ida. Naturally, everyone presumes they are mother and daughter and, when they coo, it is to Ida alone they turn their eyes.

Ida accepts their compliments with a little nod and a side-ward glance at Henry.

'Have you ever believed in this sort of thing, Ida?' Jack asks. 'The psychics? The mystics? You don't strike me as a believer.'

'Can't say I am,' Ida replies, shaking her head. 'Although, having been awake all night, I might be quite receptive to anything.'

The two share a smile.

Henry does not comment on how comfortably they converse, Jack and Ida – two supposed strangers. But he notes it. Perhaps it is something he can mention to Miss Brown, if she doesn't seem a total phoney.

The café is busy. At every table, there sits at least one man, bending his bowler-hatted head over a broadsheet, or one lady, red lips puckering around the end of her cigarette holder as she attempts – or so it appears to Henry – to stave off the urge to indulge in a sweet tea and a chunk of toasted bread: it is an urge Ruby would never have fought. Dawn light spreads through the wide windows and into clouds of bitter smoke, draping the room in nebulous veils and obscuring those people on the furthest side, who are crammed back to back along the peach-coloured Vitrolite walls. Behind the counter, three girls skitter about, pinched fingers snatching browned bread from the metal cages of electric toasters and flinging them onto plates; pouring from tea or coffee pots, their heads held back to avoid the steam scald rising from the spout; brushing loose strands of hair back with their forearms. They are accompanied in their chaotic dance by the whirring of electric appliances, the tinging of silverware, the gurgling of just-boiling water, and, on this side of the counter, a swelling sea of chatter and calls for service.

Against Henry's wishes, Jack and Ida had decided they should order breakfast: they had an hour to waste. Henry had been on edge, convincing himself silently that their order would not come, and that they'd be late to Sybil's and that the lady medium would refuse to entertain her tardy clients. Now though, with the smell of toast settled in his nostrils, Henry is glad Ida insisted on two rounds for each of them.

Jack, tired but no less enthusiastic for it, had declared that it did not feel like breakfast time and ordered two slices of the pineapple upside-down cake. The waitress, frowning, complained that the cake was for later in the day and that cutting it now would make the edge go hard, but a grin and a 'please' was all it took for Jack to persuade her into ruining the creation.

He possesses, Henry has observed, a matchless talent for charming women. Men, too, it seems. Hadn't everyone liked him last night? Henry both envies him the quality and wishes it onto him. It is another echo of his wife.

Finally, their order is plonked before them and Jack immediately shovels in a mouthful of cake. He demolishes one slice in the time it takes Ida to butter her toast, then starts in on the next, speaking between chews.

'What are you going to tell her?' he asks Henry, and the three grow still as they each contemplate the question. Their surroundings suddenly seem so much louder.

'Not a lot,' Henry answers. 'If she's genuine, she won't need us to tell her anything.'

'If she's genuine,' Ida agrees, nodding.

'Monty wouldn't have put us onto her if he thought she was bogus,' Jack says.

'No,' Henry replies. 'Maybe not. Hopefully not.'

He lifts his coffee cup to his mouth but does not drink, and Jack raises his eyebrows at Ida, who purses her lips in response.

They can see his doubt beginning to show: in the new groove at the bridge of his nose, and the small crescent-shaped wrinkles which dimple his cheeks. He is tense. They have agreed, though – earlier, in the few minutes it took Henry to escort Vivian back upstairs – to just let him do this. They understand it is what he needs. They are willing to allow him his belief in anything Sybil Brown tells him.

Why not? If it stops him hurting.

———

Some hours earlier, Grayson reclines and counts the individual squares of glass in the window. He does not know if it is because of some trick of the panelled design, the light bending around the wood perhaps, but he is positive it is always sunnier in Sally's flat than in his own. Next to him, Sally lies on her front, propped up on her elbows, and kisses the ball of his shoulder. The day shines her long back almost to pure white, and Gray runs a single finger unthinkingly up and down the dip of her spine. Already he has broken his word. Monday was to be his last visit. He has now visited twice since.

Today, though, he blames Matilda for that. The way she behaved last night. He had been humiliated.

He is not ready yet to think about Henry and this Jack character and the truth of the situation. And really, it is not his business anyway. What it has done to Matilda though is obvious, and despite himself, Gray does feel a little sorry for her. To be passed over for a man, however handsome or charming – and Jack Turner is certainly those things – must surely be the worst possible insult for a woman so hopelessly in love.

She had not spoken a word on the way home. And Grayson had not prompted her to. The beats of their mismatched steps on the pavement, hers sharp, his more muted, were their only accompaniment. Inside the flat, he had simply navigated her to their bed, tucked her in, and left her there to sleep off her shock. Then, once her breathing had slowed, he had ducked out and headed straight to Sally's.

Sally – who, upon opening the door, had jumped up and wrapped her legs around his waist. Sally – who makes him feel like the most exciting man in the world.

'Tell me about when you were young,' she demands now.

He adjusts his arm so she can press herself right up against him, ribcage to ribcage, hip to hip, thigh to thigh. Though it wouldn't have twenty years ago, this simple contact excites him these days. He is more of a man, somehow, when a beautiful woman wants to know the intimacies of his body.

'How young?' he asks.

'I don't know. My age.' She grins as she says this, the tip of her tongue playing right to left along her teeth. She knows Grayson enjoys her teasing.

'Ah,' he says. 'Well, when I was your age, they hadn't yet figured how to hitch a horse up to a cart, so they'd employ boys to run deliveries around London. Five or six of us, sometimes, if it was a heavy load, all trussed together with rope. And we'd have a real lark, you know, spilling the food deliveries so we could eat what was ruined and ...' He stops once he has her laughing.

Sally brushes her hand through the greying hair on his stomach, sweeping it back and forth as though she is polishing some dull surface. She plucks one of the hairs between thumb and forefinger and tweaks it out, making Gray twitch.

'Now seriously,' she says. 'Tell me about your first love.'

'You don't want to know about all that.'

'I do,' Sally protests. 'Please.' She reaches forward and kisses his neck. 'Please.'

He huffs and settles himself more comfortably. 'All right. There was only one woman,' Gray recalls, 'before ... Before. Her name was Helen. She was all of twenty. I was only just seventeen so I thought her a real adult, at the time. In fact, I thought her a marvel.'

'Did she break your heart, Gray?'

'Yes, I suppose she did.'

'Do you regret it?'

Grayson sits up a little and pulls Sally with him, bringing them face to face.

'Having my heart broken?' he says. 'No. It didn't last all that long. It got itself back together again.'

Sally scowls at this. 'Do you think that's because you didn't really love her?'

'Maybe,' he concedes. 'Or maybe I just wasn't ready to love her. Wasn't committed enough, or wise enough, or honest enough.'

'Is it really so important,' Sally muses, 'honesty?'

'I think so.'

'And yet,' she answers, 'you're here.' And rolling away from him, she gets out of bed and slinks across the room, dragging his eyes with her.

As she skirts around the desk, feet pointing and bending like an acrobat's, her hand hovering over books piled into toppling towers, Grayson watches the easy sway of her shoulders and tries to guess at which exact moment she will turn around. Not that he wants her to. He enjoys the back of her neck, slender as bone, and the light honey-quartz sheen of her hair. He enjoys the red flushes on her skin, like flower blossoms, where he has held her too tight. And, perhaps most of all, he enjoys the fact that she wants him to watch her. Matilda has never performed for him like this.

Sally picks a book from halfway down one tower and swivels it out.

'Do you know what I love about books?' she asks.

'What?'

'It's not so much the reading them. It's not the characters or the images or any of that stuff I talk to the children about. It's not even about the look of words on a page – although I do love that, don't you?'

She flips the book open and holds it out towards him, demonstrating the black on white text, and Grayson waits in silence for her to continue. She is not finished yet. He knows this. Despite his intentions for his particular affair to pan out otherwise, he has come to learn things about Sally Emory during their too-brief meetings: things he did not want to know, like whether she has had a bad day, or whether she wants to talk before they make love, or whether she will be frustrated with him for pretending to be a better husband than he is. He is savouring solving the puzzle of her, slotting the pieces together in one arrangement only to have to break them up and begin again. And he is too far into this now, he realises, to cease before he has all the pieces set in their proper places.

'What I love most,' she explains, 'is being able to stop wherever you like.' She flicks through the pages, then lets the cover fall shut and places the volume back on top of the pile. 'You can go so far as the lovers declaring their love and then leave them, forever happy, forever wrapped up in each other. You don't ever need to know that one abandoned the other, or that one died young and left the other alone.'

'Who says one has to leave or die?'

'One always does,' she replies, sadness thick in her voice. 'Otherwise, what would be the point of writing the book?'

'But ...' Gray sits forward and scratches at his cheek. He needs a shave. 'Don't you want to know what happens?'

'Not always,' Sally says, and then, finally, she turns around. With only the sun to clothe her, she looks as peaceful and perfect as a Renaissance nude, and Grayson actually gasps.

'You are incredible,' he tells her.

Sally lowers her head to hide her smile. 'So are you,' she whispers.

An hour or so later, Grayson is called from bed by his rumbling stomach. As he fumbles around for his clothes, Sally speaks from between the rumpled sheets.

'What was she like?'

'Who?'

'Helen.'

'Helen. Oh, haughty of course,' Grayson answers with a laugh. 'But that was just for show. When we were alone she was very quiet. Not shy, you know – just serious. And she was ambitious. God, she was a dreamer. Why do you want to know?'

Sally shrugs.

When she speaks again, he is fully clothed. 'Grayson?'

'Yes?'

'What did you imagine being, when you were a child?'

He sits on the end of the bed to think this through. The mattress springs creak under his weight. 'Honestly?' he says eventually. 'A father ... What did you imagine being?'

Sally crawls forward to kiss him, long and deep and more

honest than he's yet known her. 'Needed,' she murmurs.

Gray kisses her again, to create some time for himself before asking the question he must next ask. He is not sure if the answer he is imagining is the one he wants, but something in his gut is telling him to carry on, utter the words: that is the only way he can find out.

'And what about now?' he says. 'What do you want to be now?'

Sally's answer bounds back at him. 'Yours,' she says.

———

Sybil Brown does not rise to meet them. They are invited inside by a door left partly open and the glow of candlelight through a small archway. The flat is dark notwithstanding the weather. Heavy curtains have been drawn across the two windows, and in this first reception room, there is only one small lamp to illuminate the way: it reveals little beyond the deep green colour of the carpet and a nearby vase of silk roses. Henry, Jack and Ida file towards the archway in silence. Libby too, balanced on Ida's hip and perhaps discerning the mood, is quiet.

'Miss Brown?' Henry calls.

A slightly husky, disembodied voice replies. 'Yes. Come in, Mr Twist. You're welcome.'

They sneak, the odd three, through the archway – which has been knocked out crudely around an existing doorframe, Henry notices – and stop to assess the room. Ida stands between the two men and makes shushing noises at the baby, who has still not uttered a sound.

Sybil sits at an undersized but obscenely ornate table. Square-topped and shining, its single leg has carved into it masses of unusual and grotesque creatures, each pushing and stumbling over the creature beneath in some desperate upwards scramble. On top of the table, a single candle lights Sybil's face eerily from below, and Henry sees that she is younger than he had been expecting: perhaps around his own age. To welcome them, she unknits her fingers and spreads her hands, creating in the simple arrangement of flesh a single pale butterfly. It is only then, and because of the movement of her arms, that Henry notices her fudge-coloured hair, rippling, as though shivering with cold, all the way to the floor and then some inches further. She wears it like a cloak. Beneath that, she has on a plain black dress and, combined with the intense shadows in the room, the latter makes her body almost indistinguishable.

She is, Henry thinks, acting the part expected of her. He reserves his judgement, though, as to whether that is for their benefit or her own.

'Please,' she rasps. 'Sit.'

There is a chaise longue set before the table, the green material just light enough to avoid clashing with the carpet. Henry, Jack and Ida sidestep along the length of it. If nothing else, Sybil Brown has a certain command over people: they are obeying her with a silent mechanism. At the nod of her head, they sit in unison, making the candles lined up along the walls flicker.

Henry squints into the darkness beyond Sybil, looking for the detail; any detail which might make him believe she can be trusted. There is nothing much in the small cubic space but a narrow bookcase, filled with glasses and jugs and vases of the same silk roses he saw in the reception room.

Beside him, Jack coughs into his fist.

'So,' Sybil begins. 'Who are we looking to speak with today?'

'Shouldn't you know that?' Henry replies quietly. 'Either she's here or she's not. That's how it works, isn't it?'

'Henry,' Ida warns, putting a hand gently to his knee.

'Don't fret, Miss,' Sybil says, opening her palms again and launching that pale butterfly into lazy flight. 'Let him speak freely. She was your wife then, Mr Twist?'

'Yes.' Henry pushes his left-hand knuckles across his

forehead, leaving red tramlines on the skin there. He is starting to perspire.

Sybil considers Libby, her eyes moving baldly over the child. 'And she was taken suddenly.'

Henry's head hangs lower. He breathes loud between the grill of his fingers. Jack touches his back: as though, Ida thinks, he is guiding a woman through a doorway.

'Yes,' Ida answers.

'But not on account of the child?'

'No.'

'Is there … Can you see anyone?' Jack asks, his voice too loud. He is either scared or impatient – Henry suspects that even Jack could not say for sure which. 'Can you hear her?'

'No,' Sybil replies.

'Then how did you …?'

'I am simply ascertaining the facts, Mr Turner. These things are apparent on the faces of the people sitting before me. *They –*' she indicates Henry and Ida, '– are mourning this woman, this … Ruth. No, Ruby. That's it. Ruby.'

'That's right!' Ida nods.

Sybil hums, as though she is agreeing to some solemn pact, before falling silent. She closes her eyes, but she does not affect the twitching and shaking Henry is expecting. She does not roll her eyes or mutter inaudibly. It is as though she has just settled down to sleep.

Ruby was never an easy sleeper. She found the state effortlessly enough, yes, but once there, she would turn about and about, legs kicking, arms thrashing. Sometimes, caught unawares, Henry would receive a significant blow and half-wake thinking himself caught again in the clinging depths of French or Belgian mud, sinking, sinking forever downwards, until it was possible he might just break through the earth and plummet into hell itself. The only sweet relief during those moments was that the sky – pink and warm as a blush, or a far-off flat blue, or even a blasted mess of buckled steel-grey

– was still visible above him. What fully woke him each time, though, was not the mud or the bodily panic or the desperation for a glimpse of the sky, but the fact that he had promised his father he would not fight this war. He had offered the old man hope. Hope that theirs was a bond which could be rebuilt. Hope that Henry would live to do the rebuilding.

With each gasp into consciousness, he would find Ruby somehow already leaning over him, her hand pressed to his heart, her lips mouthing words he could not hear but which he now decides he must have been able to decipher all along. *Let it fade, Henry. It's just an echo. Let it fade.*

The great fear now, of course, is that it is she who will fade.

'Let it fade,' Sybil whispers. 'Let it fade.'

Henry does not react to the words. He thinks them within his own mind still, because inside the private black blink of his eyes, he is lying on cold sand with his wife – the one time they went to the beach together – and he is waking again from nightmares. He is waking to a sky sliced through with shards of icy pink; he is waking to the always-surprising fact that he survived it, he is alive while Bingley is not; he is waking to Ruby.

They had walked every grain of the beach that evening, then stayed in a little B&B on the front and done the same the next day, exchanging plans with every rolling slosh of the seal-coloured sea. Ruby possessed some vague idea that they would travel Europe, visiting – though she didn't actually say as much – all those places Henry had once fought his way across. They both knew they would never afford it, but Henry appreciated her need to share in the locations he had suffered through. He showed her his appreciation with his body, there on the beach, hidden by nothing but the temperatures which were keeping everyone else away, which were persuading every other fool to rush indoors, to light fires, to envelop themselves in layers of wool, to waste their winter evening in the pursuit of simple, unsatisfying heat.

Henry felt then that he had been gifted some knowledge the rest of the world had failed to acquire.

'I feel,' he'd mouthed into Ruby's neck, 'like the wisest man in the world.'

'You are the wisest man in the world,' she answered. 'That's why I chose you.'

They unwound onto the sand, turning their faces to the brightening moon.

'You didn't choose me,' Henry said. 'I chose you.'

And Ruby had laughed at that. 'No,' she said. 'No, you didn't.' And, of course, she was right.

Sybil speaks again, more clearly, yanking Henry out of his daydream. 'It's just an echo,' she says. 'Let it fade.'

'What did you say?' Henry stands, and four heads follow his movement.

Sybil's eyes flutter open. 'Only what I could hear. Does it mean something to you, Henry?'

'It's what I'd been thinking.'

'Exactly what you were thinking?' Jack enquires.

'Exactly,' Henry confirms.

'Then I'm sorry,' Sybil says, standing to catch his eye. She is, he notices, quite tall, though nowhere near his equal.

'Why?'

'Because that's all I could hear,' she explains. 'Your wife is not here.'

'You know that?' Ida says. 'So quickly? Don't you need a little more time?'

Sybil lowers herself back into her chair and motions for Henry to do the same. Again he obeys. Once he is seated, Sybil puffs out the candle between them, turning her face to grey.

'To a certain extent, I give people what they expect when they visit me,' she says, demonstrating the room with her hands. 'But if I don't hear anything, I don't report anything. No amount of money could entice me to lie. Especially to a friend of Montague's.'

'But you ...' Henry cannot bring himself to say, 'read my mind'. He leaves the words suspended in the air. Sybil, it seems, will hear them if she wants to.

Sybil smiles. 'It's a gift,' she says. 'So, you doubted me, Mr Twist.'

'I did,' Henry replies, smiling slightly in return.

'And have I persuaded you that you were wrong to?'

'Yes.'

'Then why not just ask me what it is you want to know?'

He almost pauses to consider his question, but then he thinks better of it and pushes on. He knows what he must ask. He has been asking it of himself for months now.

'I want to know if it's possible for her to be trapped. No, not trapped. Caught, voluntarily, in someone ... inside ... Could she be using someone else's body?' he blurts.

'Using?' Sybil replies. 'What for?'

'To stay. With me.'

Sybil takes a moment to ponder her answer. She leans back in her chair. She knots and unknots her fingers.

'There is a belief, amongst some, that certain souls, however many times they might visit Earth, are meant to be together. That they will find each other, so to speak, regardless of distance or age or –' she flicks her eyes at Jack, '– gender. Linked souls, you might call them.'

'A belief amongst *some*?' Ida asks, frowning.

Sybil nods.

'And are you one of those some?' Ida pushes.

Sybil sighs. 'I'm not one to observe rules or beliefs,' she says. 'I hear what I hear, and I share it with people. That's all. I'm no philosopher.' The sentence ends uncomfortably. They all hear the 'but'. Eventually, Sybil continues. 'But it is a theory most practitioners would subscribe to. It is said that a soul might return, through many different channels, to help a soul they are linked with.'

'And then what?' Jack asks.

'Then,' Sybil shrugs, making her hair shimmer. 'Who knows, Jack? You tell me.'

Henry does not miss the wink. He does not react to it, either. He does not feel capable of an awful lot at this particular moment, except nostalgia. Who would have thought a year ago that he would be sitting in this shabby flat, his wife's sister and his daughter to his right, a man he could call his lover to his left, and a pale-skinned psychic medium directly in front of him? Ruby would laugh at his desperation to find her. Laugh, or cry – Ruby Twist was afraid of neither. Henry is perhaps afraid of both.

'Do you suggest we come back?' Ida is asking now. 'I mean, might it be different, at another time maybe?'

Sybil shakes her head slowly. 'I'm sorry,' she says.

'Don't be,' Henry says and, standing again, he extends a hand to her. Jack and Ida, taken aback by how readily he has accepted Sybil's failure, slowly mirror his movement, and Henry nods encouragement at them. The meeting is over. Ruby, as she was – young and Welsh and abundant and female – is not here. And that, he has only just realised, is exactly what he wanted Sybil to say. Of course Ruby's spirit is not here. How could it be? Hasn't Henry known all along that it only journeyed so far as the next available body?

All he has to do now is find a way to prove it. Surely, there are others with gifts similar to Sybil's. He could consult them, too. He just needs to keep asking questions. Eventually, someone will give him the answer he wants.

'Can I ask about the roses?' Henry asks as he and Sybil shake.

'The roses?'

'They're all silk,' Henry explains. 'I was wondering why they're all silk. Why not get some living flowers in?'

Sybil nods as she answers, her lips just considering a smile. 'It's as you think, Mr Twist,' she says. 'It's because living flowers die.'

It is a surprise to find the sun still shining when they step back through Sybil's darkened flat, down a flight of wide faux-marble steps, and out through a pair of light wooden doors into the day. It is a surprise that the city is still there, ploughing onwards, when they have been so cocooned – for such a short time, though it feels like hours – within that quiet, womb-like flat; just them, a medium, and all the spirit world.

They bunch together on the pavement, not knowing what to do next. A Dalmatian on a lead pauses to sniff at Jack's trouser leg before being coaxed away by its tolerant master.

'Well,' Ida says through a long exhalation.

'Well,' Jack answers.

'What now, then?'

Jack grins and slips his arm into Ida's, as though they are the best of friends. 'I for one could do with another slice of pineapple cake,' he says. 'What do you think?'

'Why not,' Henry answers. 'Why the hell not?'

A BIRTH *and a* STRIKE

I n the very first minutes of May the 4th, 1926, Britain's blood stops flowing. The Tubes stop rattling, trams stop screeching, bus wheels stop turning, cars crowd themselves into stillness, and with a creak and a splutter, every man and woman in London is stranded. The Trades Union Congress demands strike action and its members take to the streets, determined, in not doing their jobs, to save them. The country, without its transport, regresses to a time when nights were silent and the sky was black. And Henry and Jack lie shoulder to shoulder in bed, enjoying a morning which they have begun, not separated by crowded city miles, but together.

Just that. Together.

Ida left for Wales the same day King George welcomed his granddaughter, Her Royal Highness Princess Elizabeth of York, into the world, and, though they knew this child would never rule their great country, the nation was briefly buoyed on the 21st of April. It was, for millions, a happy day. For Henry, it was a day of pure relief.

At Paddington, Ida, pushed up onto her tiptoes, had kissed first Henry and then Jack on their cheeks before boarding her train. Then, hanging from the window, she'd grinned and instructed them to 'be good daddies'. Since, they have received a letter. *Dear H and J*, it reads. *An interesting trip which I hope to soon repeat. I could not be more convinced of the health and happiness of my niece — though I have been forced to promise my parents that you, H, will bring her to visit us soon, which may not do much for your health or happiness. What if I baked you a pineapple upside-down cake, J? Could you help persuade him then? With affection.*

Despite the easy tone of her correspondence, she still could not resist the formal, *Sincerely, Ida Fairclough* to end. This had amused Henry.

Now, he is composing a letter of his own, scratching his awkward hand into Ruby's fine writing paper.

It is time, he informs his sister-in-law, for them to give up the flat. The money is running out. He and Jack have spoken to Monty and the old man has agreed to put them up, temporarily at least. Henry relays his news this simply, painting an easy picture for Ida. He does not mention that he doesn't even know where Monty's home is exactly, or that Monty made his offer drunkenly and may have forgotten it yet, or that he is fairly sure Matilda has lost her mind. He writes only cheerful words. Then he folds the page into an envelope and throws it onto Ruby's dressing table.

He does not imagine for a moment, as it glides away from him, that he will never post it. Or that he will have to rewrite it, two full weeks from now, and that the words will have distorted in the interim from happy, not only to sad, but also to desperate. That by that point, Jack will have very nearly lost his life.

How could he possibly imagine that?

The strike turns violent almost immediately. Whether it is a policeman who first raises a baton and clouts a striker, or a striker who first lifts a fist to a policeman's jaw, the distinction becomes, in the main, irrelevant. With the *British Gazette* branding the strikers greedy revolutionaries, and the *British Worker* refuting the *Gazette*'s every inflated claim, it is inevitable – those stacks of tiny printed words become physical clashes.

Soon, motorcars sit nose to tail all along Stratford Broadway, locked in the pointed shadow of the Church of St John the Evangelist's spire, their engines chugging uselessly. Soldiers stand around the city, arms and legs clamped in military tension, rifles and bayonets thrust towards the foamy clouds. As barricaded, barbed-wired buses edge through London's clogged arteries, their volunteer drivers gripping steering wheels with aching fingers, massed men march across Blackfriars Bridge towards Memorial Hall, their coats buttoned, their banners crackling when the breeze catches them, their footsteps beating away the sound of the Thames which meanders greyly beneath them.

The days, chaotic, meld one into the next. On occasion, Henry and Jack take to the streets, their intimacy made invisible – or so Henry believes – by the thousands of other men who stand side by side, shoulders bumping as they stride or shuffle towards their collective aim. Nobody questions their motives as, some nights, they wander about together under jolly spring moons, and they take increasing advantage of the situation.

They see lorries being relieved of giant milk urns by stony-faced men. They see food packages being stockpiled in the temporary army barracks which appear, as if by some magic spell, in Hyde Park. They see men sitting in rings around park benches or tables they have carried from their homes, smoking and drinking and planning, stubbing their cigarettes out on the soles of their boots and tipping back their hats as the conversation grows more frustrated.

And they happen to be milling about amongst a large gathering one morning when a lady striker is arrested and the crowd turns on the police.

It is not yet midday and the strikers are crushed together at a crossroads, watching a procession of volunteer-driven trucks creeping away from the docks to deposit their emergency cargos. At the strikers' backs: an untidy mix of little bars and larger restaurants, lights off and doors locked, the occasional face visible fleetingly in the glass; a sign above a window which reads *Wittenberg's Leather Goods* and another which shouts *Oysters!* Before them: tyres too close to their feet, beeping horns, a fruit-seller wheeling a near-empty barrow, students walking their bicycles and, closer still and more intimate, the scent of their neighbouring union members – an offensive blend of alcohol, cigars, sweat, and the sickly pervasive perfume of the women present.

Far from the front of the crowd, Henry and Jack's best view is of shoulders and hats – bowlers and pork pies and, most numerously, flat caps. But both men are tall and they catch glimpses of the odd pale-faced volunteer in the cavalcade. They notice, too, a concentration of domed police helmets, moving together in an organised diagonal. And behind them, a trail of people which, as it travels, swells outwards like pooling water.

Henry turns to the man next to him.

'What's going on?' he asks.

'Lady striker, they're saying,' the man answers with a sniff and a twitch of his mouth. 'The pigs'll be making an example of her. Done nothing more than the rest of us, far as I know.' He shrugs his shoulders and, pulling one hand from his pocket, offers it to Henry. 'John,' he says. It is Ruby's father's name. Henry doesn't know, though, whether he has been offered a forename or a surname. 'Railways. What are you, son? Building I'd say by the look on you.' With a nod he indicates the breadth of Henry's chest, which is level with the top of John's head.

'Henry Twist,' Henry answers, covering both bases. 'And no, I'm not anything. Jack's down at the docks.'

He thrusts a thumb at Jack, and Jack and John lean around him to pump hands.

'Will they jail her?' Henry asks.

'They'll arrest her,' John answers. 'After that, who knows? Even if they've got nothing to hold her on, that lot always do what they want. And they're starting to get scared, too. Have you seen what they've been writing in the *Gazette*?'

Henry shakes his head. He takes little notice of the newspapers these days. He had never been able to understand why they should report on what they called 'society' in the first place, but when, some months ago, he'd stumbled across an article about Mr Montague Thornton-Wells and his 'garden of depravity', he had given up on them altogether. Of course, Henry couldn't bear a single one of that uppity lot Monty so enjoyed playing his games with, but really, who needed to know about what did or did not occur in one man's private garden? All Monty was guilty of was trying to make himself happy. And Henry couldn't think of a single person who wasn't guilty of that.

'Rubbish, all of it,' John explains, his sneer obvious even beneath his stiff black moustache. 'Revolutionaries, they say. Want something for nothing, they say. And it's possible half the country believes it. What do we know?'

'How long do you think it can last?' Henry asks, meaning the strike.

'Oh, a long while yet,' John assures him. 'We've got a lot to say, and they're going to have to listen. Especially now the King himself is speaking up for us.'

Everyone has heard rumour of King George's plea to his countrymen, to try living on the miners' wages before judging them, and Henry thinks this a particularly bold and wonderful statement for a man born in a royal mansion house to make. The King and the common man, unified in their disgust at the government. It hints at the possibility of another birth in Britain this spring – the birth of choice.

The rich have always had their choices, Henry knows that. He even argued with Ruby about it once or twice. But here, right in the hands of a mob whose palms are blistered and scarred from decades of real work, is the opportunity to extend that luxury to even the poorest; an opportunity which might, eventually, lead to he and Jack being able to share a home together, free from the spectres of fear and shame. Henry's excitement can carry him to no other conclusion. This strike, if successful, could mean a whole different life for them. That is why he has been insisting, since the start, that he stand along-side Jack amongst these men and women from time to time. Every body is a welcome one when the police are bearing down with batons poised, and Henry is determined to lend the weight of his body to this particular fight. It is an investment in his own future.

Despite his optimism, he does not speak these thoughts to Jack. There are things Ruby might have coaxed him to say that he cannot conceive of saying to another man. He knows, for instance, that he will never tell Jack that he loves him. Never that, however sure he might be that if he looks far enough into Jack's eyes he will see Ruby looking back.

'Well, well,' John says. 'There she is. Have you got sight of her, lads?'

John cannot see over the heads before him, but from the roar that has just gone up and the forward surge of the crowd, it is apparent that the lady has been seized. Henry stretches to catch a glimpse of her and sees a flash of fair hair unravelling from its pins as her hat is knocked to the ground and trampled by the pursuing protesters, the few inches of skirt which show beneath the hem of her coat rippling as she is rushed away, the sharp angles of her elbows, jutting out – her own tiny protest – at the men who hold her. He shoulders himself between the men in front, to keep her in his sights.

'She looks a tough one,' Jack tells John, and silently Henry agrees. Though she is becoming dishevelled, she has not once lowered her chin. Neither has she craned around to see the people following her, their arms high as they shake eager-knuckled fists at the constables, their mouths open to words which, heard together, melt into a growl.

John knows the words, though. He takes up the chant which, in the last week, has become the most familiar sentence in the country.

'Not a penny off the pay, not a minute on the day!'

The phrase is well written. It beats easily off the tongue. It drums. Jack joins in immediately, his arm brushing against Henry's side as he struggles to lift it in the jam of people, and Henry tries hard to disguise the shiver this contact sends through his shoulders. Always this. Always the same need. He closes his eyes to it, as he has become accustomed to doing, but it is not the usual thought that blares through his mind, chanting almost as loud as the workers that surely he cannot be a gay man. Instead, and for the first time, he thinks only *later*.

'Not a penny off the pay, not a minute on the day!'

It's different when they are at home, when they are alone. You can be anything you want, in secret. There are no repercussions, no validations, in the privacy of your own bedroom. But what is Henry, here and now?

'Not a penny off the pay, not a minute on the day!'

Is he a man standing next to his lover, or a man standing next to a delusion? He had never once considered that his life might transmute this way. And perhaps, perhaps it is just his grief. It's one thing to admit Jack to those idiot Bright Young People.

'Not a penny off the pay, not a minute on the day!'

But in this crowd … In this crowd, they'd be killed, both of them. And would Henry be willing to risk his life for this man? Would he stand before the police and be identified as a deviant for a ghost? Now, right now, he would.

'Not a penny off the pay, not a minute on the day!'

The voices rise and rise, crashing against the surrounding buildings and echoing off again, shaking the windowpanes, shaking the ground itself, it seems, since Henry can feel each syllable in his stomach: a low, even buzz. It is, he thinks, something like charging into war. And that is why, as the traffic is brought to a standstill and every last man and woman gets their chance to storm after the retreating police, Henry goes with them.

This is the old camaraderie, the old thrill. He is advancing again towards a necessity, and it quiets his mind. He almost feels young Bingley alive once more in the throng. Bingley, the sapper who has haunted him most in the years since: a boy, really, who found himself a man of twenty-six, stronger in the arm and back, to fight with, and in whose shadow he thought he would be safe.

'Not a penny off the pay, not a minute on the day!' Henry cries, and Jack, surprised, turns to him with a smile. He has never before heard such passion in Henry.

'So,' he says into Henry's ear. 'There it is.'

'What?'

'Your voice,' Jack answers. 'I've never heard you like that before. What's it about?'

And Henry realises then, inversely, that there are things he will say to Jack that he had failed to say to Ruby. Later, when they are alone, he will tell him about Bingley. About how badly he failed the boy. About how, when it came down to it, self-preservation was more important than the half-drunk promises he'd made with such ridiculous bravado. Of course he would not die for Bingley, brothers-in-arms or not. He would not have died for anyone then.

'Something I need to tell you. Later.'

'Later,' Jack nods.

There is another surge from the crowd, Henry and Jack stagger forward into sudden space, and it is not long before John is lost to the jostling. For long minutes then they sway and shuffle as one, the gathered strikers. Until, that is, they pick up a certain momentum and advance towards the police, who instantly form a line and raise their batons. Henry and Jack are somewhere in the middle of the pack, out of reach of the flailing batons but close enough to see, and hear, the blows they land on heads and shoulders and defensive forearms. Close enough to see the blood.

The chanting speeds up, quickened by adrenaline, and perhaps a little fear.

'Not a penny off the pay, not a minute on the day! Not a penny off the pay, not a minute on the day!'

The arrested woman has disappeared, ushered through waiting police van doors which were promptly slammed behind her, but still the men push on. Their voices strain. Their fists pummel the air. And when each man meets the police wall awaiting him, they stand their ground proudly as foot-long wooden weapons are swung at them. The constables not employed in causing injury blast shrill notes from their whistles, which sound in frantic pairs. And then comes the clattering of horses' hooves on the pavements, a rapid triple beat, growing in volume until the horses, the musculature of their chests tautening and twisting, crash into the strikers, their eyes rolling in fear, their legs as sure as their training.

'What should we do?' Jack rasps, and Henry turns to see that Jack's eyes, too, are flickering about in panic.

What Henry wants to say is 'fight – we should fight', but he cannot. Whether it is because of some ingrained fear the war worked into the man Jack once was, or because he was never a soldier at all and does not know the sensation, it is obvious to Henry that Jack will not fight. That maybe he is not capable of inflicting that sort of hurt. Henry does not think for long.

'Just stand your ground,' he says. 'They'll go without you.' He indicates the crowd with a nod. 'Keep your legs locked, stand straight, and let them go.'

Jack, silent for once, obeys. He straightens up, braces himself against the weight of furious people, and waits, his teeth working back and forth across each other as he concentrates on his stillness, the risen hairs on the back of his hand brushing against Henry's. And even here, Henry cannot help but wonder if the contact is deliberate. How suddenly his whole life is shaped by these thoughts. How easily he is lost to them. But then, perhaps Henry Twist is a man who finds it easier to lose himself than to face what he might otherwise find.

He snatches Jack's hand within his own and holds it tight. Here I am, he thinks. He is here, and he is keeping Jack safe, and that is enough for now.

It happens as Henry said it would. They stand braced against the flow of people and in time, they are released from the crowd. They are able then, Henry and Jack, to begin the walk home to Libby, leaving the strikers to plough on through the streets in pursuit of their hope. It is the hottest point of the day. The sun, large and filmy and white, glides about behind gossamers of cloud. Henry measures his and Jack's shadows on the pavement before them as they walk. Their steps fall out of sync and, as each man takes his next pace forward, so his shadow bobs ahead of his companion's.

'Jack,' he says eventually – one of the rare times he uses Jack's name. He is thinking still about the choices which could bloom out of this strike. 'Do you think the best things always start out badly?'

'No,' Jack answers. 'I think the good things just happen to be good and the bad things just happen to be bad. I don't want to think of anything beyond that.'

'Why not?'

'Because,' Jack says with a grimace, 'that's how men drive themselves insane, with too much thinking. Far better to just do and be and hope for the best.'

'And what about the worst?' Henry asks.

Jack shrugs. 'Avoid it like you'd avoid the devil,' he says.

'How would you avoid the devil?'

'With your gut, of course,' Jack replies, punching at his own stomach. 'With your gut.'

Though Grayson tells her she shouldn't be out and about during the strike, every day at nine o'clock Matilda Steck bursts through the front door of their building and marches the morning streets to Monty's – or at least, that's where she goes first. She holds her head high, so that passers-by will catch her eye and wonder at why she does not return their smiles or greetings. She steps quickly, so that her heart thunders in her chest and her upper lip moistens. And, most of all, she carefully ignores the weather. Even when the rain wakes her by battering her windows, she does not bring an umbrella. She is feeling sorry for herself, and it would not do to attempt the misery she is aiming for with the comfort of such an apparatus so readily available.

It is an art, misery. One Matilda is well practised in. And she knows that the most miserable do not consider their attire, or the weather, or any similar trivialities. They are too consumed by their hurt. She has taken therefore to wearing the same ensemble every day: a cotton square-necked day dress in an unhappy shade of faded rust, a cream cloche with a ribbon to match the dress, and a pair of cream shoes.

Despite Matilda's pain being quite real, though, she cannot bring herself to descend into the dirty depths of true carelessness. So that she may wash them, she has bought two identical dresses. The spare one she hides from Grayson in the back of her wardrobe.

After what he has done, she will not allow her husband any reprieve from his guilt.

At Monty's, she lets herself inside with the key she carries and heads straight towards the tree, where she lies on the ground – filling the very space Henry did on the day of the funeral – and smokes until the coughing forces her to sit up. This is where she plans her next move. And she has had to plan carefully, since involving Ida did not work out as she'd expected. She has had to exercise more patience. She feels she ought to have a pen and a notebook, like a spy in an old story, so that she might scribble each new facet of information down, but that would give her away, of course. This plan shall have to be retained in only the most elusive way, in her memory. There have been days when she has been crazy over it all, she sees that much; when the image of those two men, lying together, has ripped through her body like a sickness, weakening her. But she is thinking more clearly now. She is reordering herself. She is becoming Matilda again.

Today, as she smokes her way towards her next decision, she stares at the pallid sun and listens to the fracturing of the city. It has grown so much noisier this last week, the city, broken by shouts and plots and the bulk of tanks rolling through its narrow streets. It has grown chaotic. And it was that observation which first gave rise to the idea she has been nurturing of late. Initially, it was only a feeling: a vague sort of thing which took up residence somewhere at her middle – the place where a child should have grown – and begun, like a new-built clock, to tick towards an unknown chime. People, she had realised, can be bought when they're desperate. People can be persuaded to provide certain information when they feel the order of their lives slipping away, when they have only dirt left to bargain with. And she has used their desperation well. Soon, she thinks, soon, she will be able to take real action.

Two days later, when she hears news of the Flying Scotsman being derailed near Newcastle, she realises that those clock hands are approaching their chime. And now she can see the inner workings of it, as though she has prized the back off a pocket watch and bared all the tiny wheels and cogs whirring away within to the world. And yes, yes, she thinks. This is just the time for derailing things.

DERAILMENT

A different day. Night, in fact. Matilda sits again beneath the sycamore in what the newspapers have dubbed the Garden of Depravity and sucks at the end of her cigarette holder as she watches the staff setting up around the summer house at the other end of the lawn. But for a smattering of stars stuttering through an odd-shaped break in the clouds, the night is black. The garden, though, is beautifully lit. Miniature gas lamps, perhaps four feet in height and of a sort Matilda has never before seen, have been placed all around; she imagines for a moment that they have been especially made for the occasion, before dismissing the idea as too extravagant, even for the Bright Young People. Though that kind of extravagance is exactly their style.

Tonight they are making up the garden as an open-pit mine, complete with empty wheelbarrows, detached and abandoned wheels, planks of wood painted to resemble the side panels of trucks, and strewn-about stones and rocks some poor girl of Monty's must have carried in.

Secretly, Matilda is disgusted by it all. These people are the victors, really: indirectly. It seems they always are. They are happy, though, to celebrate the victory the losers should have known – *and* just one day after the loss. There are still working men wandering about London this very evening, mourning their futures. Matilda has heard a couple of small gangs stumble past on the other side of the wall, voices loud with drink, searching out another pint glass to stare their disappointment into.

She also knows, though – or suspects at least – that once the party begins, she will delight in it as much as any of them. She will toss back cocktails and dance and forget all those people the guests have come dressed as. There are certain varieties of guilt which can simply be pushed from the mind and left to fall to their destruction.

She takes another long drag on her cigarette. She is convinced that, after all these weeks, the scent of the smoke has begun to feel its way into her skin, like a cream rubbed over and over the face until it fills in all the little cracks around the eyes and mouth. Had she wanted that to happen the day she picked out the tortoiseshell holder? Presently, she can't recall what her intentions had been. And nor do they matter. It's not a choice any more. The tobacco has her.

She squints through her own weak-grey exhalation at Monty's staff, scurrying around in the middle distance, filling glasses and wrapping beef sandwiches in brown paper and string to drop into the scrubbed-clean wheelbarrows. There are four of them – four girls, all clad in identical dresses. Matilda knows Monty keeps them around more for their looks than their abilities, but still the dresses are ridiculous. Not in the least bit practical. They remind her of the china doll she was gifted on her fifth birthday. Her mother had already christened it – Marianne – and initially Matilda had loved it. Loved *her*. At night, however, when the curtains were drawn and the nursery door was pulled shut and Matilda was deserted to the darkness, Marianne used to stare at her, those little glass eyes gleaming, hypnotising her into staying wide awake. And so, after two weeks of hardly any sleep, Matilda had subjected Marianne to a violent and unfortunate end. The shattered china pieces she left at the bottom of the staircase, for her mother to discover.

Monty appears at the gate and, with a wave for Matilda, begins showing around a tall, spectacled man. At short intervals, the stranger releases an emphatic laugh, tipping back his head and flicking a back-handed slap into Monty's upper arm.

The Victory Party has been dubbed such by requirement. Fun can't be had at a Defeat Party. Having been organised in such a rush, though, it does not boast the usual parchment paper invitation. An envelope heavy with the thick black lines and curves of calligraphy has not been delivered to anyone's door. Instead, a time and theme have been agreed in passing conversations and the usual crowd is expected at ten o'clock. Grayson is expected beforehand, at nine, but Matilda supposes he will be late. He is forever late these days. Since her.

Matilda has not yet discovered her name. She has considered that she should let the situation run a while, to see if perhaps Gray will give the woman up of his own accord. But there is an obvious risk to that strategy – namely, that Grayson will give her, Matilda, up instead.

She ought to be fine with it all, of course. She remembers now. *That* was what she'd hoped for when she'd sat at her mirror practising how to flourish her cigarette holder. She had wanted to be like the girls who party at Monty's, swapping lipsticks and husbands. What she hadn't anticipated was how painful it would be to share Gray. Her Gray, as he has been for so many years.

Had been. *Had* been. That is an idea she will have to get used to.

Matilda beckons one of the girls, motioning for a drink: *anything will do*. She does not know what to do but calm herself with intoxicants. Once, she would have been able to confide in Ruby, but Ruby – only five and a bit months dead, not even rotted to bone yet – feels like a much more distant memory. To Matilda's mind, the poor girl should already be a skeleton, her flesh taken as quickly as her future. But she knows it is much more unpleasant than that; that perhaps Ruby has passed that stiff, blue-tinged stage and is already beginning to fall away, her perfectly dainty features distorted and then stolen by feeding insects. Matilda has no idea how long all that will take, but she refuses to contemplate it any further. It makes her feel that, somewhere deep in her own stomach, one of those insects is going about its work, hollowing her out. God, she misses Ruby sometimes. Before envy had grasped hold of her, Ruby really had been able to make Matilda smile. Drink in hand now, she hums to distract from her thoughts, pushing the notes up and down a major scale as though they are physically heavy. Mercifully, her horrible singing voice is not heard by anyone. The city sucks it up and silences it, along with her hurt.

Later, the temporary miners flow over the garden like particles caught in the same current of water. They are identically dressed – men and women – in brown slacks, creased grandfather shirts and newsboys. As they dance, the women's bobbed hair falls out from under their caps to swing around their jaws, but they do not pause to re-pin it: they simply sweep it behind their ears and carry on, shifting from partner to partner, from dance to dance. They are a thoughtless mass, the temporary miners. They move on instinct. They have none of the organisation the real miners boasted.

The point around which they eddy is a four-piece jazz band: three men, on drums, saxophone and double bass, and one extraordinary woman, whose voice seems to find empty splinters of air through which to lace itself.

For Matilda, the scene moves too fast. Where others seem to see hands to grasp, she observes only streaks of pale motion; where they find a space to kick their legs into, there is, to Matilda's eyes, a thickly populated forest of rippling brown slacks. Because rather than concentrating on the dancers, she is thinking closely on her drink. She is using it to quiet herself. With each sip, she imagines she can feel it swilling down her throat and vortexing around her bloodstream. She cannot drink too much tonight, but she wants to feel tipsy. She wants her eyes to swim aimlessly around, lost in their sockets. She wants, as ever, to feel not that she's sinking, but that she's floating, floating towards something new. Tonight, a single, slow-drunk drink and her imagination must be her medicine.

She closes her eyes and when, some time later, she opens them again, Monty is sitting beside her. He does not wear a costume. Instead, he has on an everyday grey suit.

'Well?' he says.

'Well, what?'

Monty glances over at the guests. These are not his parties any more: not really. Ever since he revealed his secret little plot to the Bright Young People, they have increasingly treated it as their own. Treated him as their own. At such close range, all that is visible on his face.

'What will we do now?' he asks.

'Grayson's doing one of the teachers at his school,' Matilda answers.

'No!'

'Yes.'

'How do you know?'

Matilda shrugs. 'I just do.'

'Ah, I'm sorry Tild,' Monty says, shuffling closer and hooking an arm around her shoulders. They lean back against the tree trunk together. 'Are you certain, though? I mean, Grayson. I wouldn't have thought he'd ...'

'Positive, Monty dear,' Matilda says. 'I'm definitely positive. He shuffles off somewhere late at night. And he never comes straight home after work these days. It's more than that, though. It's as if I can see it on him, almost as though he's *wearing* her. It truly is the most awful thing.' She sips at her water.

'As awful as Henry and Jack?' Monty whispers.

'Of course.'

'Equally awful?'

'Yes.'

'More awful?'

Matilda pauses. She has never conceived of pain being comparable along a scale, but it's quite a thought. It might be a good way to order things – because if pain is comparable, then surely love is too. It doesn't have to be, I love Henry therefore I do not love Grayson, or even the reverse. It might simply be, I love this man so much and this man so much. In which case, it is quite possible for her to be hurting for two different men at the same time, equally or unequally.

'They're just as awful as each other,' she says slowly.

'You're smiling,' Monty replies, frowning at her. 'Why are you smiling?'

'They're just as awful,' she says again. She knows now that she's right in what she has been planning. Before, she had been distracted by the new jealousy she was feeling at Grayson's betrayal, but Monty has focused her. He has made it simple. She has to follow up on what she's found out about Jack. She has to. 'What time is it?' she asks.

'Gone eleven,' Monty answers.

'Gone eleven? Already?'

Monty nods and Matilda snaps into a standing position.

'I have to go.'

'But Gray's not here yet,' Monty protests.

'Exactly,' she answers. 'Exactly.'

Monty stands and puts a gentle hand to her waist. The smile has worried him and he is suddenly remorseful. 'Listen,' he begins. 'I need to talk to you … You're not going to do anything silly are you, because really, I need to –'

'Montague,' she says. 'Whatever it is, tell me tomorrow.' She cups her palm around his cheek, letting the bristles of his beard scratch against the soft skin there for a moment. 'You're a good friend to me. Tell me tomorrow.'

And before Monty can blurt out his regrets about how unfairly he has treated her – in those opportunistic moments when he has teased her about Henry, when he has tricked and persuaded her into feeling more than she ought to – she is walking away, and Monty cannot bring himself to call after her. Back straight, arms stiffened into oars which drive her forward, in the last minute she has somehow acquired a kind of ferocity; a determination, perhaps, which he has never seen in her before. She reminds him, just a little, of Ruby. And he'd never want to change that. Whatever the cost.

⸻

Though he knows he has now been late for nearly three hours, Grayson checks his watch again. He is breathless. Lying on his back, wrist held up to his face, he matches his inhalation, then his exhalation, to four ticks of the second hand. In, two, three, four. Out, two, three, four. With each count, he makes a little bob of his head, as if he is a swimmer, timing carefully those strokes he uses to surface for air. He is surfacing for air, really. His marriage has been a hand on the back of his neck, holding him under, and Sally is the force which has loosened the grip.

He sees her watching him from the corner of his eye and smiles at her silent laughter.

'What are you doing?' she asks.

'Breathing.'

'Is it something you have to concentrate on?'

He does not stop counting. He speaks in the transitions. 'At. The. Moment. Yes.'

Sally rolls nearer to him, tucking the sheets tightly around them, and laughs into his shoulder. Grayson is beginning to feel embarrassed that every hour they spend together is spent here, in bed. It cheapens her, he thinks, but Sally doesn't seem to see it that way.

'What time did you have to leave?' she asks.

'Half past eight,' Gray mutters.

Sally props herself up on her elbow and slaps at him with her other hand. 'Half past eight? Jesus, Gray, it's got to be near midnight. She'll kill you.'

'She'll already be too far gone for that.'

This is what his wife has become to them: a 'she' they mention only when they are not making eye contact. The triteness of it rankles Grayson. He has to be careful not to snap at Sally on the odd occasions they do mention Matilda, but those occasions are rare and mostly he manages not to upset her. And it's new to him, this: being able to think and speak freely, without argument, with reproach. It is as though he is a performer onstage, who can act just exactly as he pleases, because the audience will never see him for what he really is. Sally does not see him for what he really is.

But then, does he really see her? They are performing for each other, surely. She cannot be this sweet. She cannot be this in awe of a paunchy, middle-aged schoolteacher. There must be some benefit in it for her that Grayson has as yet failed to recognise.

He turns onto his side to better breathe Sally in. She leaves talcum powder and coconut shampoo in his nose.

'Let's go out somewhere,' he says.

'Where?'

'Anywhere.'

'We can't, Gray, you know that. What if one of the children sees us?'

'It's the middle of the night.'

Sally smiles at the ceiling. 'And if you think they're asleep, you must be getting old.'

'But they wouldn't be about so soon after the strike. Come on, Sal. I want to show you off.' He leans in and kisses the soft, always-warm bend of her elbow joint. This is his favourite part of her: smooth as blood.

'All right,' she says. 'All right. Give me ten minutes.'

Grayson doesn't believe she will be ready in ten minutes. He settles back into the pillow to doze, but just as he feels himself growing light and careless, she speaks. 'Let's go then.' And when he opens his eyes she is pulling on her hat.

Outside, they walk for a while, away from that square of London which contains Grayson and Matilda's flat and Monty's garden and most of Grayson's recent memories. They link arms as though they are an honest courting couple. Sally starts to laugh again and Grayson realises, when she indicates it with her eyes, that he is strutting like a pigeon, chest puffed, head high. He truly is showing her off. To an empty street.

Gray smirks. 'All right,' he says, stopping. 'There's nothing else for it – we're just going to have to stay here until someone passes.'

'And what will you do then?'

'I'll nod my head and say "good evening" and make sure they see the beautiful woman on my arm.'

'And will you introduce me as your wife, Grayson Steck? Will you say, if asked, this is Sally Steck, my wonderful lady wife?'

Grayson considers the pavement, then the tiny toes of her shoes, then the undulations of her legs. His pupils crawl up her body until, eventually, he is eye to eye with her again.

'I'd love to do that, Sally.'

'Because you think me beautiful,' she prompts, shaking her hair.

'Because I love you,' he replies. And there he is, saying those words again, and never, never, knowing if they are true.

———

At some lonely minute past midnight, Matilda storms through the docklands, moon-eyed, her mascara leaking down her cheeks on account of the wind. At measured intervals, she wipes it away.

She is here on serious business. She has to look proper.

To her side, the Thames slops towards the sea, its noisy surface twinkling like it is home to a thousand fallen stars. Little fishing vessels, roofless and engineless, cluster around the bows and sterns of larger boats, jostling for space, their wooden bodies creaking with the effort. The larger boats sit more calmly in the water, lounging, their tall funnels open to the bitty rain. In the distance, Matilda can see Tower Bridge, spanning the river with its two giant's footsteps.

She would, she thinks, have brought Victoria here, to walk hand in hand over the bridge with her mother on a sunny day and look down at the boats. And at her side, Victoria – her black hair pigtailed into two red bows, her shoes shone to perfection, her skirt pushed out into a shuttlecock about her slender legs – would have been admired by every passing stranger. She would have been a delicate, otherworldly child, Victoria Steck, with pale skin and bright green eyes. She would have been a sprite. But, God, she'd have been tough. Tough enough to play at soldiers with her brothers; tough enough to refuse the boys who would try their luck when she reached her teenage years; tough enough to grow into a woman so beautiful, so sure of herself, that men feared for their sanity around her. Yes, Matilda's daughter would have driven men mad, if only she had managed to battle her way into existence – Matilda is sure of that. Just as she is sure that she would have been happy, if only she could have birthed the children she so frequently dreams life into. She would have been happy.

She walks past a huddle of men, arranged in a circle, their heads bowed conspiratorially inwards so that they resemble one dark, wilting flower, and is whistled at. She pulls her coat tighter over her chest, huffs, and is careful not to break her hurried stride. Luckily, none of them follows her. She does not speculate as to whether this is because they are too drunk and apathetic, or because she is no longer worth the effort.

She moves on. And as she goes, she tries to remember the

last time she was truly happy. There must have been times, with Grayson, but she has lost any enthusiasm for the memories and they hide now, like scolded children, amongst her bad feelings. Before that, though. Before that … There had been a night, near the end of her time at training college, when she and her girlfriends had bunked at Miriam's parents' house while the couple were taking their holidays. Miriam. Matilda has not thought of the name in so long that it snags in her mind. In fact, she has not thought of any of them – Miriam, Bernadette, Joan, Eileen – in years. Peculiar, since they were her best friends that night. They were her confidantes, her allies, her support network. She could not envisage her life without a single one of them.

It was the sultriest night of the summer. The air outside the flung-open doors was still and thick as porridge. In the garden, a hedgehog snuffled along the hedgerows; a rat scurried worriedly back towards her den; the grass did not move. Beyond, the neighbours tossed about under their bed sheets, almost asleep and yet denied that easy state by the fidgety, pressing heat. The city was quiet, mostly. If the girls had listened, they might have been able to hear one lonely motorcar, chugging its way home, or a couple squabbling at the end of the street. But they were not listening. They were all of them nineteen, full of ambition and expectation and drink. They were sprawled over the arms of big, cushioned chairs, pencil-slim legs kicked up to catch the falling moonlight. They were comfortable, and too ready to smile, and they didn't care about anything, just then, but themselves.

'I can't wait to see the end of this bloody training,' Bernadette said, tipping her head back and pouring more wine into her mouth. 'I'm going to teach for two years, at the absolute most, then I'm packing it in to get married and have hundreds of babies.'

'Really?' Eileen said. 'But, you don't even like the children at school.'

'Exactly,' Bernadette replied. 'I've discovered I haven't the tolerance for other people's children. So I thought, better my own than theirs.'

'Better none at all, I'd say,' Joan, the straightest of them, suggested.

'The thought of it,' Eileen put in. 'Of it *ramming* its way out of you!'

'Perhaps 'ramming' isn't the best word to use,' Matilda said. And they'd laughed at that, as they had laughed at everything else that night, because what else was there to do but laugh? At the heat. At the dark. At the drink. At the approaching end of their teacher training. At the boys they had courted. At the men some of them were only now beginning to court. At the prospect of one day owning a house like Miriam's parents'. At the prospect of failing to do so. At the frightening vastness of what their lives might become.

They were in it together, though. Perhaps that's what made it a happy night.

After they'd drunk themselves into a torpor, then recovered from it slightly by shovelling down an entire apple and raspberry tart, Miriam dragged them all out into the rear garden, where they sang and danced, catching hands and twirling around each other, until lights flicked on in the neighbouring houses and they were urged, not at all politely, to keep it down.

Grayson, Matilda thinks, probably can't even remember the girl he met shortly afterwards. Matilda was a different character altogether before she became Mrs Steck, before she fell in love. It is possible that she was just never strong enough for that sudden descent.

She picks up her pace, stomping the thoughts out through her feet.

As she had suspected, there are plenty of sad huddles of men dotted along the embankment. They might be lingering in last night, mourning the failures of yesterday. They might be anticipating the dawn and the opportunities of tomorrow.

Matilda isn't sure. But their presence here convinces her that they are desperate. And desperate men are just what she needs. Desperate men will talk at only the slight persuasion she has to offer.

Grayson does not expect his words to be answered with tears. And yet, she cries. Sally cries. She stands in the street and she looks up at him and she cries.

'I'm sorry,' he says, hands curled around her upper arms.

Sally shakes her head. 'Don't be sorry.'

'Then don't cry,' Gray pleads. He can feel the ridiculous expression on his face, the desperation, the panic all men wear when women cry. It is, he thinks, the result of some trick of nature that men cannot cope with a woman's tears; it is what weakens them, what brings the two sexes that fraction closer to parity.

Sally smiles. 'It's too late for that,' she says. 'But, if it helps, I feel like an idiot.' She struggles to keep her voice steady. 'Take me home, will you?'

They step slowly back in the direction of the flat, wound into each other, Sally's ribs pulsing outwards now and again as she tries to calm herself. Gray waits and waits for her to say something. Hadn't she wanted, after all, to be his? Hadn't she said so? But then, he is used to people saying one thing and meaning another. Tilda has long since perfected the practice. Each morning, when Grayson leaves for work, she says she is going to Monty's, but she can't, surely she can't be spending every day there, alone, just waiting for him. Gray is convinced she goes directly to Henry's. And he doesn't want to imagine what happens there. Nor does he feel able to challenge her, considering what he has done – is doing.

Leaving Matilda is an idea which wades about his mind, heavy, like a fisherman slumberously setting about his early labour. He sees himself and Sally, always busy, always laughing, in a house with enormous windows; the sun leaning in to settle in her gemstone hair; every wall painted white so that she – strawberry-lipped, emerald-eyed, milky-skinned – would shine all the more. They would sing while they prepared their breakfast in that house. They would host dinner parties the guests would refuse to leave until they had forgotten the chime of midnight. They would rush home from work just to slump onto the settee together, Sally half-reading a book, her head cradled by Grayson's legs, Gray watching the top of her head for clues as to whether the story was funny or sad or frightening. They would knock ornaments to the floor chasing each other about and not care when the porcelain smashed and scattered. They would miss appointments because they refused to rise from bed. They would giggle and cry and moan and fight, and Sally Steck – as she can never be – would be a wonder.

When they reach the flat door, Sally has still not broken her silence. Gray wonders if she too has lived an imaginary lifetime in the minutes it has taken them to walk past the Rose Inn, along a length of stacked-up terraces, and through the shared hallway of Sally's building. He wonders how you might communicate such an old man's idea to a woman in her twenties. Then, finally, she speaks and his thoughts melt to nothing.

'I've spent my whole life afraid nobody would ever say that to me,' Sally whispers.

And Grayson laughs: he shakes his head and closes his eyes and truly, unapologetically, laughs. 'But Sally, you lovely girl,' he says. 'Why?'

When those groups of nestled men grow scarcer, Matilda turns and walks back the way she has come, the Thames on her left now, the men to her right, her ankles aching in her high-heeled shoes. Ahead of her, ramshackle warehouse buildings shove black shadows out over the water, and Matilda tries to avoid looking at them. For a long time now, she has felt her shadow to be her only company. She has come to regard it as a sort of friend, an attachment unique to her. She does not like to think of a thing so lifeless as a building possessing one.

It is a paradox, she thinks, that loving another human being – two, even – can make a person feel so isolated. But then she supposes Henry is a sort of paradox, in a way. She loves him though he will never love her. She needs him though she understands now that he will never need her. She thinks of him constantly though he probably never thinks of her. And, God she hopes for him. She knows beyond any doubt that she will never have him, and yet she cannot stop hoping for him. Her body – her tingling skin, her opening pupils, the roaming of her eyes over his waist and his back and his shoulders, the pathetic tightening at her core when she sees him – her body acts without her permission, and it hopes, hopelessly, for Henry Twist. Matilda enjoys as much control then as a fish caught on a hook, or a sparrow stuck in an updraft. And that, surely, is one of the cruellest things about unreturned love – it is the loved person, the person who is not hurting, who gets to make all the decisions.

She considers the nearest bunch of men, finds them wanting, and immediately scans the next. What criteria she is measuring these men against she does not know. She is working on instinct, really. But she is sure she must choose cautiously, find the right mix of age and sense and anger.

She stops before a clutch of four. They cease talking and turn slowly towards her, moving as one, their faces flat, their anger burning off them like real physical heat. It feels, Matilda guesses, like being sized up by a pride of lions. There is nothing she can do now but press on with her plan. She steps close and – having decided to play it bold long before she arrived here – plucks a just-lit cigarette from between thick, poised fingers.

She takes a deep drag, battling the tickle the unfamiliar brand starts up in her throat.

'So,' she says. 'Any of you gents in need of some business?'

The one she has relieved of his smoke smirks at her. His head is as smooth as eggshell; his teeth thrust chaotically through his gums; his shoulders, clearly well-used, push out through the torn-off arms of his shirt. He's good for the job. An easy job, really. He does not immediately answer her, though. Instead, he bends down to retrieve something from a cloth bag which sits between the men's feet. As he rummages around in it, she sees, low on his back where his shirt has ridden up, a small tattoo of a misshapen anchor. When he rights himself, there is a fresh cigarette dangling from between his lips.

'We're not looking for any more trouble, missus. The strike, it's over. We don't need no more –'

'Who mentioned trouble?' Matilda answers. 'All I'm asking for is a little favour. You do something for me, and I'll give you a wage in return. I'd call that an honest day's work.' She takes another pull on the cigarette, hoping it will stop her hands from trembling. It doesn't. Never before has she known this sort of fear. The immediate sort. The sort where there is a chance, any minute, of her being really physically hurt. Killed, even. She is surprised to feel a knife edge of excitement, cutting through her stomach. She wishes she was drunk.

There is a prolonged pause before one of the other men nudges his friend with an elbow. 'I could do with the money,' he mutters.

And Matilda seizes on his need. 'There we are, then,' she says, as though a deal has already been struck. 'Let's keep talking. Perhaps we'll find ourselves in perfect agreement.'

The larger, bald-headed man, clearly the fellow in charge, emits a short laugh. But his eyes give him away. He needs this, no, any opportunity. He needs a break. He leans towards her.

'Go on, then,' he says. 'What is it you want?'

'I'm looking for some information,' she says, 'on a man

called Jack Turner.' She pulls a scrap of paper out of her handbag and holds it out to them, loath to let go. It had taken all her charm to obtain the few shreds of information which led to this address. 'He's not at this address any longer, but I need you to get in there, find all the information you can on him. It's a bar, so there should be a certain ease of access.'

The men trade glances.

'You're looking for anything on a Roderick Miller – I believe that's the name he went by then. Roderick Miller.'

MISSING

Henry tumbles into the morning on the back of a horrible dream. In it, he is standing beneath the vaulted ceiling of a gloomy church, dressed in his wedding suit, hand in hand with his bride. To his left, a stooped priest bumbles through his lines, dropping the words onto the floor where they scuffle away to hide under the pews. To his right, a dark pack of people wait, heads thrust eagerly forward, for him to utter his promise. Henry feels them, pressing him small. He glances about, seeking some detail with which to secure himself in the scene: the stem of a flower in a nearby arrangement; a guest's hat; the soothing curve of a baptismal font; an image of Christ; the outward flick of Ruby's eyelashes. But he can see nothing clearly. He can only feel, and what the church feels is tomb-like.

In reality, Ruby had worn a long fitted dress, decorated with the tiniest pearls, which other girls might have teetered about in, fearful of ripping or bursting or tearing or snagging. But Ruby had soared about in it. She had danced and thrown back drinks, sworn and kicked off her heels, laughed until her eye make-up wiggled down her cheeks. She'd worn too, for an hour or so anyway, a birdcage veil which left intricate criss-crossed shadows on her skin, and when later she'd grown frustrated and unpinned her hair to remove it, Henry had basked in how easy and wonderful it was to see that deep brown hair unwinding down her back and be able to reach out and touch it, whenever he wanted, forever.

In the dream, Ruby is invisible, buried beneath the puffs and creases of an extensive, pure white gown. Still, Henry recognises the size of her under there: her diminutive height, the inward arrows of her waist, the sweet swell of her hips. Here is his Ruby, brought back to him, and he needs to touch her, just once more, so he puts out his hands to turn back her veil and reveal her face, to trace his fingertips along the length of her neck, to brush his knuckles over her lips, to press his wrist to that place beneath her collarbone and feel their pulses beat out of sync. But of course it is not her. Things are never as they should be, in dreams. The face he first sees is Ida's, and then it is as if the record sticks, the dream plays on repeat, and always Henry is lifting that veil to see someone different staring back: Monty, Matilda, Jack, Grayson, Vivian, Bingley. And when he runs short of familiar faces, he sees instead all those abandoned faces he'd caught sight of, or averted his gaze from, or stopped to stare at in Belgium; their eyes screwed shut or shocked open; their mouths clenched closed or forced wide by a final scream; their noses releasing bloody rivulets; the skin of their cheeks blasted away or hanging from the bone, limp as just-cut beef; their freshly revealed bones glinting in weak sunlight or shining slick against misty rain; their jaws decimated; their ears ruined and peeled from their heads; their tongues stripped naked; their necks impacted into loose, stringy things, incapable of supporting the weight above. Their entire selves removed, from the outside in.

He surfaces with a gasp into near daylight. At his side, that newly familiar weight sleeps on, curved in on himself like a baby. *Cwtched*, Ruby would have said. Jack is *cwtched in*, but – and perhaps because Henry wills him so hard to wake – he soon stirs and stretches out with a groan. In her cot, Libby slumbers, peaceable, the way she does when they all lie together in the same room, Henry and Jack and Libby, held safe.

'Is it early?' Jack susurrates, his eyes still closed. 'Please say it's early.'

'Not for you,' Henry answers. 'Sorry, but you're probably late.'

Jack's entire body creaks as he stretches again. Henry catches, spilling from under a raised arm, the stale smell of a night's sleep on the other man's skin, and attempts, subtly, to inhale it.

'I'm always late,' Jack says.

'Then don't go today.'

'I have to go. You know I do. It's the first day back. Besides, how else would we afford to stay here?'

Henry hums in response to this, unwilling to say what he must say. The fight has gone out of him rather, now that the strike is over, now that the changes it was to bring have become impossible again.

'Go to sleep,' Jack suggests. 'I'll wake you when I come back.'

'I won't sleep,' Henry answers. 'I might take Libby for a walk.'

Jack, dragging on his clothes, nods, and Henry wonders again whether this is the sort of conversation Mr Turner once exchanged with a Mrs Turner — that woman in his dream who laughed so happily as her sons played in the garden. He wants to ask Jack if those dreams still come to him; if, perhaps, his sleeping hours are cheerier than his waking ones. But he doesn't, in case the answer is yes. Instead, he proposes they make that trip to Pwll, to see Ida and John and Elizabeth.

Jack, halfway into his trousers, pauses. 'Both of us?' he says.

'Yes,' Henry replies, sitting up. 'Well, no, I mean, we could travel down together, and you could stay nearby while Libby and I visit, and then maybe we could, I don't know, take a look around.'

Secretly, he is still harbouring some part of that idea which sustained him through so many monotonous shifts at the bank – that he would one day go to Wales, and stay. He imagines choosing, over many weeks, just the right grassy spot and beginning to dig out his foundations, his head wet with the effort, his shirt removed and tossed aside, his shovel cracking like a fired gun when it hits something hard in the earth. He sees himself building a small stone cottage, the cold scratch of the stone turning his palms red, the labour leaving an ache in his lower back which would persist into old age, the repetition of lifting and laying sculpting the muscles in his shoulders so that he resembles again the man he was when he fought for his country. He fancies himself sitting atop the rafters, placing slates and hammering them down and hunching like a tired crow against the grey rain which slices into him. Jack would mock him for that, for battling the weather when he might have just waited for a fine day. He would stand on the grass below and cup his hands around his mouth and shout something like, 'Come down, you idiot. If you have to build something, come and build us a fire.' Because that is what Jack does for him. That is what Ruby did for him. They make him stop and take his time.

'Look around at what?'

'Just … the place. The sea. Do you like the sea, Jack?'

Buttoning up his shirt now, Jack considers the question. 'I don't know,' he answers. 'Maybe.' He pulls his braces up over his shoulders with a wink and a grin. 'I'll let you know when we get there,' he says, and then he disappears, like a shadow, into the very first fissures of the day.

Henry rubs his hands over his face once, twice, three times, coaxing himself to rise from bed and go through to the kitchen to prepare a bottle for Libby. There is always something to prepare, something to wash, but he doesn't curse the endless need. It is better, he has found, to keep moving when you are afraid. And that – afraid – is undeniably how he feels about visiting the Faircloughs. He doesn't know what he will say to them, or how he will manage to hand Libby to them and declare that here is their granddaughter, or how he will explain that he hasn't been tending Ruby's grave. In the kitchen, he listens for a city sound beyond the trickle of birdsong, but he can hear none. London is quiet. The calm before the storm, he thinks, though he doesn't dwell on the idea. It is only a bit of bad feeling, left behind by his dream.

He cannot know that, short feet away, deposited carefully near his front door, flashing brighter with the emergence of each new strand of sunlight but as yet unseen, there waits one small clue that, in fact, a storm is coming. She left it there just last night, so that it would be easily found when the police arrived. She had to stack the odds. But Henry cannot know, and so he can do nothing to prevent what will happen next. He stands in the kitchen of his Bayswater Road flat and spoons SMA formula into a bottle. In the next room, Libby snuffles in her sleep and he returns to her, answering her every noise, the way his body has taught him to. He has no reason to suspect that Matilda Steck's wedding ring is positioned just outside, waiting to be discovered. Why would he? He has never thought her capable of what she has done.

Because it is Saturday, Matilda does not expect Grayson to wake early. Especially considering how late he arrived home: later, even, than she had. But it is only when he slides out of bed at half past six that she realises just how much she'd been hoping he would lie in this morning. It is only as she watches him swing away through their bedroom doorway that she understands she had wanted them to make love.

There was a time when she could have spoken to Ruby about the affair. When she could have met her friend at a coffee shop on Oxford Street and let the words run out of her, hidden by the scraping of chair legs and the chatter of strangers and the chinking and rattling and squealing of hot drink preparation. Matilda knows how Ruby would have reacted. She would have arched an eyebrow when the news was delivered, she might even have grunted in disgust, but she would have made sure to stay quiet until Matilda was finished and she was in possession of all the information. Only then could she offer her instant and unalterable opinion.

Matilda smiles at the thought. She was always so stubborn, Ruby; always so certain. If she had found out Henry was being unfaithful, she would have battered him with her words then walked out, gone back to Wales or Strawberry Hill or gone somewhere new entirely, and left her husband heartbroken.

But Matilda is not so brave. And she is not convinced that Gray would be heartbroken if she walked out now. She is afraid he might even be relieved.

In the bathroom, she hears the tap creak on, then the first crash of water into the cast iron tub. She knows too well the bony ankles above the feet which will step into that bath, the slight inward pull of the knees, the scar which had speared his left thigh when he'd fallen off his bicycle as a child, the rose petal of pigmented skin just above the concentration of pubic hair, the lately developing paunch, the odd heart-shaped arrangement of chest hair, the slow-narrowing shoulders. Grayson's body is still mostly strong, but it is beginning the slip into old age now. That much is undeniable. Matilda does not think him irresistible, particularly to other women, but there must be something, something charming perhaps, which makes this teacher of his think him worth the risk to her reputation.

Oh, she wishes she could tell Ruby. Ruby would know what to think, what to do, how to make him love her again. Though it oughtn't, considering her behaviour, this thought seems to come to Matilda along her very bloodstream. Of course she has to make him love her again. What else is there? There will certainly be no child now. There will certainly be no Henry. She climbs out from under the sheets and steps through to the lounge in her peach cotton nightdress, the morning cold clinging to her calves and the tops of her arms. She pulls the neck tighter over her chest and bows the string. It is not her most elegant nightdress. She should make more of an effort.

She studies the street below from her third-storey window. She knows this view. She knows that the straight line of the pavement is interrupted, for a long way, only to permit entrance to the skinny side streets which leak away from it, London's little veins; she knows that, just a short distance away, there hides a cramped and dingy café which accommodates artists and writers and the poor unfortunate like; she knows that if she looks directly ahead she can see eight rectangular windows, arranged with soldier-like uniformity; and that in those windows, net curtains are drawn and opened and removed and cleaned and replaced with such regularity that the aspect of that building is nearly always different; and that sometimes, when those curtains do not spoil her view, she can see into other people's lives and decide whether she has anything, anything at all, to be jealous of.

At this early hour, all the curtains are closed. Today, in any case, she doesn't want to consider anyone but herself. There are questions she must find answers to.

She focuses her attention down to the place where the kerbs rise up from the road: there yesterday's rain has amassed into two canals which reflect the new pink faults of the sky. Funny, she thinks, that in looking down she might be forced to look up.

When the taps stop running and the flat is silent again, Matilda returns to the bedroom and, pulling her nightdress up over her head, ponders her bared body in her dressing table mirror. It's not all bad. If she turns sideways – she does – and sucks her stomach up, just so – she holds her breath – her silhouette might pass for a woman's ten years younger. Failing to bear children has at least brought her this: a body she might be able to bargain with. She leans in towards the glass, studiously avoiding the reflection of her breasts, hanging forward with her, pendulously, as though they are, by degrees, dissociating themselves from her body – a good cami would solve that – and uses her hands to stretch out the skin of her cheeks, her forehead, her eyes. She grabs the heavy jar of Pond's Vanishing Cream off her dressing table and, choosing to believe, for now, in the promise of the bold red C on the packaging, sweeps a cool palmful of it over her face. She pinches her cheeks red, clamps her eyelashes in a curler and teases the tips outwards with a dab of Vaseline, bites her lips until they plump slightly. Then she reaches for a brush and drags it hard through her hair: seeking volume, she tosses her head upside down and shakes her fingers through the roots. And when, finally, she has done all she can, she rummages around for her prettiest camisole and step-ins. It has been so long since she made this sort of effort that, once she has pulled her undergarments on, she is surprised to find herself quite excited. Hadn't they loved each other hard, she and Gray, when their nights had been filled this way? Couldn't they do so again?

She tiptoes over to the bathroom and, without knocking, pushes open the door. She is ready to use her hands – gently, expertly, as she had in the beginning. Upon entering the room, however, she discovers that Grayson has taken to using his own. His eyes snap open when he realises he is being watched.

'Isn't it enough?' Matilda screams, and Gray is struggling to sit up now, to get out of the water, but he slips and slides in the tub, sending the water swaying and sloshing over the lip and onto the floor with a pathetic wet slap. 'Isn't it enough to *be with her*? Jesus, Grayson, you have to be *thinking* about her too. In *our house*! When I'm in the *very next room*!'

She spins around and slams her way through the flat with a sudden physical strength, banging the lounge door against its frame, flicking a vase to the floor where it releases just one sharp fragment of china and rolls away, kicking the legs of the dining table so that they screech over the floorboards, thumping the window with the heel of her hand. She knows he will follow her. He always has. And perhaps that is all she needs. Perhaps that is why she moons over Henry, and flirts with Monty, and neglects Grayson – because that is the only way to secure the devotion she needs, to feel like a woman, to survive. She does not stop thumping the glass until she is sure Grayson is standing behind her. When she turns, slowly, he is on the opposite side of the room, stock still and naked, the bath water streaming down his body like so many rivers, seen from a distance. He is goose-bumped all over. His penis is a tiny thing. And he is about to say *I'm sorry. Forgive me. I'm a fool.* Matilda is certain of it. But when he opens his mouth, different sounds come out.

'Why did you stay quiet so long?' he asks.

Matilda answers the question the only way she knows how – with her hands. She strides across the room, lifts her arm, and slaps his face as hard as she can. The whip-crack of it bounces across the flat, already an echo. And then she is kissing him. She is grasping that familiar face, and tasting those beautiful lips, and she is kissing her husband, her Grayson, until she runs short of breath, because she doesn't know what else to do. She doesn't know how else to say, *It's me who is sorry.*

———

By three o'clock that afternoon the mid-May sun has transformed number 101a Bayswater Road into a tropical dwelling. The streets are busy with wealthy Londoners revelling in the first real heat of the year, most of the strikers have resumed their jobs and sweat now down at the docks or in the factories or over a row of just-laid stones, the birds have stopped singing and retired to the shade, Jack is many hours late back from work, and Henry is sitting at Viv's kitchen table, cradling a cup of her over-sugared tea. He is used now to the sickly sweetness, to the residue it leaves on his teeth. He quite enjoys it.

Viv's kitchen door is flung open, but the breeze comes at longer and longer intervals, barely disturbing the nets at the window. Henry fiddles with the collar of his shirt. The temperature is worsening the panic swirling about in his stomach.

'How is he?' he asks Viv in a whisper. Henry wants to distract himself, yes, but he does care about Herb. In the next room, the old man snores and snorts. Viv glances through the open lounge door, as though she might find a better answer there, in the precious space which contains her husband.

'Still here,' she says. 'He hasn't left me yet.'

Henry reaches across the table and captures Vivian's hand. She is not, he knows, a woman who appreciates these sorts of gestures. But then, he is not a man who readily offers them. They understand each other perfectly. Henry nods and, when Viv nods back, he retracts his hand again. That is enough.

Though really, there is a secret part of Henry which wishes she would hold onto him, just for a minute, because Jack is so many hours late back from work.

He should be used now to these short absent spells. They'd happened, hadn't they, at the start? But Henry knows that the gut-roiling sensation – of fearing someone leaving, of waiting for their return – is one that cannot simply be put aside. He knows because, as a boy, he'd spent countless nights waiting on the rodent-like scratching of his mother trying to unlock their front door when she returned from the pub.

'You know, we're going to have to leave, Libby and I,' he blurts. He'd been meaning only to think through how best to arrange the words, how gently he could tell Vivian that, once again, a child was being taken from her.

'No,' she says, and Henry swears he sees her skin fade by a shade or two. There comes a point, he supposes, when your life starts to fail you; when you must rely on other things, other people, to keep you going.

'I'm sorry, Viv. I know you love having her, but –'

'And you, Henry. I love having you, too.'

Henry's mouth turns downwards into one of those inverted smiles. 'I really am sorry.'

Viv's hand flies up to silence him. 'Oh, I know, I know,' she says. The beginnings of tears roll her words into softer version of themselves. 'And, really, I can't bear apologies. Our whole lives are so full of sorrys and goodbyes, I think I've decided to give up on them. Let's just pretend you're not going, can we, for a little while?'

'I'd like that.'

'Me too.' She gulps her tea too quickly and coughs, shaking her head. At length, she speaks again. 'A friend of mine did it once, this pretending, with her sister. It's the best way, I think, to just pretend everything's going to go on the same; that nothing's changing. She was dying, the girl, you see. Eleven she was, when the TB got her. And all the way along they just kept pretending, nothing was happening, nothing was changing. And do you know what the last thing she said to her sister was?'

'What?' Henry obliges.

'She said, 'I've got us a basket ready for tomorrow, and we're going to go blackberry-picking.' It was the middle of winter, Henry, but I'd swear that little girl believed she'd be going blackberry-picking in the morning. I'd swear it because I want to swear it, do you see?'

'I think so.'

'Don't you wish you'd pretended more, Henry?'

The answer, Henry supposes, is yes and no. He remembers a night in particular – though there were undoubtedly many quite similar nights – when he and Ruby had gone out to dinner. Afterwards, Ruby had wanted to go dancing. Ruby always wanted to dance. But Henry had refused.

'I have to work in the morning,' he'd said. 'I have to wake early.'

They were walking past that theatre where she'd once stood him up. Between the streetlamps and the theatre lights, she was a cacophony of reflected colour: raspberry and indigo, sea blue and sunshine yellow, lime and a deep, expensive gold. She looked like some sort of ancient queen, smothered in jewels. And, on account of the whisky he'd drunk at dinner, Henry was thinking stupid thoughts like, Wouldn't Ruby make a wonderful queen, and, Ruby might just be made of gold underneath. But still he would not take her dancing.

'You, Henry Twist,' she said, crossing her arms, 'are a miserable old sod sometimes.'

'And you, Ruby Twist, are a bother.'

'I am not.' She frowned and stepped a little heavier: a toddler, pouting.

'You are, but I love you for it.'

'*And* I love you for it,' she corrected, but Henry didn't understand.

'Sorry?'

'*And* you love me for it,' she explained. 'Not but. You shouldn't love me *in spite* of something. You should only love me *because* of something.'

'Ah, so those are the rules, are they?'

Ruby paused, just momentarily, to nod her head and smile. 'Yes,' she decided, 'I think they might be.'

'Good to know,' Henry answered, playing at seriousness, and though they did not go dancing, he knew he had managed to keep Ruby happy with that touch of ribbing. He knew because she did not keep on at him for being miserable that night. He knew because, when they arrived home, she threw herself onto their bed, kicked off her shoes, flung her arms out wide and called 'Quick, husband, take my clothes off me before I rush out and find another man to dance with'.

But even so, yes, he wishes now he'd pretended he didn't have work the next day and just taken her dancing. It would have meant a night spent pressed together – surrounded by people of course but also, quite blissfully, alone. It would have meant another memory.

'Sometimes,' Henry tells Vivian finally. She finishes her tea and stands to clear the cups. She winces against the stuttering movements her thinning bones force her through, and Henry averts his eyes. 'But we can't choose what to believe.'

At the sink, Viv takes a long time about arranging the cups and saucers, then turns to smile at him.

'Sometimes we can, Henry,' she says. 'Just sometimes, it's good for us.'

THE HEAT

The heat swarms across the country with a plague-like ferocity. In Pwll, Ida Fairclough wakes into a muggy morning and, unable to ease the headache it brings on, finds herself walking along the beach, shoes hooked over her right-hand fingers, toes kneading the sand, before the postman has deposited the first of his letters. In the valleys, the miners allow themselves to be glad, for a few very secret hours, that they do not yet have jobs to return to and share cigarettes and newspapers with their buddies, sitting outside their own front doors. Hundreds of miles away, in Hyde Park and Kensington Gardens, horse hooves rattle the otherwise still air as ice-cream carts are dragged out and cleaned up and taken on their first outing of the summer. Lovers sneak away from their offices on their tea breaks to rush, giggling, down quieter city streets. Cats flatten themselves under beds and dogs give up on barking and pigeons strut slower than before. Down at the docks, the men wipe their greasy brows in their shirt sleeves and curse that Jack Turner chap for not turning up, today of all days. And at his desk, beneath the single too-small window of Classroom F, Grayson Steck hides his face in his hands and decides that this is the first time, the very first time, that he has welcomed the building's eternal cold.

He peeps through his fingers to check his watch. The children will not arrive for another hour yet, but the next sixty minutes cannot last long enough for Gray. Readying himself for the day ahead seems suddenly an impossible task. He has such a choice to make that his brain refuses to consider anything beyond his two conflicting options. Surely, he cannot think about history. Or rather, none but his own.

Saturday, with Matilda, had been difficult and wonderful and terrifying all at once. They'd made love right there against the dining table, Tilda draped back over the wood so that her chest bucked up and her neck grew long and her ribcage opened up like the wings of a swan. Gray's body, still drying from the bath as the morning snuck through the window to warm them, only spoiled hers, casting its lumpy shadow, but he could not move away to admire her. Not for a second. He was too desperate for this. When they had finished, they had taken a moment to laugh at each other, at their urgency, then they had gone to bed and done it again, playfully this time, slowly, reminding each other of tricks and peculiarities the years had stolen.

'Do you remember the first time?' Matilda whispered, and Grayson laughed again.

'Wasn't it awful?' he said.

'Truly awful,' Matilda replied.

'I don't think there was any need for the *truly*, thank you very much.'

'Oh, no, there was.' Matilda pressed her cheek to his shoulder, like a pet waiting to be fussed. 'There really was. In fact, I nearly gave up on you after that first time.'

'That is a lie!' Grayson protested. 'I clearly remember *you* pursuing *me*, actually.'

'Now that's a lie. A great, whopping one.'

For hours they joked and messed like that, twisting their memories into funnier things than the reality ever had been. As the day aged, they kicked their sheets down the bed and lay naked, trying to ignore the bubbling temperatures, the streamers of sweat leaking down their necks, over their stomachs, along the creases of arms and legs and buttocks and breasts. Lacking the energy to make love a third time, they resigned themselves to kisses and touches and words: words in the shapes of promise and hurt and hope and regret. And eventually those words, all those words, led them – naturally, painfully – to Sally.

Grayson baulks now at the way Matilda had avoided her name, unable to lend her voice to those five simple letters, unable to bear the pain. He is ashamed to think that he too had avoided it, that cowardice had silenced his truth. He loved Sally. Hadn't he told her so? Wouldn't he have to tell Matilda the same thing?

He stands and drifts between the rows of desks, dragging a finger through the dust on their hinged surfaces and watching the furry little particles scatter through the air. As a boy, he would have marvelled at the complexity of their tiny flight, the same way he marvelled at the crunch and stretch of a caterpillar's walk, or the first drop of rain to flop heavily onto your head, or the way that sometimes, when you went to sleep at night, you woke an instant later and it was day again, as though someone had thieved away your darkest hours. Grayson frowns. When had he lost that way of seeing the world? With the first shooting hair on his chest? The first time he slipped his hand under a girl's dress? The day he got married? He doesn't know. But had he had children, he thinks, he would have rediscovered it. He would have observed the same inclination in them when, waking one morning, he found them pressing their noses to the window pane perhaps, inspecting the mass race of condensation beads down the glass and wondering at why the winner won. He would have remembered, then, how to be the boy he once was.

And now – now it seems he will be given the chance to do just that.

They had agreed, he and Matilda, that he should visit Sally

that same night; that it would be the kindest way; that the girl would understand, wouldn't she, that it couldn't have gone on forever. Hour by hour, they talked themselves into belief, and when Grayson finally dressed and stepped outside to begin the walk to Sally's flat, he felt fall over him a curious sort of anticipation. Here was his answer. He would call it off with Sally. He would tell her that he was sorry, that Matilda had come back to him, and Sally, being Sally, would not fight for him. She would, with all the dignity he knew she possessed, wish him well and say goodbye, probably with one last kiss. And then his life would be right again. He knew it. They could find their way back, he and Matilda.

As he walked, London buzzed into life around him, as loud and intense as the crackly opening note of a theatre performance. It was Saturday night, after all. People had important business to attend to, like fun and frivolity and living. And the heat! The heat had drawn hundreds onto the streets. Groups of giggling couples tumbled out of dances and flowed over the pavements, their feet still moving at triple time, their smiles burning their cheeks. Restaurants flung their doors open to bring their failing waiters some relief as they squeezed between customers, trays held high, top shirt buttons surreptitiously undone. Men sat in doorways, skimming paper hearts and clubs and diamonds and spades at each other. And in one water trough, three boys stood, kicking passers-by wet. Probably, Grayson thought, Sally would not be home. But if she was not home, where was she, and who with? Jealousy reared up in him like a frightened horse. Sally might be out on a date.

As it happened, she was home. She opened the door before Grayson had even begun to consider a second knuckle-tap on the paintwork, and he was free to breathe again, temporarily. Though it was only nine o'clock, Sally was in her nightdress. Her hair, undone, hung about her face. Her eyes were light and soft-lashed without mascara. And, wasn't she pale? Yes, definitely. She was definitely pale. She was ill, then.

Grayson cupped her jaw in his palm. 'Are you unwell?' he said, his concern making him forget, for the minute, the reason for his visit. He'd vowed not even to go inside.

'No.'

'What then? What is it?' Grayson urged, taking her hand and sliding through the door. 'Tell me.'

But Sally would not, and when her tears welled up and threatened to drop, he began to understand.

———

At nine o'clock that same morning, Henry finds himself hunched in the curve of his bay window, his back to the light, the chain of Ruby's sapphire necklace looped through his fingers. He holds the pendant at eye level and lets the jewel swing, as though he is attempting to hypnotise himself. The sun sparks somewhere deep down inside the blue, and each time the chiselled stone reaches the high point of its arc, his mind chants out a syllable of her name. Ru … by … Ru … by. It is like the ticking of a clock, though Henry knows he must not wait for the relief of a chime. It will not sound. Ruby, as she once was, is not coming back.

And hadn't he always feared this? He is ashamed to recall how angry her absences had made him in the beginning. The first time she had stayed at the flat, Henry had woken the next morning to find her already gone. It was the only night in many years that his nightmares had not dragged him into the dawn, and he'd wanted to turn over and find her there, waiting for him, ready to make his every day better. Selfishly, he had expected that of her. All she had left in her place was a note, wound out in her hasty hand on the back of an old bus ticket. *Daisy will have missed me. And how will I explain! Tomorrow.*

But Henry had not wanted to wait until tomorrow.

He had fathomed later – though only because Ruby had explained it to him – that she had rushed home to Daisy because she was happy. She had let herself in, stumbled through that jumbled attic flat, jumped onto Daisy's bed, laughed herself weak when the poor girl woke with a squeal, then proceeded to talk for two whole hours about the man she was going to marry.

'So, what exactly did you tell her?'

'What?'

It was the 'tomorrow' Ruby's note had promised and they were sitting on a bench in Hyde Park, knotted into each other. The grass was crispy with cold and shone white under a murky crescent moon. Their breath misted the air.

'What did you tell Daisy about me?'

Ruby shrugged her way further into her scarf. 'Oh. I don't remember.'

'Yes you do.'

'All right. I said you were quite good looking, but you certainly weren't to everyone's tastes.'

'Honestly?'

'Of course. And I said that really you were a bit too full of yourself, considering you were a little on the chubby side, you know, and starting to bald.' She motioned to the top of her head and clamped a smile away between her lips.

'Ruby, tell the truth.'

'No. I can't remember. Truly, I can't.'

'Ruby!' he pestered. He wanted her to keep playing now that she had reassured him, now that she had sworn to him she would always come back.

But when she met his eye and sighed, 'Henry,' she had finished with the game. She untangled his arm from around her shoulders and sat sideways, to better see him. 'I told her,' she whispered, 'that I'd found the man I always wanted to walk into rooms with. That I'd found the man I wanted to do tedious things with, like take long train journeys or straighten the bed. That I'd found the man I hoped would sit next to me whilst I listened to the gramophone and dozed, because just feeling him there, without us speaking or looking at each other or touching, would keep me from ever feeling lonely again. And I told her how frightening it was even to hope for any one of those things. Are you happy now?' She was not whispering any more. 'Or do you need to know all my secrets before you'll just believe that I'm not going to leave you? Because, you know, Henry Twist, a girl isn't so easy to love once she's lost her mystery. And haven't I agreed to marry you? Isn't that enough?'

Before she could reiterate her questions, Henry stood and pulled her up off the bench. He held her to him and kissed her, in that way he had learned made her weak, their lips barely touching for the longest time. Then they walked along the Serpentine, her arm hooked into his, and listened to the secrets of the water instead of their own. Ruby taught him how.

'Listen,' she insisted. 'I'll bet this lake has heard all the city's best secrets. Don't you think?' She looked up at him with a grin. He was forgiven. 'I'll bet it's heard them all, and that the sound of the water is really just the sound of all those naughty tales being whispered back to us. Isn't that a lovely thought?'

He closes his fist around the necklace and rests his head on his knees. He is not crying, but he is, he realises slowly, emitting a low sort of groan; a sound which throbs from his middle, to the rhythm of his pulse perhaps. It is redolent of some animal call, but he cannot think which. It is an idiotic sound. He is glad no one can hear it. No one, that is, except Ruby. Ruby's ghost. Because now that Jack has disappeared again, Henry has begun to suspect once more that the man is nothing more than a puff of imagination. Naturally, the proof he had presented himself with previously was flawed. That Jack had interacted with that costermonger, and then with Libby, and later with Monty and Tilda and Gray and Ida and Viv – that was not conclusive. If Henry had managed to invent an entire man to hold onto while he clambered out of his grief, then surely he could have invented all those exchanges too. That is what lunatics do. And, of course he should have invented a man. It makes perfect sense now that Jack is no longer here to distract him from the truth. Henry Twist, so recently a widower, would not have allowed another woman into his bed. Henry Twist, so guilty a soldier, needs to bring men back to life almost as much as he needs to resurrect his wife.

A knocking jolts him out of his thoughts: an uneven four-beat. It makes Libby cry. When he lifts his head, he finds the room an odd place: too light, too square, too real. He wants to close his eyes again, to fill the infinitude behind them with pictures of lost people. But the knocking continues, and his mind echoes each knock with a single word: Jack, Jack, Jack.

He struggles to an upright position and steps towards the hallway, slow on his feet, his past making him heavier than he really is.

He is careful not to look into the mirror as he passes; she never stands before him in it any more.

He opens the door to a figure he ought to recognise, but can't. The man – possessed of one or two too many chins – has a soft, swinish face, upon which he has balanced a pair of spectacles so dainty and round that they must surely belong to a child. The arms of the spectacles squeeze around the sides of his face and disappear into the tufts of blunt, thick hair which shoot out uniformly from his skull. He does not wear a hat. Beneath his chins, a tie secures his head directly to his chest, and Henry entertains the idea, fleetingly, that were he to unfasten that tie, his visitor's head would simply pop free and float away. Henry would not like to be left with custody of the body it would leave behind. It is a body familiar with good food, and probably good drink, and it does not look easy to move.

A hand is offered, which Henry takes up.

'How is it, Twist?' the man says. And still Henry cannot place him.

'Fine,' he answers. 'Good, you know.' He does not know how to speak to this man.

'Yes, well.' The man's head drops. 'It's a funny time.'

'It is.'

'Which, incidentally ...' the man appears increasingly apologetic, '... is the reason for my visit. You know, you've always been a reliable tenant, Twist.'

And there it is. Of course. Mr Larkin – the landlord. Henry steps aside and pushes the door fully open.

'Come in, Mr Larkin,' he offers. 'I'll get you a cup of tea.'

As Henry places Mr Larkin's tea down in front of him and awaits his scolding, and Grayson tries desperately to remember just how all those figures fighting the War of the Roses had been related, and Ida checks the post for news from her brother-in-law, Matilda is spreading herself star-shaped over the grass in Monty's garden. She pushes her arms straight out, as though she is a bird in flight; she sets her legs as wide as her skirt will allow. Beyond the walls, London is hot and busy and loud, but here – an increasing rarity – it is quiet. There is no one present but Monty, who sits nearby, his legs crossed as if he is a Sunday-school boy awaiting his lesson. Matilda stares up at the flat blue sky, searching a crease, a wrinkle, anything. But there is nothing. It is perfect. Everything is perfect.

Except, of course, for her. Matilda Steck, née Fellows, is a criminal of the highest order. Her guilt, like a rolling snowball, gathers weight with every passing second. It is as unstoppable as that sequence of events she has initiated. At some point, it will crush her.

'I don't think I can recall such a sudden heat, Monty dear,' she says, fanning her face with a flattened hand. She is attempting her usual aloofness, but she cannot keep the wobble from her voice. Monty – attentive at last to this woman, though it is younger women, merrier women, he needs to keep him going – catches it.

'Do you know what I miss about Ruby?' he says, after a long silence.

Matilda lifts her head and, when they lock eyes, she notices that Monty appears softer than before: it is as if his edges are starting to blur. Old age, she thinks, but she swallows the thought. It is another fear she doesn't have the energy for just now.

'The sight of her chest?' Matilda suggests, attempting a joke. It comes out bitter-sounding. 'Sorry,' she says. 'What?'

'Her honesty,' Monty answers.

'Yes,' Matilda agrees, nodding. 'Her honesty.'

It was perhaps on account of her youth that Ruby felt able to say pretty much anything she wanted. She might, given the opportunity, have grown out of it. But, no, Matilda decides. It was an essential part of her, that way of being able to deliver a truth, any truth, with so much sincerity that it could not cause offence.

'So,' Monty advises. 'Why don't you say what it is you need to say? Ruby would have.'

Matilda sighs, loud and long. 'Because I can't,' she replies. 'Because it's too many kinds of awful.'

———

'Is there any chance,' Grayson pleads, 'any chance at all, that I can get a date out of you, Mr Pollock?'

Pollock – a skinny, freckled boy with a mess of stringy blond hair – glows red and, near the back of the classroom, a couple of the other boys snigger. Ordinarily, Grayson would punish them for that. He would order them to stand in front of the class and recite facts to childish nursery rhyme tunes: humiliation, he has always found, is a far more effective deterrent amongst boys than a sharp whack to the palm. But today he is too busy bullying Pollock. Poor young Pollock. He has blundered onto the wrong side of Mr Steck today and it is in no way his fault. Grayson cannot stop thinking about what awaits him down the corridor.

'1485, sir,' Pollock answers finally.

And Grayson, taken aback, can't for the life of him think whether this is the correct answer. He turns to the blackboard for help: there is nothing written on its dark plane. He scans the faces of his students, seeking, in the curl of a lip or the roll of an eye, confirmation that Pollock's response is wildly inaccurate. It might be; Gray doesn't know. He finds no clue. In the end, he resorts to that tactic all the worst teachers must employ – he forces the children to teach themselves.

'So,' he says, tapping the board with a snatched-up tip of chalk-stick. 'What do the rest of you chaps think to Mr Pollock's answer? Is he correct? Is he correct and why is he correct? I want evidence, gentlemen.'

The puzzlement this task brings about allows Grayson to be silent again for a time, and he resumes his place behind his desk, the chair hard under his backside.

For once, they hadn't gone to bed. At least, not in the manner they usually did. Sally had shown Grayson inside then sat down on the edge of her mattress, facing the window, refusing to properly meet his eye. She had developed, quite suddenly, an odd way of moving: mechanical, almost, as though Sally Emory had been left out in the cold too long and stiffened. Gray perched next to her, his arm tight around her shoulders, but she did not thaw into him.

'What's upset you?' he asked. He didn't want to give his suspicions access to the conversation. Not yet. He had to keep talking until she interrupted him. 'Something's upset you. You can tell me.'

But Sally wouldn't speak. Or couldn't. She shook her head, considering the floor as though intrigued by the arrangement of their feet there: hers bare and slim and grey in the moon-light; his larger, shoed, and altogether clumsier. When he gave up trying to look at Sally, he took to staring out through that enormous sash window and attempting to ignore that it was forcing him to see the world through a series of small rectangular frames. Hadn't he been doing that his entire life? The answer was yes, of course. He lived inside a box. He always had.

Sally had been his only stab at escape.

'Tell me something else, then,' he said. 'Anything at all.' He couldn't say exactly why, but he wanted so much to hear her voice. She had uttered only one word since he'd arrived. 'No,' she'd said. 'No.' And Grayson needed more. He needed her to be that force he watched walking the school corridors, a sway of colour in the drabness. He needed her to be the woman he'd been to bed with, so poised and self-assured. But something had drained all that from her, and he suspected that something was him.

'Tell me,' he insisted, '... about a time when you were so embarrassed you thought you might explode if you were stuck in the situation for one second longer.'

Sally very nearly smiled.

'Go on,' Gray pushed. 'Then I'll tell you mine. It's a good one, I promise.'

'It was that day.'

'Which day?' He rested his chin on her shoulder and pressed the tip of his nose to her jawbone.

'*That* day. The day I came into your classroom.'

Grayson kissed her cheek. 'That was very brave.'

'I knew all those boys were laughing at me.'

'Not for long they weren't.'

'What was yours?'

Grayson kissed her again. 'I didn't have one in mind,' he admitted, smiling. 'I just wanted to hear your voice.'

'Sneaky. Think of one.'

But he hadn't been able to. His mind was racing ahead to the revelation he was dreading and aching for all at once.

'Sir.' One of the boys, Hunt perhaps, is calling to him, as

though he is a man who has collapsed in the street, as though he has not been present for some time. He can't imagine why. Here he is, discussing the War of the Roses, and trying to recollect long-ago dates, and struggling not to snap at the children who are temporarily in his care, and avoiding contemplating the fact that, though Matilda thinks he has, he still has not broken it off with Sally, and all the while his son or his daughter is just down the corridor, sprouting into life. His son or his daughter. His daughter or his son. A tiny seed of a thing who could become just about anyone: a doctor or an artist or an explorer or the prime minister. Grayson is uncomfortable thinking in these terms. He has never indulged his hopes like this before, but already names are darting into his mind. He considers them as though they are some fragile antique item he might want to purchase: he seems to hold them in his hands, the letters solid and heavy, and turn them about, looking from all possible angles, searching for the faults. Just this morning he has found four options he wants to share with Sally.

And the thoughts are exciting, of course they are, but they are also laden, laden with guilt. At some point, he is going to have to tell Matilda; his poor, unknowing Matilda. And he has no doubt that the words are going to kill her.

AN ADMISSION

I t keeps them out of their homes that night, the sluggish, slow swirling heat. It calls all of London onto the streets. Cafés stay open. Theatres hasten to throw together an additional late-night performance. Jazz bands cram extra venues into their schedules, for the right price. The city plays. And Henry walks the long path from his flat to Monty's garden, not wanting to admit why. He has so much to do tonight that he cannot afford the time to sit to drinks with any man, especially a man so unhurried as Montague Thornton-Wells. Part of Henry is hoping he will not be there; the other part is desperate for the company. But more importantly than that, he has a favour he must call in.

Ruby's echo walks alongside him, five months pregnant, talking about the baby.

'I don't think I'd want a Welsh name, you know. I mean, it would grow up here, wouldn't it, and imagine having to explain how your name was pronounced, over and over again.'

They had been on their way to lunch. The late November day was low, charcoal-coloured and damp. As they stepped along the pavements, little droplets of fallen rain arced up to wet their ankles, motorcars splashed through puddles, a constellation of magpies beat their way noisily across the sky. Ruby was all in burgundy: a woollen dress with matching court shoes, a calf-length coat, a small hat beneath which she had tucked most of her hair. Her hands – which she waved about as she spoke – were warm inside brown leather gloves. Her lips were dark with cherry lipstick. It was as if someone had cut open the day's chest and Henry was looking at the beating heart revealed within.

'And I was thinking I'd like it to sing, Henry. Properly. It could have music lessons, and ...'

Ruby was forever singing: whilst she bathed, whilst she pressed on her face powder, whilst she cleaned the flat. She sang as Jack whistles, to fill the day's silent spaces. When she was not thinking about it, she sang in Welsh and the words, though he could not decipher them, were beautiful to Henry: they sounded, he thought, like they were closer to the soul than their English counterparts. They set his skin tingling. And not only because his wife released them so expressively, but because one night, uniformed and hunkered in a bullet-holed barn, he'd stayed in the shadows and listened as four Welsh men gathered around a fire and sang themselves back to their country, their voices hushed, yes, but strong too; as strong as the earth they sat upon.

Gwlad, gwlad, pleidiol wyf i'm gwlad.

He could have told her what a blessing it was, to feel those voices trembling through his body. But he had found reasons not to. He had convinced himself that it would spoil her mood to interrupt her speculations about the life ahead of them with stories of the life behind him. Now, he is certain she would have loved hearing about those four men. He had been cowardly, not speaking of them.

He had been cowardly a thousand times.

It is edging towards twelve when he reaches Monty's. He stands for a while on the pavement, trying to decipher sounds on the other side of the wall. He doesn't want to go in if there's a party on. And he can't bear to rid himself yet of Ruby: not now that he is missing Jack, too. She had still been making plans after they had eaten their lunch and made their way to Monty's for drinks. She had stood on this very spot and said, 'And I want it to look like you. Just like you. Our baby is going to be a Twist, right down to its soul.'

'But, you're a Twist now,' Henry had pointed out.

'Yes,' Ruby had replied. 'Yes, I suppose I am. Funny, that. *Twist*.' She'd tested the word, tasted it. 'I love that word.'

'Do you? Why?'

'Because it's the sound of you.'

And Henry understands that now. It is important, the sound of her. 'Ruby Twist,' he whispers. But no one answers him. She is gone. And now Jack has gone with her.

Again, he listens for life on the other side of the wall then, hearing nothing, lets himself through the gate. Grayson, Matilda and Monty sit around a large wooden table which is a new addition to the garden. They are illuminated by a line of mismatching candles. On top of the table are a bowl of red apples, built into a pyramid; a square of cheese, already cut into; an empty vase; and three wine glasses, their grape-white contents at various glinting levels. There is a fourth vacant chair, pulled under the table. There is also a spare wine glass. They are waiting for him.

As he steps towards them, he raises an awkward hand. Suddenly, he feels stupid, an imposition. What if they have each been pretending all this time? What if they've been acting a man into their lives for him, the crazy soldier, the lunatic widower? What if, when he sits down, they acknowledge Jack Turner as present amongst them? If it happens, he thinks he might go along with it, out of shame.

'Twist!' Monty calls, expansive as ever. 'Come and sit down, man. For some obscure reason, we're discussing the economy, and I don't know that I can take much more of it. Come and save me.'

Matilda gives a little smile and rolls her eyes. 'Is there any need for such exaggeration?' she asks.

'Always,' Monty replies. 'Life is one long series of exaggerations, don't you think?'

'I'm not sure about that,' Grayson puts in.

Henry drags out his chair and, settling into it, pours himself a glass of wine.

'Of course it is,' Monty argues. 'I love you, I need you, I hate you, I want you! It's all such a drama. You can't disagree with me, Steck. I saw the way her eyes lit up when you arrived. Something's afoot here.' He winks at Matilda, who puts her hand – her right hand, so as not to draw attention to her missing wedding ring – over Grayson's.

Grayson breathes deep, fighting hard against the urge to remove it. Though Matilda doesn't seem to notice, all the intimacy of a few days back has been lost.

'There might and there might not be,' Matilda teases. 'I'm sure it's a private matter.'

Now it is Monty's turn to roll his eyes, and he exults in the opportunity, tossing his head back and letting his mouth gape open. They laugh, then release a collective sigh, the four of them, their breaths the coolest thing in a hundred-mile radius. Somewhere not too far off, they can hear music playing: a trumpeter is meandering his way through 'Tin Roof Blues', the heavy four-four beat perfect in the heat. They begin nodding their heads to the lazy rhythm, their chins lifting and falling in exact synchronisation with the bundle of people who lounge about, invisible to them but just a few buildings distant, before five perspiring musicians. Under the table, Grayson's foot drums the grass flat. Henry's fingers tap the wooden dining surface. The air cracks under the strain of twenty-one midnight degrees.

'So,' Monty enquires, 'no Jack tonight?'

And time stops.

Matilda has been waiting for this question. She has been dreading and wishing for it since that moment, down at the docks, when she shook hands on her deal; since she stepped, already sorry, out of the police station. A blush begins at her feet and scuttles up her body, insect-like, reaching her face before she has a chance to turn away or hide it behind a tilted wine glass. She does not turn her eyes on Henry. She sits, quite still, and she waits. This she will have to gauge carefully.

She had insisted on making the full payment only after the job was done. She had had to offer a small deposit, an incentive, but she had hoped she would appear a shrewd business-woman in withholding the rest. The truth was she had simply needed time, to decide on what she should sell to meet the sum. She had settled, in the end, on a brooch of her mother's: a hideous thing, really, in the slinking shape of a cat, its eyes two slanting garnets jammed amongst a mass of minute diamonds. Its ugliness did not excuse her behaviour in selling it, though. It had been gifted to her, after all, in her mother's will – to pass on, down the female line.

Since, Matilda has attempted to convince herself that, seeing as there will be no female line – no line at all, in fact – its sale does not matter. But she knows this is not true. If it were, she would not have been forced to fight tears as she exited the jewellers. She had remembered then, the memory coming too late to save her from her actions, that she had played dress-up with that brooch as a very small girl. She had stabbed the pin through her nightdress and balanced a great flopping hat on her head and staggered around in her mother's heels, admiring herself in every mirror as she paraded from one room of the family townhouse to the next.

She had sold that memory.

She chances a glance at Henry. He is lifting his glass to his lips, tarrying over taking a gulp. She wonders if her blush is visible in the candlelight. She wonders what Grayson thinks of it.

And the answer is nothing. Nothing much. Gray is struggling to concentrate on the sense of the conversation, let alone his wife's response to it. He feels as though he is floating away – from the garden, from London, from the planet, even. He is a balloon, cut free of its string. But no, he is heavier than that, more cumbersome: he is a hot-air balloon, too weighty, too prone to sinking down the sky without that necessary burst of flame.

It has taken him all day to work out where, or rather when, he recognises this feeling from. He has it now and it constricts his throat. He recognises it from the months after he lost his mother. It feels like grief.

He notices a certain feeling of anticipation around him and it causes him to swim back to himself temporarily. But everyone's attention is fixed on Henry: they are waiting for him to say something. No one has noticed that Grayson is growing absent, and that is useful, very useful indeed, because already he feels closer to that sinuous trumpet melody, the angled confusion of slate roofs surrounding the garden, the rich orb moon. Monty and Matilda and Henry are small, far away. He is gliding apart from these people. His life is becoming a separate thing. And there is nothing he can do to stop it.

'Not tonight,' Henry says.

'Got a better offer, did he?' Monty teases. 'I wouldn't be surprised. We are, I suppose, exceedingly old in Jack's eyes. How young is he anyway?'

Henry does not know how to answer. The first thought in his mind is, twenty-five. He's twenty-five; must be. But perhaps he's twenty-six. Or twenty-eight. Or perhaps Henry is just making this up. He stays silent. He has not yet waded through the relief that swamped him when Monty asked that simple question. *No Jack tonight?* Because no, there is no Jack tonight, or last night, and it is worrying, painfully so, but at least now he can safely assume that the man is real. Monty would not ask after a glitch in his imagination.

But if Jack is not here tonight, where is he? It might be that his memory has failed him again, or that those people who beat his identity loose in January have returned to finish the job, or that he's had an accident at work, or — the realisation of Henry's newest fear — that his memory has somehow been restored and he's gone back to wherever he came from. He might just be Jack. Mr Jack Turner: husband, lover, father, worker, criminal, drunk, campaigner, believer. He could be anything. He could have pushed that glimmer of Ruby out. He could have robbed Henry of the person he loves for a second time, and Henry does not think he can endure it. He is not sure he wants to. Not again.

When the silence grows uncomfortable, Henry plumps for 'Twenty-five. Around that.' But he cannot think about conversation now. He is cold all over. He has to find Jack.

'Around that?' Monty laughs. 'The man shares your bed and you don't know old he is. I never appreciated what a tart you were until now. Bravo, Henry. Bravo!' Monty claps his hands twice in quick succession. The sound is dulled by the warmth.

'Monty!' Matilda protests, her voice a semitone shriller than usual.

'What?' Monty pretends at innocence, opening his eyes up wide.

'You know.'

'Oh, I think we're past sensitivity, aren't we?' Monty

answers. 'Haven't we been friends long enough?'

'I'd say so,' Grayson puts in.

'So would I,' Monty agrees. 'Now, how long are we all staying? There's this Dawn Party happening tonight. Or in the morning, rather. They're arriving around four and drinking until the sun comes up.'

'I'll have left before that,' Henry answers.

'Why not stay?' Monty says.

'I'm not in the mood for a party.' He has more pressing matters to attend to: like packing up his belongings, getting Libby ready, finding Jack. He has not paid the rent. He has promised Mr Larkin he will be out by the morning. While the Bright Young People dance and flirt and laugh, Henry will be saying goodbye to the home where he built his family; where he lost his wife and found her again; where, for however brief a time, he raised his daughter.

'Well, then,' Monty replies, 'I'll have to keep pouring you drinks until you find yourself in a better mood.'

'Yes,' Matilda agrees, holding out her drained glass. 'Please do.'

'There's no risk of that,' Henry answers. But he smiles sadly as he says it, because now that he must give up the flat, this is the place where he is closest to Ruby; here, where other people remember her too. His smile falters and Matilda reaches over and pats his hand.

'You don't like it, do you Henry, darling – seeing so many people here, trampling over her memory?'

He shakes his head. 'No, it's not that. It's just ... I came to ask a favour, of Monty.'

'Go ahead, then,' Monty urges. 'I'm going to say yes, I'm sure of it.'

'Don't be. It's big.'

'I don't care if it's bigger than Buckingham Palace.'

'Well,' Henry lowers his voice and begins mumbling. 'I was wondering ... the thing is, I'm going to be made homeless very soon, and I was wondering whether, Libby and I … whether you might have room, for me and Libby … at yours … For me and Libby. And Jack.'

'You want to stay?' Monty enquires.

'Just for a short while. I mean, we'll go as soon as possible.'

Monty sits forward. 'You'll go when you're able,' he says. 'And not even then, if you don't want to. It's a big old house, Henry. I'd be glad of the company.'

'Really?'

'Really.'

'All of us?'

'Of course all of you,' Monty replies. 'Surely it's all of you or none of you, isn't it? That's how it is, with family.'

'Yes,' Henry replies, standing. 'Yes it is.' But is that what they are now, a family? Are he and Jack really going to grow old like this, living the half-life the rest of the world will allow them? He holds out his hand. Monty takes it up and they shake, too roughly for Monty's thinning bones, but the old man laughs anyway. He is happy to have made someone else happy. That is all he hopes for now. That is what keeps him alive.

'Will I see you before the night's out?' he asks.

'Yes. But, I don't know where –'

'Ah.' Monty feels around inside his jacket, finds an invitation detailing the particulars of the Dawn Party in a coiling cursive, holds it up, turns over the envelope, and points to the address scrawled on the reverse.

'It's you!' Matilda almost shouts. '*You* organise all the parties. But, it must be so exhausting. I thought you only provided a venue. I thought *they* organised everything. I thought –'

'We all thought,' Henry agrees.

'Thinking is a dangerous game indeed,' Monty grins. 'And I don't organise them all, Tilda dear. But some, yes. I'm a lonely old man, and sometimes I want to watch young, beautiful things pretending at life. You can understand that, can't you?'

Henry shakes his head, smiling lightly. He does under-stand. 'And we weren't young and beautiful enough for you.'

'No,' Monty replies. 'No you weren't. Not without her.'

Henry nods. 'That I can understand,' he says. Then he turns and strides away across the garden. He needs to find Jack. He needs to tell him the good news. And he needs to collect Libby, and pack up his belongings, and thank Viv, and say goodbye to Herb. He needs to sit one last time in that window where his wife sat, missing her parents and her sister and the rain, and touch the pane her breath once misted over and promise her that he will do the best he can; that he will take their daughter home; that there is not a single thing he will forget.

———

At Henry's back, Matilda releases her husband's hand and swivels away from him. Though she ought not to have, she has felt Monty's words. She feels them still, hard inside her stomach and tight around her windpipe. They are not enough, without Ruby. *She* is not enough. She never has been, never could have been, never will be. That Henry should ever love her was a ridiculous idea. That Grayson should continue to love her is preposterous. She is a revolting human being. She has grown ugly on the outside. She always was ugly on the inside. And perhaps that is why she cannot give her husband a baby – because nature recognises her as an awful thing.

'Well, that was fleeting,' Monty says, taking another drink.

Grayson grumbles something in response, but Matilda doesn't hear it. She doesn't want to. She stands.

'Wait!' she shouts. In the heat, her voice is weak, listless. It jams on the air. She is afraid it will not reach Henry, but then perhaps it oughtn't. She sits again with a sigh. And as she does, so Henry stops, turns, and waits – as she has asked him to. His face is pale under the moon, his hair silvered, his shoulders so straight that it makes Matilda ache. There he is, that brave man. The man she has cried and longed and hurt for. And still, even now, he is someone else's man. Perhaps he always will be.

Henry shrugs, asking her what it is he is waiting for. At her side, Grayson crosses his arms over his chest and cocks his head. Across the table, Monty shoves a sigh out through his nose. Saturated city yards away, that trumpeter takes another run at 'Tin Roof Blues', stretching it longer this time, loving it harder, worshipping it. He had not done it justice before. It had not been right. He is asking his instrument for the chance to try again. And Matilda is asking for the very same – the chance to try again – and she must ask for it boldly.

'It's Jack,' she says. 'It's about Jack.' And Henry takes a single, involuntary step towards her. 'I know he's missing. I know where he is.'

THE SEARCH

Head down, eyes up, Henry marches through the heat–blotched darkness, one white shirt sleeve descending in slow rotations, one brown shoelace undone and rippling, both fists clenching and unclenching metrically at his sides. He does not know where he is going. He has not yet heard Matilda's confession. He knows only that he must move, and keep moving, in the same way as a shark must keep circling the seas if he is to continue to breathe. Moving, in any direction, might bring him closer to Jack.

Behind him, Matilda scurries along, pumping useless words out from between wine–slicked lips.

'I'm sorry, Henry, darling … I thought it was for the best … Won't you listen to me, Henry, darling? Please?'

Her footsteps punctuate her pleas, marking irritating little commas. Her breathing is growing heavier. She is struggling to keep up.

'Go away, Tilda.' Henry pushes the command through ground teeth. She has done something terrible. He knows it. He always has been wary of Matilda Steck.

Naturally, Ruby had been kinder.

He recalls how, one late night, they had left Monty's and taken the Tube to some unfamiliar part of the city, keen to be free of Matilda. They had sat in an empty coach, Henry straight-backed and wide-legged on the dusty green upholstery and Ruby curled into him, her cheek resting on his shoulder.

'You shouldn't be so cruel,' Ruby said. 'She has a thing for you. She can't help it.'

'Well, she should try.'

Ruby, sleepy, yawned through her next words. 'I, for one, don't blame her. Who wouldn't want you?'

'Anyone with a bit of sense,' Henry muttered, and Ruby sighed out a laugh.

'You have a point there, husband. You are terribly difficult, at times.'

'Is that so?'

She nodded her head and they sat for a while, listening to the lopsided two-beat the train was rocking out, inhaling the stale, damp smell rising out of the seat fabric. Soon they were both asleep, pleated into each other, Henry successfully fending off his nightmares for a trice, and Ruby dreaming – or so she told Henry when they woke – about she and Ida, standing on the rocks at Burry Port and watching the waves flick their bleached manes at the shore.

'I don't even know if that really happened,' she said.

'Why would you doubt it?' Henry asked. They were off the Tube and walking, seeking a café that had yet to close. They had agreed, upon leaving Monty's, that they would not return home until the sun pushed open the next pale morning. It would be fun, Ruby had assured Henry. They could watch their past fade and their future colour, just for the hell of it. They could pretend that there was nothing but them and that – the slow turning of their life together.

'I don't know,' she answered. 'It just seems too easy for a memory, you know. I feel like there'd be something unpleasant in it, if it was real. An argument I'd had with someone, or a fear, or a worry. There's always something. Nothing is that pure.'

Henry understands that sentiment now. Isn't his every memory of her tainted, in some small way, by her loss?

But he cannot think on that now. He has to find Jack. He has to. Jack is in possession not only of the only sliver of a future Ruby might now have; he is in possession, too, of Henry's future. Henry will not lose him. He would not survive it.

Behind him, Matilda is still talking; pleading rather, her voice louder than before.

'Stop, will you! Just stop and let me explain!'

And because Ruby is gone, and Jack is missing, and Matilda was his friend once, he does. Henry stops and turns to consider her. He allows her the opportunity to explain.

Matilda stands perhaps five strides distant, a shaky figure in too few clothes since her hat has been discarded and she did not stop to pull on her shoes when they left Monty's. She is girlish in her stocking feet. She is small. She is, Henry realises gradually, audibly sobbing. And she looks, well, she looks calamitous: her fingers have worked tangles into her hair; her mascara strikes black lightning bolts down her cheeks; her lipstick, dislodged by a frustrated swipe of her hand, is a scarlet bruise, bleeding across her chin. Any onlooker would think her the wronged party here. Any onlooker would see an injured woman, not a plotter, a schemer, a ... what? Henry doesn't know. And yet he is aware that he soon must.

He breathes deep, trying not to reach the worst possible conclusion. But what if she's done it? What if she's reported Jack to the police, had him arrested? He'd be killed in prison. Henry would have to find some way to break him out.

'Henry —' Matilda begins, but Henry silences her with a single glance. He can't stand any more of her whining or imploring. He wants – no, he needs – only the facts. He closes his eyes to a fleeting prayer. Then, breathing deep, he voices the question he must.

'What have you done?' he asks.

Between the grey stone walls of Monty's garden, his suit jacket draped over the chair he sits on, his feet crossed at the ankles, a deep two-pronged ache spreading down the back of his neck, Grayson stares at his own elongated reflection in the thin curve of his wine glass. He does not rise to chase after his friend, or his wife. After all, he knows nothing of Jack's whereabouts – he cannot help Henry. And he has no desire to help Matilda. She has, once again, done something he will be ashamed of. That much was obvious in the way she ran off, without a single glimpse back in his direction.

'So, Steck,' Monty murmurs. 'She's gone again. I'm sorry, old chap.' He stands and reaches across the table to clap Gray's shoulder, and Grayson falls into the older man's grasp. He closes his eyes against the ghost in his wine glass: that ageing, unloved thing. He grabs Monty's elbow and holds on, tight. He is, he is discovering, a man in need of mooring.

'Yes. She's gone again.'

'And you?'

'Me?' Grayson considers the question for a moment. He holds himself in his mind and ponders his own physical weight, the mess of bone and blood and flesh and muscle that has somehow knitted itself together into him, Gray, a husband who has found himself in possession of one miserable wife and one frightened mistress with a child on the way. On the way. Even the phrasing stirs up a panic at his middle. It is an unstoppable force, this child: it is *on the way.*

'Yes, you,' Monty says.

'I have somewhere I need to be,' Grayson answers.

'You too, hmm?'

'Sorry, Monty,' Grayson says, standing now. He has seen the sadness in Monty's face: the droop about his eyes, the downward shuddering of his lips. It's clear he does not want to be left alone.

'I really do have to go. You'll be all right, won't you?'

'Of course!' Monty waves him away. 'Go. Do what you must.'

And though he ought to be a better friend, Grayson does go. He leaves Monty to his loneliness, and within half an hour he is again knocking at Sally's door.

She lets him in with one of those tight downward smiles more inclined to be accompanied by tears than joy and, still standing in the hallway, starts unbuttoning his shirt. Gray kicks the door shut with his heel and tries to kiss her, but she won't allow it. She dodges him. So instead he watches her go about her work, the graceful way her fingers liberate one button and then the next breaking his heart because she is so fragile, this woman; she is so small and fragile. And yet, in the half-light which spills outward from one green-shaded lamp, she is also a thing that sparks. She is a jewel. She has the deepest sort of strength.

'Are you drunk?' she asks.

'A little.'

'Good.'

'Why would you want –'

Sally closes her eyes and presses her cheek to his chest. 'Sssshhhh,' she says.

And Grayson, as usual, obeys. When she links her hands around his middle, he echoes the movement. When her breathing slows, he matches his respirations to hers. He catches, emanating off her skin, the clammy scent of too much mois-turising cream. She must be covered in it, he thinks. Beneath her nightdress, she is surely slick to the touch. He lifts the nightdress over her head and, dropping it to the floor, runs his hands over her bared back, but it is not the beginning of a sexual act, this: it is simply an exploration. He is exploring the woman inside whom a part of his own self has attached itself and begun, unbelievably, to grow. He brushes his palms over her upper arms, he loops his fingers around her wrists, he measures the gentle tapering of her waist, and only then, when he has touched every other possible part of her, does he turn her around, pull her tight to his chest and stroke the still-flat plane of her stomach.

'Sally,' he whispers.

'Yes?'

'We're going to be parents.'

'I know.'

He hears the smile in her reply and, taking his cue, speaks into her ear, her hair shifting where his breath hits it. 'I've been thinking of names,' he says.

This – a slow coming together, words she'd been waiting to hear – would have weakened Matilda. She would have turned into him and smiled and waited to hear his suggestions. But Sally is new and different, and he still has so much to learn about her. He must remember to adopt a more observant approach. Starting tonight, because he has just learnt, this very moment, that talk of names, pacification, is not what she wants. He has felt her stiffen in his hands.

'Don't do that,' she says. 'We can't do any of that, not until *she* knows, Gray. I'm sorry, but not until then. It's too hard.'

And there she is again, the woman he promised his whole life to, standing between them, reduced to a 'she'.

Grayson wouldn't have thought it possible for Matilda to fade so far from his considerations before he met Sally. The day they'd married – no, before that even – Matilda Fellows had scorched herself onto his brain matter, like a brand mark on the rump of an animal, so that every thought he had, every idea or concern or whim, was laced through with her. She was the rings that run through the trunk of a tree. Or the layers of rock which stack up to form a cliff face. She was part of him, good or bad. And he was part of her. And even when she stormed, even when she lashed him with her tongue or battered him with her eyes, there she was. Immovable. However much he might have wanted to rid himself of her, Matilda was tangled in his person. Was that love, then?

He tries to think of other things he has loved, to draw a comparison, and ridiculously he can come up with nothing but his Lee-Enfield. Excepting a palm's worth of women, he has never loved anything so much as that rifle. But then, it did keep him alive through the long slog of 1916, so he supposes that's excusable. He feels for the smooth eight-pound weight of it, still familiar in the muscles along his hand and forearm ten years on. He could shoot that thing blind, even now. He knows the flat polish of the butt, the womanly curl and flick of the trigger. Gray had clung to that rifle as though it was made of gold. It was gold, to him. He had cleaned it daily, checked its every function near-hourly. At night, he had slept with it tucked along the length of his body, the butt against his ribcage, the whole item warmed by the blanket he shared with it.

He'd lost it in Malta, when his sleeping battery had been shelled and they'd had to dive for cover, every last one of them. Of course, Grayson had gone back to his makeshift bed to retrieve it later, but it was gone – pilfered, he suspected, by someone in close proximity. For weeks afterwards, though he'd found himself a replacement rifle relatively quickly, Gray had looked suspiciously on any man who lifted a Lee-Enfield. He was convinced he would know his rifle on sight. He knew its every nick and indentation, the particular shade of its wood. His very own fingerprints were imprinted on it. Hadn't he shed a secret tear for it that night, for God's sake?

But that was need, not love. And he does not need Matilda or Sally, not in that essential way, not to survive. He never has. He is a man, it seems, incapable of anything more than want. And perhaps that is adequate, so long as he makes a secret of it: why not let them, both of them, think he would die without them? It is only a small deception.

'I am going to tell her,' Grayson says.

'Really?' Sally lifts her face to his and he nods.

'Soon,' he promises. 'I'll tell her soon.'

'And what then?'

'I don't know,' Grayson answers. 'I don't know yet.'

———————

Though she cannot guess where they are going, Henry and Matilda are travelling again. Fast. Matilda hangs just a step or two behind him, no longer pretending that she cannot keep up. Her wallowing had transformed into true, deep-seated dread once she'd said the words, observed the new set of Henry's face. Never before has she seen him look so volatile. And that is why she must stick with him – because it is her responsibility now to ensure that he doesn't do something stupid.

She does not plead with him to slow down or talk to her. Unusually, and but for the wheeze of her breath, Matilda remains silent. She has done real wrong. She has to right it.

Running to match Henry's quickening strides, she stays with him as he rushes down the centre of Fleet Street, the jostling buildings which are the stones in its claustrophobic walls rising above them, the streetlamps dangling pendulously from their strung-out cables to light up the asymmetric sign for the *Yorkshire Evening Post*, the square temple-like frontage of Newspaper House, the palatial columns of the Daily Telegraph building. Matilda cannot concentrate fully on which streets they turn on to, then off, then back on to again. The hot, honey-coloured summer moon gleams over the pavements and shows her a stall, closed for the night, which boasts Gateway Tobacco, and, above locked doors, signs for Haircutting and Shaving, the Cottage Tea Rooms, Baker's the Tobacconists, A.B.C Tea Rooms, Judge's Postcards, Finch's Wines from the Woods. But Henry is running now, running, and she is running after him, and she has no time to think about where all these turns are taking them.

On the corner of the Strand, they career past a J. Lyons.

Then, before she knows it, they are tearing towards the Hippo-
drome, and for a moment she is loosely aware of the names
presented on its sandy exterior – Rosie Moran and Robert
Hale, who might just be performing in a musical comedy – and
then the names disappear, because it is busier here, and there
are more people to stop and gape at she and Henry, thumping
by, and Matilda is both embarrassed and thrilled to be, ever so
fleetingly, at the very core of their attentions. There is no need
to enter the theatre. Here it is. Life. Happening right in front
of them. And she has made that happen. *She* has. Matilda Steck
– though she would adopt Twist as her name, of course, if she
were truly a character in a drama. Why wouldn't she? After all,
fiction is the only freedom a person who knows unanswered
love is ever offered.

But this is not a theatre show, and Henry does not eventually tire and fall exhausted into her, the woman he has just
realised he adores. Panic keeps him running. And regret keeps
her chasing him. And smog pools about them as they veer onto
narrower streets, and steer around tighter corners, and stumble
and rick their ankles, and soon, Matilda fancies, they are lost.

Henry slows to a walk.

'Where are you going?' she manages to gasp out, but
Henry does not answer. He stops and glances one way then the
other along the street, he straightens his shirt, he fidgets with
the waist of his trousers, he stoops to tie his shoelace, he wipes
the sweat off his forehead and upper lip, he coughs. He does
everything he can to avoid looking at Matilda.

'To Sybil's,' he says.

At the mention of a woman's name, Matilda's skin goes
cold. It is her eighteenth birthday again, and she is watching
her cousin Annabel sneak bare-footed into a large storage
cupboard, her fingers jumbled in Elliot Condon's – the first
boy Matilda had decided to love.

'Sybil's?' she asks, because she can't not ask, and Henry
nods. He paces back and forth, nodding. He pinches his lips

between his thumb and his forefinger – the way he does when he feels he is not in control – nodding.

And this, Matilda fathoms now, is exactly why she loves him. Not because he is handsome and brooding, though he is undeniably both of those things. Not because he can send a particular frown at a person which makes their heart start beating faster. But because she has found someone who holds inside himself the same levels of fear as she does. They live off it, she and Henry. Their blood runs with it. For that reason alone, she knows they could never be together. But then, she does not love him because he is good or clever or right, or because he would make her happy. She loves him because she loves him. It is as simple and as impossible as that. She loves him because she doesn't know how not to.

***

'Sybil will know,' Henry says. 'She'll know for certain.'

'Know what for certain?'

'What do you think?' he shouts. 'Where Jack was taken. Where you had Jack taken.'

In the stillness, Henry's words snap and spit, and Matilda flinches as though an electric shock is passing through her. Perhaps it is painful for her, receiving his anger. Henry doesn't care. She deserves every bit of it, and more, but he makes an effort to calm himself all the same. He can't spare the time, even to hurt her. He has to speak to Sybil.

A cat, blacker than this particular night, tiptoes along the pavement towards him and Henry pauses to watch it for long enough to realise that he does not know which building is hers. He can't remember. And he can't believe he can't remember. It has been only months since he first sought her out. The door numbers must be there somewhere, buried in his mind, but no, he thinks as the cat draws level and hisses at him from the back of its throat, he can't access them.

Coming to Sybil's is a long shot in any case, he knows that, but he can dredge up no better idea. And when Henry can think of nothing positive to do, he acts. That is his instinctive response – to do, good or bad.

It had been the same when Bingley was killed. The boy was still spilling ropes of bloody intestine when Henry decided he had to find a woman that night. And it sounds callous, Christ it sounds callous, even in his own mind, but it's true. Bingley was still breathing, battling when Henry started planning what he would do once the boy was dead. Even as he was encouraging Bingley to 'Hang on in. Just hang on in for a few more minutes. Just until someone comes to help. Just until then,' Henry was thinking that she must not look anything like his mother, this woman he would pour his guilt into; she must be small and shy and dark eyed, and nothing at all like his mother.

Bingley had not attempted to speak at the end. But Henry, selfish Henry – unable to stand the deafening, gun-blasted silence – had pulled the words from him.

'Tell me about Hawthorn Road,' he coaxed. 'Tell me about your sisters.' Then, when eventually he felt Bingley go slack in his hands, 'What's your name, Bing? Your first name?'

Bingley's reply rattled up from his core. 'Jack,' he said.

And Henry took off then. He left Bingley, Jack Bingley, there on the ground, his middle blown to bits, his eyes dulled by staring up towards hopes of heaven, his helmet removed to reveal his perfectly intact, smooth-skinned face, and he walked away. He walked until he was out of sight, and then he ran. He ran over other bodies, bodies that had not been his friends; he ran until the mud beneath his feet grew harder and he could move faster; he ran into a thicket of thorny bushes, which clawed at his hands and ripped free thin strings of flesh, but which led him towards trees, lots of them, and the opportunity to run harder; he ran through centuries-old tree trunks until his legs were burning and his eyes were streaming and his lungs were fit to explode, and then he kept going, he kept going, because he'd known that they'd stumbled into the path of mortar fire, he and Bingley, he'd sensed the descending whir of a shell, and he'd ducked, he had, he'd thrown himself flat to the ground, he'd saved himself, and though he could have given a warning shout as he dropped, or grabbed Bingley's arm and dragged him down too, he hadn't. He'd thought only of himself. He, Henry Twist, had killed Jack Bingley.

In the early hours of that morning, Henry found his woman.

He had travelled perhaps fifteen miles across a country he did not wish to know and discovered himself, moonlit, in a mostly abandoned village. He did not bother to attempt to hide, or to remove his uniform before stepping through the streets. If he got shot, well then, hadn't he been expecting that bullet for two whole years now? Hadn't he imagined the specific spot where it would enter his body, just below his ribcage, left side, obliterating his birthmark? But there was no one around. No one, it seemed, could find the energy for killing at this time of night.

He did not have to search out a woman. He did not have to haunt hotels or pubs or walk his lady home pretending at innocent concern that she make it there safely. As he wandered along, the shutter of a house window opened and someone called to him with a 'Pssst!'

Henry spun around, seeking the sound.

'Go out of the streets,' a voice said. 'You shouldn't be in the streets.' Then, when he did not move, 'Wait. You wait.'

Seconds later, a door opened.

She was around thirty, he supposed. Older than he. She wore a loose cotton shirt and what appeared to be men's trousers. She leant against the doorframe, one bare foot tucked around the opposite ankle, her head tilted to the wood, and gestured for him to come closer. Henry did not oblige. It was unrealistic to think this woman, with her meandering, thickvowelled accent, meant him anything but harm. He was in a foreign country. He was a soldier. He was ruining great long bands of her birthplace, churning up chunks of the land with boots and bullets and hatred. He had not washed in nearly a week. He was covered in other men's blood.

'It is dangerous,' she said.

'Then why did you open the door?' Henry asked.

In other circumstances – circumstances Henry could hardly recall – the encounter might have been considered flirtatious. They had turned to face each other. Their eyes were busy measuring the other's body. There was a crackle, a pull in the air between them, drawing them towards each other, which they might yet decide to fight.

'Because you are not the dangerous.'

'How do you know?'

'Because I see you.'

Henry took a single step towards her. She answered it by dropping her gaze briefly, playfully.

'What do you see?'

She smiled, for the first time, and it was a brilliant thing to see. Her cheeks rose, her eyes crinkled at the corners, but what made Henry go inside was this: that smile undulated through her entire body. Her shoulders slumped, her chest fell, she dipped a couple of inches lower as she shifted her weight from one leg to the other, and then she righted herself again, returned to her full height, showed him the woman she wanted to show to the world. Henry couldn't remember the last time anyone had smiled so honestly at him.

He stepped across the street and took one of her hands as she answered.

'I see,' she said, 'a man sick with hurting. A man who wishes not to hurt any longer.'

'Yes,' Henry nodded.

'A man who wants.'

'Yes,' Henry nodded again. And of course it was too easy.

Afterwards, she would ask for money, her eyes filling with the regret which would persuade him that she hadn't done this before the war; that she hadn't been this before the war; that when he told her he didn't have any money, and she held on to him anyway, pressing her head to the top of his so that her neck cradled his jaw, it was just because she wanted to.

That night, with that woman, had been the saddest of Henry's life. Until Ruby, of course. Until that. And he had promised himself he would tell Jack about it – Bingley's loss, not the Frenchwoman – but he hasn't yet. He hasn't had the chance.

'Henry?' Matilda says again, and Henry wonders how many times she has spoken his name; how many times she has uttered it to herself. She voices it like a prayer.

'Yes?' He studies the cat, which, having had a complete change of heart, is orbiting his ankles now, releasing its mechanical little purr. A madman, he supposes, might see his lost wife even here, in the bony body of a straying cat. Is it any more rational, then, to see her in a man? Perhaps not. But either way, he cannot be without that man. He cannot. He has never known it so clearly as he does now.

He turns to Matilda, who has not yet responded, and forces himself for once to look straight into her eyes. She withers a tad. Henry knows he could have her any time he wanted. He also knows that that time will never come.

'I need to get him out,' he says.

'I know.'

He pinches his top lip between thumb and forefinger as he speaks, as though the words need the support. 'Then help me.'

'I don't know how. Truly, Henry darling, I don't.'

Turning, Henry looks both ways along the street, deciding on a direction. In the distance, a clinch of party-goers stumble over the pavement. To Henry, they are five shadows, two taller and broader than the others: two men, three women.

One of the men sings loudly, carelessly, his arms flung out into the shape of a crucifix. One of the women hangs around the singer's waist, laughing at his atonal performance. And for a moment, Henry envies them, this easy couple, on their way to or from a party. Later, they will make love and forget all about the rest of the ugly world.

He waits for them to vanish into the night then steps carefully over the cat and, as the animal slinks away, begins walking, then marching, away from Matilda. Then back towards her. Then away again.

'Sybil,' he calls. 'Sybil!'

His shouts and his footsteps beat a desperate rhythm. He wheels around and re-treads the same path, calling over and over. Matilda stands and watches, biting at the inside of her cheek in an attempt to stem her escaping tears. Sybil's name clogs up the air like chimney smoke.

'Sybil!'

Soon, Henry's voice is growing stringy, strained, but he does not stop, and then, abruptly, there she is — Sybil Brown — standing before him, her hair shining its way right down to the ground.

'Is she right?' Henry demands, pointing at Matilda. 'Did they take him?'

Sybil nods.

'Are you certain?'

'As I can be.'

'Then where? Do you know where?'

'Pentonville.'

The word winds Henry and he staggers backwards slightly, as though he has taken a blow to the stomach. He wasn't ready for it. He wasn't ready to believe it.

'Thank you, Sybil,' he says slowly. 'Thank you.' He moves forward to clasp her shoulders, to kiss her cheek, but Sybil shakes him off.

'Go on, then,' she says. 'Go and find him.'

Matilda waits until Henry has receded into miniature before acknowledging Sybil. The woman wants to speak to her, Matilda can feel it. It is as palpable as the pulsing and wheeling of birds overhead, or the cling and drag of water around your feet. Matilda is sure she does not want to hear what Sybil has to say. She does not want to hear what anyone has to say. But Sybil speaks anyway, her voice soft as daydreams.

'I understand why you would love him.'

'No you don't,' Matilda answers. 'Not really. How could you?'

Sybil does not argue against Matilda's snappy answer. She only puts her hand to Matilda's shoulder, smiles, and continues.

'And I think he must be a very difficult man to love. You have my sympathies.'

'I do?'

When she had last been offered anyone's sympathies, Matilda cannot recall. She has been fighting, it seems, for so long. Even when she had gone to bed with Grayson, she had been fighting, hadn't she? Fighting to remind him. Fighting to keep him. Her every touch, however affectionate, had been a battle strike. And so had his. She sees that now.

'Why would you be so kind to –'

Matilda is about to say 'me' – that tiny, massive word. But when she looks to the place where Sybil was standing, the psychic is gone. There is still a warmth at Matilda's shoulder, though: an unmistakeable warmth, on the spot where Sybil laid her palm. Matilda presses her own palm to it.

'Me,' she says finally, releasing a small laugh into the tacky air. 'Of course, me.'

JACK

It seems to him that this must be the state people enter into immediately before they die.

He can conjure no other explanation for his feeling at once heavy and light, for his being capable of seeing both everything and nothing, for his being able to hear the smallest sounds whilst the loudest blur and get lost. Beneath him, he feels black water tilting and overbalancing, falling gently about on itself, but he knows he is nowhere near the docks. No salt wind touches his skin. No rats scuttle away from the seesawing tide. He is inside. He is surrounded by four brick walls, which hold him in darkness, but he cannot lift himself to the task of seeking an escape. He cannot find the strength. His body is broken. They were not careful when they threw him in here. They were anything but careful. Jack flops around on the edges of sleep or unconsciousness, aware always of the pain in his neck, his stomach, his jawbone, his fingers; aware always of an anger within him.

But somewhere above this, more acutely felt, is another, surging sort of pain. When Jack Turner cries out, the sound low but unstoppable, it is not because he is bruised and bleeding; it is because the person he needs is not there.

Now and then, night sounds jolt him into proper sentience.

The small window above him is barred, but bars cannot keep out the crunching and tittering of prostitutes stumbling into nearby disused buildings, or the scratching of city foxes sniffing out scraps, or the clatter of motorcar wheels over the road outside. Though his has been suspended, life continues, and it drags open his eyelids. But it is not long before he sinks back into his hallucinations. And there he meets the woman from his dream. And a hell of a woman she was, too; a hell of a woman. But she was not his. Not really. She was Fred's.

He sees her always in the same place, on a long wedge of garden which slopes up towards a turreted, ivy-clad house. On the grass, two small boys play, knuckling each other's heads or shooting each other with invisible weaponry. Through the windows of the house, nothing much is detectable: there is no lonely housemaid peering out from behind the glass, no arrogant butler guarding the threshold, no sounds of scurrying or squabbling staff leaking out of the front door. There is only her, standing at the doorstep, her hands on her hips, half a smile telling him that she has been waiting for him, only for him, and the knowledge fills him with a certain unpleasant sort of pride. He should not be proud of what he does, and yet, there is satisfaction to be found in a job well done.

'Freddy Boy,' she will call him later, into his ear, to tease him. The certainty of it does not make him want it any less, because Fred Abbington really does have it all this time. This woman, this widow, is still young enough, still attractive enough, still rich enough to keep him for many years. He might just be Fred, Freddy Boy, for the rest of his life. She whispers plans to him which make him think this is an option. 'We'll have children of our own one day, Freddy Boy,' she says when they lie next to each other in bed, limbs thrown out like starfish. 'We'll marry, you and I, and I'll make you take me away from London so that we can grow old in the country-side.' She has presented him with all manner of promises, in those gluey minutes when she is partway into sleep, when it is near impossible to conceal your deepest truths.

And in return, Fred has told her his secrets. Or so it would seem. In reality, what he tells her is exactly what she needs to hear. Fred has no past to share. He has been in existence for only three months.

But these are memories within a memory, or imaginings within an imagining. Because it is in that garden that he sees her still, her hands on her hips, half a smile reminding him of how beautiful and spiky and wilful she is. And she was all those things, despite being a mark. But haven't they argued? Didn't they argue the last time they spoke? Didn't somebody discover that there are always secrets to be told?

A pendulous movement brings him back to himself. As far back as he can manage to get, in any case. His prison is swaying, he thinks, until he remembers that the motion must be originating from within him and not without. He is not at the docks any more. He attempts and fails to open his eyes. The effort makes the swaying worse, and he starts to move with it, shifting back and forth as if he were standing on board a ship, though he is lying, as he has been for hours, horizontally. Left and right. Left and right. Forever and no time at all – that's how long he has been here. And for all he knows he could be here forever more, because Henry does not know where to find him.

If nothing else, Jack is sure of that. Henry does not know where to find him.

A moon as big as a Ferris wheel greets him when he wakes again. It pushes its way through his window, then between his eyelids, and props them open: he sees for the first time in ages. The entire, tiny world is built from black shapes and shadows which shift riotously and giddy him. It's the night after a party then, and he's drunk the place all out of whisky, and that glaring moon is nothing more than a hanging ceiling light. Yes, that's it. He's flat on his back. Flat drunk. He must be. They're leaving him to sleep it off, poor thing.

But who are they, this *they*? He rummages around his woolly brain, searching the faces of those people he's danced with, smiled with, toasted and flirted and played with. They must be stored in there, filed alongside so many snippets of easy childhood and torturous youth and beautiful, ugly adulthood. He finds a still amongst the rest – a man, a darky, bending back over a long note, dragging it up along the length of his spine like a weighty thing, his trumpet pointed straight up towards heaven, his cheeks bursting, his eyes shut tight and watering, pushing out the very last scraps of his endeavour.

Gradually, Jack's eyes drop again and, held now in the black behind his lids, the musician comes to life. He springs upright then dives forwards, threatening to plunge his trumpet straight through the floorboards but saving it with another upwards whip just in time. And as he bends and blows, blows and bends, so Jack sees the people around him, arms flung out like boat sails as they black-bottom across the foot-polished floor; so Jack smells the clog of too many cigarettes, smoked too quickly, caught on the air; so Jack hears, beyond the cry of the trumpet, chatter and laughter and, somewhere close by, a woman sobbing; so Jack feels, at his neck, lips whispering over his skin.

'Henry,' he says. 'Henry?'

But there is no one here, and that party was long ago, it must have been, and Henry cannot hear him. How could he? Jack's voice, fluttery, is carried away on passing strokes of silence.

It must be audible to someone, though. It must be, because he is being answered now.

'Henry?' someone is saying, as though the name is the punch line to a brilliant joke, and that someone is laughing hard.

Jack peels back his eyelids, the movement so painful that it seems splintered glass has shattered through his mind, then, his vision only partly functional, he attempts to probe the darkness, sweeping his eyes back and forth like lighthouse lamps. A face quivers slowly into focus: a face held disembodied in a gap in the wall. It is some paces away, enjoying an elevated position, and it laughs and laughs; he laughs and laughs. His words swim towards Jack, losing their order in the course of the race, and Jack struggles to straighten them into their intended sequence.

'Turner's back with us, boys,' the face says, and Jack realises then that he is not laughing but coughing. The face falls away, downwards, as the man hangs forward over his own knees to cough, protractedly, worryingly. He's ill, then. He needs help. But Jack can't think how best to offer his assistance, swaying here as he is, flat out on someone else's bed. He is not a doctor. He is only a barman. A waiter. Of course – that's him! He's Roderick Miller. Roddy, to his friends, who can pour three Queen of Shebas in as many seconds, who can balance four Old Fashioneds along his forearm, who has been known on one occasion to successfully juggle a couple of brimming Mint Juleps. How could he have forgotten that? How could he have confused himself with a man called Fred Abbington?

The face in the wall reappears and divides into two as Jack – Roddy – squints at him. He speaks softly, not wanting to be heard.

'Didn't think we'd see him take another breath.'

'Yeah, I thought we might've gone too far there.'

'Seems like he's a tough one.'

'Surprising.'

Jack is only half listening to this exchange. Instead, he is rolling two names over and over in his mind, like two marbles held tight in the palm. Jack or Roddy? Jack *and* Roddy. He can choose the man he wants to be.

Roddy Miller asked a woman to marry him once. He did

not do it well. It was not planned. And, more importantly, he did not love her. It had happened on impulse, because Roddy knew she wanted him, and because in a way they were happy as they laughed their way home from a concert through spears of rain, and because she provided him with everything he needed. There was a house – a large house, big enough to hide from her in. And all the food he could crave. And all the attention he could want. There was a promise, too; a promise of forever; a promise that he wouldn't have to struggle again. She was, in the worst possible way, irresistible. Roddy knew without the tiniest doubt that he would never love her.

She knew it, too. That was why he had assumed she would answer his proposal with a resounding and emphatic 'no'.

They'd met at the bar, on a night made quiet by the volume of a storm. Outside, hailstones pelted the window-panes until they rattled; pigeons flapped around in search of safety and, finding it on sills, huddled down together to wait out the squall; umbrellas sprung inside out and forced their owners to do battle as they trotted through inch-deep puddles; kerbs turned to waterfalls; newspapers released themselves from rubbish bins and, having discovered the liberty of flight, soared away over the city. It was a night for listening to the wireless and drinking sweet tea, for wrapping yourself in two extra blankets, for making love. Roddy, wet from the walk to work, was not feeling particularly friendly. He wiped violently at the inside of already-clean tumblers and tried to persuade himself to take up a whistle. Whistling usually cheered him. Tonight, though, he could not settle on a tune.

June was one of Roddy's five lonely customers, and the only one sitting at the bar.

'I thought barmen were supposed to always be happy,' she said, by way of initiating a conversation. Roddy had been hoping she wouldn't. She was, he imagined, about forty years old, crinkled at the edges. He had no intention of taking her home.

'I thought girls only drank in pairs,' he replied.

'Oh,' she smiled, 'girls might. Women, on the other hand – women can usually be relied upon to do pretty much whatever pleases them, don't you think?'

It was a brave thing to say, in a bar containing no other females. It was interesting. Roddy couldn't help but smile in return.

'And what is it that pleases you, Mrs ...?'

'June will do,' she answered quickly. 'And, hmm, how to answer such a leading question ...' She tapped at the corner of her mouth with a manicured fingernail as she thought. 'Music, funny men, and wine. In that order, too, I think. Yes.'

'Three good choices.'

'I agree. And what about your choices?'

'A drink, a smoke, and a well-roasted chicken.'

June laughed. 'That is a terrible lie. Consider it properly.'

'All right.' Roddy set down the tumbler and leaned on the bar top. June's face fell into sincerity. 'Cold mornings ... swimming ... and ... listening to people talk in foreign languages.'

'Oh,' June replied, 'that's a good one.' Her brow furrowed as she thought about it. 'But ... why? If you can't understand what they're saying –'

'That's exactly why. Because I can't understand what they're saying. And if I can't understand, then they could be saying anything. They'll never disappoint me. I'll always be able to decide for myself if they were discussing whether or not to return to their country, or declaring their love for each other, or just wondering whether to have another coffee.' June was smirking at him. 'For instance,' he added, embarrassed.

'Ah, don't blush, son,' she said. 'Can't you tell when a woman is hanging on your every word?'

Roddy knew how to charm, of course. It was his job. He knew how to spin sentences that caught the imagination, how to exchange looks containing mostly false promises, how to draw people over his bar and into his bed. But somehow, June was managing to reverse the roles and here he was, leaning close, falling for it, getting sucked in.

'Yes I can,' he said. 'Yes.' And that was the answer she'd been looking for.

They spent six months together in the end, Roddy taking advantage of every comfort she offered him and providing her in return with almost every part of himself: every part but the truth. They squandered Saturday mornings tangled in her bed sheets, telling lies and hooting at their absurdity. They sauntered into cafés and restaurants and waited for the gossip to start, then substantiated it by linking fingers or feeding each other playful portions of their meals. They vowed they would never quarrel, and they kept that vow, because they did not want to quarrel, there was no need. They were fooling around with life, weren't they? They were the ones in the know. They were having fun.

'Oh, I adored him, Son,' she said, holding her arms out like wings and spinning through the rain. She was talking about the pianist they'd seen. She had called Roddy 'Son' since their very first meeting. 'It was like listening to God Himself, just sighing. Or it was like hearing what the stars would sound like. Or, I don't know ...'

Roddy stood to attention and coughed into his hand. 'The thrill of walking in the rain with a handsome man?' he suggested, grinning.

June did not grin back. Instead, she crept closer and, cupping his jaw, kissed him hard and swift, her eyes fixed on his. 'You,' she said, 'are the most beautiful man I've ever known, Roddy Miller.'

'Maybe you should marry me then,' he returned.

'Maybe I should,' June answered. And she fully intended to. Surprisingly enough, Roddy fully intended to let her. Until he happened, one mist-strewn evening, across a younger, richer, sadder woman, and realised what it was that June had taught him to do.

He did not stick with any one of them for long, after that. He tired of them so quickly. And new opportunities presented themselves almost every day – all he need do was check the obituaries. He tired, too, of the men he turned himself into. Thomas Grove had too traumatic an invented past: he would have to remain depressed for years. George Emmanuel took up with a woman who lived too far outside London and grew restless of the quiet life within weeks. Robert Charles claimed to be an accountant then had to make a swift getaway when he could not drag a particular estate out of its financial predicament. But he got better at it. He smoothed out the deception, with practice. And he has been good to the women, and the occasional men, he has cheated since. He has treated them well, right up to the moment when he has abandoned them, because he has appreciated what they have done for him, truly he has. He has not dwelt on it until now. Frightened of the shame, he has denied himself the occasion to. But he is thankful. He is. And he needs to tell Henry that, and that he is sorry, because he has behaved unforgivably. No wonder he has ended up this way – his brain shaken, his sense spilled onto a dirty floor – for a second time. He deserves to. And he needs to explain it all to Henry, because him he will not abandon.

'Henry,' he says again. But he does not murmur the word this time. He shouts it, as loud as he can. He needs Henry. Just that. Jack needs Henry, and he does not care who hears it, so long as Henry does.

When the door is cracked open then slammed shut, it is as though an axe has been taken to the planet. The impact thunders through Jack's brain, pounds along behind his eyeballs. He wakes to find himself wholly in the present. He knows now where he is, why he is here. He does not flinch when a plate of hacked bread slides across the floor and rattles to a stop against the far wall. He will not eat.

Borrowed time – that's what he's been on for years. Borrowed time. He is not surprised that the police have caught up to him. Although, he suspects, they have had at least a little assistance. After all, he left no trail behind him. Of that much he is sure.

Lifting only his head, Jack begins feeling his way up and down his body with gentle palms, like a man soothing a frightened animal. He is investigating the damage, and he is glad to find that there are no fractured bones this time. The pain sits at tissue level. It will heal well, given the chance. There is a tenderness in his bladder, though, which tells him that he needs to relieve himself. It has been hours, days even. He rises, cautious of the movements; cautious, too, of making any noise, though he is unsure why. None of the other prisoners are attempting to stay quiet: they aim kicks at the undentable steel of their cell doors; they bash their fists or feet or heads, Jack cannot tell which, against their lavatories; they moan and scream and thrash against their incarceration. And they are punished, no doubt. But what further punishment can there be, for a certain type of human being, than being trapped in a thirteen by seven foot hollow for a year, a decade, a lifetime?

He manages to hold his balance long enough to take the three steps required to reach the lavatory then, one hand pressed to the brickwork and one swollen eye on the door which appears to have been wrought in hell itself, exposes his penis. Why he should feel ashamed to do this is unclear. The best postulation he can manage is that the threat of being watched, mocked, interrogated makes him feel powerless. And a powerless man must keep his back to the wall and his fists up. A powerless man must find a way to reclaim his agency. Jack looks down at the wretched dribble of urine he is issuing and considers that no man can reclaim anything resembling agency when he must drop his trousers for a potential audience.

When he has finished and righted himself, he turns to the window and, climbing up onto the corner of the bed, peers out. He is angled towards another block – identical, he presumes, to this – which is one, two, three, four, five storeys high and long as a steamship. Its exterior is the colour of dry earth on a summer's day. Its roof is a shallow black peak: above which, stealing low along its apex, Jack can just pick out the first grey fronds of morning. Another day. His second or his third? He does not know. Only now is he grasping the circular order of time again. Only now is his brain beginning to repair itself. And he marvels at that.

The last beating, the one that had brought him to Henry, had been worse. It had muddled his mind for a longer spell. Oh, he had recovered his senses before he appeared at Henry's flat – he cannot pretend he happened there by accident. But he was still shaking off the hiding Fred Abbington had so narrowly survived the day he hobbled along Oxford Street and heard a double decker scream to a stop, the moment he felt that bristling horror run through the crowds, the minute he stopped to watch as swarms of shoppers rushed forward to gawp or cry or help the young woman who was so evidently dying right there on the road.

'Not much use looking out,' a voice says, and Jack steps down off the bed and turns to view his warder through the opened hatch.

'Maybe not,' he replies. 'But it's never very pleasant looking in.'

The warder, the one who coughs so badly, lifts his chin and turns down his lips, considering this. He is large and wrinkled, but the dome of his head is stone-smooth. He has the appearance of an ageing bulldog.

'You might have a point there, lad. Now pass me your plate.'

Jack bends to retrieve the item, moving swiftly: he will not reveal that he is in pain. The warder, clocking this, nods his approval. And Jack, so accustomed to affecting some scheme or other, immediately starts thinking of how he might forge a friendship with the man. He is going to need allies here.

'You ought to eat it, you know,' the warder says, holding

the plate still momentarily to allow Jack to take the bread. 'You'll be given work soon enough.'

Jack shakes his head. 'I don't need it,' he says.

'Why not?'

'Well, to be honest, the furnishings aren't the most comfortable, and the service leaves a lot to be desired. I don't think I'll be staying long.'

Despite himself, the warder smiles. 'Don't push it, Turner,' he warns.

In return, Jack winks. 'I fully intend to,' he says.

Because this is what Jack does when he is scared: he talks, he performs. Really, he should have been an actor. That way, he might have hurt a lot less people. But how could a boy like Roddy Miller have ever clawed his way into the theatre? That was a richer child's dream. Roddy had learnt, by the time he turned fifteen and set out on his own, that his dreams had to be smaller, more immediate than other people's. He had been taught that in the cruellest possible way.

Still, all that fear, all that pretending, had secured him a position in a butcher's shop, and then in a kitchen; and that had led him to the bar, and June, and his most successful career yet; and so it had continued. He'd kept on and on, pretending. And that's how it had been with Henry. Or at least, that's how it had begun. Henry though, Jack is starting to realise, has dragged what was hidden out of him and dotted it all around the flat, about Monty's garden, across perhaps the whole rowdy mess of London.

The last time they had gone to bed together, it was Henry, strangely, who had fallen first into sleep. Ordinarily, Jack slumped into that heavy state long before Henry had managed to slow the churning of his mind, and Jack, unused to the silence of the sleeping flat and rendered fully awake by it, had risen and snuck towards the window seat to watch the city spinning chaotically into the next day. Across the street, the park was empty and ominous as a night spent alone. The hopeful hours were far off yet. These smallest hours Jack knew to be the bad ones. He'd endured them unaccompanied many times before. But there, with Henry's snoring slotting into a steady rhythm behind him, and Libby's cotton-breath warming the cool air, he had not been afraid. In place of the worst things, he had remembered that earliest night when he and Henry had slunk over to the park together and joked their way through the darkness; and the party they had attended, at Monty's, when Henry had been brave enough to claim Jack as his own; and the way, during those thumping, surging minutes when the strike had grown truly dangerous, Henry had fitted his hand into Jack's and pressed reassurance to the sweat there.

Yes, that is what Henry has done – he has scattered happy little parts of Jack all over this city, like paper confetti thrown for a newly wedded couple. And that is why Jack will not leave him, whatever that might make him. He no longer has a choice. He has to find a way out. He has to find his way back to Henry.

CONFESSIONS

Henry's approach is far from hushed. He steps fast, allowing his shoes their uneven click–click, click–click. When his lungs start to burn he realises he is not breathing, and he gulps at the air like a newborn tasting it for the first time, his nostrils pumping, his lips pursing to drag in more oxygen, more oxygen. His breath, cut short, is loudened by his fear. These sounds are of no consequence, though. They are disguised by the constant grind of the city, of business owners sweeping their front steps clean and flinging open their doors, of gramophone needles carving out songs, of people slamming their doors as they set off for work or throw out their cats or wave goodbye to their lovers. And no one is searching for him anyway, as far as he knows.

In the eerie flat-light of predawn, Henry charges unnoticed along Wheelwright Street, following the high brick wall which marks Pentonville's perimeter. Beyond it, at intervals, the blunt end of a particular block flashes into view then out again, in then out, but Henry takes little notice of it. He does not know which block it is, or which Jack is being held within. Pondering the prison's exterior will not help. He needs to get inside.

He veers right onto Caledonian Road, the heavy thwap-

thwap-thwap of his footfall echoing the thud of his heart. With each beat, he sends an appeal of sorts to Ruby: a prayer, perhaps. Please don't ... Please help ... Please come. Each plea starts with the same word. They all end, too, with the same word: Jack, Jack, Jack.

Further down Caledonian Road, he stops. Before him a large, ornate archway leads to a locked wooden door. He stares up at the façade which looms over him: windowed and ivied and proud, it is an exaggeration, a grim fairy tale. The outrageous idea he had been entertaining as he stormed here – of clambering the walls, of appearing at the bars of Jack's cell – he has already had to relinquish. The entranceway alone is impenetrable. Of course it is. It's a prison, for God's sake.

But from the second Sybil nodded 'yes' and confirmed the fears he'd been trying to dream away, Henry was a soldier again. He will not give up yet.

To his left, he knows, is a mostly empty road: just one man lingers in a doorway, leaning into the shadows, kissing a cigarette and watching; a worker, perhaps, spat out by the strike. To Henry's right: Matilda. He flexes his knuckles and tries to think his way to an adequate plan, but his brain is failing both him and Jack. It had been the same in France, in Belgium – he was a fighting soldier, not a thinking one. That had always been his biggest weakness. What he needs now is a strategist. And evidently, here she is. Matilda Steck, it would seem, is the most cunning strategist he knows.

'Tell me what to do,' he says.

He breathes deep, trying to still himself. She has caused this. She has. He will never forgive her, whatever her reasoning. For now, though, he might be able to use her.

'I don't know, Henry darling. I really –'

He hisses over her nonsense. 'Tell me what to do, Matilda. You did this. You. You can put it right.'

'I can't ... I don't ...'

She snivels between words. Henry cannot turn to face

the flowing self-indulgence. He concentrates on the aspect of Pentonville prison, counting the windows to pacify himself.

'What did you report him for?'

———

There is so much she could say now that Matilda has to pause to take control of the words. She holds them like a heap of apples too abundant for her arms, and though she tries and tries to balance them, she fails: she can only watch them as they roll out of her reach.

She reported him for being what he is: a conman.

And that is what she ought to tell Henry. She had begun with the docklands, walking every last inch of them and talking, talking to man after man after man, searching for anyone who might have known Jack Turner before he paraded into Henry's life. It was exciting, really, letting the workers whistle at her and sometimes winking in return, feeling the deep heave and drag of the water so close by, growing accustomed to the burly stink of the sea at the back of her throat. At St Katharine Docks, the scents which invaded her nose were even more peculiar. She couldn't pinpoint them until she recalled knowing, in some neglected part of her mind, that the trade which floated into St Katharine's was of the most exotic kind: casks of wine, perfumes and ivory, piles of sugar and rich-coloured spices, shells and rum and marble. These were whole new worlds, held tight within her London, and she came to love exploring them. She was a detective, a private investigator on a case. She was, as always, the main character in her story; except now she was in full control of it. She could make this game as small or as big, as playful or as serious, as she wanted.

As it transpired, she was good at inviting information out of people. Matilda had always been possessed of a certain human intelligence: her parents had been proud of it; her mother had mourned her relinquishing it, so soon, to marriage. But here she was, putting it to use, and it was thrilling. Every new fact or guess or rumour spurred her on to seek another. And by and by, Matilda Steck unveiled Jack Turner.

'Matilda,' Henry says again. 'What did you report him for?'

Henry knows the answer to his question. He knows it because he was part of it. But presently he is helpless, and he needs to talk his way into believing that he can undo what she has done. He needs words to dislodge the preposterous pictures his mind is showing him of Jack, beaten and beaten again, until he can no longer speak sensibly and Henry is just another tangle in the mess that's been made of his brain. Or Jack, held not in prison but behind other bars, in a human zoo: an exhibit displaying the perversion of nature, positioned alongside a hunchback or an albino. Or Jack, made so sorrowful by his incarceration that he begins to simply disintegrate, parts of him breaking off and folding away into the loneliest depths of the nights, until nothing remains but the clothes he once stood in and the implications of his crime.

The images are asinine. When removed, though, from the person you love, Henry knows that even the most beautiful thoughts can be disfigured.

The person you love. The person he loves. It is the solitary occasion on which he has considered Jack in such simple, complicated terms, and the thought jars inside him. The person he loves. Is that really who Jack is? Suddenly, he cannot imagine what should come of it. Even if Jack is pardoned, they cannot be a normal couple. And surely, they cannot choose to live forever on the run from themselves. They cannot share a home, or raise a child, or expect people to believe that they are only bachelors keeping each other company. They cannot risk, always, being locked up. There are pansies all over the city, of course, but those men have wives and respectable jobs and enough money to pay for private places; they quell their desires only to resurrect them at the right kind of parties. Yes, there are pansies all over the city, but Henry is not one of them.

Perhaps he should recognise this as an opportunity, then. He looks to Matilda. She has shrunk into herself, like a piece of rotted fruit. She stares at the ground and says nothing. Yes, perhaps this is an opportunity for Henry to remove himself from temptation, because he has never wanted any other man. It has only ever been Jack. And ought he to chance losing his daughter to be with a man whose past and present and future is an unsolvable mystery? No. Jack Turner could be anyone at all. Henry could walk away now; he should walk away. He could start again, with a woman like Ida, and watch Libby raised as Ruby intended. He could … He could …

Matilda's heart is fighting so hard to ram its way up her throat that temporarily she cannot speak, cannot tell Henry what he needs to hear.

'Tell me …' he keeps saying. But Matilda cannot decipher the rest of the sentence. The words are muffled by a new and peculiar distance between them: most parcel themselves up and flit away to hide in London's smog. She will not hound this man any more. 'Tell me …'

What? she wants to yell. That his real name is Roderick or Fred, or George or Robert or Thomas? That he is just a barman who pulls scams on grieving spouses? That she has tracked down men he worked with, and then paid dock workers to seek out the women he fooled with, and that they have all of them confirmed that Jack Turner is a total phoney? That she has reported all of this to the police because she was jealous, and because she wanted Henry to love her, and because she will never, never believe that two men should raise a child together.

But she will not say any of it. She vows it to herself there on the street outside Pentonville prison. She will not make those confessions, because, in spite of all the rest, she cannot watch Henry's heart break again.

'I told them,' she says, shoving her voice past the constriction in her windpipe, 'that I'd witnessed him … sodomising another man.'

'And,' Henry prompts.

'And that I couldn't identify the other man involved.'

'Because that other man was me,' he says, needlessly.

'Because that other man was you,' she confirms, her voice quivering. Abruptly, she is cold. Her teeth chatter frantically; her shoulders stiffen; her veins run to ice. Another word, or a sound, is trying to escape her. *No*, perhaps. Or maybe *Stop*. Because it is entirely wrong, this. All she has wanted, all these months, is for Henry to hold her the way she saw him hold Jack. Nothing more. And she has tried to ruin them for it. She has. And they were never hers to ruin.

Her thoughts shoot across the city, to Grayson, and she turns immediately to go to him: he, at least, is hers to wreck. He, at least, is hers.

Henry does not watch Matilda rush away. He does not notice her go. He is caught in a budding recollection of Ruby: of a summer dusk when he had arrived at her Strawberry Hill flat with a bunch of white tulips. They had arranged to meet an hour later, at Richmond Park, the Roehampton Gate. Ruby had asked if they could go the week before.

'I want to walk and walk in there,' she told him, 'until we are hopelessly lost.'

'Why?'

She scowled at him. 'Because I want to see the deer.'

'Why should we need to be lost for that?'

'We're just people, Henry,' she answered. 'We're not going to be able to track them down; not if they don't want us to. We'll just have to get lost, and hope we stumble across a deer who's a little bit lost, too.'

The sentiment was charming, and Henry had agreed to the funny plan. He had wanted, though, to bring her flowers. And he hadn't wanted her to traipse them, wilting, all around Richmond Park. That was why he'd come to the flat. His knock was answered by a faraway call, then an invitation inside. She spoke to him, invisibly, from her bedroom.

'You are offensively early, Mr Twist!'

'I know,' he answered, perching on the arm of the settee, the tulips held at his chest like a bridal bouquet.

'Then why are you here?'

'I couldn't wait to see you.'

She popped her head around the doorframe and crinkled her nose up at him, the way she did when she was happy. 'Aw. You're forgiven then.' She disappeared again. 'And thank you, for those.'

'I'll just –' He was going to say *put them in a vase*, but she spoke across him.

'No! Don't come in here.'

Henry laughed. 'I wasn't going to, but now I'm curious, Miss Fairclough.' He crept nearer, teasing her. 'What are you hiding in there?'

'No!' she shrieked. 'Don't! I'm only half put together.'

'What?'

'I'm only half … ready. I've lost a stocking and now … Henry!'

Unable to resist her, he was already standing at the doorway, looking in as she rummaged around in her crumpled bedclothes for the missing item. She wore only her one found stocking, her brassiere and her step-ins, and God, she was so much shapelier, so much more beautiful then than she was hidden beneath those box-shaped dresses, that he wished she would never clothe herself again. Kneeling on the bed, she lifted her pillow and aimed it at him.

'Out!' she ordered. 'You can't see me in pieces like this.'

'You've never been more beautiful than you are in pieces,' Henry said, smiling.

'Oh.' She dropped her sham anger with the pillow and stood still before him, letting him see her body: the perfect inverted parentheses of her waist; the cream-smooth swell of her hips. 'I suppose that's because you want to put me back together, is it?'

He didn't. Ruby did not need Henry to fix her.

But, he thinks now, if the best he can offer Jack is that he'll be there to piece him back together when he gets out, he will not deny him that. He'll wait. If the only way he'll ever reach Jack again is by pressing his palm to a barred hatch in a steel door for an hour or a minute or a heartbeat, that is what he'll do. He'll hold Jack. And Jack will respond by meeting him the only way he can, by matching his hand to Henry's. And there they will stay, pressed one to the other, holding each other together, until time or contempt forces them apart.

UNCONSIDERED PROMISES

Grayson is not at home. As thick pillars of dawn butt through the window he finds himself, half awake and heavy, in Sally's bed, the bedclothes lumped up around his middle and indecently white in the early light, a dribble of sweat creeping down from behind each ear. Sally is curled naked around his hand, which she clasps inside both of hers, fast asleep.

Grayson tilts his head to better see her: the soft place where her eyelashes arc out from the lids, the reptilian bump of her vertebrae through her skin, the uneven lines of her fingers. He needs to ask her a thousand questions – about the things she is scared of, and her first kiss, about her earliest recollection, and her greatest ambition, about people who have loved her, and words she's regretted, and all the ways she has hurt. He imagines all these moments and memories, smiles and tears seeping into his child, working and reworking it like the most intricate clay sculpture. He or she will be built from scraps of Sally's life, and Grayson wants to know it all, so that he might understand some fraction of the person she will bring screaming into the world. He knows it does not really happen this way. But it is a nice thought to begin his day with.

'Sally?' He shakes her shoulder gently. 'Sally?'

Eyes still closed, she groans at him.

'Oh,' he says, 'you're awake.'

'No. I'm very, very deeply asleep.'

'Then don't be. I need to ask you something.'

'What?' she whinges.

'Everything,' he murmurs.

And that is how they spend the next hour – talking of everything and nothing and trying to ignore the approaching minute when they will have to get up and ready themselves for work. It is Tuesday morning. They have to go in. There is no good reason for them both to be absent.

'Listen,' Gray begins. Sally, hooking her arm into a grey day dress now, raises her chin at him. The dress has the soft hue of fog about it: in comparison, her hair glints like a polished coin. 'I'm not going back home.'

'You can't just say that and think everything will work out fine.'

'I know ... Can you stop, please?'

'Stop what?'

'Getting dressed.'

Loosening finally, she smirks and turns to face him, the buttons of her dress undone to expose the sheen of her petticoat. 'Better?' she teases.

'Much.'

'You mustn't look like that at a woman who's with child.'

'Who's going to stop me?' Grayson asks. And the answer neither of them gives, the obvious answer, of course, is Matilda. His wife.

Where she might be, Grayson can't begin to imagine. Whether she has made it home, whether she ever intends to, are questions he cannot find any enthusiasm for. He has fallen too far into the daydream of he and Sally, strolling through the city in the anthesis of summer, a perambulator rolling ahead of them. Now and then, he supposes, ladies will pause to poke their head around the pram's hood, to coo and smile and say the baby is beautiful – and they won't have to pretend for Sally's child. If she is a girl, she will look just like her mother, and the very sight of her will draw gasps. And really, Grayson can envisage only a girl: his entire experience of infants consists of just the smattering of days he has spent with Libby.

The thought that perhaps it was Libby who drew Matilda to Henry flashes again across his mind. It's a thought he's comforted himself with before. Maybe it was just the child she coveted. But no – he forces himself to remember – she loved Henry long before Ruby died.

'I wonder about Ruby,' he says. He doesn't intend to say it aloud. It just falls from his mouth, the way it would have from Ruby's, without very much prior thought. It is as though that lovely girl's spirit got into him for an instant.

'Ruby?' Sally answers, her eyes cast away from him as she resumes dressing. 'I like that. Where did you get that from? Ruby Steck.'

No, Grayson wants to shout. No. Ruby Twist. Has everyone forgotten Ruby Twist? But instead, he explains.

'She was a friend.'

'Was?'

'She died.'

'Oh?'

'This last January.'

Sally, stepping past the bed to lift a lipstick tube off her dressing table, drops a kiss onto the top of his head. Grayson traps her within his looped arms and presses his forehead to the seemingly empty dip which marks the centre of her ribcage.

'Do you miss her?' Sally asks. Gray can hear the frown on her face.

'I suppose I do, yes.'

And he understands it, then, all of a sudden. He knows what Henry sees in Jack. He sees what he wants to see, what he needs to see. Christ, isn't it obvious? He sees an echo of her, poor sod.

Sally slides her hands around his jaw and lifts his face to

hers. 'Then you should talk about her, Gray,' she says. 'Did you love her a little?'

'No. Nothing like that. She just ... Do you believe in ghosts, Sal?'

Sally shakes her head slowly. 'I don't. And I don't think you do, either.'

'I don't,' Grayson confirms. 'I just ... I think Ruby's husband might be in need of some help. We might need to help him.'

'Then we will,' Sally answers. 'All right? We will.'

'All right.' Grayson nods and is quiet again.

What he doesn't admit – what he doesn't want to admit, even to himself – is that his reasons for dragging Sally into his friends' company are almost entirely selfish; that they have nothing much at all to do with Henry, but everything to do with him, Grayson Steck, a man who is finally chasing what he wants.

Matilda reaches the flat not long after day has broken over London. Its streets, its buildings, its trees, its motorcars, its people – all are shattered by splinters of rose-pink light. Before unlocking the front door, she steals half a minute to turn and study her corner of the city, to commit to memory the illuminated portions of it. She feels, for some reason, as though she is never coming back.

Pressing her palms to the door behind her, she ponders what Grayson is doing inside. It is not yet time for him to leave for work. He'll be sweating out last night's drink, then: perhaps dangling halfway out of their bed, perhaps stretched across the bedroom floor. He'll have the smell of wine and cigars on him and, binding those two scents together, the smells of him, just him – a unique combination that only she knows.

Or that only she and this Sally know.

They have not yet dared talk about what happened when he visited the girl. Matilda is exercising a new restraint. She is waiting for him to come to her, volunteer the details. Gray, she imagines, is stalling so as to reinvent the story, make it more palatable: he'll be trying to find a way to deliver it without once mentioning the girl's name. That damn girl! Though she has no right to her jealousy, Matilda cannot pretend it does not exist. She cannot keep her mind from painting pictures of Gray and *her*, flinging insults and teacups at each other, cowering from the smash before rising to rearm themselves, getting weakened by their anger and falling into one another, coming together for a final kiss, deciding that they can't give this up after all.

Her brain rumbles on, inventing scenarios, because he hasn't told her what really happened. He hasn't told her. And he hasn't told her because he hasn't told her! The realisation hits Matilda like a moving vehicle. It sprawls her across her own doorstep and she winces at the thud of her back meeting her front door, the sharp crack of her tailbone against stone, the crick of her ankle turning the wrong way underneath her. She stays down for only a second or two, long enough to see a gentleman approaching, his hurried strides flapping the sides of his black coat, his hand moving to remove his hat. He is about to break into a run, rush to her aid. Horrified, Matilda grabs the door knob for leverage and, dragging herself up, clatters inside before he can reach her.

She slams shut the door and presses herself to its cool surface – as she had the other, warmer side short moments before – and attempts to slow her breathing. She does not know why she is breathless, in any case. Then, having only partly calmed herself, she hastens up the stairs, her heels landing with a sound as hollow as her stomach feels.

'Grayson,' she shouts, bursting through yet another door. There are so many doors suddenly between her and her husband. 'Grayson!'

She knows instantly that he is not there. The air is unbroken. The flat has been empty all night. But still, she searches for him. She goes about and about their dining table, circling as though she is riding a fairground ride, before flying into the bedroom, the bathroom, then back again. She throws the bed sheets to the floor, she knocks a ticking clock from its shelf, she slams a fist into the bathroom mirror and, when she fails to break it, removes it from its hook, sets it down at her feet, and proceeds to stamp her way through its glassy face. Matilda turns the flat inside out, seeking nothing but relief, and when finally she accepts that there is none to be found, she coils herself up on the bed, their bed, and closes her eyes to the blackness behind them.

They were supposed to be arguing now. She'd disappeared, been gone all night. And they were going to argue long and hard and loud about it – that much she'd been prepared for. Then they were going to draw a line under it. She had decided so on the walk home. They were going to forgive every argument they'd ever had. They were going to continue in a new way.

For once, it is Gray who has denied them their chance at contentment.

As Matilda drops into sleep, though, she cannot sustain her swollen anger towards him. She is already half-dreaming, about a years-ago day when they did not yet know they couldn't have children and they had suspected she might be pregnant. Gray, too excited to stay still, was skipping around the flat, singing some invented song and whipping his arms about as though he were a famous tenor. And Matilda, laughing, laughing, was reaching out for him. Just that – reaching out for him.

They meet, as arranged, at the Rose Inn that early evening. Sally is already seated near the door when Grayson arrives, her hands tucked in her lap as though they are the shell around a pearl, her eyes roving anxiously from person to person. When she spots Gray, her whole body softens with relief, and Gray is careful not to laugh at her as he approaches and bends to kiss her cheek. He hasn't seen her like this before: edgy, nervous. He likes it. It makes him feel more of a man.

'Drink?'

'Please.'

'Relax.' He smiles. 'I'll be back in a flash.' Immediately he regrets the choice of phrase. It makes him sound old. But Sally doesn't seem to notice. Or perhaps she does. Perhaps she just expects it of him, because he is old, to her.

'But what if we,' she pauses, flicking her eyes left and right, then drops her voice to a whisper, 'see someone we know?'

Grayson, one hand on her shoulder, leans closer to her ear.

'Then we'll ask them to congratulate us.'

'On what?' Sally is horrified. Her eyes bulge: surely, they can't tell anyone about the baby?

'Us,' he answers, winking. 'And just how spectacular we are.'

'Don't joke, Gray.'

'Then don't worry,' he counters.

He smiles as he kisses her again, his lips meeting the top of her head this time, because suddenly he is not sure he wants to look further into her eyes. They are not as scared as they should be. They do not match her newly timid body. He suspects another performance. But if he has been played from the off, well then, he has been played too well. What choice does he have now but to finish the game? What choice does he have but to embrace it?

When he returns from the bar, a cold-misted glass held in each hand, he motions for her to take a new table and they settle in a duskier corner, sitting shoulder to shoulder now so that they can both see the movements of the room. It is still early, just a tick or two past six, and there are only three customers in: a pair of old fellows, swapping insults like cards, and, perched at the bar, a habitual whisky man, his yellowed eyes rolling from the bar top to the barman to the bar top as he murmurs to the devils in his glass.

The Rose, Gray decides, is a nice enough little drinker. The lines of round tables shine, cleaned and cleaned again. Broad sunbeams infiltrate the shadows, searching dust spots to drag to the ground but finding none. The air, so often stale with booze in other pubs, is made rich by the recent grinding of coffee beans. Tricked or not, he could spend his entire life here, watching Sally begin to unfurl, avoiding his wife and the hurt he must inflict on her.

Here, he will have to say, is everything I've ever wanted. Here, within my grasp, finally, is everything you've failed to give me. And that Sally has given it so easily – accidentally, probably – that is what makes it so cruel.

He watches her sip at her fruit juice; the ripple of her throat as it descends towards her stomach; the turn of her wrist as she sets the glass back down on the table.

'Do you know,' he says, 'when I was about eighteen, I set myself up in front of a mirror with a gin and a cigar – an unfortunate mix if you ask me – to teach myself how to look like a grown-up.'

Sally smirks: the intended effect. The admission is entirely true, though. He'd been in his parents' otherwise unoccupied house, prowling around his father's desk and wondering whether he would ever buy himself a decanter; whether he would ever possess the patience, the willpower, to lock himself into one square room, his back to the only window, and work for hours on paperwork his family would never know the true purpose of; whether he would ever meet the expectations they had had for him, Mr and Mrs Steck, long before he was conscious of the strange ambitions parents submit to in their most private minds.

'All right,' Sally says, 'so you got me to smile. Why are we here?'

'I needed a drink,' Grayson answers.

'And you knew that this morning, did you? Before you'd even left for work?'

'Yes.'

'Gray!' She slaps at his leg, her palm finding the jut of his kneecap.

'What?'

'Stop being so cryptic.'

Laughing, Grayson pours back another gulp of his pint. He folds up his tongue and uses it as a barrier, to keep the liquid in his mouth and let the cold of it tingle against his teeth. The words he needs have not yet come to him. He does not know how he will explain it to her, what he intends will happen next. He does not know how it will all pan out. He does not know, either, why he is so inclined to laughter. This is no laughing matter. He is taking Sally across town to present her to his friends because he has to, doesn't he, if she is ever going to be welcome amongst them? And because, if he's honest, he wants her to know Henry as he now is, locked in his delusion and his strange new relationship, so that there is no chance of her too falling in love with him. And because he wants to be able to tell them – doesn't he, very soon – that he's going to be a father. And, most importantly, because he wants to break Matilda's heart in company.

He's thought hard about this, and he knows that it is only in company that she will be able to bear it. Whatever his faults, Grayson has been an attentive enough man, in the past, to know his wife. And what he knows is this: Matilda Steck is a woman who is better with an audience; a being better seen, whatever the circumstances, than unseen.

Matilda is woken by a shifting of the light: a flattening perhaps, which – she will decide momentarily, when she rises and moves to the window to consider it – marks the end of the heatwave. It is warm still, but the sky has dropped lower, paled to white. She must have slept for hours, for presently the day is drifting away over the city, carried seemingly on the backs of the birds, in their hundreds, which fleck London's wide-arched ceiling. Tomorrow, the morning will be chill.

Matilda's sleeping hours have brought her to a decision. A very simple one, really, though she knows she will struggle with it. She will make no more unconsidered promises: not to Gray, not to Henry or to Ruby's ghost, not even to herself.

She had expected Gray would be home by now, so that she could put her hand to his neck and force his eyes onto hers and tell him, but as she wanders back into their bedroom to pick out a dress, something, something tight and low in her stomach, is telling her that he will not return to the flat today. She will have to seek him out. And where better to start than at Monty's? That's where he'll be, seeking refuge, the way she has so often done lately. She's certain of it.

She pulls a light coffee-coloured dress from her ward-robe. Somewhere, she has a pair of shoes, and a cloche in the softest cream, to match it; and there's a stole, too, a fur stole which will do nicely. Demure is the look she is aiming for. It is just one small part of her apology. Or it is just the beginning, rather, because she is aware that this apology must be a lengthy one. She supposes it will last for the rest of her life.

It strikes her, as it invariably does now, that the thought is lazy. The rest of her life. How many times did Ruby have that same thought and envisage herself as an old woman, with an even older husband by her side; as the cotton-haired mother of a beautiful daughter, or maybe two, out there in the world, building lives for themselves that would make her proud? How awful for her that she has missed all of that. And how awful of Matilda to be wasting her time with spiteful actions, with the pursuit of misery, when her time might have been cut short just as easily as Ruby's. *Can you forgive me, too?* she thinks, and she closes her eyes to picture the question as a string of airborne letters, floating up and up, through the dark-ening firmament, through the black endlessness of space and towards, finally, some vague idea of Heaven. She knows that Ruby would pardon her. Ruby would extend that kindness to anyone earnest. What Matilda does not know is whether she deserves it.

But enough! She cannot right it all in one afternoon. She has begun – that is what is important. She has begun. She pulls on her shoes, then pauses to consider herself in the mirror. She removes her cloche, fluffs up her wilted hair, replaces the hat and steps towards the door.

'Enough,' she says to the empty room. 'That's enough.' Then she descends the stairs, walks out, with the deepest of breaths, into a new evening, and sets off on the march towards her husband. Always, now, she will move towards her husband.

First, though, she must make her apology to another man.

———

At Notting Hill Police Station, Matilda marches towards the desk where first she reported Jack Turner's crimes, and demands to speak to a Constable Howard. Her stomach is loose with dread and it is quite possible, she thinks as she waits, that she might vomit right here on the station floor if the man does not hurry up. She swallows and swallows, trying to shift the saliva pooling on her tongue, but it returns, as though somewhere inside her a tap has been left running. Her eyes, too, are threat-ening to leak. Perspiration pours from her hairline and down each side of her face.

If she does not play this right, it is she who might end up in a prison cell.

Constable Howard appears fast through a flung-open door, his uniform sharp as the most brutal of words, his buttons shining like sovereigns, the polished MP at his collar flashing. He is an impressive man: tall and black-haired and serious. He knows without the slightest of doubts that his is the most important, the absolutely most important, of jobs.

'Mrs Steck,' he says, offering her his hand. 'What can we do for you?' He is frowning, confused by her reappearance. He wants to help. Guilt swirls at Matilda's middle. She does not want to embarrass him, but how else can she do it, without implicating herself? There is no other way to free them all.

'You,' she begins, her chin high, her eyes narrowed, 'made a mistake.'

'I'm sorry, Mrs —' Constable Howard begins, but she cuts him short. She does not want him to voice her married name again. It does not belong to her any more. She has not yet earned it back.

'You made a mistake!' Her words are too big in the crammed little entrance space: they slap the stone walls, crack against the tiled floor; they bring heads snapping up to inspect their authenticity.

'But, I don't understand.'

'I came here to report a crime,' Matilda begins. It will not be difficult to grow hysterical. Truly, she feels it. It is not Constable Howard's doing, poor man, but Matilda Steck is hurting, and she is scared, and she wants to rant and bawl the fright away. And here is the perfect excuse. It will lend her story credibility while it ruins Constable Howard's. 'I came here, to report a low-down sort of crime ...' She lets the tears come. 'And to see a contemptible man removed from the streets. And you, *you*, promised you would help.'

Glancing about himself, Constable Howard, already rose-cheeked, motions towards a room where they can speak privately, but Matilda shakes her head.

'No. No,' she says. 'I shan't stay.'

'But, a drink of water, perhaps …'

'I am not in need of a drink of water,' she replies. 'I am in need of having my faith restored.'

She is gaining an audience now. Three other constables, clearly rattled by her behaviour, have abandoned their duties and stand awaiting her revelation, wondering what it is they could have got so wrong.

She continues. 'Some days ago now, I informed you that I had uncovered …' she riffles through the catalogue of words she had considered on the way here, '… deplorable behaviour in a certain individual! I told you that the man involved was a thief and a trickster and you, Constable Howard, assured me that you would arrest him that very morning.'

'And I ensured that the man was —'

'You did not!'

'Mrs Steck. The man in question is at Pentonville —'

'Is he? Is he? Are you sure, sir? Because I have seen him just last night, with my very own eyes, strutting along Piccadilly without a devil's care.' She flaps her arms as she speaks, like a prey animal scaring off a predator with more noise, more bravado.

Constable Howard leans in closer, speaks quietly. 'That's impossible, Mrs Steck,' he says kindly. 'The man has been —'

Matilda lifts her left hand and thrusts it into his face to silence him. The ploy works.

'Didn't I report this ring stolen to you, Constable? Didn't I tell you that fraudster had taken it from me?' She had retrieved it no more than an hour ago, scrabbling around on her knees on Henry's doorstep. She was lucky no one had noticed it, glinting there in the dirty guttering, and plucked it from the ground. She has been lucky in that much, at least. 'Clearly you did not even investigate my claims.'

'We were coming to it,' Constable Howard replies. 'We were. But the strike has left us rather overwhelmed. I'm sure you can understand —'

'Well!' Matilda spins around. He is offering the correct responses to her accusations, but Constable Howard's anger is rippling off him now, like heat from an open fire, and whilst she trusts he will stay true to his training, she knows that it is time to make her exit. She sashays towards the door like an actress in an epic film, executing her last devastating goodbyes. 'I'm sure you feel glad that I have a husband brave enough to bargain this back for me,' she says, flaunting her wedding ring again. 'But believe me, constables, the real Jack Turner is still out there, as free as you and I, and I've warned you where his interests lie. Perhaps you might think about paying a little more attention to the moral integrity of this city. When you have the time, gentlemen. When you're not quite so busy.'

And with that, she squalls out of the station and back onto Ladbroke Road, where she can breathe again, where she can breathe.

A PRIVATE PARTY

On the gate which separates Monty's garden from the rest of London, a note hangs from a piece of string looped around one of those elaborate iron whorls. It has been hastily written – that much is apparent in the hand, which slopes downwards and grows larger as it progresses across the paper; in the improvised way the two holes accommodating the string have been punctured with a pen nib, leaving inky trickles of evidence. Despite its unattractive appearance, however, it proves an intriguing note, to those it was not intended for. A number of times already today, passers-by have paused to read its words, to puzzle over them, to imbue them with invented meaning. Some hours ago, a lady walking a small black poodle had lingered there for minutes on end, wishing it was clearer, longing to follow its clues towards some naughty adventure or other. She'd read about the Bright Young People. Incidentally, she'd whispered about them with a luncheon companion only yesterday: she had been seeking them for months, hoping to secure an invitation. Gentlemen, too, have stopped to scan the message, some deciding it a silly love riddle and moving on with a grin or a tut, others checking about themselves for onlookers before turning it over in their hands, seeking more information. But none of these passers-by can make any real sense of the thing. This note on a gate in a London street, though seen by many, belongs to only a select few. It reads:

M, G, H and J,
You are all, without the most miniscule of doubts, some of the
most idiotic people I have ever had the pleasure of knowing.
You could create a drama in a nunnery.
Now, kindly convey yourselves to the house. I'm expecting you.
I'll provide refreshments, but only if you're good!
M T-W

Matilda, appropriately enough since hers is the first initial, is the first to happen upon it. She does not stop to give it a second read. She turns, as instructed, and makes her way directly to Monty's house, the address of which she knows by heart, of course, from the back of those parchment paper invitations.

She finds the place just as grand as she had expected. She understands then why Monty doesn't invite just any friend back here: to show anyone this much wealth, you'd need to trust them completely. It is a townhouse set over five storeys, and, when she tilts back her head to take in the full scale of it, she finds her neck aching with the strain of sending her eyes right to the top. It rises forever, this house. It frowns down at you. At street level, two Corinthian columns guard a black front door, set amongst panels of glass. Above that, on the upper four floors, the stretch of smooth white paint is interrupted by windows lined up in triplicate, which glow orange in the sinking twilight and open onto neat white-balustraded balconies. Number 8, Matilda thinks, is stacked up like the tiers of a royal wedding cake. And so naturally does the image sit in her mind that when she approaches the door and lifts the knocker, she almost expects it to yield to her touch, as sugared icing would.

The door is opened by a footman, as tall as he is young, who stands puffed with pride in his white shirt and dicky bow, and instantly Matilda loses her words. Why is she here? She can't be sure. Her mouth opens, eager to fill the silence, but she finds no explanation. Thankfully, a breath or two later, the footman comes to her assistance.

'Mrs Steck?' he ventures.

'Yes!' Matilda replies, too loud. 'Sorry. Yes. How did you know?'

'It's a private party,' the boy smiles, stepping backwards to usher her inside. 'We're expecting just one lady guest this evening. Please,' he continues, 'allow me to show you through to Mr Thornton-Wells.'

———

Henry and Jack are walking through their city, roughly ten counted strides apart, burdened by piles of stuffed-full bags. Jack is ahead, limping heavily but trying hard not to. Already his bruises have ripened, mapping the right side of his face with three colourful new continents. He is scattered all over with scrapes and lumps and splinters of split skin. Back at the flat, Henry had attempted to clean his wounds, but with access only to cold water and a cloth, he had not made a great job of it. In the fading light, Jack is pitiful.

Behind him, Henry moves in half-steps, not wanting to rush him along. Moving slowly makes it easier, in any case, to be watchful of his surroundings. He is hyper-alert now: in soldier mode again. It was easier than he'd imagined it might be to snap back, to glance down a street and calculate the number of people on it, the quickest route off it, the length of time it might take to march down it. He knows, for instance, that presently there are nine people within range of a rifle: two couples, married he decides, who strut arm in arm, their feet precisely matched; a line of three men, each of them smaller than both Henry and Jack, who are likely on their way for an after-work tipple; a lone man, who fairly clips along, a rolled newspaper held in one hand and a cane he doesn't seem to need in the other; and, nearest to them and travelling nearer, a lady in her early fifties, Henry would estimate, who keeps her silvering head low as she whistles her way home, or away from home. Henry plots them all on his mind like constellations of stars: those closest to him, the greatest threats, burn brighter than the rest.

He clears his throat, once, significantly – the ridiculous code they have concocted. Jack answers by echoing the sound. A single cough means he is all right, he can carry on. Two would mean he was struggling, he might have to stop. Three – the emergency cough – was to be used if and when Jack felt under threat. Henry considers now that the order should perhaps have been reversed. In the case of an emergency, Jack might not have time to discharge the rapid tripartite Henry has forced him to agree to.

He sneaks a glimpse at Libby, tucked into the pram he pushes, her snub-nose reddened to a slight glow in the chilling air, her round eyes sparking at him. They are like worlds, this little girl's eyes. They are like deep dark worlds. They had smiled at Viv when they had said their goodbyes, exactly as her mother's would have.

Henry had hoped to spend more time with Viv and Herb. He'd wanted to set Libby down on the floor of their flat and murmur through some purposeless conversation as she crawled about, dragging her blanket and easy joy in her wake. He'd wanted her to make Herb smile one more time, for Viv's sake. But they had had to rush, he and Jack. They have not spoken yet about what really happened in Pentonville, but what choice did they have but to move fast? After all, it seems Matilda only tricked the police into releasing him. They might realise the deception, want their revenge. Someone else, spurred on by her apparent bravery, might make an accusation of their own. Either way, Bayswater Road does not feel safe any more, and so he had been forced to leave Viv with nothing more than an embrace.

'You'll write me, won't you?' she'd said, holding on tight to the tears in her eyes. 'You'll let me know where you end up?'

'Of course I will,' Henry had answered, folding his arms around her. 'Of course I will. I promise.' Then he'd kissed her cheek, shaken hands with Herb, locked up 101a Bayswater Road for the final time and walked away.

And now here he is, trailing Jack across London, armed with nothing much more than a vague plan, a bundle of clothes and his family. He touches a tentative hand to the back of his neck. His anxiety is a dull pain which pulls at his brain, pulse-like, making clear thinking impossible. But this much he knows: he is walking towards his future. That is what he needs to tell Ruby, what he has to explain to her, what he hopes she can forgive him for. That is the sentiment he'll be carrying when he visits her grave for the very first time. And, God, he hopes there will be flowers, deposited by some kindly hand before the stone on which her name is written, because he cannot stand to look down and remember the way he last saw that square of ground – opened to the sky and too many eyes and his wife. He cannot stand it.

Darkness drops like an anchor. And luckily so, for they need something to hold them in place, this eddying collection of people. They are strewn about the room as though deposited there by an accidental tide. Monty stands before the double windows, smiling through closed lips, an untouched drink held up on an idle wrist. Matilda perches on a chair edge, her head lost in her hands. Across the room, sharing a two-seater settee, Jack and Grayson look in opposite directions, one man biting at a thumbnail, the other sucking furiously on a cigarette. On the rug in the centre of the floor, Sally Emory crosses and uncrosses her ankles, straining not to reach out and touch

Libby, who has been set to sleep there. And Henry, back to a shut door, watches them. He watches them, and he finds, in the spaces between the words they are shoving back and forth, his decision. The letter he will write later, to Ida, gathers in his mind as insistently as storm clouds, the words finding their own unstoppable way together.

'You won't stay?' Matilda asks. 'Not even ... Not for anything?'

Henry shakes his head. *No.*

'But –'

'Tilda,' Grayson warns. They can feel, all of them, that she is about to start begging. They can feel it, and they are embarrassed by it. But Matilda does not care one jot for their embarrassment. She is facing a future devoid of this man and this child, and despite her best intentions, she cannot deny that the pain of it is already at her stomach, gnawing deep. Ahead of her stretches the rest of a suddenly empty life, during which she will never again sit opposite Henry to a meal while he and her husband drink and laugh and drink; never again lift Libby to her shoulder and know that smell she has, like the heat of sun on stone, present in her nose. She cannot conceive now of why she had needed more when she could have had, and continued to have all those things, those wonderful things, those real things. She could have taught that little girl just how incredible her mother had been; she could have helped to raise her, in her own way. Why, then, had she had to push? Why had she been so greedy? She is aware of the reason. She is aware of it though she wishes she weren't. She, Matilda Steck, is selfish – she always has been.

'You can't stay where you're not welcome,' Jack says, his words gentle. Henry has implored him to remain composed, just through this one last night with these people, just so that they can stay off the streets until morning. And Jack is trying, hard.

'But you *are* welcome here,' Matilda returns, deliberately

misunderstanding. 'Hasn't Monty said so? Haven't you, Montague? You want them to stay, don't you? Don't you?'

Monty responds at his leisure. He's enjoying this: the heart-break, the tension. 'I've said so,' he answers.

'But not everywhere,' Henry says. 'We're not welcome everywhere. We never will be.'

'You don't know that!' Matilda almost wails.

Henry growls back at her, his voice low but rough. 'You've proved that.'

'Well, I'm sorry, I'm sorry I –' She stops when Sally adjusts her ankles again and the movement catches her eye. She cannot look at the girl without feeling physically sick. How can she, knowing what she now knows, having noticed what she has noticed? She cannot believe Grayson was so ignorant as to think that she, Matilda Steck, barren Matilda Steck, would not sniff out a pregnant woman. She would be the country's most successful detective, if the only suspects she had to seek were expectant mothers. 'I was trying to help.'

'Who?' Henry asks.

'*You.*'

'Me, or yourself?' he mutters, blushing at the words. They have never acknowledged her feelings this way: verbally, soberly. Not Henry or Grayson or even Matilda. Doing so now makes them feel like she is standing in the middle of the room howling 'But I loved you'. Each of them, excepting Monty, stares at the polish of the floorboards, listening to the silent rumour of that awful, beautiful sentiment, caught on the air.

Sometimes, Henry wonders whether he should have spoken those words to his parents, whether he'd have grown into a better man if they had ever spoken them to him. But, no – the idea is a wasted one. The last time Henry saw his father he was slumped on the front doorstep of their home, spittle hanging like slung ropes from his lips to his chest, his shoul-ders crumbling into the sleeves of his shirt, one foot removed from its shoe, one knee drooling streamers of blood down the length of a bony shin. Henry had extricated him from a street brawl that night. He'd been rewarded with a blow to his left temple, delivered by a hand near-identical to his own: that he had accepted. When the old man had drawn a knife, though, and started sculpting the dark with it, Henry had been forced to show his father just how much strength he had acquired since his boyhood.

Later, Henry said goodbye to him without being heard, while he slept off the lesson his son's fists had taught him, and in truth, he does not know for sure now if the old man is alive or dead. He suspects, however – and he accepted the suspicion as fact a number of years since – that the bloody fool drank himself to death. Remarkably, the only comfort Henry can pull from this is that the news of he and Jack will not reach Alfred Twist. Never will he have to begin an unresolvable argument with the man he always hoped for, even through that final fight.

In Monty's drawing room, there is a shift in the conversation. Somehow, despite his fear, his anger, Henry had managed to mute the exchanges crisscrossing him for a minute or two. Monty's voice finds a way to reinstate his attention.

'I suggest a game,' he says. 'Wouldn't a game ease the mood, friends? Don't you think?' He steps towards Sally and Libby, so that he is standing at the heart of the gathering, pivotal – the position where he is most content. The suggestion is ridiculous enough to silence them. 'How about poker? Just a couple of silly hands, no money? Anyone?'

Grayson, eager to soften the encounter, responds first to the invitation.

'If not money,' he enquires, his lips spilling cigarette smoke, 'what will we play for?'

'Ah,' Monty smiles. 'How about truths?'

'Truths?' Jack asks, and Monty smiles wider.

'What else is there?'

They allow themselves to be ushered into a room which

Monty has surely had designed as a gambling den. At the room's middle, beneath a five-armed chandelier and atop a woven circular rug, there sits an enormous round table, already laid with playing cards. The remainder of the space is largely empty: there is an alcove piled with books, the battered spines of which are crammed together at every possible angle; beside it, a leather armchair; and against the opposite wall, a leather settee, a standard lamp and a drinks trolley, its treasures glinting in the candlelight. Henry imagines Monty insists on candlelight only in this room, for the drama of it, for the added tension a flame made to stutter by quickening breath would create.

They take the places Monty allocates them in near silence, uttering occasional words of apology as they bump elbows or chair legs. He does not organise them accidentally – Henry sees that right away. He puts Matilda alongside Sally, he sandwiches Grayson between Henry and Jack. As usual, he is playing more than one game.

'I'll deal,' he announces, settling in his own chair, and, like fools, they wait for their hands to be dealt. There is a stretch of time then interrupted only by the shuffling of cards between fingers, of glances over the top of fanned hands, of coughs and sniffs and hums and obdurate looks. Ridiculously, they are nervous. They are sitting to a game of poker, nothing more. But they feel, somehow, that what each of them is playing for is their life.

Sally folds first, hands trembling. She is followed by Jack and Monty and, not far behind them, Matilda. Only Grayson and Henry show their cards. Grayson lays a two pair across the table: two kings, two sevens. Henry trumps it with three of a kind and the slimmest hint of a smile.

'So,' Monty says, like a schoolmaster leading an assembly. 'The truth must be one of yours, Gray.'

Grayson glares at Monty. 'What do you want me to say?'

Quite why they feel so bound by the rules of this game,

Henry cannot fathom. He is aware though that, had the losing hand been his, he would not have refused to reveal his truth. He would not have spoiled the game.

Monty takes a slow sip from his glass, holding the liquid in his mouth for a moment or two before swallowing.

'How long have you been sleeping with our new friend here?' he asks, indicating Sally with a flick of his eyes.

'No,' Matilda interjects, before Gray has chance to draw a breath. 'No, I've got a better question ... How long have you known, husband, that she is carrying your child?'

She chases the question with a slug of red wine. A few droplets of it escape her lips and scatter across her chin, like beads of fresh blood. She dabs them away with a napkin then folds it neatly back onto the table.

Grayson gulps and gulps again, trying to loosen his throat, but still the words, the only small words he can manage, are emitted as tight, knotted things. 'Not too long,' he replies.

Though Matilda had been sure from the start, this confirmation of her suspicions is too much and she wretches into her cupped palm, the convulsion starting low in her stomach and rippling all the way up to the back of her neck. She is a bird, regurgitating its hunted food for its young. Except, of course, that the regurgitation is for someone else's young. Not her own. Never her own. She stands and staggers from the room, her palm still pressed to her mouth, holding in her shame. She slams the door behind her and then she is out in the hallway, invisible to them, and they are listening to her throwing up on the other side of the wall. They are listening to the hot expulsion of her grief. They are listening to something so private that each of them bows their head and stares at the table before them, as though they are engaged in prayer.

One of Monty's staff approaches. They hear the clip of his footsteps, parroted by the walls. They hear him tell Matilda that she mustn't worry; he'll have it cleaned up in no time; she should get back to her friends. And, unbelievably – though not one of them is her friend now, not really and truly, not the way Ruby once was – she does.

She re-enters the room with a straight back and a new, hastily applied sweep of lipstick.

'I should offer you my congratulations,' she says, her eyes pressed against Sally's for the first time. 'My husband has always wanted to be a father. Evidently the only thing stopping him was me.'

'Tild –'

'No,' she says, putting up her hand to stop him. He is silent, as she wants him to be. 'It's true. I mean it. Congratulations, Sally.'

Shamelessly, Sally locks eyes with Matilda when she speaks. She has come here to make her claim, to secure her future with Grayson. She is not returning to school. She cannot. But Grayson will keep her through her pregnancy, she knows it. Matilda, in her stoicism, is almost giving him permission to do so. 'Thank you, Matilda,' she says, and the words are sincere. She means to be kind to the woman. After all, she has committed to the hand she now holds for life. She does not want unpleasantness.

'Right. Of course,' Matilda continues. 'Now, we have a game to play, haven't we Monty dear? That is what you want, isn't it?'

'Always,' Monty replies, apparently not in the least bit discomfited. 'If there was ever a generation who ought to do nothing but play games, it's yours. You've seen enough serious-ness to last a hundred lifetimes.'

'Do you not imagine it a serious thing,' Jack puts in, his lips small, his eyes narrowed, 'to watch a marriage be broken?'

'Oh, I do, I do,' Monty answers. 'But there is nothing so broken within a game, Jack Turner, that it cannot be mended once the game is over. That is the beauty of games. They are for the playing, not for the living.'

Jack looks to Henry, apoplectic, his jaw tense as strung

cable. He is seeking permission, Henry realises, to challenge Monty, to argue his point, to cause a fight. Surely he
has kept his cool long enough. But Henry shakes his head.
No. Because, he thinks he understands now what Montague
is doing. He is trying to heal them. He's going about it in an
odd fashion, certainly; he's getting a little too much enjoy-
ment out of it. Doesn't he look, in fact, like a man reclining
post-coitally, spent, that subtle grin always flitting about his
lips, that lethargic lift of his wrist as he brings his glass to his
mouth and opens his throat to the liquid? His aim, though,
is not to injure them, but to keep them. Or some of them, at
least. Henry is sure of it. He'd seen the hurt Monty was made
of that night in the garden, when he'd swung back and forth
like a child in his swing and told Henry of his decades-old
heartbreak. All he wants is not to be left alone. And that is not
a wicked want. That is as natural as falling in love, or fearing
the dark, or curling your back against the cold cut of the wind.
That is as understandable as one man finding comfort with
another.

'Deal another hand,' Henry says.

'Really?' It's Jack. He hasn't yet grasped the purpose of the
game.

'Really.'

Henry nods at Monty. And Monty, smiling, nods back.
'That's my boy,' he says, then he squares the pack and readies
himself to begin again.

They play until the midnight moon sprays silver beams across
the floors, until that same moon dips down the clock towards
three, until they are drunk and sober and drunk again, until
they cannot tell any longer whether their tears consist of sorrow
or amusement or some unnameable mixture of the two. They
bump and bruise each other with ugly words. They punish

each other with flushes and full houses. They talk their way back towards true, honest friendship.

'Ooh, Jaa-ack,' Monty sings. 'Your turn to spit a truth.'

Jack sits back in his chair and crosses his arms. He grins. 'I'm always game, Monty.'

'Indeed. But what to ask? What to ask? ... All right, I know ... What's the cruellest thing you've ever done?'

'The cruellest ...' Jack frowns as he thinks on the question. 'The cruellest ...'

'You're thinking a long time for a man with no memory,' Matilda slurs.

'A man with no memory ought to think longer than a man still in possession of one, don't you think?' Jack answers.

Matilda laughs, slow and vicious. The drink has drowned all her good intent. She will not manage this gracefully now. 'Well, I don't know. What exactly is it you're thinking on, if there's nothing *there*?' She taps at her temple.

'An answer to the question.'

'Ha! This isn't a game of fiction, *Jack*. It's a game of truth. Do you remember what that means?'

'Do you?'

She stands and saunters around the table, staggering gently now and then, as though she is aboard a ship and must constantly re-seek her balance. Her left index finger traces a route along the chair backs: a circular trail which will return her only to herself. She's going to say it. Why shouldn't she? Henry needs to know. They all need to know. She won't be the villain in all this. Jack Turner is a criminal, for God's sake.

'Tilda,' Henry says quietly. 'Why don't you sit down?'

'But,' she replies, still staggering around and around the table, 'aren't you interested to know why the police were so willing to *lock*,' – she stabs a finger at Jack – '*him*,' – another stab – '*up*?'

'I know why.'

'No, you see, you don't.'

Henry pushes his palms over his face and speaks into his own hot skin. It is sticky in here. He wants to step outside. 'Then I don't need to know.'

'Yes,' Jack says, and all eyes drop on him. He is a lone prey animal suddenly, and they are a tight, bristling pack. 'Yes, since she mentions it, I think you probably do.'

And so he recounts it all – mostly – one woman, one name, one lie at a time. He does not hide his cowardly night-time flits. He does not deny the money, the trust, the hopes he stole and kept for himself. He does not pretend that he was sorry, at the time, for breaking all those hearts. What he neglects to say, though, is that there were men too. That admission would lessen Henry, and he will not have Henry lessened. Never that. The man has lost all Jack will let him lose.

Uninterrupted, Jack talks and talks and talks, laying out all the falsehoods of his life so that Henry can make a map from them and navigate his way to veracity. He talks until his voice dries up and rasps. He talks until he thinks he hears, outside the window, the twinkling fall of birdsong – though he might, he supposes, be wishing for the sound. He needs this night to be finished with. He needs to know whether Henry will still look at him tomorrow the way he is looking at him now. He does not shift his gaze from the other man's to notice that Monty is nodding and grinning his way appreciatively through every part of his story; or that Sally, exhausted presently by the prospect of her pregnancy, is battling not to soften into sleep; or that Matilda is slumped again in her chair, made empty, empty as the loneliest bed, by the events of the previous months; or that Grayson is dragging at one cigarette after another, suffocating the room with skulking tendrils of smoke.

Grayson is suffocating himself, too. That is his intention. He had arrived at Monty's front door struggling for breath. Now, at least, he has a reasonable excuse for the affliction. He cannot admit that it was the thought of telling Matilda about Sally which had stolen the air from his lungs.

And that has gone as well as can be expected, hasn't it? Though he hasn't actually told Matilda anything: not about his plans or his hopes or his regrets. He has been a coward. And he will continue to be, he supposes. After all, what he wants to happen, what he hopes will happen, is the most cowardly possible outcome.

'Well,' Monty sighs, tapping the gathered deck against the table top now that Jack's tale has trundled its way into silence. 'Will we risk another hand after that?'

Gray glances at his watch. 'It's quarter to four,' he points out, though he's not sure why. He has no intention of moving. He does not know where he might go. He knows only this: he wants them to raise the baby together. All of them. The three of them. He has just fully realised it.

'We should go,' Henry says.

'Where?' Gray asks.

Henry considers Jack a moment, then the baby. 'I'm not exactly sure yet,' he says, though he is, isn't he? Really, he was sure of it in that paused pulse of time when Jack stepped out of Pentonville prison, grinning like a man leaving a party. What comes next, though, is his and Jack's secret, and he wants to keep it that way for a while.

'Did you ever have a plan, Henry?' Grayson asks. 'I mean … a big life-plan. Did you decide what you wanted years ago?'

'No,' Henry answers. 'Of course not. How could I have ever planned this?'

'But before this. Before Ruby died.'

Henry shakes his head. 'Not really.' He ought to say, *not after the war*, but he does not. Grayson must understand. He lived it, too.

'Best way,' Monty puts in.

'Oh, I don't know,' Sally begins. Now that they are all drunk enough, she is willing to offer her voice. It has not yet been trampled over. 'A plan not working out doesn't mean the plan wasn't valid. Making the plan is still what brings you to a certain outcome, a certain place.'

'Wise words from a woman who's carrying an accidental child,' Matilda swipes.

'Isn't she right, though?' Monty asks. 'Isn't she absolutely spot on? It's the planning that gets us to wherever we end up, whether we intended it or not. Bravo, young one!'

'And what did you intend, Monty dear?' Matilda asks.

'I intended to enjoy myself.'

'How is that going?' Gray laughs.

'Splendidly,' Monty answers, though the response is less than convincing. It is late, and he is tired, and it is causing him to grow transparent. Even his eyes, right down to the pupils, are greyed by fear: of growing old, of being alone. They see it, now that the alcohol has stripped them all free of themselves. 'At my age, people are expected to expect only comfort,' he says. 'But I decided to expect more, and I've done a bloody good job of getting it, if you ask an old sod like me.'

'You've never done anything the *right* way, have you Monty?' Grayson says.

'I've never done anything other people's way.' Monty points at Gray as he speaks, his finger and his head ticking to emphasise the gravity of his perspective. 'But I did things the right way for me.'

'That's all any of us can do,' Jack concludes. Henry can tell by the lilt in his voice that he is mocking them. He wants now to be free of them just as much as Henry does. They need to be alone together, so that they can offer up the new promises they will have to consider and accept or discard.

'We really do need to go,' he says.

From her place at the table, Matilda speaks. 'Why the rush?' she murmurs. 'You're never coming back.' She does not lift her head to catch anyone's gaze, but stares out through the window to her left, at the lightening of the sky. Grayson follows her look. There is a frill of grey at the night's edge, revealing itself like a stocking top. It is an exciting thing, this new day. It is flirtatious. It might lead anywhere at all.

'No,' Henry says. 'You're right. We're not.' He does not look to Jack as he speaks, but he feels Jack watching him.

'But where will you go?' Monty enquires. 'You have to tell us. You simply must.' Monty, though, is struggling to concentrate on Henry. He can't keep his eyes off Sally, who may or may not be squirming slightly under the weight of his attentions. She's a hard one to read, this Sally. Henry shakes his head — that dogged old man! But he will not condemn him. He is trying to keep himself alive, that's all. He's just trying to stay alive.

'Somewhere new,' Henry says.

'Lovely,' Monty answers. 'That'll be nice.'

'Yes.' Grayson manages to stand and, shoving aside his chair, moves around to press his palm against Henry's. They clasp each other tight. 'I suppose it's good luck, then,' he says. 'And I mean that. I really do.'

He wants to say more, Henry can feel it, but he waits until they are drifting towards the front door, all of them, Matilda and Sally carefully avoiding each other, before he steals a second to give voice to his thoughts.

'I'm well out of my depth here, Twist,' he whispers, leaning close. 'What do you suggest? I've been thinking about —'

Smiling, Henry holds up a hand to quiet Grayson. 'A better soul than me told me once that men drive themselves insane with thinking; that it's better to just do and be and hope for the best.'

'And that's what you're doing,' Gray concludes.

'That's what I'm doing.'

'But ... how? How do you decide what's —'

'With your gut, of course,' Henry says, reiterating Jack's words exactly. 'With your gut.'

They stand in a little pack on the doorstep as Henry and Jack step out into the rupturing night, Libby bundled between them. An ethereal scent, like that which rolls over chill water, is suspended on the air. Their breath paints vapour peonies before them. At this hour, the city is curled in on itself like a sleeping cat. They are held within that briefest crotchet beat of rest, when the partygoers have just retired and the workers are on the brink of rising and the only people awake in London are the troubled, the homeless, the misfits. He and Jack, Henry supposes, are all three now.

They stare straight ahead as they walk, so that the people behind them cannot discern the movements of their mouths, read their lips. Their words are murmurations.

'So, it's Wales, then,' Jack says.

'It's Wales,' Henry confirms.

'Why?'

Henry narrows his eyes, the way he does when he's planning his next words. Still, Jack thinks; still he cannot just speak freely. Perhaps he never will. 'Because we've both got lives to leave behind,' he says finally.

'But, you love this city, Henry. Are you sure?'

At their backs, Monty descends his front steps and shuffles a little way after them. 'Good luck!' he calls. 'Good luck, you handsome buggers!'

Already some strides away, the two men turn, to wave their thanks, to smile their most assured goodbyes, and then they withdraw into the withering darkness and are lost to those other people, those old friends.

'Henry?' Jack says again. 'Are you sure?'

'Not at all.'

Jack laughs, and Henry, noticing again how easily it loosens his face, hopes silently that he will never stop laughing; that he will never cause him to stop. 'Me neither,' Jack says. 'Let's do it.'

On the doorstep, the depleted party deflates a little. Monty sighs, loud and unsubtle as a disappointed child. He should have liked to have kept Jack. But the night is over now, and the boy is lost, and really, there is nothing left to do but fold into sleep. In coming together, though, they have denied themselves their usual sleeping arrangements. Grayson cannot go home with Matilda. Sally cannot be expected to slink back to her flat unaccompanied. Grayson will have, finally, to work up the courage to ask the question he's been orbiting since they arrived. He breathes deep, counting himself into it.

'Mont —' he begins.

Monty's head snaps up, sensing some new to-do. 'Always,' he says. And that's the perfect answer, isn't it, Gray thinks. Always. Always, Monty is ready to distract himself from the dimming of his own life with the blaze of someone else's. Always, Monty will find a way to cling to this, the whirling pain and joy and rush of existence.

'Is there a chance we could stay?'

'Of course! Why not?'

'But —'

'But, all of you? I believe I've extended that offer to one new family already. It's equally open to you and your dears, if you want it. If *they* want it.' Monty nods at Matilda, then at Sally. He is brightening again, standing straighter. He likes the idea. He is enjoying, no doubt, how neatly the two women have been trapped in a decision which must be reached mutually.

Grayson watches as they risk one swift look at each other. Matilda is crying soundless tears, though he is not sure when this started. Sally colours, but holds the look just long enough for them each to lower their head, almost imperceptibly. They are agreeing. They must be. What can they do but say yes? Wrapping herself up in the hurt his betrayal has caused would mean only one thing for Matilda, and being alone, that awful reality, that is the realisation of her most primitive fear. Matilda cannot survive alone. And neither, now, can Sally. To raise a child without a father would prove impossible for so proud a woman. Soon, she will have to give up her teaching job, and how would she survive without it? And then there's the shame, of course; the lifetime of shame. No, there's nothing for it but to stay with him. Grayson is overly aware that he has placed them in an impossible situation. He is aware and he is sorry, but he is not about to offer them a way out. Not if he can keep both of them. Not if he can keep all three of them.

Monty turns back into the house, pausing in the hallway to consider the three people still standing in his doorway.

'So, then,' he says, grinning. 'That's that. And just look at the three of you. You really are a sight, you know.'

As he speaks, he winks at Sally, and Grayson understands then why they have been invited to stay. Of course, it is because of Sally: only Sally. She is young and beautiful and fresh enough to keep Monty entertained. She is his new game. She is going to get eaten up by him. And really, Gray should warn her about that; he should remove her from the situation; he should tell Monty that whilst they appreciate his offer, they ought to try to find some other home together first.

'One more drink, then?' Monty asks and Sally, agreeing, steps after him along the hallway. Even here, even now, Grayson is rapt: that feline way she has of walking; the long, pale delicacy of her limbs. His child will stretch and rip and deform that body. He will ruin the girl, inside and out. And he needs to tell her how sorry he is, truly, before it begins. He starts after her, but as he does, so Matilda steps forward to fill the new space at his side. He tenses slightly. He does not know how long she will stay calm like this, but he's sure it cannot last forever. Nothing ever does, with Matilda. Then again, didn't he fall in love with a woman who was unpredictable? Didn't he commit to that constant worry? He supposes he did. He supposes he had been excited by it once.

'I am sorry, you know.'

Matilda, sobering now, smiles sadly. 'I do know.'

Grayson nods and waits, unreasonably or not, for Tilda to return his apology. Because, yes, he deserves that much. He does. He did not destroy their marriage on his own. She is just as culpable, with her ... But before he can complete the thought, there is a movement at his side – a little fluttering, which puts him in mind of a butterfly, its wings folding on and around the air, its tiny form propelling itself bravely towards the sky. And it is Matilda, saying sorry the only way she knows how. It is Matilda, tangling her fingers into his and holding his hand.

AN OVERDUE VISIT

If he narrows his eyes just far enough and keeps his head high, it is possible to see in front of him only trees – a fine, unnaturally straight line of them, pulled along the boundary of the place like one long strand of a cobweb. Beyond that green periphery, there is, he knows, a street, carrying motorcars toward and away from countless unknown destinations: he can hear the low grind of their wheels turning, their exhaust pipes rattling. And beyond that street sits London – a hotchpotch of houses and pubs, department stores and courts of law, churches and hospitals and prisons so full of people that he cannot stand to think of it. Everyone important is in London. So he's heard it said, anyway. And he supposes that must be true, because here – no longer visible perhaps, no longer corporeal, no longer able to stop his tears, but here all the same – is Ruby. She is beneath the ground at his feet. She is still a part of her adopted city, still as close to him as she can manage to be, still wearing his name like a crown. She is still Ruby Elizabeth Twist, wife and mother, though her husband cannot extend his fingers to touch her and her daughter never will.

He indulges, now and then, in daydreams where they grow older together, the three of them. He imagines Libby as she will be: round-eyed and round-bellied as she sways from foot to foot, discovering the freedom of walking; or dancing about to show off the new ribbon looped around the base of her slow-growing ponytail; or, later, rushing in from the garden to open her slimming hand and present him with a ladybird or a caterpillar or some less appealing variety of insect. And there, next to her, always next to her, is Ruby, crouching down to smile into her daughter's face, or lifting the little girl to her hip to allow her a better view of a cat tiptoeing along a wall or a rainbow cupping a grey span of the world.

He'd seen her like that with a child once. They'd been sitting on the steps in Trafalgar Square, the National Gallery at their backs, watching a warm summer moon rise. The little boy had appeared from nowhere, barrelling frantically amongst the remaining light crowds. He was perhaps four and ran on a forward tilt, his head working faster than his feet as he cried out for his Mummy. Before Henry could even think of what to do for him, Ruby was squatting before him and gathering him together, as naturally as though he was simply coins spilled from a purse, in need of collecting up again.

'Come on, little man,' she said. 'Come on, bachgen. You're not hurt.' But even as she spoke the words, she was checking him over, searching for cuts and bruises. She was fussing. She was mothering.

Afterwards, they walked the child about the square, his left hand held in Ruby's, his right hand in Henry's, until his mother discovered them and bombarded them with thank-yous, her blue eyes drowning in what Henry imagined to be equal measures of fear and gratitude ... But, were they blue, those eyes? He's not entirely sure. He recalls that the night had been muggy, and that the air had been shot through with the vinegary tang of jellied eels a nearby hawker was selling, and that he'd sniffed at the dip of Ruby's collarbone, at that postage stamp of skin on which she always dabbed her perfume, searching the more pleasing scent of vanilla, and that that had made her laugh and clutch the back of his head and call him her 'sniffer dog'. Whether that woman's eyes were blue or not, though – he really would not be willing to wager a penny on it now. And if he cannot accurately remember that simple detail, then there must be a thousand other things he is misremembering.

The idea that his memories of Ruby might be flawed, even on the most microscopic level, floods through him like a cold current of water. He might be fooling himself, about the way she looked at him, or the timbre of her voice, or the texture of her hair, or how happy he made her, or how much she loved him … But no, never that. There is no doubt about that. Ruby had loved him. Ruby had loved him so honestly, so fully, that he could have crushed her with a single word. He'd known that, and he'd revelled in it.

'Ruby,' he whispers now. Still, he does not look down at her headstone, but glances around the cemetery, checking that no one can hear him. Only one other mourner is visible, perhaps ten rows away, her head bowed over her clasped hands, her hat obscuring her face. She is not listening to him.

He clears his throat and continues. 'I'm sorry I haven't been before, I just … I couldn't, you know, and … I –' He stops, scrubs his hand through his hair. He speaks to his knees. 'Ah, woman, how can it be that I can't have you?'

Ruby would laugh at such a question. She would position herself behind him and brush her hands across the wing-shaped width of his upper back – easily her favourite physical part of him – and, leaning into his neck, say something like 'I am not for the having, Henry Twist. I am for the wanting.'

Always, Ruby had made him understand that he thought in the wrong way.

The woman to Henry's right concludes her mourning and steps away between the gravestones, her feet swishing through the grass. Henry watches her until she is gone.

'There's something I have to tell you,' he begins. What he had intended to explain was how Jack had come to haunt his every moment; how, when he looked at that man, he saw his wife staring right back; how he had decided, in that fraction of a heartbeat when he first spotted Jack leaving Pentonville, to forgive Jack Turner anything. It is, he knows, the only way to love – to decide beforehand that you will allow your lover their darknesses, their absences, and wait quietly for them to return to you. That's what love is made of, staying silent while you hurt. And so how can he protest now at having to make this sacrifice for Jack? It is no sacrifice at all. It is just another duty of love to know that Jack has chewed up and spat out all those poor grieving souls, that he had planned to do the very same thing to Henry, that his life has been one long string of lies, tied one to another with broken hearts, and to forget it, as best he can. That's what he had wanted to tell Ruby, because that way, she would understand that he'd been listening all along; that he'd heard every last word she'd said to him.

But of course he has nothing now to tell the girl he buried here. There is nothing worth saying except, 'I'm taking her home, Ruby. To Ida. I'm taking our baby home.' And so he utters those sentences – he manages to keep his voice steady, just, long enough to speak them – and after that, he says nothing more. For hours, he says nothing more. There are no words big enough for the thoughts he needs to voice. There is no way to converse with his dead.

The rain starts. It falls soft as feathers and settles on Henry's shoulders, in Henry's hair, and Henry does not move. London grows rowdier for a time then quietens again as morning surrenders to afternoon, and Henry does not move. The sky thickens, like stirred paint, before thinning into evening. All over the city, women are puckering their lips to sweep on their lipstick, men are buttoning their shirts, jazz clubs are unlocking their doors and awaiting their crowds. London strips off its day clothes, ready for another frantic night, and Henry does not move. How can he? He is being separated again from his wife.

Jack appears with the fattening of the rain, pushing Libby ahead of him, a fedora tipped jauntily over one eye. He flashes Henry a smile.

'Do you like it?' he says. He means the hat: it is not his.

'Where did it come from?'

'You might say I liberated it from a life of slavery and torment,' he answers. 'You might also say I stole it, but that would be a far less attractive perspective, if you ask me.'

Henry smiles. 'I always did suspect you were a thief. In a previous life.'

'In a previous life,' Jack returns, 'this hat sat atop a very ugly head indeed. So perhaps all previous lives are to be improved upon.'

He positions Libby's pram so that it is stationary on the grass in front of them, then, sitting down next to Henry, shuffles closer until their thighs touch. Jack's leg is slighter than Henry's, and Henry wants to put his hand around the slender width of it, to feel the heat of that man's body against his skin. But he refrains. They can gamble nothing now. They are making their way out. He trusts Jack was more than careful about the hat.

'How long has she been sleeping?' he asks, to distract himself from the need that is pulling through him now, stronger than any man he ever fought beside: the need to turn to Jack and pin him to the ground with want. It is a need which quickens his breathing.

'An hour or so,' Jack answers. 'She's not moaned all day, not once.'

'Where did you take her?' Henry knows that Jack has simply been walking the city, gifting him some time alone with Ruby. He must have walked twenty miles in all these hours.

'Around and about. Just, showed her the sights, you know. Told her some stories.'

'Really? Stories?'

'Of course. She's going to be a scholar, our little girl, and I thought –'

Jack stops when he realises what he has said. Our little girl: it is a phrase Henry has never yet been able to use. He catches his nose between his forefinger and thumb and breathes through the shock of it. It is as if he's been winded, caught unawares by a kick from a standard-issue boot, perhaps, or the butt of a gun, turned around in close combat and thrust into his stomach. He is compelled to lash out, to meet force with force, as his service years taught him. This compulsion, too, he breathes away.

'I'm sorry,' Jack says. 'I'm sorry, Henry, I just ...'

'No,' Henry replies. 'It's fine. It's ... It was a shock, that's all. But, I suppose ... that's what she'll be, won't she, in Wales? Ours. Ours and Ida's.'

'Ida's?'

'She'll need a mother, Jack.'

'And what will you need?'

Henry considers this carefully. Need is such a tricky thing to him now. All he had needed as a boy was for his parents to stop screaming each other into unconsciousness every night and fall quietly towards sleep instead. All he had needed through the mess and noise of 1915 was a hot meal and to be free, for a solitary fleeting heartbeat, of the itching. He and Bingley had spoken once about what they would sacrifice for those simple pleasures. Bingley had opted for nearly all of his digits. Henry had decided on a limb, but definitely just the one. And then he'd come home and there had been only Ruby. For those few easy years he had needed only Ruby. But what of now? Perhaps he has it all, right here beside him. Perhaps all he will need as 1926 ages into summer and autumns away, is his baby, and this man, and the ghost of his wife. He braces himself to take a glance, finally, at that baldly worded head-stone. Wife and mother. Wife and mother. Why hadn't he opted for 'everything'?

He is scared, though, of the enormity of everything. He

had been everything to his parents, and he had not managed to make them happy. He had been everything to Bingley, and he had not done enough to protect the boy. He had been everything to Ruby, and he had failed, hadn't he, in his promise to keep her safe? He'd failed in the most spectacular way.

He answers Jack finally. 'Nothing more than I've got,' he says. And he means it, because here, within reach of his fingertips, is his family as it now exists. He has his everything.

They begin, Jack and Henry, two men designing a life together, on the pavement near Paddington Station. They have walked and walked some more, deciding on a place to stop and talking stupidly about what will happen in Wales. Stupidly because neither of them has ever visited, they have admitted, and now, as Jack tweaks another newspaper into its individual sheets and lays them over the ground, they are taking turns to propose some imagined truth about the place. They have it, so far, as a country far less populated than it truly is, and flatter too, with mountains only at its very middle.

'I'll bet you can see the sea from almost any part of Wales,' Jack says.

Henry nods, not knowing whether he agrees or not. 'I'd like to wake up to the sea every morning.' He crouches in the concealed doorway they have chosen, rocking Libby's pram gently and watching Jack build their bed for the night. They had had to leave even their pillows behind, being unable to carry all of their belongings and unable to pay for their conveyance. What is left of their money they will need for the train.

'Me, too,' Jack replies. 'Happen we could catch fish for our breakfast.'

'And farm meat.'

'Ah, but who would kill it?'

Henry smiles. 'Well, maybe not then.'

'Coward,' Jack teases.

'In that case, you can kill it.'

'I cannot! Perhaps we could train Lib up to do it. She can be a real little country girl.'

Henry adjusts his position to look into the pram at his still-sleeping daughter. God, the impossibility of her! Just months old, only now starting to strengthen into her developing body, and already she has endured a lifetime's difficulties. And Henry is about to ask her to start her life all over again, in a new place. How is that fair? He leans closer to breathe in the powdery smell of her. Her hair has grown fast in these last weeks and it is long enough now to curl at the ends: he threads his smallest finger through the largest shining coil and wears it like a ring. On his opposite hand, his wedding band sits loose about his knuckle. He has lost weight. But, he finds himself promising Libby, in Wales he will eat until he grows broad again. In Wales, he will always be strong enough to protect her.

Just then, as if she has felt someone watching her, Libby opens her eyes. She does not cry. She only blinks a few times, finding her focus, and recognising Henry above her, smiles for him. And yes, he thinks, it must be for him, not at him, for she has no reason to smile for herself.

'I promise,' he says.

Jack, pulling a blanket from their bag and testing the news-paper bed he has made, questions the sentiment with a warning glance. 'What are you promising her now?'

And Henry, without heeding the warning, answers, 'Everything.'

Jack sighs and stands again, then, putting his hands to his hips and scanning his surroundings, declares that they need something thicker than the newspaper to keep the cold off their arses.

Henry laughs. 'Will you be so indecisive when we build our cottage?'

What had begun as a vague daydream has become, for

Henry, a near-certainty. He cannot shake the image now of he and Jack lugging stones towards some grassy scrap of land, measuring out their boundaries, stopping when their hands are blistered to sit in the shade of a wall they have raised from the ground and drink beers, sweat darkening their hair and shirts. This will be his reality. He has decided to make it so.

'What?' Jack asks.

'When we build our cottage.'

'We're going to build a cottage?'

'Of course. What else would we live in?'

'Well ...' Jack abandons his task and moves to stand behind Henry, where he too can look down at Libby. He speaks in a whisper. 'I wasn't sure if you'd be willing to brave it, you know – living under the same roof. I mean, we might even be safer doing that here still. There are certain circles to move in, aren't there ...?'

'I just don't want to be here any more.'

Jack nods. 'All right,' he says. And, with a vigilant check down the street, he puts his palms to the width of Henry's back and runs them slowly, impiously, across the plane of his shoulders and towards his neck, which he bends to kiss. 'All right,' he murmurs. 'Wales it is.'

And, 'Yes,' Henry answers. 'Yes.' Though he can't say for sure what it is he is agreeing to.

At some biting hour of the night that follows, Henry wakes to find himself face to face with Jack. For a few sweet moments, he believes them in bed together on Bayswater Road and he watches the other man's nostrils pulsating: the only evidence of the slow dance that is his breathing, the only evidence that he is alive. It is when he reaches to pull the blankets over his shoulders that he remembers where he is, and why. They are curled around Libby like the shell of a clam, Henry and Jack, their meeting foreheads the hinge joint of that protective casing. And isn't this how it will be from now on?

Henry has always been wary of thoughts that come so easily. He's long known how dangerous they can be.

But his ideas about a future in Wales are just as easy, just as dangerous. He is making untenable assumptions. He is imagining, just as he did during the strike, that there is something better ahead of them. What a senseless man he has become. Then again, Henry thinks as he sags back towards sleep, isn't that what love means – becoming hopeful and senseless and ridiculous all at once? How else could you pour all your life into another human being? And that's what he'll do in the morning, when they board their train – he'll pour all of his life into Jack's, and they will sit in the empty must of a carriage occupied only by yesterday's scents at that hour and wait for the ticket man to ask them where it is they are travelling to. They'll watch occasional strangers parading along the platforms, coats hung over their arms, hats removed in the developing warmth of the morning, and, wanting to make Henry laugh, Jack will invent lives for them so outlandish that they could never be true. They'll listen to the mechanical workings of Paddington: the clicking and cranking, the hissing and whistling. They'll sniff all the flavour from their steaming coffees. And, when they tire of waiting for the train to lumber out of the station, they'll snap open second-hand newspapers and attempt to distract themselves with other people's words.

Henry is sure of all this. He has to be. And when, one long exhalation later, sleep finally claims him again, it does not even stall the thought, which continues unimpeded, the same way tomorrow's early train out of Paddington will along its track. And on it will be Henry and Jack, rolling away, rolling away fast, and it will all be behind them, all of this. Behind them, turning to smoke.

ELIZABETH

As she strolls up the path towards the cottage, Elizabeth Foster peels off her thin white cardigan and hangs it over her shoulder from one erect finger. Even here, where there is always a cool wind, the air is thick, weighted-down. The grass fails to tremble. Heat gathers itself up into long planks and beats down against the earth, insistent as a pulse. It is July. It is 1971. Elizabeth moves at a crawl.

A few steps later, she stops and turns to look over the village. Her village, as it once was; and continues to be, she supposes, though she has not lived here in the last twenty years. Today, it is pretty. House windows spark sunlight back up into the mountains. The slate roofs gleam as though polished. Elizabeth also knows it as it might be, ragged with clinging to the valley floor when the weather storms through, throwing trees about, dislodging chimney bricks, running the streets into rivers. But this does not prevent her from loving it. She knows this place. She became Elizabeth here.

Below her, a red mini rattles out from between the houses and into open space, then turns towards town. Though it is moving away, the puttering of its engine spoils Elizabeth's mood a little and she resumes her walk, the steep incline creating a balled-up pressure in her calves which is both painful and pleasant. She doesn't get much exercise these days. There is satisfaction in that ache.

In front of her there appears to be nothing but grassland, but Elizabeth knows that when she reaches the next turn in the path the cottage will become visible. Two-storeyed but low to the ground, its walls are the white of freshly washed sheets: it sits in the rough landscape like a fallen cloud. A washing line, nearly always full of men's clothes, runs parallel to it, and as Elizabeth follows the curving stone track she sees that today six or seven pale-coloured shirts are pegged out, hanging still and dripping dry. She thinks she can hear each individual drop tapping the ground, but it might just be the insects clicking. There are so many infinitesimal noises up here on the mountain. Sometimes, when she visits, Elizabeth stands out in the garden and just listens, believing she can hear the squelchy throbbing of her own heart. She does it to silence the worry which swamps her whenever she calls on her father.

She hoists her handbag further up onto her shoulder. Inside, she has Emma's university photos: the celebrations of the end of her first year. Elizabeth had asked her father to be there when Emma got home for the holidays, but as usual, he had refused. He didn't want to spoil anything, he said; he was too old for that sort of thing. Elizabeth knows what his refusal was really about. Like so much else in his life, it was made by fear.

She pauses again, the cottage in full view, and pulls at the front of her blouse to encourage some air inside. There is a line of stickiness between her breasts she wants to wipe away, but will not, in case one of them is watching from the window.

The back door swings open, the dark wood moving away from the walls like a tiny wing, and Jack steps out, another load of washing cradled under his arm: trouser legs dangle over the sides of the basket. Still spry in his seventies, he whistles as he descends a couple of steps, crosses a strip of lawn, and sets the basket down beside the line's side pole. It is as he lifts the first pair of trousers and flaps the water from them that he sees Elizabeth.

'Libby,' he says, his face spreading out into that happiness only children ever summon in their parents: that silly, wide-open sort of delight.

Elizabeth wonders if she smiles that way at her daughter; if it embarrasses Emma. It used to embarrass her when she was a teenager. Her own mother, opening the front door as she arrived home and grinning that way. Her own mother, walking past whilst she was lingering at the bus stop with friends and grinning that way. 'Mam,' she used to breathe, before bundling her backwards into the hallway or waving her away.

Despite having brought up her own daughter in England, Elizabeth instilled that sound in Emma before there was even the slightest chance of her repeating it. *Mam*. She would not answer to the softness of 'mum'.

Elizabeth smiles and pushes herself to resume her walk. Already, her mind is on a long glass of lemonade and the bench which waits in shadow on the other side of the cottage. She and Jack often sit there during her visits, watching the stirrings of the village below and passing fragments of their lives back and forth. Sometimes, with a lot of careful work, she unearths some hint of the man he was in London: a unique scent at a party he once attended, or a name to which Elizabeth can attach no face. And sometimes, in those moments, she sees Jack as he must have been: tall and slim and handsome as anything with his dark, curling hair and his deep, brown-marble eyes. Only now has his hair started to splinter into grey.

He laughs at her when she speaks of the Jack she imagines, strutting about the city with an unbreakable smile and some scheme always in the working. She does not know how accurate this image is; how exactly she envisages the way he would shove his hands into his pockets as he walked, or the easy loping movement of his body before the years got hold of it. Jack will not tell her. There are a thousand things Jack will not tell her.

'Here,' he says as she reaches him, passing her a pair of trousers to peg. 'Help an old man out.'

'Haven't seen any old men around here,' Elizabeth answers, lifting her hands to the task.

'Ah, always the charmer,' Jack smiles. 'You must get that from your mother.'

'Which one?'

She says it too quickly; she knows she does. She does not want to sound flippant. Jack pings a sideways glance at her, fast as a freed spring, then smiles into the clothes. He understands this battle: they have been play-fighting it for thirty years.

'That's hers, too,' Jack says. 'That tenacity. You're a grown woman, Lib. Stop being so nosey.'

'Never,' she replies, smiling back.

What Jack sees when he looks at her, Elizabeth cannot suppose. An elegant woman at five foot seven, she is, she knows, still attractive at forty-five. Men still watch her in the street. Her hair, which curls at the ends and is lighter now, in the summer, moves between a sandy colour and a more even brown. But her eyes are dark, almost as dark as Jack's, and she has concluded – though she has tried to avoid such conclusions her entire life – that she resembles him a lot, not least in complexion. Odd, that she should look like this man. Her thoughts make her overly aware of her appearance, and she pushes out her bottom lip to blow her flick of fringe away from her forehead. Emma had talked her into chopping into her hair so that it rose up around her face this way, and she likes it now. She likes the feel of it, just brushing her shoulders. It makes her feel younger.

'Em will be down next week,' she says, to change the subject. She cannot tackle it again until she has had that lemonade. She is too hot.

'She shouldn't waste her time with old sods like us,' Jack murmurs. Elizabeth knows he says it only because he feels he must. He doesn't want anything for Emma but parties and dancing and fun. He hardly even wants her to study.

'She wants to spend time with you old sods,' Elizabeth tells him. 'She can't forever be flitting around with her friends, anyway. They've got families to visit, too.'

'Is there a man?'

'Not that I know of. I don't ask, though.'

Jack nods seriously. They have finished pegging the clothes now and they wander around the side of the cottage to stand facing the lazy-bodied sun. It bleeds white hot across the sky. In the distance, a flock of unidentifiable birds fold into each other and then disperse, as tiny and weightless as pollen on the wind.

'Jack,' Elizabeth whines. Funny, how being home strips the last forty years and calls back that particular whine: the rising tone toddlers use for 'why'.

'Yes, love.'

'Are you ever going to talk about it?'

'No,' Jack answers. 'I made a promise.'

Elizabeth leans back against the cottage wall and closes her eyes. There is a film of moisture on her eyelids. Soon, she will go inside and splash her face.

'Have you kept every promise you've ever made?'

'No,' Jack says. 'But I'm keeping this one.'

'Are you ready to go in?'

'Absolutely not. Look at this. You've got to appreciate this, Lib.' She laughs as he pleats down onto the ground and stretches his legs out in front of him, shaking his feet left and right like a pair of windscreen wipers. 'I spend far too many days looking down there into cloud soup.'

'Maybe you just shouldn't look,' Elizabeth replies, settling next to him, the stone path hard against her backside, 'on bad days.'

'Actually, I think maybe you grow out of good days and bad days when you get to my age.'

Elizabeth does not want to tackle the subject of ageing, not now, not with the sun on her face and a thirst in her throat, so she lifts a hand and taps at the window above her right shoulder.

'I'm here,' she calls.

'And we're always glad of it,' Jack adds quietly. But Elizabeth's greeting is not answered and they do not rise to go inside. Not yet. There is plenty of day left for that.

———

In the kitchen, Elizabeth sits at the dining table and stares at the cupboard door of the Welsh dresser, which has been left ajar to reveal a thin slice of darkness. Her eyes are still adjusting to the indoors light, and she squints at it, trying to distinguish exactly how wide it is. It is an innocent enough action – she wants to see clearly again – but she is also aware, in some secret part of her mind, that hidden inside are hundreds of photographs, slipped messily into various albums. Elizabeth knows they are there, not because she has viewed the photographs lately – or at all, in fact – but because she holds a memory, perhaps thirty-five years old now, of opening that cupboard door and discovering them, leather bound or cloth cased, and all coated with a layer of furry dust; of being told, quite definitely, that they were not for her eyes; of having to pull her hand quickly away from the slam of wood against wood. Never, before or after, had she been so frightened by her father. The set of his face that day made her imagine them ugly things, those photographs; disturbing things.

To her right, not fully in her sightline, Jack is busying himself with pouring that tall lemonade she'd been craving. One for her, one for him. No third glass.

'I've got some photos of Em for you,' she says. She is distracted, not really thinking through the words. As she speaks, she pushes one hand into the handbag which hangs off the back of her chair and retrieves them. 'Perhaps you've got an album to slot them into somewhere?'

'Perhaps,' Jack answers. 'Or I could hang them. I'll find a couple of frames ... So, how's work?'

He bangs two glasses down on the table then, with a flick of his wrist, spins one dining chair around and straddles it, the way a twenty-year-old man would. As he settles, he winks at Elizabeth. Libby, as she has always been to him. When she had gone through that teenage stage of wanting to change every last thing about herself, Jack alone had refused to revert to her full given name. 'You were Lib the day I met you,' he'd said, 'and you'll still be Lib the day I die.'

'Fine,' she answers. 'Good. Nothing new.'

'There's always something new. Every single day.'

'Is that so?' she smiles. 'We're feeling philosophical today, are we?'

'Am I ever anything but? I am a wise man, Libby Twist,' – he never has used her married name – 'and you'd do well to remember it.'

'Maybe I would remember it, if you behaved accordingly.'

'Maybe I'd behave accordingly, if I were a boring old man.' He pops his eyes and swigs from his glass, hiding his smirk against its rim. The rush of bubbly liquid down his throat is too fast and he starts to choke, bending forward over the table.

'That'll teach you,' Elizabeth laughs, but her heart isn't truly in this teasing – their own private ritual – today. She's started something, in mentioning the photo album, which she does not feel able to stop. Whilst Jack recovers from his bout of coughing, she stands and moves towards the cupboard. There, she drops onto her heels and catches the knob between thumb and forefinger. The albums, she finds, are neatly stacked: not the chaotic towers she had been recalling. She lifts one from the top of the first pile and carries it back to the dining table.

'Don't, Lib, please.'

'Why not?' she shoots back, but Jack cannot answer this one and he stumbles over his words.

'It's not … Because … I just … Ah, come on. Looking in there is just going to make you maudlin.'

'I solemnly swear not to become maudlin,' Elizabeth recites, one hand pressing her oath to the air, the other already opening the covers. The very first photograph breaks her vow.

In it, her mother – her first mother – is sitting on the edge of a small pier, her legs dangling over sharp-peaked water. It must be cold, for she is overwhelmed by woollen layers: her hands, which grip the pier's edge, are lost to the sleeves of a dark, calf-length coat; her chin juts over the doubling of a thick scarf as she peers down into the spiking sea; and her legs kick out – the right forwards, the left back as this particular image is snapped – so that her skirt folds up a little and reveals her ankles to the blackening sky. Her feet, Elizabeth notices with a smile, are bare. Though the puff of breath rising from her mouth betrays the bitter temperatures, she looks as though she is about to jump in. Perhaps she did. Elizabeth scans the photograph for her shoes and finds them discarded in the foreground, one tossed onto its side, the other sitting the right way up. She wonders if she put them back on before she left, or whether she wandered along the seafront like that, her arm hooked into her husband's, her feet collecting millions of sand grains onto their soles.

The stories she's amassed about Ruby over the years convince her of the latter.

She lifts her head to find Jack staring at her, his hands spread flat halfway across the table, his lips making a sad smile. He exhales, loud and acquiescent. Something is different today – she'd felt it even before she got here. Something has changed, or is about to change. She waits.

'All right,' he says. 'I give up.' Henry has never actually forbidden them from talking about Ruby, but they know, they've always known, that he is incapable of sharing that particular past with them. 'She's magnificent, isn't she?'

Shouldn't you say beautiful? Elizabeth wants to ask. Isn't

that how women want to be described? But Jack is right. Just
sitting there, at the water's edge, her face in profile, her legs
moving forever with the sea, Ruby Twist is magnificent. Elizabeth nods her head. She wouldn't even know how to spark
like that.

She flicks to the next page. Here she finds images of Ruby
and Henry: sitting outside a café, leaning into each other as
a waiter or a diner captures the way in which her confidence
only complements his shyness; wound around each other at
some dance, Ruby showing him off by looking at him and only
him when the rest of the room surely couldn't have resisted
the pale drape of her dress over her body. They are magnet-
ised, these two. They cannot function, it seems, unless they
are in physical contact. They are the most intense of lovers.
Elizabeth had known, of course, that Henry and Ruby were
married, but she couldn't have known how deeply they had
been embedded in one another. Naturally, there is no sign of
Jack in the photographs. Or her mother. And perhaps that's
partly why she's never been allowed to view them. It under-
mines all their memories, those four people who have each
claimed her as their own, to be reminded that only two of
them were there to begin with.

She is aware, of course – though only in the blurriest
possible way – of how her family came to be what it is. What
she has always wanted, though, is to be able to feel it; to be
overwhelmed by the sounds and the smells and the sights of it;
to be able, though it might seem as maudlin as Jack suggests, to
mourn what everyone else mourns without having to invent
the details.

There is no discovery now which can satisfy Elizabeth.
The glamorous dresses Ruby wears; the way her nose crinkles
when she smiles; the way she glares sometimes into the camera,
serious as a schoolmistress – none of it is enough. Elizabeth's
questions have gone too long unanswered. Still, she is thrilled
by the images. She turns another page. Jack, she's sure, will

soon slip up and start telling her the stories behind each one.

'Oh,' she says. 'I'm in this one!'

'Really?' Jack asks.

Elizabeth points out the small but visible protrusion, the way Ruby is glancing down at her stomach and the unknowable thing held within. At her.

'There.'

It is a shock, this evidence of her existence. The photographs seem so long ago, the clothes and the settings and the poses so strange to her, that Elizabeth can barely reconcile the people who fill them with her own life. How can that woman, with her curled brown hair and her smile and her love, have created her, Mrs Elizabeth Foster, Professor Elizabeth Foster, who walks from her front door to campus every morning to begin lecturing on the books which saturate her brain; who shares hours-long phone calls with her own, lovely, grown-up daughter; who needs her husband so painfully that his presence in a room still soothes and excites her as completely as it did when they met twenty-six years ago; who, whenever she is out of the country, misses the particular kind of rain that falls over her fathers' cottage; who has known more parents than she's ever been capable of coping with? Surely she could only have been a disappointment to the woman in these photographs.

She turns another page. They are sitting in a garden now, Henry and Ruby and another, older couple. Elizabeth pins them with an index finger.

'Who are these two?'

Jack spins the album around to face him. 'That is Grayson Steck,' he says, pointing needlessly at the man grinning into the camera. 'He was a friend.'

'Of Henry's?'

'And Ruby's. That's his wife, Matilda.'

'Did you ever see them, after you left London?'

Jack shakes his head.

'Why not?'

'She was dreadfully in love with Henry,' Jack answers. 'It was better for her to stay away from him.'

'Was there anybody in London not in love with Henry?' Elizabeth says, pulling the album back towards her.

Jack laughs. 'Not many people.'

'But he chose you.'

'I suppose so.'

Elizabeth huffs. Always this vagueness with Jack. And maybe it's because of the heat, or because she is impatient for Emma's visit home, or because she's been at the cottage for nearly an hour already and Henry still has not opened his study door, but she does not think she can stand it one second longer. She glances through the kitchen window at a rectangle of the world split equally into flat blue and bright green. It's too good to be true, that view. It annoys her further.

'Jack,' she says, propping her elbows on the table and pressing her bunched fingers to her temples until the skin whitens. 'Please.' And Jack, recognising her exasperation, decides to disclose some truth. Elizabeth can see it moving through him – the fact, kicking its way to the surface. He is about to say: 'Your mother was a showgirl', or, 'Your father was rich as a king'. He is about, perhaps, to reveal where he came from. And that is the biggest mystery, isn't it? Jack Turner did not spring into life already grown: once, that man was a child. But he doesn't say anything at all, in the end. Because at that exact moment, as if he divines that there is something happening he must put a stop to, Henry cracks open his study door and steps into the kitchen.

Instinctively, Elizabeth slams the photo album shut.

———

Her mother once told her that Henry Twist had more fear running through him than blood. The war did that to some men, she said. It pushed them in on themselves, silenced them.

Henry, though, had not always been silent. Elizabeth can remember days – and not enough of them, perhaps, but there were definitely days – when she would go up to the cottage to visit her fathers and find him as loose and easy, almost, as Jack. She knows that once, at least, she'd climbed up onto the slatted pen fence as Henry was feeding the pigs they'd kept then and that they'd pretended at throwing each other into the boot-sucking mud within. She can recall the blue-and-white striped dress she was wearing, the ankle socks, the way the wind dragged her ponytail across her eyes. She can see the smile Henry wore as they messed about at that fence, laughing at the snuffling of the hungry pigs then putting down more food so that their noise never subsided. She knows also that he used to come down off the mountain occasionally. When she was very small, a woman called Viv had written to tell him that her husband had died, and he had gone to the funeral. Elizabeth remembers her mother explaining that one of her fathers would be away for a few days; that he had to travel to London to say goodbye to a friend. She remembers that clearly, because she had never seen Henry away from the cottage and she couldn't imagine him in any other setting. He was as essential to that mountain as the sky above it and the town below as far as Elizabeth was concerned. In bed that night, she had worried that without him the whole thing would crumble; that she'd wake in the morning and open her curtains to find a great gaping space where once her fathers' mountain had stood.

And that's how she thinks of it still – her fathers' mountain – because no one else has lived on it, before or since. Henry and Jack built this cottage with their own hands. They have told her of that late summer a hundred times over, but today, Elizabeth wants to hear their words again.

'Really?' Jack asks. 'Haven't we bored you with this story enough times?'

'You haven't *bored* me with it once.'

From his place across the table, Henry smiles. 'You're a beautiful liar, you know. We bored the life out of you when you were a child.'

Elizabeth wants to stay angry at him, for only now emerging from that stuffy old study, for having wasted so much time he could otherwise have spent with her and Jack and Emma in there, for becoming the obsessive creature he presently is. But he smiles, and those soft-green eyes disappear into creases, and she can't. He is an old man now, her father. He is inching towards his end.

'How so?' she asks. She just wants them to keep talking. She wants them to do that thing they sometimes do, when they talk their way so far into their past that they forget she is there in the room. It was such a definite part of her childhood, that vanishing act they performed together. It is comforting still.

'With all our stories,' Henry answers.

'I love your stories.' And she does. She just wants more. She wants to know it all. She wants to know what came before their arrival in Wales.

'You're humouring us.'

'No,' Elizabeth protests. 'I really do love them. I'm made up of your stories.'

Jack rolls his eyes. 'You're made up of getting what you want, Miss Twist.'

She grins and settles back into her chair, knowing that soon they will begin to tell her of how the summer had been a long one, and lucky for them it was, because when September strolled in all they had were four exterior walls, an open doorway and two badly aching backs. They would work until, degree by slow pink degree, the light deserted them. Then they would lie in the grass like inverted stars, taking turns to knead their way down each other's spines. They would return to the beds – two singles, of course – Ida had secured them with a local unmarried farmer by the name of Gareth, only when they were sure the man had long retired for the night and they could attempt to silently slide the heavy wood-framed objects into a double.

Here, they would smile, and Henry would blush a little, and they would admit that the attempt was never very successful: the bed legs would thump against the floorboards, and they would spook themselves into laughter, and Gareth must surely have known their game. But Gareth was a kind-hearted fellow and he said nothing through those weeks they spent sitting to a toast and bacon breakfast with him each morning. He was as gentle in his manner as he was strong in the shoulder, and perhaps that contrast was what Ida loved about him in the end. With Henry and Jack and Libby to bend her life around, she had needed the simplicity of a man like Gareth. She married him the Christmas after the Twists arrived, and fell in love with him slowly, over so many years that she could never say for certain when the feeling had begun. It was like an ancient tree, she would say, her love for Gareth: everyone knew it was old, but no one could tell you its exact age.

Most times, when they tell her of that summer, Jack's narrative drifts towards this claim of Ida's. Perhaps, Elizabeth thinks, it's because he wishes Henry could love him so simply. And she hopes he includes that part of the story today, because she misses Ida. She misses her badly. She is still counting her absence in months. And one day, she thinks, Emma will grieve her this same way. The thought drags through her middle, like a balloon tied by its string to a newly dropped stone. Just the idea is unbearable. She attempts to talk over it.

'Start with the owl,' she says.

'We told you about the owl?' Jack replies. 'See, you have heard this too many times.'

But Elizabeth insists, and she is able to listen for long minutes then as the two men describe how the barn owl had taken up residence in a corner of their unfurnished home, and how, once they'd watched her float in for two or three nights, like a tiny snowdrift, her pale chest proud and puffed, her dark eyes round and fearful, they hadn't the heart to chase her away. Instead, when at the conclusion of their work they reclined on the grass to rest, they waited to catch sight of her, a spectral dot closing slowly in. Aged around twelve, Elizabeth had asked, precociously, how they could possibly know it was the same owl, returning each night. And Henry had informed her, patiently, that their owl had not had the normal tan and steel mottled wings of other barn owls; their owl had been pure white.

She thinks now that perhaps they had seen it as an omen, that owl, all white and unnatural – as unnatural as they were. Henry and Jack have endured their fair share of trouble since they arrived on the mountain. And that summer, that first hopeful summer, filled with the constant satisfying smart of physical labour through their muscles, and daily picnic visits from Ida and Libby, and the fresh olive and emerald promise of a new country unfurling before them, they must have feared it. They must have felt it coming. They must have been searching reassurance. The appearance of a beautiful, ghostly bird must have seemed like just that.

'Have you seen one since,' she asks now, 'a pure white one?'

Jack shakes his head.

'We still look, though,' Henry says. 'Most nights. At dusk.'

Elizabeth sits up, excessively shocked by this. 'Do you?'

'Yes,' Jack answers, laughing. 'Why not?'

'I don't know. I just ... I hadn't imagined ...'

'What?' Jack jokes. 'That we like each other?'

'That you ... stand outside watching the sky. Romantically!' She slumps back into her chair. She feels a little drunk. Because of the heat, she supposes, and the exhausting week she's just blundered through at work, and the fact that, for some reason she doesn't wish to examine, she is finally pulling some truths from her fathers.

'We've had a good life, me and Jack,' Henry confides, his words turned about on themselves by four and a half decades in Wales. 'I don't want you to ever think otherwise, Lib. Okay?'

'Okay.'

'No, really, I need you to understand.' He reaches across the table to grab her hand and, though the sensation is odd with all these years of careful father–daughter distance between them, she lets him. His skin is loose and fragile: it reminds her of that flimsy packing paper, so easily torn. She studies the fingers wrapped around hers. The width of the knuckles betrays that these hands were strong once. Now, they are growing weak: it is visible in the veins which push away from the flesh, as though their connections have gone slack; in the smattering of darker spots which map a messy route up and under his shirtsleeves; in the ease with which his wedding ring swings around and around the digit. All these years and still he hasn't removed that ring. She wonders if it bothers Jack.

'I do understand,' she says, catching Henry's eye. She nods solemnly. 'I promise I do.'

'Good,' he replies. Then, rising, he rounds the table to kiss the top of her head. 'We've had a good life, us three,' he mutters. 'It's been a good life.'

When thick, eye-widening darkness finally scales the mountain, sticky with the effort, Elizabeth decides she will stay the night. She can visit Gareth in the morning, when the walk down is safer. He would beg that of her, Gareth, the third man who has acted as her father, though she has never named him as such.

'You don't mind?'

'Of course not,' Jack answers. 'I'm glad of the company.'

Henry curled into sleep hours ago and they sit now, Elizabeth and Jack, one either side of his sleeping form, on the armchairs flanking the settee he lies across. The lamps which light the room trail shadows like bridal trains, and they whisper into them, enjoying the naughty atmosphere they are creating. All of Elizabeth's naughtiest childhood memories involve Jack. They would infuriate Henry and Ida by taking unplanned jaunts into the mountains and not returning until the bats led them home; by sneaking to the sweet shop and charming Mr Doyle into filling paper bags to bursting with toffees which they'd sit on the pavement outside to demolish, ruining their dinner; by always, somehow, managing to acquire a bloody nose or a bruised shin or a scraped knee.

'Jack ...?'

He returns her whining intonation. 'Yes ...?'

'Is there a photo of you in that album, from back then?'

'No.'

'Liar.'

'Oh, all right.' He pushes himself out of his chair and goes to retrieve the album from the kitchen table. Elizabeth rises to follow him. They bend over the table together as he flips from page to page, years cartoon-flickering by. He stops near the back of the substantial volume and slides two fingers cautiously under the top edge of a photograph of Ruby and Ida, sitting before their parents on the shore, at Pwll she supposes. It pops free of its four corner-tacks. Beneath, there is a second image: a boy just spilling over into manhood, perhaps seventeen years old, in uniform.

'Jack,' she says. 'How old were you?'

'Sixteen,' he answers. Then, with a wink, 'Though I was claiming eighteen, naturally.'

'Always misbehaving.'

He laughs. 'Always. I think we might have had that in common, your mother and I.'

'It's funny you never met her,' Elizabeth says.

'I know. I think I'd have liked her, you know. She had sass, that girl.'

'It won't be long before Emma's as old as she was.'

'Make a man feel his years, why don't you?'

Elizabeth smirks. 'Isn't that what daughters are for?'

She wanders towards the light, photo in hand, and tilts it this way and that, searching its every detail. He is beautiful, this younger Jack. He stands straight, pleased with himself and the uniform he has managed to cheat his way into. There is a gleaming point of pride on each of his cheeks, where the flash has caught his smile. His eyes are dark, brilliant, deep as love itself. It's a wonder so many of those London women fell for Henry when there was Jack, too, standing beside him.

'Why do you hide this?' Elizabeth asks. 'It's brilliant.'

Jack shrugs and, turning away from her, begins shuffling the items on the table around: a salt shaker, an empty glass vase, the cold teapot she abandoned there an hour ago. He moves them from their places then slides them back again.

'Oh, come on, Dad. It's been so good today, getting to know things.'

'Then why can't you be content with it?'

'Because there's always something more.'

'Of course there's always something more. There always is. You can never know everything, darling girl.'

'You know everything about Henry,' she says.

'I do not. What would make you think that?'

'Well,' Elizabeth pauses, lost for a moment in where her argument is going. 'All these years ...'

'In all these years, Lib, he's only ever shown me what he wanted me to see.'

She leans against the Welsh dresser, the wood a hard truthful line across her back, and crosses her arms. 'That's not true.'

'It is. I'm certain of it. Do you want to know why?'

Elizabeth nods.

Jack reinstates the whisper they have just lately discarded. 'I know because I wasn't Jack when that photo was taken.'

'What do you mean?' Elizabeth hisses. 'Who else could you be but Jack?'

Jack runs two hands up the back of his neck, rubbing at the bars of tension there, and bit by bit he explains it all again, the same way he did forty-five years ago, right up to that last night at Monty's, when they drank themselves honest and dealt themselves new lives. He explains it all again, except this time, he tells the whole truth.

'Come here,' he says, indicating the back door.

Outside, they take a few measured steps away from the cottage, their feet cautious over the uneven ground. The moon is the perfect end of a telescope, pointed down at them. It is as though they are spotlit, standing centre stage. And they are, really, Elizabeth supposes; they are at the pinnacle of their own life stories. Everything to come, all of it, is unknowable. The future must be plunged into on faith alone. For no particular reason, she imagines herself taking a few steps more into the darkness, towards some precipice she might fall from. The thought of that endless freefall turns in her stomach. It is a peculiarity of human nature, she knows, to fear falling when we are safe. It is how we fight the drop into sleep. It is how we surrender to love. We fall and fall and fall.

At her side, Jack takes one long, hard breath, like a man readying himself for a dive into the deepest water. Perhaps he feels it too. Perhaps whatever truth he is about to speak will be his fall.

'Jack ...?' she prompts.

He closes his eyes to find the words. 'I never went any further backwards,' he says. 'I never went all the way to the beginning, and he never seemed to notice. Or he just didn't want to know.'

'And where was the beginning?'

Jack shakes his head.

'It was so long ago,' Elizabeth prompts. 'It doesn't matter now.'

'Of course it does. All of it matters. All the jobs I worked, and all the people I conned, and all the days I fought in that uniform. They're what Jack is made of. You said it yourself. You're made up of our stories.'

'That's —'

'Different? How?' He does not wait for her to answer. 'No. He can't ever know, Libby, but there were men. There were men *before* there were women. Do you see? It's important, the order. There were men when I wore that uniform — that's why I don't show him the photo. He can't know. He can't guess.'

Elizabeth responds slowly, unable to marry the two pieces of information Jack is offering her. 'Why? I don't understand why the photo …'

'I don't know exactly, but I can't let him see that boy. It frightens me — that he might see it in my eyes, sense it. He doesn't want to know who I was before Ruby died. He pretends we've never discussed it. He needs to believe I wasn't there before. He has to, to find what he wants …'

'But, what's he looking for?'

'The impossible,' Jack answers. Finally, he opens his eyes. Elizabeth notices the rim of tears along his lower lid, but pretends she has not.

'Jack, please. Clearly.'

He turns away from her slightly, so that he can deliver his next words to the night instead of his daughter. 'He's searching for proof,' he says, quietly. 'I'm just part of the search.' He stops and shakes his head. 'I'm nothing but evidence. Don't you see?'

'No.' She steps around him, so that they are face to face again. She doesn't see, not completely. She can't contemplate anything now but how distressed Jack is. She has to stop her interrogation. 'No,' she says. 'That's not all you are. Far from it. You're my father, Jack.'

'But I'm not,' he answers. 'You've always known that.'

She exhales protractedly. 'Yes, I've always known, but it's

never mattered. It hasn't.'

'You kept asking, Lib. Even when you were tiny, you needed to know it all, to see it all.'

'Yes. Yes, I know. I'm sorry.' It has always been her curse, this need to fathom the nastiest depths of every situation, to be in possession of the absolute truth. Henry, it seems, suffers from the same affliction. 'How can I make it up to you, old man? How about ...' she loops her arm through his and twists them both around so that they stand with their backs to the cottage and their eyes to the rest of the world, '... we keep a look out for that owl together?'

'Yes,' Jack says, rubbing away his tears with a quick swipe of one hand. 'I'd like that.'

She leans in to touch her head to his, temple to temple. 'What,' she asks, 'no cutting comment?'

And, 'No,' Jack answers. 'No, not today. Today, I'm just going to be good to my daughter.'

'Well, well,' Elizabeth smiles. 'That's a first. I wonder how she'll take it.'

———

Rather than go to their bed alone, or wake Henry, Jack settles in an armchair and falls into sleep in the most peculiar fast–slow way. His every movement is calibrated, careful. It is a task, this folding into a chair to rest. Even closing his eyes is a chore which seems to take minutes. And yet, he is asleep before Elizabeth has left the room. She watches from the doorway as her fathers' breathing drops into sync. They are like the pendulums of two grandfather clocks, these two, positioned side by side; they swing time away in perfect unison.

Above the living room there is a spare bedroom, and soon Elizabeth will creep up to it, step by cautious step, one hand held between frame and closing door for too long because she is trying to muffle her every sound, because she does not want to wake those sleeping lovers. She has long imagined that when they go they will go together, as though their hearts are linked by some message system which will conspire and agree as to when to stop beating. It is her secret fear, every time she climbs towards the cottage now, that when she opens the door and moves inside, she will find two bodies, pressed together in the coldest sleep. And she is not ready for that yet. Not so soon after Ida's mind took her body away.

It was the saddest possible ending for Ida – a woman who had decided, when her sister was lost, to become everything they both should have been; who had loved and laughed and given with every part of herself. Ida would wake each dawn with her husband just so that they could drink that first cup of tea together, then, while Gareth tended the farm, she would bake breads or knit jumpers to give away. She would organise boys to come in and work the farm so that she and Gareth could disappear for a week, to walk along the seafront on grey Swansea days and share single ice-cream cones. When the snows arrived, and they often did so high above sea level, she would take a shovel and dig her way around the village, clearing little paths all through the streets, and when men waved her down and offered to take over, she would laugh and continue and explain to them that so many years as a farmer's wife had made her grow strong in the back. And she'd been a fun mother, when Jack was not thoughtlessly infuriating her. While the other girls were enduring a ticking-off for wading through the river at Witches' Wood, Ida would be sitting beside Elizabeth as she towelled her feet and asking if she'd stepped on a fish. When, later, they started sneaking off to dances and returning home after dark, their lipstick shamelessly smeared, Ida did not punish Elizabeth for kissing boys but wondered instead if they were handsome or if they were good dancers.

She had been, in short, the mother Elizabeth has failed to be for Emma. But, God, isn't she there, in Emma? Doesn't Emma possess that very same simmering spirit her grandmother did?

That's a Fairclough woman right there, Henry had commented absently once, when Emma was perhaps fifteen and just beginning to brim over into her brightest, most buoyant self. *Full up, she is. Full up with the world.*

The memory pulls at that deep, lonely place where Elizabeth grew her daughter. Already, Emma is so much older than that girl they'd all smiled at. Already, and it has only been a minute.

Elizabeth is not yet ready for sleep, so she steps through to the kitchen, where she runs her flattened palm over the photo album. There are lives in there. Lives she will never really know. Lives already extinguished. She wonders how many of those people Jack has told her about today are still breathing; and whether Matilda and Grayson ever worked things out; and if Sally's baby was properly loved; and how happy Monty really made himself with all those Bright Young People whose spark he fed off. She wonders what she will look like when she is nothing more than a photo in a photo album in a cupboard.

But she does not like the thoughts. And so she walks again about the house, brushing surfaces, putting glasses and teacups back on their shelves, humming an unidentifiable song. It is only when Jack has been asleep for an hour, and Henry many more, that she admits to herself why she wanted to stay the night.

There is no need for a lock on the study door. It has been an unspoken rule, this last forty-five years, that no one enter. And, as far as Elizabeth knows, no one has. Though surely Jack must have sneaked in, some late night or other, to discover how far his Henry's work has come in more than four decades. Surely he has done that much. She pauses to listen for a movement, any movement, but there is only the long, dark swish of windy mountain nothingness passing outside the cottage and, abandoned on a cupboard top to her right, a watch, ticking out its own incessant rhythm.

'Nothing,' she whispers, and the shadows whisper it back.

Ridiculously, her hand is nervous on the doorknob, but she turns it all the same, and pushes the door, and is confronted within by stacks of books so high, so dense, that immediately she finds it difficult to breathe. Three walls are lost to the piles of bound pages. Jack's words had led her to suspect this, but still the extent of it is shocking. The stacks sit four, five volumes deep, nudging their way towards the middle of the room. That spying moon strays through the window to Elizabeth's left, bleaching the scattered surface of Henry's desk, the scrawled-on papers there, but Elizabeth does not want to read them: she does not want to spell out her father's madness.

She closes the door behind her. With only the dust for company, she edges along and reads the words on each spine which sits at her eye level. *The Transmigration of the Soul. Metempsychosis: Studies from Life. Samsara. Rebirth, Renascence, Reawakening.* She realises she is crying only when the letters of one particular title melt into incomprehensibility. The poor man. The poor man has wasted a lifetime in pursuit of certainty without once realising that it's been there the entire time, sitting in the next room, waiting for him.

When she can taste the dust, heavy and bland on the back of her tongue, she slides quickly out of Henry's study and through the side door of the cottage to stand under the slumping sky. She breathes out. New, fast-rolling clouds tumble over the mountainside, their bruised-purple edges hardly visible against the hour, but Elizabeth strains to see them. She needs to see them, to know them. She has been afraid, all her life, of not knowing. Somewhere in the darkness embracing her, a fox yowls for her mate, and Elizabeth wishes she could yowl for hers now; that, if she called to her husband, he would hear her and come. But of course he wouldn't. She's on her own. That fear rolls over her again – that inside their cottage, the same cottage they built with their own sweat and love, Henry and Jack are breathing their last breaths together – and, though there is a cold cut in the air now, she cannot risk going back through the door and discovering them gone. So instead she lowers herself onto the bench she has sat on so many times with one father or another and decides that when she and Emma visit next week, she will show her daughter those old photos. She will introduce her to her past. Then, she will let it go.

For now, though, she might simply sit here and keep watching for that bird, the way Henry and Jack have done for so many years. She might sit here, another of Ruby's ghosts, until the sun shatters the night and she can appreciate the flushed rose ascent of the morning. She'd like that. It's something, she's sure now, her mother would have done.

ACKNOWLEDGEMENTS

My sincerest thanks go to my parents, for their generosity; to my wonderful friends and family, who support my endeavours by reading (or pretending to read) my words; to my lovely agent Chris Wellbelove, who is obliged to read them, and does so with a keen and kindly eye; to the brilliant people at Serpent's Tail, who have made publishing this novel a joy, particularly Rebecca Gray, Anna-Marie Fitzgerald and Valentina Zanca; to the many thoughtful writers I've met in recent years, whose honest encouragement of new writers is a credit to them both personally and professionally; to Peter Florence and the staff at Hay Festival, who have offered me such exciting opportunities; and, as ever, to my readers – I hope you will fall in love with Henry and Jack and Ruby as easily as I did.